LOVE AMONG
THE SINGLE CLASSES

Angela Lambert

BLACK SWAN

LOVE AMONG THE SINGLE CLASSES
A BLACK SWAN BOOK : 0 552 99740 4

Originally published in Great Britain by The Bodley Head

PRINTING HISTORY
Bodley Head edition published 1989
Penguin edition published 1990
Black Swan edition published 1998

Set in 10pt Melior by
County Typesetters, Margate, Kent

Black Swan Books are published by Transworld Publishers Ltd,
61–63 Uxbridge Road, London W5 5SA,
in Australia by Transworld Publishers (Australia) Pty Ltd,
15–25 Helles Avenue, Moorebank, NSW 2170
and in New Zealand by Transworld Publishers (NZ) Ltd,
3 William Pickering Drive, Albany, Auckland.

Printed and bound in Great Britain by
Cox & Wyman Ltd, Reading, Berkshire.

This book
belongs to
H.J. *v.* K. B.

Table of Contents

Acknowledgements   9
Cast of Characters   11
Part I: The Librarian's Obsession   15
Part II: The Polish Obsession   157
Part III: Dissolution   227

Acknowledgements

Several poems are quoted in this book, both English and, in translation, Polish, but the poem from which I have taken the greatest number of lines is *Exequy upon His Wife* by Henry King (1592–1669).

The name Iwo Zaluski has been borrowed, with his surprised but generous permission, from a Pole whom I last knew thirty years ago, when we were both seventeen. Everything else about the character is imaginary.

I am grateful to Kris Kalinski for his help and suggestions for this book, and in particular for his careful translation of Iwo's words on page 145.

Cast of Characters

In London:

Iwo Zaluski	'Monty', a Polish political refugee in his mid-fifties, living in poverty in Earls Court; formerly an economics teacher at Lodz University
Constance Liddell	a divorced librarian in her mid-forties, living in north London with her youngest child
Max	Constance's twenty-three-year-old son, living in a south London squat with his girlfriend
Cordelia	'Cordy', Constance's twenty-one-year-old daughter, at college and living in digs in South London
Kate	Constance's thirteen-year-old daughter, living at home
Paul	Constance's ex-husband, an advertising man in his mid-forties, living in a flat in Hampstead with his girlfriend
Steve Linda	Constance's colleagues at the library
Fred	an unsuccessful, unemployed would-be writer who uses the library and is having a desultory affair with Constance
Tadeusz	a widowed Polish friend of Iwo's, in his mid-sixties

Joanna	Tadeusz's unmarried daughter, in her mid-thirties
Marina	an ex-student of Iwo's, in her late twenties, now living in London and working as a waitress
Peter	Marina's English boyfriend; in his mid-thirties
Lulu	Paul's live-in girlfriend from the advertising agency; in her late twenties
Andrew	an unmarried friend and Oxford contemporary of Constance and Paul
Judy	girlfriends of Max
Danuta	
Ben	Cordy's boyfriend
Magda	Constance's Polish teacher; in her late seventies

In Poland:

Katarzyna	'Kasia', Iwo's wife; still living in Lodz
Henryka	Iwo's elder daughter, married to Stanislaw
Alina	Iwo's younger daughter, married to Janek
Jerzy	Marina's former Polish fiancé, now dead
Kika	a one-time student of Iwo's, now dead

To Francesco Algarotti
Turin, May 1741

When I had a frantic passion for you the desire to please you
(although I understood its entire impossibility) and the fear
of boring you almost stifled my voice when I spoke to you,
and all the more stopped my hand five hundred times a day
when I took up my pen to write to you . . . I have studied
you, and studied so well, that Sir Isaac Newton did not dis-
sect the rays of the sun with more exactness than I have
deciphered the sentiments of your soul. Your eyes served me
as a prism to discern the ideas of your mind. I watched it
with such great intensity that I almost went blind (for these
prisms are very dazzling). I saw that your soul is filled with
a thousand beautiful fancies but all together makes up only
indifference . . . Because I am dull enough to arouse nothing
better, and I see so clearly the nature of your soul that I am
. . . much in despair of touching it . . .

Lady Mary Wortley Montagu
(*Selected Letters* edited by Robert Halsband)

I

The Librarian's Obsession

1

I fell in love with him the moment I heard him on the telephone. I had no idea, then, what he looked like, so it can't have been sexual chemistry – unless chemistry can work solely on the sound of a voice. He was Polish, and his English was stilted, with a heavy accent, so it wasn't even an obviously attractive voice. Certainly it gave no clues about his age or status. Yet from the moment I first heard him speak I was in a fever of anticipation, counting the days to our meeting.

It's true that I have a susceptible heart – but then, we who are members of the single classes, unmarried and unattached, are always waiting to fall in love. We live in a state of emotional vulnerability. Every day and each encounter holds out the possibility of that momentous flash which will change everything. This is what makes us different from people who are already one of a couple. It doesn't seem to matter how old we are or what we look like: our antennae probe constantly, tentatively, hopefully for that marvellous someone with whom to share an unknown future. It's because women are more honest with themselves than men, and better able to admit their needs, that they are even more exposed to the tantalizing, invisible proximity of love.

He rang me last Monday evening. Today is Saturday. We have arranged to spend the afternoon on Hampstead Heath, which is near to where I live. It's one of those miraculous September days, when the sun and clouds ride clear and high and the trees combine the leafiness of summer with the colours of autumn.

He said on the phone that his name was Monty Zaluski; but something about the way he said it made me wonder if perhaps he were lying, or concealing his real name from me until we had met and he felt he could trust me. Or perhaps he was a bit ashamed of it. 'Monty' is not a very distinguished name, though it could derive from some Polish Christian name I've never heard of. I know next to nothing about Poland, although in the few years since Solidarity raised its banner against the Soviets I have learned to feel a generalized admiration for the Polish people, dropped my fifty pence into their collecting boxes, and watched the shipyards on television news with anxious, ineffectual sympathy.

Our first meeting takes place at a bus stop near my house. I too am wary, despite my impatience to see what he is like, and I know better than to give my address to a stranger. I recognize him at once, and my heart clenches like a fist inside my chest as I walk up to him and say, 'Mr Zaluski? Hello. How nice of you to be punctual. My name is Constance Liddell.' His face is high-boned and serious, his head most beautifully shaped, and he somehow looks intensely Polish – perhaps because of his clear, pale blue eyes: the eyes of that actor who used to play the tortured parts in the films of Andrzej Wajda that I saw at Oxford, more than twenty years ago.

'I remember seeing *Ashes and Diamonds,* years ago . . .' I say, to cover the awkwardness that follows our handshake.

'Sorry?'

'I suppose it must have had a different title in Polish. The film made by Wajda.'

This puzzles him too, until we work out that the name I am pronouncing 'Wider' sounds like 'Voyda' in his language. He smiles at me as the bus arrives. We sit side by side as the single-decker trundles its way through Highgate towards the Heath, jammed together like an old married couple out for their weekend breath of fresh air. This sudden closeness is overwhelming and I sit as still as the movement of the bus allows, in case he should think I am pressing up against him and being what my mother would call 'fast'.

'What is Monty short for?' I ask, filling the conversational gap as usual, since I feel guilty about silence.

'Nothing. It is not my real name. Real name is Iwo. But the fellows at work think that is funny, "'eave 'o!", they say, so they call me Monty instead. They say I look like your General.'

Not to me he doesn't. He's much too tall, for a start, and his elegant, patrician features are quite different from Monty's stern little gnome face. But they were probably just making a friendly joke to try and show him that he was welcome, in spite of being a foreigner. 'So your proper name is Iwo Zaluski?'

He turns swiftly and smiles again, apparently surprised that I have remembered his difficult surname.

Of course I have. I've had it written down like a talisman ever since Monday and have already searched for it in the London telephone directory. I wanted the reassurance of knowing his telephone number and address too, but he isn't in the book. Probably he's only just moved in.

'Yes . . . Iwo Zaluski. That's very good. Many English persons cannot remember it.'

The bus slows down to climb the hill that leads up towards Kenwood. Already the trees look more intensely green and gold.

'What do you do?'

'Here, or in Poland? In Poland I was economics teacher at Lodz University.'

I've never heard of anywhere called Woodge, but I can ask him about that later.

We stroll – formal, apart – through the spacious Georgian rooms of Kenwood House. I point out the Gainsboroughs and he admires their haughty English faces. We look at the Adam library – already I am showing off, prattling about books – and the Rembrandt self-portrait. Outside the windows the lawn drops away from the gravelled terrace down to the ornamental lake. The brilliance of the afternoon puts me in mind of Traherne – *The corn was orient and immortal wheat* – and my mood of quivering expectancy heightens everything: the colours; the people; the landscaped view; above all, him. I have no way of telling if he feels the same. We leave the house and walk outside to where families are sitting on the grass and children rolling over and over down the incline, laughing. Couples stroll arm in arm or interlaced: *young men glittering and sparkling angels, and maids strange, seraphic pieces of life and beauty! Boys and girls tumbling in the street and playing were moving jewels.* Traherne was in love with God, but I am in love with Iwo.

This meeting is the result of a small ad which he had placed in the *New Statesman.* It said: 'Polish gentleman, 50s, political refugee, seeks intellectual woman for marriage.' I was attracted and touched by its economy and truthfulness. It contained no word of romance. He might have softened his request by describing himself as 'handsome', 'tall', 'lonely' or 'cultivated', or indeed any word that might strike a chord in some female heart. He could have requested a 'kind' or 'attractive' or 'younger' woman. Most persuasively of all, he could have inserted 'for love and' before 'marriage'. He did none of these things. All he asked was that she should be clever. Perhaps he simply didn't care what she was like, provided she earned him the right, in the eyes of the Home Office, to remain in England. So he stated nothing beyond his bare need, and I could not resist the appeal that I assumed must lie behind those words. I didn't seriously contemplate marrying this unknown, fiftyish Pole, but I thought I could befriend him, introduce him to people, give him a good Sunday lunch occasionally.

As it turned out, his advertisement was so terse that mine was the only reply. This was just as well, since had the response been any larger he would surely never have followed up my letter. I had written, with self-deprecating embarrassment; surprised, really, to find myself answering at all:

Dear Polish gentleman, [this after toying with 'Dear Box 543']
    For a start I must warn you that I'm no intellectual,

20

although I did somehow manage to con the examiners at Oxford into giving me a First (in English). But that was many years ago, and since then marriage and children and a humdrum job as a librarian have softened the brain! However, [lest he take this too literally] I am still an avid reader and I also go as often as possible to the opera, theatre and cinema – meaning, as often as I can afford it! I have been divorced for six years and the scars are healing nicely. I have three children: two are grown up but the youngest still lives at home with me, but not in the usual state of armed neutrality common to most parents and adolescents. I'm lucky: we get on pretty well. I've also got lots of friends, many of them politically oriented, whom you might be interested to meet. I have a large house which I used to share with my husband but is now all mine, on the wilder shores of north London. I cook quite well and entertain quite a lot. If you think you'd like to meet, give me a ring and ask for
Constance.

PS I'm afraid I've never been to Poland.

Iwo told me many weeks later that he had found most of this letter incomprehensible, because it used so many idioms that were quite unknown to him. He thought I had gained my degree by cheating. 'The wilder shores of north London' led him to believe that I lived on the edge of a lake. He had also assumed that my husband beat me and this was why I had divorced him. However, what had appealed was my failure to mention either my age or what I looked like. He had read between the lines, and been touched that I seemed ready to offer him my home, my friends, and my cooking.

On this fragile web of allusion and implication, spoken and unspoken need, distanced on both sides by pride, on this unlikely basis we met.

Outside in the crisp blue sunshine our feet sink into the spongy tussocks as we walk steeply downhill. Already I lean towards him, so as to be as close as possible, though without daring to touch him or take his arm. His face is immobile, his movements taut. His skin is hardly lined, though he must be over fifty, he said so in the advertisement, so I assume that he is always self-contained, his face always this smooth and expressionless. I on the other hand am filled with emotion, galvanized with energy; and, because he is already so important to me, nervous in case I am asking too many direct questions. I get round it by asking him about his advertisement, and whether he has ever been married before.

'Yes, once. We were happy for a short time, maybe three, four years. Then I learned that we hoped for much different things from marriage.'

'What did *you* hope for?'

'I was young and the young have big ideals, so: everything. I wanted from one person all my needs. Love, sex, another mind to talk with, nice home, happy family, good friends to come to our house . . . everything! I even wanted her to like same ideas and books as I do; also to have thoughts and visions same as mine, so you see I was very young! But we . . . she . . . I am sorry', he sighs, and slumps his shoulders, '. . . I could say better in Polish. My English is no good. But, I wanted to be interested in her more than any person in my whole life. And to be the same for her.'

There is a long pause. I count the seconds. One and two and three and, 'And?'

'It is a young man's dream. When I began to be grown up man I see that this is not possible.'

'Do you want me to call you Iwo or Monty?'

'Iwo is my name.'

'All right then: Iwo. How old are you now?'

'Fifty-four.'

'Well, I am forty-four. I was married for fifteen years. And I still believe it *is* possible. Perhaps not like you imagined when you were young, or I did, but it is the *only* thing I have ever really wanted out of life. More than to be successful or beautiful or rich or powerful or whatever the things are that people want, I would rather be *truly* happily married. And Iwo, you do occasionally see people like that. Middle-aged, even old people who really seem to talk to each other still, who hate to be parted, who *love* each other, with a real strong love. Oh Iwo, you mustn't think a good marriage is impossible!'

'No?'

'But you do?'

'I hope not, but I think so.'

I am eager to discover as much as possible, and take for granted that he must feel the same about me. So I ask him bold questions, like: 'Obviously you can quarrel and still love each other. But do you think people can be unfaithful and still be happily married?'

'Taking another person to bed is not the worst thing. Boredom is worst. Not to care, not to listen, not to look at wife or husband, not to see when he changes. That is worse.'

They can be astonishing, these conversations between two people who have only just met, yet who sense vistas unfolding before them. Filled with hope and freshness, one says things that even one's best friends might be surprised to hear. I have never admitted to my women friends that this desire for a good man and a good marriage is still the most powerful dream of my life. We rejoice in our candid, necessary friendship and yet I keep this secret from them all.

Iwo and I reach the crest of the Heath and gaze at the views across London. We watch the children fly their kites, the young parents pushing babies in prams (already they have stopped holding hands), the couples who kiss and bicker. We look at one another and smile and draw breath carefully, slowly, in case something goes wrong. The autumn sunshine throbs with fading brilliance. There is one particular beech tree that, by some trick of the light, stands out in three-dimensional clarity from all the others, its foliage a burning orange that reflects the sun like fragments of gold leaf. I think, I shall remember that tree until the day I die. *Eternity was manifest in the light of the day, and something infinite beyond everything appeared: which talked*

23

with my expectation and moved my desire.

I feel that I have never in my life had such a momentous meeting, and that it will alter me for ever. Life *is*, after all, kind and good. You endure trials in preparation for its key moment; but then it comes, and everything is all right. Yet I am not naïve. I have lived through a complicated marriage and seen it disintegrate against my will. I have brought up three children, which is not a simple matter. I have had a number of affairs and relationships since I got divorced, some of which have put me on my guard. Yet this afternoon with Iwo I feel overwhelmingly certain that he is my heart's desire, and life will grant it. Why? Partly it must be his extreme physical beauty. He does not look young and not every woman would find him attractive: his face is not striking enough; the colour of his skin and eyes and hair is pale and subtle, rather than masculine and emphatic. But the curves and angles of skin across bone, the energy and grace with which he moves – these are perfect. Not in some aesthetic, passionless sense. He is overwhelmingly erotic. I shiver with the desire to see his naked body and touch his smooth skin and feel the hardness of his muscles as they tense. It is usually the physical that first blinds me, so that I stumble and fall into love.

Something else is important, too. He wants – needs, at least – to marry. In the six years since my divorce, eight since Paul, my husband, left me, I have seen my chances of becoming a wife again diminishing fast. The brave ideals of feminism, which I discovered and embraced whole-heartedly as a single woman, can't alter the ageing process, or the bitter truth that very few men consider women over forty to be desirable. Younger men are an exception but they have their own reasons and none of them are to do with marriage. Of course women in their twenties and thirties are firmer and tauter in face and body: but can that make up for the lack of parallel experience? I grew up with Hungary and Aldermaston and the Beatles; the deaths of Marilyn Monroe, President Kennedy and Winston Churchill. These were my formative public events. How, then, can one overcome the time-slip with someone whose teenage passion was *The Rocky Horror Show*, whose first political memory was the massacre at the Munich Games or the Watergate scandal? Evidently this is unimportant to men. Nowadays, if they're my own age they seem to regard me as an older woman – and why not, when the pool of younger women grows all the time?

This discovery fills me with angry resentment; but it also saps my confidence. I used to be pretty, at any rate, prettyish, and I took my looks for granted and never stopped to think that it would make any great difference when they began to desert me. I didn't need to. I was married, wasn't I? The other thing I took for granted was that my marriage would last for ever. Now I realize that as I develop lines in my face and grey hairs, the prospect ahead grows worse. I will have to compromise, if I want to marry again, and settle for a man perhaps a decade or two older than me, and to hell with contemporaneity. The chances are that he'll be pompous or cynical; drink too much or smoke too much or both; think all feminists are lesbian bra-burners; and assume that my job is to look after him and iron his shirts in return for the housekeeping and a spot of pocket-money. He won't even understand why the prospect appals me.

So? The obvious solution is not to re-marry, to stay a member of the single classes and take love and sex wherever I can find them: one or the other, seldom both. But I want to marry again; and that means both. Whatever I may say to the children or my friends, I can't deceive myself. I am afraid of future loneliness. Kate is the last of my children still living at home with me. The other two have virtually gone, to live independent lives, and gone too is the caravanserai of au pairs and mother's helps who accompanied the family over the years. When Kate leaves home I will no longer be able to justify keeping our rambling, shabby, beloved family house. Paul bought it for us all when he got his first big promotion in a new advertising agency that quickly became rich and successful, making him so at the same time. When we parted he offered me a choice: maintenance for myself and the children, or the house and all its contents outright, and nothing else. I chose the house. Losing it would have felt like a second divorce, and I didn't want to deprive the children of its security at an insecure time. Our standard of living fell sharply, from two dozen free-range eggs, size two, to one dozen battery farmed, size four, per week, for instance, but the house was what mattered. It had seen me young and the children small. Fairly soon I shall have to sell it and shrink into a cramped, spotless flat with a spare room for the children's visits, and there I will spend my time surrounded by books and cats . . . The children have made a joke of it; yet it's not so far from the way my mother lives, now that she's a widow. One hopes it will turn out to be a caricature. All too often it doesn't.

And now here, suddenly, is Iwo; no compromise at all. His poverty – he *is* poor, if his second-hand clothes are anything to go by – doesn't bother me. What matters are his obvious qualities of grace and intelligence, and the fact that he wants to marry. Unless that was just a ploy to get women to answer his advertisement? I must know.

'Iwo . . . were you serious in your advertisement? About wanting a wife? Your first marriage doesn't sound very encouraging.'

'I need to stay here in England. I cannot go back to Poland. Is very complicated, but . . . believe me, I cannot. Home Office may refuse my next extension of temporary permit. With English wife I could stay.'

Bald, uncompromising, honest: like his original advertisement. I can hardly ask if I will do, whether any woman will do as long as she's English. Is it just a marriage of convenience he's after?

My thoughts must show in my face, for he says, 'It is not absolutely as simple as this. Of course I hope for much more, not just British passport. I make relationships more slowly now, you will be patient with me? But I am hoping.'

He looks at me and, defencelessly, he smiles. It is, I think, the last time we look at each other as equals.

Already I find myself overawed by him. I have fallen in

love so quickly, and without yet knowing what he feels, that I am inevitably at a disadvantage. Yet it is easier to talk openly now, before we have formed a definite relationship, than it may be later, when every word will become loaded. And so it happens that most of what I know about Iwo comes from this very first conversation, before my questions could seem like an intrusion or a threat. And just as I feel free to ask, so he, too, is free, even eager, to reveal himself. How lonely he must have been, I think, to be so anxious to make contact and sense an emotional response. Our conversation dips and swings like church bells, pealing the good news, and our sense of discovery is extraordinary, and mutual. I am sure it is mutual.

We walk across the Heath for hours, filled with elation, talking, still not touching one another; but at each new discovery and every shared opinion my heart soars higher. I am breathless and triumphant with love. This is his first time on the Heath, so he hasn't a clue where we are supposed to be going, and I have lost all sense of direction. I must have criss-crossed these walks dozens of times with Paul and the children. We've been coming here for birthday picnics and Bank Holiday Fairs for years, almost twenty years, and yet I'm utterly lost. In the end, because it's dusk and the air is cooling and we're both thirsty, we have to ask a passer-by for the way out. Twenty minutes later we are sitting in a Hampstead tea-room, looking at one another across a round table with an imitation lace tablecloth made of embossed paper. I feel that my eyes must be ravenously, comically wide, as they scour his face. The enormity of our emotion makes us feel powerful, important. The piped music annoys us, and so Iwo summons the waitress and asks her to turn it off, and she does. The roomful of chattering people seems silent, distant, foggy, beside the sparkling reality that surrounds the two of us.

'Let me see your hands,' he says, and although I have always thought they are ugly hands, I spread them before him across the table, clumsy and docile as a child who has just washed them.

27

'They are good hands, working hands,' he says kindly, and I withdraw them into fists. I look at my hard-working hands and he does too, and finally he extends one of his hands and places it over mine. We touch, drily, skin against skin. For several seconds we look at our two hands, and finally at each other. At last he says, 'This is . . . extraordinary.'

And I echo, 'It is, yes. Quite extraordinary.'

Nobody interrupts us, no-one wants to share our table. Even the waitress stays away. It must be perfectly obvious that we are falling in love.

By the time we leave it's getting dark, and as we walk on to the street my legs buckle under me, so that I can no longer stride out, as I've been doing all afternoon. I stumble. He catches my elbow.

'What is it?' he asks.

And I say, 'It's you.'

I am in shock. Standing beside him is more than I can bear, and I think I almost faint. He grasps my arm and we walk along in silence, arm in arm, like a long-married couple at the end of their Saturday outing.

I wish this were a short story, so that I could stop it *here*: a little abruptly, perhaps, leaving the reader to imagine various conclusions to this overheated beginning. Then I could move on to the next wry tale about something quite different. The reader needn't ever think about it again, though a critic might find fault with its structure, its lack of symbolism, even its abrupt and unsatisfactory end. But my life is not a literary *jeu d'esprit*, my feelings are not anaesthetized by words, they are savage and untidy and way off the mark. I make mistakes: most of which come from simply thinking about him too much. I study Iwo the way a chess-player studies his opponent, anticipating every possible move and its consequences, trying to enter into his mind, trying, almost, to *become* him; until I am incapable of acting spontaneously.

But I'm leaping ahead. This first afternoon, evening now, is still straightforward and happy. I am charged with the energy and optimism and sexual tension of new love. We take the bus down the hill, the trees now dark silhouettes against a slanting sky, and at our original bus stop we part. The people in the queue must take us for near-strangers. We are. We shake hands, thank each other gravely for a pleasant afternoon, and I head home leaving him to wait for his bus. Ah, but he has agreed to come for lunch tomorrow!

The greatest surprise comes on Sunday evening when he takes me to see where he lives. All he has told me is that it's in Earls Court. I don't ask whether it's a flat or a house; whether he lives alone or with friends. I know by now that he works in a repair shop for musical instruments; that he earns very little, so that the DHSS pays his rent.

As it turns out, he lives in a single room in a large, dilapidated Victorian house in one of those shabby streets behind the tube station. From the outside it looks like the sort of house where prostitutes might take their clients, for twenty minutes and twenty-five pounds a time. In fact it's one step up from that: a rooming house for travellers; a first base from which to find a proper place to live. His room is large, perhaps seventeen feet long, with two tall sash windows looking out over a bedraggled patch of grass and some mature trees. The room looks even larger because he has pushed all the furniture except the bed to one end, and concealed it behind a white curtain hanging from a ceiling track the width of the room. This is drawn across, so that through its pale, quivering fold one can just make out the shapes of the cheap chest of drawers and wardrobe behind it. The effect is eccentric, surprising, and beautiful. At the other end of the room, beside the window, stands his bed, very squarely and tidily made and covered with a clean double sheet. The windows are uncurtained, but sparkling clean. He has partitioned off the bed as well, with another pale, loosely-woven curtain which is drawn back towards the bedhead. The walls are painted white, and the bare expanse of floor is sanded and stained a creamy colour and sealed with varnish. This austere room, when I see it for the first time on the evening of our second day together, is the first thing that makes me apprehensive about Iwo.

He locks the door from the inside.

'Will you drink coffee? I am sorry I have no wine for you.'

He draws back the curtain at the far end, plugs in an electric kettle that is already full of water, and brews real coffee for us: black and strong. I sit on the bed — there is nowhere else — and watch him until he brings it over and comes to sit beside me. I wonder for the first time whether perhaps he is nervous, too. All his movements, especially here on his own territory, are so pared-down, so perfectly controlled, that it is impossible to tell. He doesn't give himself away by being clumsy or flippant, he makes no excuses for the lack of milk or sugar or chairs. When I have drunk the coffee he takes my cup and places it under the bed beside his own, turns off the light, and, at last, oh men and angels, at last, he kisses me.

His bed is crisp and white, its clean sheets suggesting that he hoped to bring me back here and make love. Later it becomes hot and seamed with creases made by our rolling bodies. At first the cold, and my shyness, keep us covered up with bedclothes, but by the end we are glistening with sweat and naked and I don't give a damn about modesty. I think to myself, rapturously, Oh *everything* is going to be all right! and my tenderness towards him is almost more than I can contain.

'Iwo, you are . . . wonderful . . . you're amazing . . . I wish I could, just . . . oh, I don't know!'

I wish I could unpack my heart's excess of words. I wish I could flower into extravagant prose, praising him and glorying in this extraordinary discovery, opening my heart about the new possibilities that stretch ahead of us. I do not dare.

He pulls the covers across us and hugs me and murmurs only, 'Relax, relax . . .' and the wild words remain unspoken.

Instead I ask the question that throbs like a bad tooth: 'Are you still married?'

'Yes.'

30

This is such a blow that it is several minutes before I risk the next question: 'So where is your wife?'

There is a recoil, so slight that if I were not lying naked with my body pressed along the length of his I would not have noticed how he shrinks from my question. There is a long silence, and I have to fight my polite English impulse to fill it by swerving off tactfully on to some safer topic. But I have to know what has happened to her, so I keep quiet, and eventually he says, 'If she is not dead then she has divorced me.'

'But wouldn't you *know?*'

'My dear, you cannot understand. You say you know nothing of my country. I am a dangerous non-person. I do not exist, and yet any contact with me will . . . infect? make bad?'

'Contaminate.'

'Perhaps. So, I can send money to my daughters' – he has daughters, too? – 'but I cannot know whether they receive it or whether it is stolen in the post office. Even to write to me they put themselves into danger.'

'It must be very . . . hard . . . for you.'

'Daughters, yes; wife, no. Wife and I were separate people many years ago. If she is sensible she has divorced me. If not, if she is still good wife, she has probably been vanished.'

'And your daughters? How many? How old are they?'

'Grown up. Married. To good Party workers, one a journalist, one an official. I hope they are all right.'

He sounds so bleak that I turn and cling to him, kissing the fluent, throbbing line of his jaw – his pulse like a soft drum – and bury my head in the hollow curve of his shoulder.

'Iwo, it's dreadful. I am so sorry. Oh God, I can't imagine . . .'

Quite melted into tears for thee.

He is touched that I should cry for three women I have never seen. He gets out of bed, walks naked across the room and, drawing aside the far curtain, reaches into the chest of

31

drawers. He climbs back into bed beside me, holding a couple of curled photographs.

'Here you have my daughters. Henryka, Alina. Now twenty-nine. Twenty-six.'

They are both tall, slim, very dark, and even in this cheap colour photograph it is clear that they are beauties. They stand on either side of a Christmas tree. In front of them on the table, in the centre of a lacy table-mat, is a home-made Nativity scene with candles burning around it.

'Are you Catholics, your family?'

'Not I, but their mother.'

'Then she won't divorce you, surely?'

'Not *that* Catholic!'

I look again more closely at the two girls, smiling obediently for the camera. How strange, what a quirk of fate, that some four or five years later *I* should be scrutinizing these private family faces. I search for clues about them. Their hair-styles are unsophisticated but becoming; their clothes look cheap, made of poor material and assembled without much sense of colour or style, let alone fashion. Most important, can I detect a likeness to him? The older daughter seems to have inherited his fine bone-structure. 'This one looks rather like you, doesn't she?'

'Henryka. Yes.'

Enough. A man's love for his daughters is a minefield. He forestalls me in any case by showing me the other photograph. 'My . . . wife.' She is a handsome woman, though almost comically Slav with her strong, square face, severe hairstyle and broad shoulders. I try to discern her breasts under the shapeless dress and flowered shawl. Large, soft, deep, a fine figure of a woman. Not like me. Iwo's hand reaches across my bare shoulder and takes the pictures from me. He leans behind him to put them on the floor under the bed. Then he folds his arm, and the blankets, around me.

'I shall have to get used to your warmth in my bed.'

I analyse those words, examining them for every shade of meaning from I am uncomfortable with you in this bed, to Now we sleep together as a couple in future. Why can't

32

I take them at face value, as a declaration of intent, a commitment to many nights together, and respond with some generous word or gesture? It must be because I am afraid. It is so long since my desire for a man has been reciprocated. Either lame dogs fall in love with me – they seem to think I must be a strong woman; or I am fucked after a party by someone I have just met and may never see again, using and being used. With Iwo, now, I hesitate in case I jump to the wrong conclusion, and find myself rebuffed. The sexual humiliation of having been rejected for a younger woman cuts deeper than anyone knows. I was the complacent wife in her mid-thirties who never stopped to think about taking care of her looks until it was too late. After many years of sexual neglect, as Paul's moments of physical need or tenderness for me became less and less frequent, I had almost succeeded in persuading myself that sex was no longer anything to do with me. And so now I take it for granted that the surge of lust that I feel for Iwo is one-sided, and don't dare to believe in the first delicate tendrils of hope and affection that he extends towards me. The moment passes. But we do make love again.

2

When I wake up in my own bed my first thought is of Iwo, just as it was my last before I finally fell asleep. But I can only lie in bed for a few moments – long enough to wonder if he will telephone me today – because it's already after half past seven, and I must launch the children into their week. He didn't say when we parted that he would ring, but, as I tiptoed out of his room hoping not to wake him, he suddenly spoke from the bed.

'Constance. That was a lovely day with you. The most happy day since I came to England.'

I turned back to the bed, and his long naked arms reached up. He held my face in between his two hands and smiled at me and said, 'Thank you.'

I can still feel the touch of that gesture against my skin.

I always love breakfast time, particularly when my children are around. I love the simple responsibilities it demands, the ritual of laying out bowls and cereal packets and jars of marmalade, timing eggs and not burning toast while at the same time doing Kate's school lunch box. When they were young and all still living at home I used to love the cross, preoccupied faces and morning smells of my children at breakfast. Paul would come down first and make a pot of coffee, gulp down a cup himself and hurry off to work, leaving me to drink the rest as I wove through the habitual dance from table to dishwasher to airing cupboard. The children too wove in and out looking for Sellotape, one glove, a lost gymshoe, or homework; later on borrowing make-up or money. It was a safe hour in my day, knowing myself to be needed and efficient.

This Monday morning all three of them are once again

34

sitting round the breakfast table, since both Cordelia and Max have been home for the weekend, as much to catch up on one another's news as to see me. Cordy, in her final year at university, lives in a student house near college and Max, who has a job, lives with his current girlfriend in a squat. At first I hated this idea. The very word 'squat' was repellent and seemed to conjure up a squalid, lavatorial image. When I eventually visited them I found to my surprise that they lived in a perfectly ordinary terraced house which they shared with another couple. All four had spent a good deal of time and care on repairing and decorating the house, and had persuaded the council to reconnect the electricity and water in return. They proudly pointed out items of furniture rescued from skips or kitchen things picked up for less than a pound at local bazaars and jumble sales. I realized then for the first time that my children attached a very different importance to their possessions. They didn't care about inherited furniture, 'good' furniture, and thought it even more absurd to spend money on buying things new. On the contrary, they were proud of the fact that they had equipped the whole house for less than £500. It would have been tactless to point out how many bits and pieces of my own I recognized about the place.

Their clothes are acquired in the same haphazard way: by borrowing, swapping, rummaging in sales or charity shops, and the end result is a faded, pouchy, comfortable look. Only their hair is elaborately savage. I am touched by their skills in dressing and living – born of the necessity for economy, but carried off with great style. I envy their freedom from the constraints that bedevilled me at their age. My clothes, chosen by my mother, paid for by my father, were safe, dull and expensive – camel coats and leather gloves and Harris tweed skirts – proclaiming me a nice middle-class girl, safe, dull and expensive. Yet I didn't feel myself to be any of those things, and I seethed under this false image.

Over breakfast the children sort out their immediate needs.

'Max, can I borrow your leather jacket for a couple of weeks?' asks Cordy.

'Yeah, great, and what am I supposed to wear?'

'I'll swap you for the Crombie.'

'I didn't know you had one.'

'It's Ben's, but he won't mind.'

'Hasn't got much choice, has he? Yeah, OK. Give it back next time I see you.'

'What time do you have to be at work?'

'Half nine-ish.'

'If you got there early we could all leave together,' says Kate, pleadingly.

'Get your skates on, then . . .'

And in a hectic ten minutes they're suddenly all gone. I should be hurrying too, but instead I pour myself another cup of tepid coffee and sit at the breakfast table, its cloth warmed by the sun pouring in through the breakfast room windows. The children had been tactful about my late return home last night, but I sensed their unspoken questions.

Only Kate voiced her feelings directly. '*I* thought he was very *foreign,*' she had said, meaning, Am I going to be supplanted? Do you still love me? We don't want him here.

Cordy, voicing my own uncertainty, had asked, 'Are you going to see him again?'

'I don't know yet, but I think so. I hope so. We didn't exactly arrange anything but . . . well, yes, probably.'

'Were we OK at lunch? Any mother would be proud of us, all that sort of stuff?'

'Shut up Max. You were fine.'

'Wait till he gets to know what we're *really* like!' said realistic Kate.

I get to work eventually, a bit late, but nobody much comes into the library first thing on a Monday morning. A few old people, anxious for company after a solitary weekend; a few who're unemployed, wanting to get to the 'Situations Vacant' first. There's the odd school child playing truant, asking about books for some project. Or maybe not playing truant at all: sitting down in a quiet corner of the library and working out how to research something, being shown how to find the way through a zig-zag of indexes, bibliographies and back numbers, from encyclopaedia to microfiche and the orderly logic of the Dewey system. This must be at least as educational as sitting day-dreaming in a noisy classroom. One of my favourites comes in, bright-eyed, pigtailed Jackie.

'Miss, we're doing a project on servants in the olden days, like, Queen Victorian times. Have you got any books I can look at?'

'Jackie, you ought to be in school. Why didn't you come and ask me on Saturday?'

'I had to help me Mum. She's on nights at the moment and so I had to do the shopping 'cause she doesn't get home till nine most mornings and then she's dead knackered.'

'Oh Jackie . . . well, where does the school think you are?'

'I told Carol to say I was poorly. Oh Miss, it's only German and RE this morning and I went to church Sunday and I *hate* German . . .'.

'Victorian servants then . . . let's see. Have you got any ideas? Did your teacher suggest anything?'

And we're off, Jackie and I, engrossed in the hardships of scullery maids and 'tweenies a century ago. Jackie herself would have been a 'tweeny in those days: who says things haven't improved?

The next one in is another regular, Mr Southgate. A tiny little man, scarcely bigger than a ten-year-old boy, he's a pensioner who has fought in two wars, though God knows how he ever passed his medical for either of them, let alone survived. Endlessly cheerful, cracking the same old jokes – 'Ask me how old I am? I'm twenty-one next birthday!' – he is a tribute to the best that harsh discipline and a sense of place can produce. Mr Southgate still lives in the house he was born into, eighty-three years ago, though his parents and his sister and his wife, with whom he shared it once, are all long dead. Now he takes in lodgers, and because he has never really caught up with the value of money today, let alone decimalization, he undercharges and is ruthlessly exploited by rascally drunken single men. He tells me his stories of cleaning up the stairs on Friday nights in a tone of respectable indignation that is nonetheless quite without self-pity. I have sometimes tried to suggest he should ask a social worker to help him to extract the rent that's long overdue, but he says, regardless of the irony, 'No, thank you; I'd rather keep myself to myself. So long as I still have my strength I'll keep the house clean without help from anyone, thank you very much all the same. Though what my dear wife would have said, if she could have seen the stairs Saturday night, after that man on the top floor had come home, I don't know. He'd had a skinful, I tell you . . .'

Mr Southgate comes in to talk to me and to read the papers. He reads the *Express* and the *Mirror,* as he has done all his life, and doesn't seem to notice the changes that have transformed them over the years. The scandalous goings-on of 'Dynasty' stars are as remote to him as stories from behind the scenes on the great transatlantic liners. Apart from his brief and violent forays out of England for the wars, his world has been bounded by the same few streets for eighty years, and everything beyond them is fabulous to him. Joan Collins, Gertie Lawrence, Mrs Simpson, Princess Di . . . they're all more or less mythical beings, who wear their heads upon their shoulders.

'You're looking nice this morning,' he says kindly. 'You look as if you got a nice rosy glow at the weekend. Go up to the Heath did you, with the kiddies?'

'Yes . . . yes. I had a lovely walk on the Heath.'

'I thought so. Does them good to have a bit of fresh air, doesn't it? I like to see a family enjoying themselves together, out of doors. Lovely day, Saturday?'

'Yes . . . lovely day,' I say.

Lovely day, lovely day, *the corn was orient and immortal wheat . . . O what venerable and reverend creatures did the aged seem!*

'And what about you, Mr Southgate? What did you do?'

'Got up to mischief of course, dear, like I always do!'

'Now then, were you looking for any particular book?'

I think I'm a good librarian. I love books, and the people who read them, and if that makes me intolerant of the video and computer age, it doesn't much matter in here. Paul was embarrassed by my job. It didn't fit in with his Creative Director image at dinner parties. He'd rather I had either stayed at home, and then he could continue to make jokes about me being the last housewife in captivity; or else that I had found some trendy, highly-paid job in the media. When I pointed out that I did work in the media, it just wasn't very highly paid, he would look pained.

I've always been addicted to the printed word. A former headmistress once said, 'If Constance had nothing else to read, she'd read the label on a jam jar!'

She meant to be scathing, and the other girls tittered sycophantically, but I thought she was being silly. You could learn a lot from the labels on jam jars . . . and besides, the other girls would only gaze into space and moon. Was that supposed to be better?

So my first thought, when Kate started school and I decided I could now take a job with a clear conscience, was something to involve me with books. I would have been quite happy in a bookshop, but the humiliation of having his wife working as a shop assistant was more than Paul could contemplate. I tried to argue that all advertising is only selling. I'd heard him propound the argument often enough at dinner parties, when smart young women fresh out of university and burning to write had asked him if it wasn't an awful come-down, when you'd got a First in English, to wind up working in *ad*vertising? The moment he heard that contemptuous stress on the first syllable, *ad*vertising, *ad*man, Paul would assume his patient, sophisticated smile and take them through his catechism about selling. But evidently the same didn't apply to me and bookshops.

'Not even Hatchards?' I'd said. 'Then I'd be near your office and we could meet for lunch sometimes. That would be nice . . .'

'My dear girl, you wouldn't stand a chance of getting a job in Hatchards!' Paul had answered.

So I did a year's course in librarianship, and started work within a month of completing it. There aren't that many librarians with a First from Oxford, and although I didn't tell my colleagues, it showed up on my c.v. and must have impressed the selection committee. They probably thought I wouldn't stay, but I have spent nearly nine years now in the same public library. It helped to tide me over the utter disorientation I felt when Paul left me, and my raging sense of pain and injustice over the divorce. My incredulity at the distortion of our marriage as expressed in solicitors' letters, and later my fury over the court proceedings, were tamed and made bearable by the sweet unvarying routine of the Dewey system and the old ladies, the truanting children and the coffee breaks.

'Have a good weekend, Constance?' says young Steve, the assistant. 'Get up to any no good?'

'Yes,' I tell him; 'lots of no good. Absolutely no good *at all.*'

'Good for you. About time.'

'You serious?' asks little Linda. 'You mean someone took you out?'

I laugh at the frank disbelief in anyone of twenty-two that somebody twice her age could possibly be engaged in the same process of nodding and smiling, becking and advancing that she pursues so avidly through the pubs and discos of north London.

'Hey . . .' says Steve chivalrously. 'Constance isn't exactly tombstone material just yet.'

'Sorry . . . I didn't mean . . . actually you *are* looking good,' says Linda belatedly, as she puckers her eyes through the cigarette smoke and looks at me properly for the first time.

'What about you, Lind?' I ask. 'Give us the next instalment. How goes passion and poverty in Kentish Town?'

'Well!' says Linda, in a great thump of remembered indignation, like a gas heater igniting from the pilot light; and Steve and I stir our Nescafé and listen to her wonderful

Thousand and One Nights with Stavros, the unemployed Greek with whom she lives. Stavros is male chauvinist pig incarnate; an overweight, sleepy-eyed figure who sometimes shambles into the library to 'borrow' a couple of pounds from Linda so that he can sit in the Greek café over Greek newspapers with his Greek friends . . . all of whom strenuously resist the idea of ever going back to Athens.

Very soon I switch my 'Really?' and 'So you. . .?' on to automatic, so that I can think about Iwo. He was reluctant to talk about Poland, yet I sensed that it was tremendously important to him, and still exerted a magnetic pull. I knew little about Polish politics, or history – though I shall go home laden with the best the library can offer and start remedying that – and anyway I was much more interested in learning about his personal history.

He had come to England as a political refugee, he said, at the beginning of 1982. He knew that opinion in the West was sympathetic to what was happening in Poland, and felt he had the best chance then, not only of being granted political asylum, but also of finding a post in some English university. 'Why England? Why not America?' I had asked, meaning, What miracle has brought you over here, within my reach, from the unimaginably distant and foreign country where you spent the first half of your life? He felt that Europe would be more congenial than America; that it would offer more of the culture that was his by inheritance. His image of English people – it was hardly more than that, he'd met so few – was preferable to his image of Americans. Also, he'd had some correspondence with academics in English universities. Not much, he would have cultivated them a great deal more had he known how crucially he was to need them one day; but at any rate he had a few names of people who he hoped would be helpful. In the event, they offered sympathy, but precious little else. A lecture or two to start with, perhaps: 'Totalitarianism and the Road to Serfdom'; 'Solidarity and the new Socialist Economics', that sort of thing. Well received by idealistic young students, or

41

coldly received by Marxist-Leninist students, it made little difference, since after one or two visits, rewarded with fifty pounds and expenses, he was not asked to go back.

'Is it my English, you think?' he had enquired; and certainly his English was stilted and his accent harsh.

But he was able to put over his ideas perfectly clearly so, 'No,' I said, I didn't think that was likely to be the real reason.

'So then what?'

How could I say, we are simple, over here in England, and we are ignorant. We think in crude stereotypes and, to put it most crudely, you do not look like Lech Walesa, or like a shipyard worker. You are not a man of the people: bluff, powerful, passionate, with a strong face and charismatic eyes. You look more like an English civil servant. You look aloof, composed, superior, secret: not the sort of exile to whom we extend our charity and a welcome. You intimidate us. Had you been a refugee from the *ancien regime,* that might have been different. Then your aristocratic appearance would have fitted in with our expectations.

Unconsciously I stretch and close my eyes as I recollect the sexual well-being of only twelve hours ago. The gesture is momentary, but it catches Steve's eye and he smiles at me, and says, nothing. How damning a silence can be, or how companionable!

Back in the library, the rest of the morning deteriorates. I am obsessed by the thought that Iwo is trying to ring me, and it becomes more and more impossible to concentrate. I decide that the earliest time at which I can say, casually, 'Anyone mind if I pop off home for a quick lunch?' is twelve fifteen. This means I watch the clock, and every five minutes slipping by, scrupulous in holding to my self-imposed deadline. Just after ten past twelve I am forced to delay, since I am singled out by a deaf and dumb woman to interpret her urgent reading needs. 'M'ha B'hahine!' it sounds like, and she aims these explosive syllables at me ever more loudly, like anybody speaking their own clear language to a wilfully

stupid foreigner, while I smile helplessly and try every possible interpretation. I *am* sympathetic; I can imagine all too
clearly that this simple encounter – let alone any social
occasion – must be an ordeal. But try as I may, her sharply
expelled barks make no sense, and in the end I have to resort
to paper and pencil, knowing that this means she has failed,
and must be infuriating.

'I am sorry to be so stupid,' I write, 'I have a headache and
I can't quite follow you. Could you write it down please?' It
turns out she wants a book on marathon running, but at least
the library stocks plenty of those, so we stand grinning and
jerking our eyebrows up and down over a selection until
eventually she leaves satisfied.

It is early to take a lunch-break, but my need to be at home
for Iwo's phone call becomes overwhelming. I leave the
counter and hurry out into another brilliant autumn day.
*The dust and stones of the street were as precious as gold:
the gates were at first the end of the world.*

I sit in my breakfast room at home once again, revelling in
the luxury of being alone. I look at the telephone as though
looking will make it ring. Needing to discharge this pent-up
energy in some action, however trivial, I write a note which
I sellotape firmly beside the phone, instructing Kate to: 'Ask
for Iwo's phone number if he rings (and don't tell him I said
so!)'

I need to recall, as far as possible, his exact words. His
unique voice is a help, for it gives rhythm and tune to what
he says, as well as words. Ah, now, here it comes: the most
important and beautiful thing he said during the weekend.
On Sunday afternoon, after lunch had been eaten and
cleared away and the children had dispersed to their rooms
to work, meaning, I knew, to compare notes about him, he
had been sitting beside me on the sofa and we were talking
desultorily.

Suddenly he said, in a phrase of beautiful tenderness and
eroticism, 'I should like you to stay with me tonight, for we
can talk to each other differently when you have seen how I
live and I have held you in my arms.' The avoidance of

43

sexual statement, his concentration on the protective tenderness of *holding me in his arms,* was devastating. It was also uncannily perceptive, for as well as wanting him to make love to me, my wish to be enclosed within his arms was hallucinatingly vivid.

What else, what else? There had been moments, during the hours we spent talking over the weekend, when statements that might almost have sounded eccentric had struck a deep reciprocal echo. It was he, for instance, who had tried to express his strange, strong feeling that inwardly he was the same person at fifty-four as he had been as a small boy, and I could hardly let him finish, so deeply did I share that conviction.

'Yes! Yes! I must have been about ten, or even less, anyhow still quite a little girl, when I first felt the central core of myself as something distinct and secret from others, and that grasp of who I am has never changed! I know *exactly* what you mean!' This odd sense of self, its lifelong unchanging integrity, is common to most people I dare say: but no-one had ever expressed it to me before, and Iwo and I had clasped hands at that moment and looked at each other in astonished discovery and wonder. We were speechless. It was one of the most profound and moving exchanges of my life . . . why?

Impossible to say. I had passed beyond words into images and the image was of a diver plunging down, down, down through sheets of darkening water. What came to the surface was the phrase, 'I am fathoms deep in love', which I understood for the first time. My heart was beating violently so that it reverberated in my chest, and I said to him, 'My heart beats so hard it almost hurts.'

I say to myself again, as the apple and cheese and cup of coffee burn in the brilliance of the sunlight that streams through the window, I am fathoms deep in love. And indeed I feel like a diver who has endured a change in atmospheric pressure. I can't adjust to the lighter, airier freedom of the world on the surface. Deep down, in that new subaqueous zone into which I have plunged, I move with an overwhelming gravity of heart and mind, my body weighted with a new awareness. Love is the oxygen I breathe, love keeps me alive, fragile and sparkling like shoals of tiny spherical bubbles. Can Iwo be undergoing a similar ecstasy of awareness? I try to imagine him bent in concentration over his work, his fingers dotting glue into the crack in a violin, perhaps, and his mind swollen with thoughts of me: and I can't, of course. If he were feeling as I do now he would telephone. Already my cheerful certainty that he is bound to ring is ebbing away. If only I can retain the confidence I had while we were together, that feeling that everything would be all right . . . I hurry back to the library, dispirited and late.

As I return to the counter I see by the rack of periodicals the person I least want to face at this moment. It is Fred, poet, playwright and critic, unsuccessful at all three and passionately unemployed. Fred has the burning eyes of a starveling, yet he dreams, not of being rich or famous, but of being *good.* Meanwhile, he devotes himself humbly to what he calls 'an apprenticeship in my chosen craft'. He told me once that he had analysed all thirty-seven of Shakespeare's plays, drawing up graphs which divided each play into acts, then into scenes, and tracing with differently coloured lines the entry and exit of each character in each play. He had also blocked in, with appropriate colours, every major speech. He had symbols for themes. The thought of this immense and pointless task filled me with pity; so that when, one afternoon as the library was closing, he invited me to come to his room and see these great double sheets of graph paper pinned up around the walls to inspire him, I could not bring myself to refuse, even though I knew what the outcome would be. And so it was.

In the two years since then, I had gone to Fred's room only a few times, when the force of his unspoken need became impossible to resist. He never put any pressure on me to sleep with him. He despised emotional blackmail: Fred was ideologically very sound, but I was fairly sure he slept with no-one else. Fred was not repellent. He didn't smell, he didn't scratch, he didn't live in chaos, although he had only one shabby room. He wasn't even a bad lover. But his lack of talent as a writer would never be redeemed by diligence or determination or luck or good timing. Fred was doomed to be forever unpublished and unperformed. The only time he got into print was when he spotted advance notices of amateur theatricals by people like the John Lewis Drama Club or the London Transport Operatic Society. Then he would write to the director or producer, requesting tickets for the first, and often only night, and promising a review. These reviews could be relied upon to appear in the house magazine concerned, for Fred was fair and detailed in his apportioning of praise or, very rarely, blame.

I hated sleeping with Fred because I felt so unbearably sorry for him. A writer's style *is* his character, and Fred's plays reflected his dogged small-scale hopelessness. I couldn't bring myself to criticize or praise his writing; though I knew he hungered for textual analysis. This meant that I had to comment on his dedication, single-mindedness, refusal to compromise, lack of materialism. He didn't know *why* his writing was bad, and believed obstinately that one day one of the fringe theatre managements to whom he sent his dog-eared typescripts would write back asking him to come in and discuss his play. Then, he had already decided, he would fight for the integrity of his work. 'I won't let them change a line,' Fred would declare, 'at least, not unless they can convince me their line is better. Which I doubt.' It is hard to feel sexual desire for a man you pity, and the margin between pitying Fred and despising him was narrow.

Seeing Fred in the library I know at once that I will never make love with him again: Iwo has accomplished that much for me already. I scribble a note, 'I have to talk to you Fred: can you ring me later at home? Reverse the charges if you like,' and feel irritated by the way his eyes light up. He smiles at me complicitly and leaves the library with an anthology of Kenneth Tynan's reviews.

There's a lull in the early afternoon. The pensioners are dozing, mothers are still relaxing at home over coffee before the toddlers and children have to be collected, so not much is demanded of me. I sort through Saturday's more esoteric requests, and ring round the other libraries to see if they have an early novel by James Hanley, an A level textbook on geology, or *The Undergrowth of Literature.* Thank God for books! The letters and words which crawl across the pages like flies or insects take off and soar into four dimensions when they are read. I always ask the children who come for readers' tickets why they like books.

'You can get lost in them and the time just goes and you never even notice.'

'It's like living other people's lives and lets you feel as though it's you.'

'Learn about things.'

'What things?'

'The olden days.'

'The stars, I like looking at the stars. My Dad says he'll give me a telescope next birthday.'

'You've got to, haven't you? For school.'

'Would you otherwise?'

'No fear. I'd rather watch telly.'

Not many of them have ever said, 'It's for the words.' Yet it is language that I love about books rather than the imaginary world to which the language conducts you.

So I am happy in the library and have never wanted to aim for the rarefied jobs to which my degree is supposed to entitle me. I lack those qualities of ruthlessness and hypocrisy which success evidently demands, and I'm not very good at self-advertisement either. Those were Paul's talents, though I didn't know it when I married him, and I was more than content to let him push for both of us. I genuinely admired his energy, the vigour with which he drove through life, achieving a level of comfort and security for all of us that I would never have aspired to. Probably that was why I got left behind. First he was embarrassed by my indifference to our new trendy status, then irritated, and finally contemptuous.

'For Christ's sake, Constance,' he had said towards the

end of our marriage, when I was at home engrossed in Kate, 'can't you at least get a decent haircut? I give you a clothes allowance, for crying out loud: what's the matter with you? Do you want more? Ask me! Shall I get Madeleine' (his secretary) 'to take you out shopping one day? I could give her the afternoon off. *She* always looks great. You . . .' His voice tailed off in despair. He didn't dare spell out for either of us how dowdy I seemed beside the brilliant creatures with whom he worked.

No, it wasn't Madeleine who had ended our marriage. Perhaps he'd had an affair with her at some time; I really hadn't thought about it. He was my husband and mine were his children and his house was our home and I looked after it and him and them: and that, I had thought, was that. The thought of bird of paradise Madeleine 'taking me out shopping' was terrifying. I imagined myself in the sort of colour combinations that suited her – green with purple; navy blue and yellow; black and grey and orange – and then thought of my own comfortable clothes. Soft shirts or sweaters with jeans for the day; red or black for evenings out. I used to think I looked quite nice. Other people occasionally thought so too. I remembered how once, towards the end of a dinner party, I had felt Ron Rendle's hand close firmly over my thigh under the damask tablecloth. I had sat transfixed with shock, neither moving my leg nor his hand, nor flirting with Ron. I had not felt flattered, or sexy, or even indignant: just silly, as the hand grew hotter, squeezing my leg spasmodically from time to time. In the end Ron took it away. Ron had been Paul's boss and I realized, looking back, that Paul might have been pleased that Ron had wanted to squeeze my thigh. Ron, with his whisky and cigarette breath, his expensively shapeless and crumpled clothes, his sloppy mid-Atlantic turn of phrase, epitomized everything I disliked about advertising, and I sent my red dress to be cleaned, asking them to do it particularly thoroughly.

Before the after-school rush of children begins, I search in the microfiche and then along the shelves for books about Poland. The magic numbers are 943.8. There, amid more famous chunks of European history – the French Revolution, the Russian Revolution, the Hungarian Revolution – stand a few books on modern Poland, with garish red covers and aggressive titles. The word 'Solidarność' with its bannered logo splashes like a blood-stain across the jacket of more than one. Avid to learn everything about Poland – when you fall in love with a foreigner you fall in love with his homeland, too – I ring up our central library.

'Maggie? Constance. Listen, would you do me a favour? Send over the best you've got on modern Poland, would you? . . . No, it's for me, personally . . . Oh, post-1940, I should think . . . Well, call it a sort of project I'm doing. Can you get it into tomorrow's delivery? . . . You're a love. You OK? . . . Yes, I'm fine, and more than fine.'

The books are on their way.

At the end of the day I take home the ones I've found on our own shelves, which have now become precious clues to the riddle of Iwo.

All my life I have tried to control events through books. When I was first pregnant with Max, even before he had become a moving bump, I was scouring bookshops for the best on pregnancy, birth and motherhood. As the months wore on, I read more and more compulsively, as though by knowing everything about natural childbirth, derived from Grantley Dick-Read, Pierre Lamaze, and other white-coated patrons of the labour ward, I could somehow earn gold stars towards my own initiation into that awesome temple. In the event, Max was a straightforward delivery. I breathed my way through the first stage just as I'd been taught, while Paul played the part of the dutiful father, sponging my dry lips and performing a strange fluttering massage called 'effleurage' on my hugely inflated stomach. I panted through the second stage, proud of the midwife's approval and of the fact that I wasn't letting Paul down by needing drugs or gas and air; until suddenly, with unimaginable force and urgency, my new-born son was there.

I discovered with my two subsequent babies that I possessed that most rare and practical female talent: instant birth. Our first daughter was born with such indecent haste that the midwife hadn't even been summoned, let alone had time to reach us. Twenty minutes from first to last gasp, before she slid into Paul's waiting hands. 'Textbook,' said her father smugly; 'total textbook.'

I was a diligent pupil, eager to learn all that books could teach. Our shelves were a reflection of my various enthusiasms, some of them short-lived – Arthurian Britain, sixteenth-century Japan – and others prolonged over two decades. When Paul left me, and his absence turned into a definite separation, and then into a divorce, we agreed very simply that he should take the car, all the records and the stereo system, which I had used so seldom that I was still inclined to call it a gramophone, leaving me all the books.

My walk back home from the library is another of the comforting rituals of my day. It's only half a mile, but I can seldom resist going via the baker to buy treats for the children's tea, even now; the Greek greengrocer, who loves to hear me say *'Endaxi'* and *'Malister'*, as Stavros has taught me; the flowershop or postershop or stationers. These few hundred yards are my village; here I am known and recognized and greeted and safe. Shopkeepers and sometimes even parents consult me about how to persuade their children to read; yet when I say, 'But do you read yourself, Mr Kyriakos? Are there books around the place?' they look baffled or offended. The Indian lady in the stationery shop tells me in her staccato, tinkling voice that it's disgraceful the way young schoolboys come in and snigger over the men's magazines, which she calls 'porny books', and how thankful she is that her own sons are safely cloistered in a fee-paying school, away from such temptations.

It's getting dark by the time I reach home – this time yesterday and the day before, Iwo and I were together – and the house too is in darkness. Of course: Monday is Kate's jazz practice session and she'll be home late. The other two are away for the rest of the week. I have the house

50

to myself, and more time to think about Iwo.

Not an hour has passed all day long without my thinking about him, but those were hurried, incomplete thoughts. Now I have time to sit down and think about him in leisurely, languid detail. I start by toying with the temptation to ring him. Even though I know I won't, nevertheless I imagine finding out his phone number: comparatively easy, now that I have his address, and then ringing the house, and asking for him, and his coming to the phone . . . and then what? My mind plays two possible conversations. One goes:

'Hello, Iwo? This is Constance.'

'Constance! My dear! How good! How much I have been thinking about you.'

'Oh, Iwo, me too . . . Didn't we have a wonderful weekend?'

'Extraordinary.' He would say 'extraordinary'. It's one of our key words.

In counterpoint to this trusting little dialogue however there runs a more cryptic conversation.

'Hello, Iwo? It's Constance.'

'Yes Constance, good evening.'

'How are you?'

'I am well, thank you. I am sorry I did not escort you home yesterday evening. I hope you arrived safe.'

'Oh yes, heavens yes, yes of course I did. Thank you.'

'So. You are well?'

'Oh fine, yes, fine . . .'

After which it peters out in humiliation and misery.

I prefer to forgo the possible bliss of the first rather than risk the rebuff of the second, so although I pick the receiver up and put it down a couple of times, to reassure myself that the dialling tone is still there and the telephone will ring if prompted, I do nothing else.

In the kitchen I feed the clamorous, undulating cats and take a couple of pork chops out of the fridge to reach room temperature. These, with yesterday's leftover roast potatoes and vegetables made into bubble and squeak, will be supper

51

for Kate and me. Then I carry my Polish books through to the drawing room and sit on the sofa by the window in the steeply falling darkness. The room is shadowy and placid, its surfaces cluttered with trinkets and trophies of twenty years. Paul's mother's collection of enamel boxes had left with Paul, and I wasn't sorry to see them go. I prefer the random assortment of objects which I have gathered . . . a saucerless cup of piercing turquoise, its porcelain so fine that each finger is outlined against the blue when looked at from the other side. A plain jug, eight-sided, with a most satisfying shape. A *bonbonnière* of a strange greeny-yellow cut crystal. Few of these bits and pieces have any value, yet they, like my local shops, define who I am and the small daily choices I make.

Iwo had said something strange, as he arrived for lunch: 'It is so long since I have been in an ordinary room!'

At the time I was baffled; now, having seen the house and the room where he lives, I understand better. He had not praised my crowded, comfortable home, any more than he had praised my children or my cooking, nor had he apologized for his room or explained its austerity.

Despite this reticence, I remind myself that I had felt sure when we parted that he *would* telephone me. The happy feeling that everything will be all right fills me again, and I turn on the lights and start to prepare supper.

3

Two nights later, just as doubts are seriously undermining my confidence, he does ring.

'Hello: Constance? This is Iwo. Zaluski.'

'Iwo! Yes! Hello! How are you? I'm so glad you rang.'

'Please, don't make me feel as if I should have rung before!'

'No, no . . . of course you . . . I didn't mean that!'

'I know, my dear, I am only teasing you. I want to go and see a film with you. Will you be free?'

'Oh *yes*! How wonderful! Yes, when?'

It is arranged. This is Wednesday; we are to meet on Friday. I warn him that, as my children always say, my ideal film would be one made in black and white before 1940 with subtitles. He laughs.

'And I, of course, am quite opposite. I like decadent Westerns and Hollywood movies, with much blood and rabbits.' *Rabbits?* Oh, robots.

'It will be difficult to find a film that suits us both, Iwo.'

'Then we may have to see two.'

I am brimming and foolish with joy. Only Kate is faintly sullen: it's clear she doesn't like Iwo, and I know I must be tactful; I must try not to talk about him all the time, must not persuade her how nice he is really, must understand that, to her, he is a tall, thin, laconic foreigner who has disrupted her mother's life.

'Kate, my honey bunch, I'm going out on Friday.'

'Yes. I know. With him.'

'Yes darling, as you heard. Now listen, what will you do? Shall I ask Laura' — my sister, the children's favourite aunt —

'to come over and cook you supper and spend the evening with you?'

'For Christ's sake, Mummy, I'm not a baby any more. I can cook my own supper. Can I have some friends round?'

'Who? Not Billy and Rocco and that girl . . . what's her name? The one who was so rude to me.'

'Well I didn't think your Polishman was particularly polite to me.'

'Sweetheart, he's got two daughters who he had to leave behind in Poland. He must miss them dreadfully. You probably reminded him of them and made him sad.'

Kate is mollified, and we negotiate our way towards a compromise. I am to ring up Suzie's mother, and Kate will spend the night there. We've had Suzie to stay here often enough: she won't mind.

Forty-eight hours until I see him again. I spend much of the time reading about Poland, realizing how little I actually know and how crude are my stereotypes of noble trade unionists, charismatic churchmen and patient, queuing women. When I'm not cramming chunks of Polish history I am fretting like a teenager about what to wear. My clothes, now that I examine them critically, seem chosen to make me look nondescript and sexless. Dusty-coloured shirts and sweaters, skirts that don't fit properly, trousers that are never very well cut, shoes that allow me to walk briskly rather than elegantly. For the first time I glimpse myself through Paul's eyes, and see what a dowdy figure I must have appeared to him and his colleagues. Poor Paul: his antennae perfectly tuned to every shift on the fashion wavelength, how depressing it must have been for him to partner me. Now that I have the promise of happiness I feel tender and guilty towards him.

On Friday evening, getting ready to meet Iwo, I indulge in narcissism for the first time in years. My vanity has only ever been focused upon my children or my husband. Now I pull clothes out of drawers and cupboards, try them on, reject them, ask Kate's advice, reject that. I can't remember when I last dressed with the conscious aim of pleasing a man; presenting myself as an object of desire. Have I *ever* worn beautiful underwear? The girls' cotton pants and a couple of sensible bras had sufficed for years. Black lace made me feel timid and when Paul gave me bits of small frilly satin lingerie I had been too shy to parade them. Now I unwrap them after their years in tissue paper. Wearing them makes me walk differently. I tremble in the secret consciousness of my sexuality and the knowledge that, when I undress tonight, it will be in front of Iwo.

Do I ever stop to consider that the violence and suddenness of my emotional commitment is unbalanced, even abnormal, or that my response is out of all proportion to anything Iwo is or could be? Am I sometimes calm, objective, cautious, sceptical? No, not for a moment. I pitch headlong into love. And yet from the very beginning I fear that I'm wrong. Love is fanned into a blaze by insecurity, and Iwo never allows me to feel sure of anything. It is not that he deliberately lies or misleads me, but he is . . . equivocal, evasive, tantalizing. He is the unicorn, alien and wary, and I the improbable virgin who may succeed in taming him. He has, after all, talked about his great longing for intimacy and trust. Alone in England, with a long lost past that he can't go back to, his vulnerability is obvious.

In the darkness of the cinema we both sprawl in our seats, almost lying rather than sitting, close but not touching. My right side burns with the imminence of contact. If I move just half an inch I could feel his shoulder, arm, wrist . . . hand . . . fingers? If I shift my leg fractionally it would rest against his. The sensation is so close that my own blood pulses faster, as though from contact with his; yet still we do not touch. He seems absorbed in the film. What stops me from simply taking his hand, or slipping my arm through his and snuggling up to him? It is, again, my sexual modesty. Indoctrinated since my teens with the belief that 'no girl ever cheapens herself by running after a man', and further intimidated by Paul's physical indifference to me, it is impossible for me to initiate any contact, however slight. At parties or dinners I used to watch enviously as other women hinted and promised and dazzled with almost invisible movements of eyes, mouth or hands. It was a wonderful female skill and I never risked it.

Iwo takes my arm. Easily, naturally, quite suddenly he turns and smiles at me in the dark and draws me closer. My heart leaps and I could sigh with joy. Instead, I frown at the film in pretended concentration.

Afterwards we have a pizza and two glasses of wine and take the underground to Earls Court and lie once again side by side, naked, cold; above and below, pulsating, warm, in his bed, under the pale London night sky.

In the sweet exhaustion and tenderness that comes just after making love, as we lie still locked together in our last grasp, returning gradually to our separate selves, I finally relax. In these few moments I can articulate my love: not as *love*, but delight in our mutual pleasure. Iwo is silent; not, I know, through disappointment, but because his form of sexual shyness is not physical but verbal. Perhaps he lacks an English vocabulary of tenderness and eroticism. I hope so. It would mean he had not slept with many other English women: maybe I am the first.

I always mistrusted men who had to lash themselves into sexual activity with a string of dirty words – 'I want to suck you and fuck you and lick you and prick you' – a ritual incantation that had nothing to do with me but was all about naughty nights at prep. school when smutty schoolboys would shock and thrill each other with all the taboo words; so Iwo's reticence does not disturb me. Yet when, half an hour later, we make love again, I am self-conscious about my gasps and high cries, which seem very loud in his labouring silence. Will the other lodgers hear? Will they pause outside his door, nudging one another as they listen to me? I decide that next time we make love, it will be in my bed. Also, I very much want us to spend a whole night together. He is drifting into sleep and so am I, and it is an effort to leave his warm body and slide my legs out of bed into the cold air and my feet on to the bare floor. I pick up my clothes from their stations around the room. Later I shall lovingly recall how they got there . . . here, just inside the door, he took me in his arms and pulled the dress high over my head; there, moving towards the bed, I kicked my shoes off; next, standing here by the curtain he unhooked my bra with one practised hand while the other curled around my breast; and right here beside the bed I pulled off this fragile slip and these tiny triangular pants . . . He lies in bed smiling as he watches me reverse the process.

'I could take you home . . .' he says.

'Iwo, you have no intention of taking me home!'

'No. But I will, if you want me to.'

'I do want you to. But I want even more to leave this room with that image of you lying there in bed, so that I can picture you here as I sit on the tube going home.'

I kneel on the floor and enfold his head and shoulders in my arms, printing kisses upon his cheek, the curve below his ear, the concave arch under his lifted chin. Now I could say it, now would be all right. Perdition catch my soul! But I do love thee, and when I love thee not, chaos is come again.

Yet I don't. I can't speak.

Early next morning, as I dawdle over coffee and oranges, he rings me.

'Constance?'

'Iwo! How are you? Did you sleep well? *Thank you* for last night.'

'My dear, I am a very guilty man. I should not have let you go out alone, so late. Next time I will stay with you.'

Next time! Oh joyful leap of the heart, oh promised bliss!

'I agree. Definitely. Oh Iwo, have you seen what a beautiful morning it is?'

'Of course. I have been up for long. I have been planning to take you a churn eye with me.'

'A *what*?'

'Churn eye. Train churn eye.'

'Oh good. I love trains. Have you thought about where?'

'I will explain when I see you. I plan to go to Newark. Are you free tomorrow? Or have you family obligations?'

Iwo, Iwo, have you no idea how I feel? You don't realize

that nothing would get in the way of the chance to see you.

'Newark? Whyever Newark?'

'Can I tell you when we meet? Tomorrow is Sunday. Are you free?'

'All right, yes, I am.'

We arrange that he will come over here this evening for supper. I am left to puzzle over Newark. Relatives? A friend? A musical instrument to collect or deliver? What matters is that we are going there together.

The night is our third together, and the first time we wake up in the same bed. I watch him wake, and doze, and wake again, and pretend to doze, for as long as I dare, and then go down to make our breakfast, leaving him to the uninterrupted solitude of a bath. We get to the station early and at the bookstall I make one of my most important discoveries yet about Iwo. I buy a Sunday paper, and a French magazine.

'Why do you read that?' he asks.

'To keep my French in good working order and my idioms up to date,' I tell him. 'And also because it has wonderful photographs.'

'So: you speak French?'

'Yes. Well, more or less. No: yes, I do.'

And thus I discover that Iwo's French is perfect, much better than mine, his accent polished and scholarly, his vocabulary so flexible that he can express the nuances that escape him in English. After this we always speak French together, and it transforms our conversations. It is like fine-tuning a radio and finally getting the voice clear of static.

'My mother's family,' he explains, 'like many Poles at the turn of the century, had a resident French mademoiselle, and children were brought up to speak French at dinner with their parents, and during lessons in the schoolroom. Their Polish was fluent, too, of course: but French was the language of civilized conversation. So when I was born my mother was determined that I should be bi-lingual in French and Polish. As well as speaking it with me, she made me read the French classics, Molière, Racine, Pascal's *Pensées*.

58

Which is why my French may sound old-fashioned and formal to you.'

That had not occurred to me; but I do notice – more and more as I become familiar with the colour and music of his French – that in it I can hear echoes of his childhood. In French, he is more tender, relaxed, and childlike than he is able to be in English, a language he learned first for academic purposes and then, here in London, for survival.

During the two-hour train journey the paper and *Marie-Claire* lie unopened on the formica table as we cross barriers of thought and feeling in our new language. Iwo's freedom with words makes him expansive and he tells me anecdotes about a family background that I had not begun to suspect. His parents, I realize, though he does not spell it out, were clearly upper-class; landowners, perhaps even aristocrats. By the time he was born their world was rapidly being destroyed, yet was still close enough to have formed the framework which influenced him most.

'My great-uncle', he says, 'used to send his laundry to Paris because he said no-one in Warsaw had the right kind of starch!' Nowadays Iwo is able to laugh at such absurd fastidiousness and recollect with some guilt the poignant figure of his mother's French governess. 'She was forever trying, like the duchesses at Louis XIV's court, to achieve tiny privileges which would bring her status closer to that of a member of the family and further from the servants; and forever being rebuffed. My grandmother was proud, snobbish, selfish, and must have been cruel because – my mother used to say – she would turn a blind eye for days to these minuscule social advances, such as the governess instructing the servant to lay a linen napkin at her place instead of the cotton ones which the children used. . . and then suddenly she would ridicule poor Mam'selle in front of the whole family, in exquisite, cutting French. It was like a perpetual game of grandmother's footsteps: only the governess never reached the front.'

Yet I sense that, beneath his contemporary perspective, deeper than he can acknowledge, Iwo is nostalgic for this lost world. His room, stark and immaculate amid the surrounding chaos he can neither control nor reject, is evidence of that. I wonder what his own home was like, and try to frame a tactful enquiry.

'And your wife . . . was she proud and fastidious too?'

'Good heavens no! Quite the reverse. She despised housework and home-making and the women who made it their life. My wife was a fantasist: a fighter in every impossible cause, a dreamer of every hopeless dream. A true, dedicated, idealistic Communist, even when it was perfectly obvious that Communism was as corrupt as any other political creed. My wife harangued meetings and distributed leaflets.'

Dare I risk the next question? I take a deep breath. 'Then why did you marry her?'

'My dear Constance, have you forgotten the force of lust when one is twenty?'

Forgotten it? Iwo, I am in thrall to it, and I'm forty-four! 'Yes, I suppose I had overlooked that.'

He smiles wryly. Did you love her very much Iwo? Or did she love you, that spare, self-possessed elegance which obsesses me? Did she use those female wiles of tantalizing and then withdrawing, blowing hot and cold, those skills of artifice that are beyond me? I dare not ask. He smiles again, this time not at the memory of her but at me.

'I am so glad we have discovered French. Now we need only speak English with your children.'

'And my friends . . . if you ever get to meet them.'

'Perhaps,' says Iwo enigmatically.

At Newark station Iwo tells the taxi driver to go to the Polish war cemetery. On the way he explains that some hundreds of Polish airmen are buried here; the men who died fighting in the Royal Air Force during the Second World War. I am surprised that he should make this pilgrimage, and even more surprised that he should want to bring me. None of the dead airmen was related to him or even known to him; it seems a strange journey for a man who has repudiated his country for ever.

Yet Paul, like so many English public schoolboys, had

been fascinated by the First World War. He knew the most esoteric details about its battles and recited with gloomy accuracy the casualties from the first day of the Somme; the battle of Passchendaele – endless figures, thousands, tens of thousands, hundreds of thousands, and finally, numbingly, eight and a half million young men killed in the trenches of northern France. On our way to some sunny holiday destination, he would insist on making the detour to walk the children over one of the battlefields or cemeteries. The mere sight of those smooth English gardens of perfectly trimmed grass, sprouting rows and rows of small headstones, reduced me to tears. The identical crosses marked 'Known Unto God' were the most distressing of all. Somewhere I supposed that a mother, hundreds, thousands of mothers, had waited with inextinguishable hope. Miracles might happen, had happened. Amnesia; a prison camp; even a disgraced son, finally coming back after years of lonely guilt to confess that he had deserted – anything, if only the young man who had once set off for France would return. These cemeteries were a dreaded prelude to our holidays, but Paul seemed to feel they were a necessary penance; after which the brightness of the sun and the south were more vivid.

Today, with Iwo, my reaction is the same. At the sight of the gaunt memorial to Polish airmen and the neat rows of graves, the tears fall down my face leaving dry prickling streaks at the corners of my eyes. My face is cold and pinched. The wind chills us both. Iwo just stands there. He doesn't pray; he doesn't speak; he doesn't approach any of the other people – the handful of, presumably, Poles placing stiff Cellophane bunches of flowers at the foot of the memorial, or in one case on a particular grave. There is nothing I can say, and in any case my weeping becomes so violent that I can't speak. I am crying, not for these dead airmen but because I am overwhelmed by the passions that Iwo has called forth.

We leave at the same time as an elderly couple heading towards a small car. Iwo speaks to them in Polish, asking for a lift to the station. In the car I hear him speak his mother tongue for the first time. It is rapid, abrasive, unsmiling. He makes no attempt to introduce me, which is a relief since I am plunged into ugly, frowning despair. It is not that I share his grief, he has shown no grief, but because ten days ago I was moving safely through my small accustomed world. Now it has been transformed into one of vulnerability and terror by my passion for him: this outsider, this exile.

In the train we begin to do ordinary things again. He buys a sandwich and two plastic cups of tea. I read the paper, and look at the pictures in *Marie-Claire*. He dozes and I close my eyes but soon, as the train flashes across the East Anglian flatlands, I open them to watch Iwo's sleeping face. I wish I dared take out my notebook and draw him. His expression is cloudless, his body relaxed. He shows no sign of the tension that has prevented me from sleeping ever since we met. My mind overflows with questions: why did he say he was an 'unperson', or 'nonperson', and what does it mean? Is he trying to tell me that he is a dissident under sentence of death, and, if so, why not just say so outright? I study his face: is he victim, or, no, torturer? I try to imagine what he might have done but can only conjure up visions of cells and pain.

We have both been subdued ever since we stood together at the foot of the war memorial. Also, of course, we are both tired. We've made love several times this week, after which, instead of curling up together into natural, animal sleep, I have had to leave his bed and travel home charged with energy. Even last night, which he spent in my bed, I was still awake when the birds began singing in the dawn. By now I am in an almost trancelike state; my perceptions abnormally acute but my body sluggish with exhaustion, dragging itself towards sleep, kept awake by an overactive mind. For Iwo it's so simple. He's tired: he sleeps. I lean against the headrest, my eyelids fall, I doze. At King's Cross we separate, going in opposite directions on the tube. I still don't know the telephone number of the house in which he lives. He might never ring me again.

When I get home I am astonished to find that it is still

only late afternoon, and all three children are having tea. It is unusual for Max and Cordy to be home on two successive weekends, so I assume Kate must have phoned and asked them to come over, to keep her company, or perhaps for a family conference: What shall we do about mother? Although the other two smile, Kate looks sullen if not positively hostile. Oh Lord, please not . . . I haven't the energy to cope with one of her moods.

'Darlings, listen, I'm dead tired: I think I'll go and lie down for a couple of hours. Wake me just before seven and I'll make supper.'

'Do you want us to do it?' asks Cordelia, but I feel guilty already at having been away all day. The least I can do is cook for them.

Later, over supper, I relax a little thanks to their warmth and normality.

'Drop your shoulders Mother . . .' says Max, and as I turn to him and laugh and do an exaggerated slump I realize that he is right, my whole body is tensed and rigid. 'What's up?' he asks.

How do I explain to my children, who have perceived me for years as a comfortable asexual figure, that I am spinning in a maelstrom of love? 'Why? Do I seem . . .?'

'Peculiar? Yes. You've been a bit peculiar ever since you got in.'

'She's been peculiar all *week*,' says Kate glumly. 'It's that bloody Polishman. Eeeevoh.'

'Kate,' I say automatically, 'don't swear please.'

'I bloody well will swear if I want to!'

I am taken aback by her sudden sharp outburst.

'You've been bloody useless all week if you really want to know, and I'm fed up with it. You just moon around by the telephone or you sit and stare into bloody space.'

'Katie . . .' says Cordelia warningly, and I recognize from her conspiratorial tone that the three of them have already talked about me.

'Shuddup Cord! You don't have to bloody well live with her! You don't know what she's been like!'

Cordelia looks at Kate, who is red-faced and shaking and after a moment says, 'C'mon up kiddo, let's have a chat about this, right?' and the two of them go out.

'*Max*,' I say incredulously to my son. 'Max, am I honestly as bad as that?'

'I don't live here any more: I don't know. You seemed OK to me last time I was here, but that was Monday morning and a week's a long time in north London.'

'No, seriously. What's Katie been saying?'

'She says you've gone all moony. She says you don't talk much, except to ask if he's rung. She says you let her watch television all evening instead of making her do her home-work. She quite enjoys it really, so don't get too screwed up about it. What's going on, though? I thought you'd only just met this Pole.'

'I have. I met him last weekend. I'm in love with him. I know it must sound daft to you, but that's what it is.'

'*Heavy*,' says Max. A pause. 'Doesn't he fancy you, or what?'

'Yes, I think he does. I mean . . .'

'Yeah I noticed.'

'. . . I think he quite likes me, really, as far as I can tell. We've only seen each other four times so far, and I might never see him again. That first afternoon last weekend, when we went for a walk up on the Heath, everything seemed all right. But it's hard to know, with him.'

'What do you expect if you will go out with someone who doesn't even speak decent English?'

'Max, belt up. Anyhow I discovered today that he speaks marvellous French, so we've been speaking French ever since.'

'Well, take it easy, Mother.'

'You're supposed to be past all that games-playing, your generation.'

'Just keep cool, that's all. Try concentrating on Kate. She's pretty pissed off. Can I have a coffee?'

'Ask the other two if they want some as well.'

Later that evening, going to bed, I sniff the towel and sniff

64

the pillow for traces of Iwo. The sheets are precious because we shared them. Luckily they were clean yesterday so I have a week in sheets that his naked body has slept in . . . I am a fool: and a selfish, callous one. How has this stranger, quite unknown to me two weeks ago, suddenly acquired the power to plunge me into such despair that I neglect – evidently ignore – my daughter? The answer has to be, not because of what he is, but because of what I need. Not for years has anyone made love to me with such power and patience. I flex and curl my hands and make myself smile and make myself relax, and make myself sleep. They who one another keep alive, never parted be.

4

Iwo and I had parted abruptly at King's Cross with no suggestion of when or where we might meet again. I have to tell myself constantly that even days of silence won't mean I'm never going to see him again. I struggle to keep some sense of proportion, and resist the hourly temptation to write him a letter or find out his phone number and ring him. I must concentrate on the things which filled my life quite satisfactorily before I met him. If I wait, he will – surely he will? – ring me again. Doing nothing is the hardest of all.

After the highly-strung emotions of the weekend, the ordinariness of the week calms me down. I make a special effort to concentrate on Kate. We do homework together, go and see a film together, I hear her while she endlessly rehearses her Grade V violin pieces. I invite friends over for lunch on Sunday, and persuade Cordy and Max to come as well, to ensure that I have something to fill my weekend even if he doesn't phone. The attempt to appear normal actually succeeds. I realize that I was lashing myself into paroxysms of emotion and melodrama which distanced me from my real feelings. Looked at coolly – 'Stay cool, mother' – what are they? Iwo and I shared a remarkable intimacy at our first meeting, reinforced since then by the happy discovery that we both speak French. We seem to be compatible, in bed and out of it, so there is no logical reason to suppose that he is not also delighted with our relationship. He has every reason to want to continue it, at least for the time being. There is no other woman in his life; no man in mine – Fred doesn't count.

Meanwhile I give myself a crash course in Polish history. Out goes the Hollywood stereotype of Chopin and Liszt, long-haired, fine-fingered heroes of the keyboard giving passionate expression to the tortured soul of the Polish nation. In comes a harsh and sober grasp of what drove Iwo away from the country where he was born and lived for fifty-odd years. I learn of the horrors inflicted by the Germans, who murdered some three million Polish Jews and half-starved the rest of the population. I learn about the post-war years of austerity and repression by the Russians, the bleak, blank, black and white and above all grey years of bad housing, bad food, no money and no freedom. It is impossible to picture Iwo in such a society.

On Friday evening he telephones.

'Constance: how are you? Shall we meet this weekend? Let's do something cheerful and irresponsible . . . what do you think? Have you any plans?'

'On Sunday I have people coming to lunch . . . you are welcome too. You'd like them. Saturday I'm free.'

'Can one be irresponsible cheaply in London?'

'With difficulty. But . . . yes. We could go for a swim. Dance. We could ice-skate. We could . . .'

'Then let us start with coffee and Polish cakes, they are delicious, tomorrow at two o'clock. There is a café just by South Kensington station. The Daquise. Can you meet me there?'

On Friday night I have my first uninterrupted stretch of eight hours' sleep since meeting him, and wake looking five years younger.

I dress in the jeans and big sloppy sweater and bright scarf in which I feel most comfortable, and stuff a swimsuit into my handbag just in case. My mood is almost manically light-hearted, and I swing along to the bus stop with a step that is nearly a dance.

At first sight, the Polish café he takes me to is disappointing. It is dimly lit and dingy, in need of redecoration. Yet it is also instantly, obviously foreign – or is it just my imagination that invests it with an air of *mittel*-European seediness? What *is mittel*-European seediness anyway, except for a few half-remembered black and white films seen with Paul in the friendly darkness of the Academy or the Scala for ls.6d. when we were undergraduates?

On the wall an oil-painting – by Feliks Topolski, at a guess – shows the Horse Guards on parade, high-stepping, plumes flying: a perfect symbol of the ambiguity of this place, a Polish enclave in a foreign city. Although my first assumption is that everyone here is Polish, I realize that in fact only about a third, at most, of the people seated at banquettes against the walls are speaking Polish. A very beautiful, black-haired young woman, chic in a moiré-patterned black raincoat, sweeps in and whirls past. Her hair is cut to curve sharply around her jaw. I ask Iwo, 'Is she Polish? Is she typical?'

He laughs. 'My dear, a girl like that is not typical in any country!'

I feel snubbed, though he doesn't mean to be unkind. I invest him with endless old-world sophistication, although his clothes are the oddments he arrived with, or has bought cheaply in second-hand shops, and his room of course betrays only a kind of pride in possessing nothing.

The people at the next table are speaking Polish: soft and yet guttural. An old man with an angular face – Iwo will look like that in twenty years' time – sits with folded arms opposite two women. Their conversation is intense, oblivious to my stares.

'What are they talking about?' I whisper in French to Iwo.

'The past,' he says, resignedly.

The food they are eating looks substantial, and everything smells of red cabbage or sauerkraut. Chunks of smoked meat or sausage are much in evidence. The Polish cakes we eat with our coffee are, as he had promised, delicious.

'Is it proper Polish cooking?' I ask Iwo. He looks at me incredulously.

'We haven't eaten like this in Poland for fifty years,' he says.

I am ashamed of my stupid lack of tact. Why would he be here, in London, with me, if the old Poland still existed? His very presence is a measure of despair with the country that has made him, and all the Poles here, exiles.

A tall, distinguished-looking man in a camel coat and old-fashioned beige Homburg enters. He greets Iwo gravely, in Polish. Iwo introduces me in French, and the three of us converse in that language. The other man, Tadeusz, is also fluent.

'We met at the Polish Club,' Iwo tells me.

Tadeusz says, 'I have lived in England for over forty years, yet I still behave like a Pole!'

Moments later we are joined by his daughter. She is slender, her face quite clear of make-up although she must be in her mid-thirties. She evidently knows Iwo already, and as he rises to greet her they kiss formally on both cheeks. As we are being introduced, my mind races. She wears no wedding ring. Have they a more than friendly relationship? In the past? Still? Am I imagining the intimacy in her voice as she addresses him in Polish?

'Il faut que nous parlons français,' says Iwo to her after a while; 'Madame Liddell ne parle pas polonais.'

'In that case,' she says easily, 'we shall have to speak English. My French never got beyond school standard.'

She is relaxed, confident, charming. I am smitten with the hammer-blows of jealousy. It has not occurred to me for a moment that Iwo might know other women here in London, or even other Poles. I suppose I thought he had been living in a vacuum, except for the workshop. I thought him mine exclusively. New avenues of torture stretch before me, peopled with Polish women as sophisticated as he: elegant, old-world, yet belonging here.

Joanna's auburn hair falls over her forehead as she leans earnestly across the table towards Iwo, speaking in a mixture of perfect English interspersed with rapid explanatory Polish. How foreign she looks! How European, in contrast to my over-anxious, over-made-up Englishness! I dare not look at Iwo or catch his eye, for fear I should see that he's as mesmerized by her as I am. I bleed. Suddenly the café fills up with a group of chattering English students, and I am grateful for their intrusion. They too are relaxed; they too are charming and vivacious, just like the Poles.

Iwo and Joanna have now lapsed completely into Polish, and he seems even more forthcoming in his native tongue than with me in our new-found French. Precise, metallic, flexible, the incomprehensible words ricochet across the table between them. I suffer. Does it show? Probably it does, because his friend engages me in conversation. In a low voice (but he needn't bother: the other two are absorbed) he says, 'Our friend Iwo is of a very old family. Poles who have lost their lands consider it bad form to use their titles. But his father was a Count. His name comes from their estate — Iwomicz, down in the Tatras.'

It is no surprise to me. I nod and smile and raise my eyebrows.

'I hope we shall see you at the Polish Club one day,' says Tadeusz courteously.

'I should like it a great deal,' I reply. Does he see me bleed? If only I could understand what his daughter is saying to this stranger whom I adore. I gaze over his shoulder at an elderly, aristocratic-looking Polish couple opposite us. This is absurd. *All* Polish emigrés can't be dispossessed aristocrats. Both are white-haired, fine-boned, with lean hands and fingers. He has a small white moustache and pale but lively blue eyes which he focuses on her as he gesticulates vividly. The coffee, in Pyrex cups, is bitter and frothy. I long to leave.

'Constance,' Iwo is saying, 'have you any change?'

I root in my handbag and extract a ten pound note. He gives it to the waitress. For the first time since we met he seems ill at ease. We say goodbye to his friends, who hold my hands and my eyes with what is either great courtesy or real warmth. Yes, yes, we must meet again. Yes, the Polish Club, soon. How glad I am to be out in the sharp autumn sunshine!

Iwo takes my arm.

'My dear, I apologize . . .'

'Whatever for?'

'I . . . today I have very little money. I was not expecting them. I could not pay for everything. That is why I had to borrow from you. I will repay you, of course.'

I had already forgotten the money I had lent him.

'Iwo! Don't be ridiculous. I don't mind paying. In fact I should have offered. I remember now: you said we would have to do something cheap.'

Now we are both mortified. I hadn't really considered how poor he must be. He must have to exist on low wages, and he said something about sending money back to his family in Poland. He probably had to save up for the train fare to Newark last weekend: was it so important to him, to visit those unknown Polish graves? For a little while I am distracted by safe thoughts about his poverty and can batten down my mind over the words, 'What a beautiful young woman . . . what a charming daughter . . . have you known Tadeusz and his daughter for long? . . . what a beautiful young woman . . . beautiful . . . young . . . woman.' They beat rhythmically against my mind in the silence between us, until I have to let them out.

'Your friend was charming . . . and his daughter is a beautiful young woman.'

Iwo feigns to be – is? – indifferent. 'You think so?'

Jealousy will betray itself if I am too enthusiastic. With great difficulty I say nothing, even though it elongates the silence.

'What can we do around here without money?' asks Iwo. Evidently his train of thought is still on the embarrassment of having to borrow from me. 'Perhaps you could show me the Museum?'

'The Victoria and Albert?' I say joyously.

'Yes. Since we are practically outside it. I have been in a few times, but it is so big, I never know what I am missing. Show me what *you* like here.'

I adore museums, and especially this mauso-museum, vast, ornate, Victorian, crammed with the spoils of Empire. A guided tour, oh, wonderful!

Once we are inside the V and A my confidence returns. I

have been here many times with the children and can find
my way around it effortlessly. Back on what feels like my
territory, I relax. I will begin by showing him the surprise
with which I first delighted my children. We go left, up the
stairs to the English furniture galleries. I used to make them
shut their eyes until we were standing directly in front of the
huge, concave magnifying mirror. Then I'd say 'Open!' and
they would laugh in astonishment at their own enormous
reflections, and lean into it and back again, to see their faces
swaying moonlike to and fro in its shiny surface. From there
we go to the Hilliard portrait miniatures, and the Grinling
Gibbons woodcarvings, and then to the Great Bed of Ware,
and then down to Tippoo's Tiger, and then, since I suddenly
realize that these are all things to delight children, but not
necessarily of riveting interest to Iwo, I take him to the room
with embroideries and antique textiles. Some are displayed
around the walls, but many are so delicate and friable that
they have to be hidden in drawers, away from the light. We
pull out the smooth-running, wafer-thin drawers, revealing
fragile sheets of silk painstakingly worked with arabesques
of fruit and flowers and foliage. The stitching is minute, the
colours subtle with age. There are babies' bonnets, shaped to
long-dead little skulls; long kid gloves for women with
impossibly tiny hands and narrow fingers, the same hands
that stitched these patient works. I used to make the children try to imagine what the ladies talked about as they sat
with heads bent over their needles; and they would come
home inspired, and I would buy some coarse modern version: a canvas with big holes to make the work quick to
finish, crudely printed with a colourful kitten or pony; and
they would lose interest after a day or two, and the piece
would be discarded full of the knots and tangles of their
impatience.

Iwo and I go down to the ground floor and stand in front
of the Persian carpets, even more minutely worked than the
embroideries, with hundreds of knots to the inch.

'They sent these all over Europe, you know,' says Iwo.
'They were very popular in Poland: there is a special type

72

called the Polonaise, because so many Polish noblemen collected them. I remember . . .' and he trails off.

Is he about to describe some priceless carpet his family once had? Or does it make him sad to recall what he had lost? Or is he too tactful to boast about his family's former wealth? 'Yes?' But he won't finish his sentence.

As we stroll along his hand suddenly tightens around my arm.

'Have you seen enough? Shall we go?'

'Of course if you want to,' I say; and we leave.

Outside on the street he says, 'Will you come with me, back to my room?' Smiling with happiness, rapid with sudden urgency, we sweep through the streets, through the dusk, to the house where he lives.

The room looks exactly as it did before. I can't imagine him ever leaving it untidy. Its geometrical order is almost ritualistic, as though he were compelled to establish a pure, impersonal, bleached environment, devoid of any sign of permanence or comfort. I gaze around it for a moment, but as he comes towards me, lifts the jacket away from my shoulders and pushes his cold hands under my warm sweater to rest against my skin, I am transfixed by the thought: has *she* been here? Has the beautiful Joanna undressed here; and let her clothes drop, like mine, on to this bare floor; and been gently propelled, like me, towards that cool white bed; and bent back across it, like this; and kissed with *this* strong harsh need? Iwo picks me up and lays me across his bed and, seeing my frown, says, 'You won't be cold for long.' I must not ask. She is the daughter of a friend, a compatriot. He doesn't have to explain her to me. I have him here, and as his long body rolls on to the bed and covers me I clutch him passionately and hold him as tightly as I can, wrapping my arms around his back, pressing myself into the hollows and curves moulded against me. My mind, behind his kisses, beats a drum-roll of questions: Was she here? Have you made love to her? Will you? Has she been in this bed, your arms? Tell me, tell me, tell me! I may relinquish control of my body, but never of my words.

But hark, my pulse, like a soft drum, beats my approach, tells thee I come.

After love comes a little sleep; and when I wake up, I see Iwo fully dressed at the other side of the room, making coffee. He brings me a cup, and sits beside me on the bed. Even in French, he never uses words of endearment, nor does he afterwards utter those tender explosions of pleasure and gratitude that I cannot suppress. They are my substitute for telling him that I love him: but he, evidently, needs no substitute. Why should I think he loves me? Sex is quite different for men, and he's probably been without it for quite some time – oh God, here comes Joanna again! I must dismiss her from my thoughts.

'Iwo, we haven't done our mad irresponsible thing!'

'No?'

'No, I mean, not *that*. We were going to be irresponsible on the cheap.'

'Constance, you have so much energy.'

'Do I? Is that bad?'

'No, not bad: it's good. I have often noticed that women have more energy after making love, and men have less.'

Often noticed? 'I don't know about that. I've just been asleep. You're the one who woke up first.'

'I wanted to make sure the bathroom was clear for you, and it is. Do you want to borrow my dressing gown?'

And so, enveloped in his striped towelling robe, redolent of him, I pad bare-foot along the linoleum corridor to the bathroom. How shabby it is, with leaking, stained pipes and peeling wallpaper. Iwo has of course left it as clean as possible, but he can do nothing about the rust marks in the bath, or the damp corners where the lino rises up from the wooden floor. How he must hate this! Is it really the best he could find? Oh, if only he would come and live with me! Hastily I wash and return to him.

'I am sorry about . . .'

'It's all right. You can't help it. Did you have difficulty getting this room?'

'I lived in a men's hostel for the first six months.'

'Iwo . . . was it awful?'

'Yes. But I was determined not to accept charity from any of the kind, well-meaning people who offered me a room in their houses. I couldn't bear to have to creep past their drawing rooms, hearing the family conversation, being invited to join them, knowing they preferred me to refuse.'

'You sound as though you'd tried it.'

'No, that is just my imagination. But we have a saying: Guests are like fish, they stink after three days.'

I laugh, but am shocked by his bitterness.

'So: this room seemed like a haven. A man from the Polish Club was marrying an Englishwoman, and he told me about it, and persuaded the landlord to let me take it over from him. Luckily he'd been a good tenant.'

'And you are too.'

'The landlord was offended when he saw what I had done in here, but I assured him that when I left I would put everything back exactly as it was. I have learned to ignore the bathroom, and I never cook in the kitchen.'

'And the other people in the house? Have you made friends?'

'They are all transients. I have been here longer than anyone now, I think. The Australians come in, and have a lot of girls and a lot of parties, and get thrown out, and others come. I am the old man in this house.'

'Iwo, don't be absurd! You're not an old man!'

'I am to them. And to myself.'

'Not to *me*. You are . . .'

How can I tell him? He is beautiful, his body attracts me like no other body since I was a student: perhaps not even then. I can't remember feeling this same magnetic pull towards Paul. We made love a lot, in the beginning, inexpertly but enthusiastically, sometimes several times a day. But Iwo's body is my North Pole. I cannot tell him that.

'You must be fit.'

'Yes. I swim a lot. Can we swim anywhere, at nine o'clock on a Saturday evening?'

75

'I very much doubt it! I've brought my swimsuit, though.'

'Constance . . . did you? Let me see you wear it.'

'What, now?'

I am shy. He can see me naked, but to contort myself into my swimsuit here, in the middle of his room: I am shy.

'Constance: put it on. I want to see you. My dear, please.'

That is as close as he will ever come to demonstrative affection, and so to please him I do as he asks. Self-consciously, I struggle and twist into the swimsuit, and stand in the middle of his floor, feeling foolish.

He smiles, and walks towards me, and enfolds me. 'You are cold.'

'Well, of course.'

'Can you dive? Do you swim well?'

'Quite.'

'I want to see you dive.'

'Not *here*.'

'No, of course not, but some other time. Now I will help you to take it off again.'

'I could always simply put my clothes on over it.'

'On the contrary. *I* am going to take my clothes off.'

'For an old man, Iwo . . .'

'Don't expect too much.'

As happens when a man is uncertain about his potency, patience and slowness prove far more exciting than urgent lust. With very great care he devotes himself to my pleasure. I move into another realm. My mind sways with images of Elizabethan embroidery, curling its tendrils like snakes through the silk. Small flowers clutch and sway, gracefully, dreamily, and long white-gloved fingers pick in and out of the soft white fabric. Time is immensely leisurely, my limbs seem stately and disembodied. He does at last lie down by me.

This time it is I who wake first, and looking at his face, relaxed by sleep into the downward lines of exhaustion, I know that I must get up and leave him. It goes against the instinctive yearning for bodily warmth and comfort during sleep. It also deprives us of the murmured conversations that only happen in bed. *Then* I could ask him, as if jokingly, about the lovely Joanna. As it is, at lunch tomorrow among my children and friends we shall be almost as remote as strangers. Sweetest love, I do not go for weariness of thee.

5

Next day, Iwo is the last to arrive for lunch. We have all been sitting around laughing, gossiping, discreetly boasting about our children, under the guise of parental exasperation, and drinking wine, so that his upright, formal figure among our sprawling ones seems incongruous, almost an intrusion. I am aware of their puzzled curiosity as I introduce him. His face is a mask of politeness; it is I who am suddenly tense, my heart racing. It is his first encounter with my world, my friends, and I want them to approve of him. Fortunately Kate is spending the weekend with her father, so I don't have to hiss and frown at her black looks, while Max, knowing my predicament, will ease the situation for me. As I disappear towards the kitchen to scatter parsley over the soup, I hear him say disarmingly, 'Iwo, has my mother warned you that *all* her friends are eccentric?' There is a shout of laughter and expostulation behind me and the noise rises to its former babble. Eccentric, *excentrique:* yes, he'll be able to manage that.

I can't bear to have Iwo at the far end of the table, away from me, so I seat him beside me, and put French Eloise next to him. Eloise is tall and blonde with a slender, androgynous figure; an ardent feminist. She works as a librarian at the Institut Français.

Both she and her husband Jack are active left-wingers, and the soup has hardly closed over his spoon before I hear Jack saying, deceptively soft-voiced, 'So: is it no longer possible to live in Poland?'

'For me, no,' says Iwo, and stops there.

'I wonder how distorted a view our media has been giving of events?'

'I am in your boat,' Iwo says. 'I have no other means of information. I read your papers, watch your television sometimes, and hear stories of other people's families from my Polish friends.'

'What about your own family? Did you have to leave them behind?' asks Eloise.

'Yes, all. They chose to remain,' answers Iwo, but only I know him well enough to detect the edge in his voice.

'Can't be that bad, then,' states Jack, who seems to have decided already that he doesn't like Iwo, and is looking for an ideological argument.

I touch Iwo's arm in a brief gesture of support. 'Jack, I am afraid, has been very hard to convince ever since he went to Moscow. He says he got his interpreter drunk on the first night and had no trouble seeing whatever he wanted after that!'

Jack grins at the oft-told tale and prepares to embellish it, but Iwo says unsmilingly, 'In that case he is lying.'

Eloise and I exchange anxious glances as the two men square up to each other, ready to launch into argument, and I try to create a diversion by getting up and clearing the soup plates. When I come back, carrying the joint on a huge serving plate, Jack stands up and, without pausing in his flow, prepares to wield the carving knife.

'You say you were a lecturer, right? In economics, right? And that you were able to correspond with your opposite numbers in universities here in England . . . yes? Hardly sounds like total intellectual suppression to me. Or didn't the authorities know what you were up to? Letters and learned articles smuggled out by visiting Westerners, thrilled at the chance to hoodwink the oppressors?'

'Constance, what is "hoodwink"?'

'Tromper?' I say, and Eloise nods.

'They were not hoodwunk,' says Iwo.

But before he can go on Jack's shout of laughter breaks the rising tension. 'Hoodwunk!' he bellows. 'Hoodwunk! Oh I like hoodwunk! Hoodwink, hoodwank, hoodwunk. That's it from now on folks: the party line says hoodwunk . . .' and he laughs again, with such gusto that Iwo has to join in.

The plates of roast pork and red cabbage circulate; Max hands round the gravy, Cordy tops up the wine, and everyone concentrates on eating. Eloise engages Iwo in conversation in French and I steer Jack into calmer waters with his neighbour at table, my old schoolfriend Sally. Sally is what New Yorkers in the sixties would have called a 'kook': and that's where she learned her scatter-brained manner and scatological humour. Jack is agreeably shocked by her language, since like most northern Socialists he is a puritan where women are concerned.

'Talking to your friend is like trying to have an intellectual discussion with a blue-bottomed monkey,' he says to me, grinning.

Propelled by wine and food, the lunch has gathered momentum and will roll forward without any help from me. I am free to watch Iwo covertly as he in turn observes my friends. What does he make of them? Spoiled, complacent left-wingers, ignorant of the realities of life beyond their privileged circle? Does he mistake Jack's energy and political commitment for naivety, Sally's zany clothes for decadence, her husband's serious, slow speech for pomposity? Well, maybe they are all these things: yet I long for him to see that they are also good, caring, sensitive people, troubled by the lives beyond their own Western comforts. Even more, I want them to like him: not just patronize him, as a member of some rare species, the expatriate from behind the Iron Curtain. I want them to perceive the anguish beneath his refusal to explain or pretend, the poignant dignity of his ill-fitting, second-hand clothes. As it is, they are trying too ostentatiously to include him, and I sense Iwo's recoil.

'Cordy, if everyone's done with the salad can you help me clear?'

In the kitchen she puts a hand firmly on my shoulder.

'Mother, stand still for a moment. Relax. Listen, it's going OK. Stop worrying about him. He can fend for himself.'

'Oh darling, he can't. In English? With a crowd of

strangers? Who he thinks are interrogating him?'

'Presumably he's been doing it for the last three years or whatever. Mostly with people a good deal less sympathetic than this lot. Now relax: you'll only make everyone tense for you. Sit down in here while I clear and bring in the pudding. Just sit.'

So I do; and when I go back in to the dining room I find that someone, Max, presumably, has handed Iwo the corkscrew and a new bottle of wine, and that while he deals with it he is talking to Eloise in French. They are discussing *Les enfants du Paradis.* Iwo has seen it three times and, overjoyed at this discovery of a mutual passion, I chime in, and Jack talks to Sally, and Cordy serves the pudding, and my panic is over.

By the time lunch and coffee are finished the afternoon is far advanced, and turns into a long, leisurely winding-down of the weekend. The room grows shadowy, and nobody stands up to put the light on. The table has been unobtrusively cleared; the dishwasher's gentle background roar has subsided, and I find myself sitting on the floor at Iwo's feet, watching and listening to my friends. Jack has warmed to Iwo, perhaps encouraged by his wife's evident approval, and the two of them are engaged in a discussion of the Polish economy: an area where Iwo's English is at its best. He talks gravely and knowledgeably and Jack stops trying to score points and pays attention.

Sally crosses the room and motions me towards the kitchen. Out of earshot she says, 'Constance he's amazing! However did you meet?'

This is a problem I had anticipated. I can't possibly admit that I found him in the columns of the *New Statesman.*

'At the Royal Festival Hall. Max was supposed to be coming with me to a concert and then he let me down at the last moment so rather than waste two tickets I went on my own and in the interval Iwo and I were standing next to each other and just started talking.'

This nebulous, uncheckable explanation is obviously plausible, for she says, 'How wonderfully romantic! He's

81

sort of impressive isn't he? Sort of terrifying, too.'

'How so?'

'He's so controlled. Look at the rest of us . . . all over the place. He doesn't move a muscle. He's so damn dignified, in spite of those – sorry love, but they *are* – frightful clothes.'

'Sally he's dirt poor. He hasn't got a bean. He buys his clothes at Oxfam.'

'Don't we all? Look at me.'

I look at Sally. She is wearing a wispy black mini-dress below which she wears yellow tights and red ballet pumps, with red satin ribbons cross-gartered around her legs up to the knee. Over the dress float two or three brilliant chiffon scarves. Yet the language of her clothes is perfectly decipherable to all of us: a bit of Greenwich Village, the black; a bit of 1960s hippiedom, the psychedelic scarves; a Shakespearian reference, the motley tights. And so the statement they make about her is not random at all, but individual and witty and charming. Iwo's clothes say only one thing: that he is poor.

'You'll have to take him in hand.'

'What does it matter! It's who he *is* that matters!'

'Constance, you're in love, I perceive . . .'

'Sal don't joke . . . it's deadly serious. It's agonizing. I *am.*'

'Well bully for you. Don't look so miserable then . . . or doesn't he fancy you?'

'He seems to fancy me all right, but apart from that I've no idea what he thinks. He's the most inscrutable man I've ever met. And it tortures me. I lie awake wondering about him: what does he want, where has he been, how long will he stay, what's going to happen to us?'

'Stupid cow. No wonder you're miserable. Just enjoy. Is he OK in bed?'

'He's . . . incredible. Just absolutely . . . I've never . . . I have not *ever* . . .'

'Spare me the details or I might start trying them out on Richard. Just keep yourself under control, if you can.'

'You're as bad as Max. He keeps telling me, "Cool it, Mother".'

'He's probably jealous.'

'He can't be jealous. He's living with that girl in Clapham, happy and domesticated: why should he be jealous?'

'Ever heard of Hamlet?'

'Oh, Sal, don't be absurd.'

'Think about it. Now I'm going to suggest to Iwo that we give him a lift home. Did you say Earls Court?'

'Sally: I'll kill you.'

'I mean it. You sit and talk to your son. He's been a good lad today, very supportive. Pay him a bit of attention.'

And so I have to disguise my agony behind a mask of social pleasantries as Sally and Richard take Iwo away, his formal kisses on my cheek indistinguishable from theirs.

With them out of the way, Jack and Eloise can question me openly. Eloise says, 'He's very good-looking: and he's fond of you.'

But before I can ask her for some evidence of this Jack says, 'Watch out lovey: he's a tough bugger. Mind like a steel trap. No nonsense. That one's out to survive. Just make sure he doesn't mow you down in his path.'

'Don't be so cynical, Jack. He's just . . .'

'I'm not being cynical. Don't be so besotted that you forget to protect yourself. Today you were handing him your house, your kids and us on a silver platter. Just take care you get something back.'

'Oh Jack, don't say that. I love him.'

'Yes, I gathered that. It's dead obvious. What does he say about it?'

'I don't know. I haven't told him yet.'

'Why the hell not?'

'I don't want to scare him off.'

'You won't scare him off. He should count himself lucky. What else has he got, apart from you?'

'I don't know. I've only just met him. He's got a job.'

'Yeah, works as a glorified carpenter.'

'So did Jesus Christ!' I mutter petulantly.

'Well, he isn't Jesus Christ, so stop acting as if he were. Look out for yourself, Con. You're a smashing girl and you've got three smashing kids and a bloody nice house. Don't underestimate all that.'

'So whatever happened to "property is theft"?'

'I'm not being political. I'm being practical. He's intelligent and he may be a red hot poker in bed for all I know, but don't look upon him as a pitiful displaced person, because he's not. There's something about him that makes me uneasy. He's got a very strange attitude towards Poland. He's a long way out of touch with reality. You get the feeling he'd have been more at home in Poland fifty years ago.'

Telling Jack about Iwo's aristocratic background won't cut any ice so, mildly offended and more than mildly upset, I change the subject. They offer Cordy a lift back to her flat in Twickenham, and the three of them go, leaving me to pay belated attention to my son.

Very much later that evening, as I'm preparing for bed, my mind languorously going over the same sequence with Iwo last night, the telephone rings.

'Hello Constance. Iwo. Thank you for a pleasant afternoon. I am glad to have met some of your friends.'

'Iwo, how lovely of you to ring! Did you really like them?'

'They are nice people. Of course I liked them. And thank you for an excellent lunch. You never told me you could make red cabbage.'

'Well of course I . . .'

'Yes. You must have worked very hard. I must not keep you from your bed.'

Oh Iwo, I wish I were in yours, or you in mine!

'Sleep well, Constance.'

'You too . . .' How lame, how cowardly. Speak your thoughts. Ask him. When shall we meet? Will you think of me? Do you remember last night? I love you. 'Good night.'

Had Iwo spoken to me gently on the telephone I would have hugged my pillow and fallen smiling into sleep. Had he not rung, I might have done the same thing, for today's lunch went well and my confidence is running high. But by ringing and being cold he condemns me to days and nights of introspection and the minute re-enactment of each hour we have spent together. Where did I go wrong? Was it Joanna? Was I too obviously jealous? Or was it the money I lent him . . . did that humiliate him in front of his friends? Perhaps it was the lunch today: should I have come to his rescue in the argument with Jack instead of walking away from it? Perhaps making love is not as good for him as it is for me. Or perhaps it's just that my body is wrong, and I'm not his type. His wife has splendid breasts. I find fault with everything, and never know when I have hit upon the crucial inadequacy, or if there is anything wrong at all.

6

I've never been a *remarkable* woman. Bookish, competent, perhaps pretty: these are the sort of adjectives people use to describe me. Yet now I am fuelled with enough emotional energy to power Antigone, Héloïse or Lady Macbeth. If Iwo were to ask me to go to Poland and smuggle his family out, I could do it. But he seems to want nothing of me except, possibly, marriage. His cruelty and my torment come from the gulf between these two extremes.

I can't believe that he is being deliberately cruel. How can I steer him towards loving and marrying me? We have known each other for less than two weeks and made love half a dozen times, but he remains private, detached, fastidious: far more so now than at our extraordinary first meeting. He discourages any show of intimacy or affection, let alone love. Since I must do something, I shall use this emotional energy to find out.

Seeking clues to his enigmatic personality, I spend hours in the library and at home looking for characters or stereotypes with one or two features in common with him, from whose fragmentary identity I can perhaps assemble a composite, sharply-defined Iwo. He becomes the focus of everything I read as well as most of my thoughts. Can anyone ever have studied him so conscientiously? My task is now to meditate on him, on him: he is the book, the library on which I look.

With no first-hand evidence of his past life and the people who figured in it – apart from what he chooses to tell me, and I have to assume he isn't lying – my task is like re-creating a whole dinosaur from a single, long thigh-bone. Random clues provide ambiguous fragments which I can start to reconstruct. Here the French governess lies in a corner, a modest heap of honeycombed bones. Over there is a double section of curving rib-cage, his wife's, big and deep. The partially assembled skeleton has his own broad, high forehead and beautifully oval skull, but there is no life yet in these bones. He is, in reality as in my imagination, like a man waiting for his life to start up again, in a state of suspended animation. Suddenly, with a guilty grin, I remember overhearing Kate on the phone to Cordelia, calling him 'the Undead'. 'Mother's still haunted by the Undead!' she had said, and they giggled together, defusing his power over me by mocking him.

In the library, pretending to return books to the shelves or look for readers' requests, I search for references to men of his type, his age, with his background, from his country: anything that can help me crack the code. I look through art books, finding in a Bellini Pope here, an Otto Dix or Christian Schad portrait there, those same marble features and impassive expression. Just as one sometimes comes across a new word and suddenly finds it everywhere, so now with Iwo I wonder how I can have failed to encounter his type before. He is omnipresent, above all in my mind.

Yet when I do see him, these spectral images seem irrelevant and misguided. The real Iwo is flesh and blood. He smiles, occasionally laughs, has corporeal appetites for food and drink and me. Mere happiness could not enslave me as thoroughly as this alternation of happiness and pain: invariable cruelty would not enslave me at all. I am not a masochist, thank God! It's the method used by torturers down the ages, which renders the victim helpless by never allowing him to be certain of anything. Since I can never anticipate what will come next, I live in a state of highly-strung nervous tension.

And the worst thing of all is that I never know whether this torture *is* deliberate on his part, or self-inflicted. Is he sadistically playing on my vulnerability, amused by my desperate attempts to hide the pain? Or am I inventing the whole torture chamber? *I never know.*

As the late autumn hardens into winter we spend more nights in my room and my bed, for his is bitterly cold, its ashen whiteness nearly as chilling as the cold sky outside. The streets gleam like black rubber under the slanting rain and street lights; the wind is blustery and stings our faces. But my house is centrally heated, the front door opens on to welcoming warmth, and my bedroom is cocooned with eiderdowns and pillows and fat lined curtains to keep out draughts. In the deep darkness of my bed during the small hours, when we can't see one another's faces, occasionally we talk with the openness of our first, rapturous meeting. Only then do I risk asking questions.

'Iwo, what do you miss most about Poland?'

'Poland.'

'Not your family, your daughters, or friends, or students, or . . .?'

'No: Poland.'

'What do you mean by Poland?'

'My country. My nationality. My history. Poland.'

'What's it like?'

'It may live – Poland may be free one day – but I couldn't stay to see it.'

There is a long silence. I lie very still, not daring to touch him. My muscles become locked and I am uncomfortable.

'How did it affect you?'

'I was one of those who opposed the government. Have you heard of KOR?'

'Yes.' I have read the papers, studied Polish history books. 'But you explain it to me.'

'KOR was originally a committee to defend workers from the factories who had protested against the government in 1976. They took to the streets in their thousands and rioted and set fire to buildings. They were punished, often brutally. Most lost their jobs, some were sent to prison. A few months later the intellectuals – writers, university teachers – started to help. That's when KOR was founded. I was a member from the beginning.'

'Was it dangerous?'

'Not really: there were so many of us, the government was scared. But from then on I knew I was watched; that a dossier was being kept on me, and that one day they would find an excuse to arrest me.'

'And then?'

'Then? Then? How do *I* know? It never happened.'

'Iwo: what might have happened? I mean . . . is it like Russia? Would they have tortured you, or sent you to a mental hospital and given you drugs? Would they have sent you to a prison camp? Put you on trial? What?'

'Perhaps all of these things, perhaps none of them. I told you, my daughters are married to good Party stalwarts; members of what we call the *nomenklatura,* which is a bit like what you call the Establishment. They might have been able to help me, or might not.'

'What did you do wrong?'

'I was an economist: we are always the avant-garde of Communist revolutions. In Poland, economists are more of an elite than historians or philosophers. We are the prophets of the future, along with poets and writers. I was not prudent in my teaching; I didn't care who heard me, and as time went on I took fewer and fewer precautions. They knew I corresponded with academics in the West.'

'Weren't you always afraid, Iwo?'

'I don't think so. Partly because I had a great sense of fatalism. Partly because many university people, students as well as teachers, were doing the same thing. Partly because it never seemed quite real.'

'*Some* people must have been afraid.'

'I will tell you about a student of mine. A girl. She was very highly-strung, even melodramatic; very clever. Her parents were factory workers in a textile mill: ordinary, solid people. She was quite different. She had imagination.'

'So? What happened to her?'

'She was arrested for knowing the names on a secret list of people in the Soviet Union – not in Poland – Poland would have been all right – in the Soviet Union, to whom she was to send copies of one of the new, in theory uncensored, but still secretly printed journals of political and economic ideas. At police headquarters they prepared to question her. Maybe nothing would have happened, she could have denied it, and been believed, and been released. But she *thought* she would be tortured, and did not know if she could keep quiet. She was young, only twenty-one. She asked for a glass of water. When they brought it to her, she smashed the glass, and slashed her jugular vein. She died. Of *course* people were afraid.'

There is nothing I can say, so I lie in silence, and after a little while realize that Iwo has fallen asleep. I am wondering who gave her the list of Russian names.

Stories like these make me more afraid of Iwo. He has areas of experience which my life has never begun to approach. I lost a girlfriend once, when I was much younger, in a motorbike accident, and one or two more of my friends have died since, but my life is as balmy and innocent as that of a child by comparison with the events he describes.

Another night I say, 'Was your wife a member of KOR as well?'

'Yes, certainly, but in a different group from mine.'

'Did you talk about it?'

'We had separate lives, Constance. I have tried to explain to you. We shared the same apartment, because in Poland we do not have the luxury of being able to find another one when it suits us. After the two girls had both got married, she moved into the bedroom they used to share. She conducted her separate life and I, in what had been our bedroom, did my work.'

'So you didn't ever speak to each other?'

'It was not as clear-cut as that. She might say, "You have used my sugar", or "my milk"; I might ask her for a stamp, or some ink. She might even tell me she had seen the girls. We did not live in a passionate silence, but in occasional banalities.'

'How long were you married?'

'Thirty years.'

Thirty years. He cannot feel as indifferent towards her as

he pretends: after all, I am not indifferent to Paul. Paul can scarcely hurt me any longer, but I can't think of him without emotion.

'Why didn't you divorce?'

'What for? Neither of us wanted, then, to get married again; we are both in some sense Catholics. And it might have distressed our daughters.'

'Then', he had said: *then.* Does he want a divorce *now*? Is he thinking about marriage? 'Polish gentleman seeks intellectual to marry': we never talk about that.

We get into the habit, when we meet, of eating mainly at my house. It doesn't cost him money, and is easy for me, and more than easy: a relief to be able to discharge some of my pent-up energies in preparing a meal, setting the table, behaving ordinarily. It means Kate eats with us, usually hostile, occasionally mollified if he talks to her about jazz or helps with her maths homework. Sometimes one of the other children joins us, but as time goes on they like Iwo less, not more, and become blatantly ill at ease. Once when Kate is with Paul for the weekend I try to arrange the table 'romantically', with candles and starched table napkins, but as Iwo walks into the room he says involuntarily, 'What's this nonsense? Why candles?' and I feel such a fool I never do it again.

Later, that same weekend, however, he insists that I come over to Earls Court so that he can take me out for a meal. I spend the late afternoon going through the ritual preparation that provides some outlet for my inexpressible emotion. First I lay out my clothes on the bed; then immerse myself, eyes shut, in a warm scented bath, trying to make my body quite limp and free from tension. By the time I have washed and dried my hair, dressed, made up, stared at my reflection, changed a few things, stared again, added scent and jewellery, and finally smiled, the whole process takes nearly two hours. It becomes increasingly necessary to me, as a counterweight to Iwo's overwhelming attraction. It is always in vain. He rarely makes any comment about my appearance, and if he does, it's totally non-committal. He has a genius for remarking on my clothes in words that avoid any hint of personal judgement. 'That hat will keep your ears warm!' for example, or, 'Have I seen that dress before?' Yes, I could say; or, a confession, No. It never occurs to me to say, How should I know? or, I don't remember; because I do, I remember everything.

He meets me at the tube station and we walk round the corner, in the opposite direction from his house into one of the dignified Victorian squares behind Earls Court Road. He stops in front of a red brick building and we go in.

'The Polish Air Force Club,' he says. 'It is a good place to eat and I can hear the radio in Polish. I've made many friends since I started coming here.'

The walls are hung with old photographs of aeroplanes and sketches of square-jawed, dashing young air-crews from the Second World War, looking exactly like illustrations for a Biggles adventure story. Just beyond the hallway there is a bar, around which a number of elderly men sit talking in Polish. They look up and swing welcoming arms towards Iwo, halting the gesture in mid-air as they see me. Iwo says something in Polish, and then, for my benefit, in the awkward English that has become unfamiliar to me since we discovered the joys of speaking French together: 'Can I present to you Mrs Liddell?'

The old men bow and take my hand; one lifts it to his lips; another insists on buying us a drink. They explain the origins of the club to me, and I tell them that I have visited the memorial at Newark and been much moved. Iwo explains that we are going to eat, and we leave their warm, friendly circle and go downstairs.

He precedes me, and at the foot of the stairs is greeted by a young woman, one of the most unusually lovely women I have ever seen. Her face is all curves and softness. Its contours are round and full, her skin and hair seem corn-coloured, though her complexion is golden-olive and her thick pony-tailed hair is golden-brown. She looks like Primavera. Her expression, when she sees Iwo, is one of surprise, her eyebrows arching above her wide eyes; followed by a puzzled frown when she catches sight of me. She is quite without artifice, and even to my jealous gaze, captivating.

'Monty!' she exclaims, in astonishment and delight. I stand like Lot's wife, wondering who she is, why she calls him Monty, and, most urgently of all, whether they are lovers.

He turns round to me. 'Constance, this is my very good friend Marina, who saved me from starvation many a time!'

She is evidently the waitress here: but no ordinary waitress. Iwo is smiling at her so broadly that he's almost unrecognizable. He has never smiled at me like that. I exchange polite greetings with Marina and after we sit down I ask why she too calls him Monty.

'One evening, soon after I had managed to find at last a job, I brought a couple of fellows from the workshop here: to be friendly, show them that I, too, am a person. And of course they called me Monty, so . . .'

'. . . to put them at their ease,' Marina continues, 'he explained to me that he was known as Monty: and ever since then it is our joke!'

Bully for you, lady, I think: that, and how many other little private jokes? Yet I don't feel the sharp agony that Joanna had provoked. Beside the sumptuous beauty and open friendliness of this young woman I am quite defenceless. Indeed, it would be odd if Iwo were *not* enchanted by her. In the basement dining room with its garish orange paint and splashy mural across the end wall, she glows with warmth, and Iwo responds by relaxing and stretching his long legs and entering into a conspiracy with her about what I should eat – for this is my first Polish meal. Together they devise the best that the menu can offer. She brings us a bottle of wine, betrays no sign of flirtatiousness towards him, and smiles at me. She seems *pleased* that Iwo is with a woman, so surely she can't . . .? I will think about it later. Marina leaves us alone to eat and Iwo explains that the club had been a sanctuary during his early days in London, as poverty and disillusionment set in: for him, and for many other Poles. They can gather here, exchange information, eat cheaply, and talk about the country they have all lost. In between eating and listening I watch Marina. She is an expert waitress, attentive without being obsequious, and it's clear that the old men love her, and doubtless see in her the daughter they never had, or had and never saw again. Finally, over coffee, Iwo persuades her to join us.

'Did you come to England at the same time as Iwo?' I ask.

'No: a few years earlier. I came in 1977. But, as you see, I haven't really left Poland yet! All Poles are the same. We simply make London an extension of our homeland, establish our little havens of Polishness here and there, and behave as though we had never left. Some people haven't learned English after forty years!'

'Can I ask . . . why did you come?'

'I came because my fiancé died. And because it was possible. I didn't know how soon they might clamp down again, and I felt I had no reason to stay, so I went.'

'What were you doing in Poland?'

'Oh, hasn't Monty told you? I was one of his students, at Lodz.'

'No, he didn't tell me.'

Why not? He must have known I would hear it from Marina. He ought to have forewarned me. Now I am plunged into speculation and despair, and can't keep up this charade of polite small-talk. Fortunately, she can.

'He didn't know I was here. He came down those stairs one day quite by chance, and I thought I was seeing a vision! Nobody had told me Professor Zaluski was here in London – I couldn't believe it! How we talked, that first evening! He gave me news of so many friends at university and in Lodz. It was marvellous for me, but it made *him* homesick.'

He is evidently pleased to hear her tell me how respected he was among the students; how well attended his lectures were, how audacious his ideas. I learn something new about him: that he likes to hear himself praised.

'Did you know his wife?' I ask abruptly. Now Iwo will be angry with me.

'Sometimes I saw her at the university. But I was just a young student.'

In a moment I shall ask her whether Iwo's wife was beautiful too, and perhaps he senses that my recklessness is on the verge of becoming lunatic, for at last he interrupts.

'I have told Marina she was far too good a student to be working here as a waitress . . .'

'. . . and you are too good a professor to work in a repair shop: yet here we both are! And if we complain Mrs Liddell will think we are ungrateful to her country which is our host, and, really, we are not!'

Grateful, ungrateful, what do I care? Must I endure this? Can't we go? 'Iwo: should I leave you two? I have to go back home tonight.' Just so that she knows I do sleep with him.

He shows no annoyance, but stands up, extends a courteous hand to me, speaks to Marina in Polish and moments later we are outside on the street.

I march along in silence. Let him speak.

We walk several hundred yards to the tube station before he says, 'Do you really want to go home now?'

I am either forced to say yes, which he will know to be a lie, or to capitulate and say no, and apologize, and be graciously taken to his bed. 'What do you think?' I say.

'I think we have time for a coffee in my room.'

'Yes, all right then.'

His room is dappled with shadows and reflections. It is impossible to imagine the life-giving Marina here. It is also impossible to imagine him refusing any comfort she might offer: and she offers so much. The comfort of her young body, her curving smile; the comfort of someone from his own town, who knows the people he knew; the comfort of recapturing Poland, in memories and ideas. How could he resist her?

'How old is Marina?'

'Constance, she is more than twenty years younger than me. She can't yet be thirty. And now, will you stop frowning if I ask you to come to bed, or will that make you frown all the more?'

I will stop frowning. I turn to him, cleave to him. Tonight I want kisses to comfort me. The body he kisses becomes the map of Poland. In a half-sleep, in a kind of trance, I cease to be my own self and become what he wants me to be, which is his country. These arms its borders, these feet its limits, these breasts its cities, and here, his home. The body of this world like thine, my little world! . . . My mind detaches itself and hovers, quite clear and rational, above the bed where Iwo is mapping out his territory. The mind reasons, Do not ask him about Marina, for he will not deign to answer, neither with truth nor kindly excuses, he will simply rebuke you for asking. Assume the obvious, that she has been here; but take her friendship at face value and use it. Make an ally of her. Talk to her. Ask her questions about him. Tell her you love him, and ask for help. But he – this self-contained and secretive man, silent even in these paroxysms – will tell you nothing.

The victim may also remain silent under torture.

7

Yet I am not always plunged into self-indulgent melancholy. At home and in the library I am quite often my normal, quick-witted self. On the telephone or with my friends I make my relationship with Iwo accessible by making it absurd: reducing it to a series of picaresque incidents in which I star as a sort of Charlie Chaplin of the heart. Then they laugh and say, 'Oh Constance, you are *hope*less . . .' and few realize that the comic melodramas I rattle off for their benefit are a painful parody. My emotions are so vast and turbulent that if I were to describe them literally people would think I must be going mad. It's easier and safer to joke.

Sometimes I try to tell myself that the relationship has manifestly failed and I might as well cut my losses. I could say to Iwo, Look, sorry, we're wasting our time: I can't marry you. Find someone else. This course of action would at least allow me to walk away with dignity and self-respect intact. Late at night, waiting for him to ring – he hardly ever does – I practise letters of graceful renunciation. Any form of action is better than aching hours of thought, and sometimes the letters are so plausible they almost convince me. I need advice, but whose? It ought to be someone who has also experienced this kind of lunatic obsession; preferably some-one who has met Iwo and could tell me whether in fact his impassivity might conceal something more than indulgent tolerance. Maybe an objective viewpoint could persuade me to take action; whether by reason or ridicule, it doesn't much matter. But whose?

An unlikely comforter turns up: Paul, my ex-husband. The children must have talked to him during a weekend spent at his flat; at any rate, he brings Kate home one Sunday evening, invites himself to supper, packs her off to bed early (she goes with unusual docility) and says, 'Can I go down to the cellar and fetch up one of my bottles?'

'*Our* bottles, Paul: yeah, sure, why not, help yourself. Good idea. Let's get pissed. I could do with a sympathetic shoulder.'

''76 claret do?'

'Christ Paul, you know I haven't a clue. I don't even know what's still down there. Just get it and open it and pour the stuff out.'

'Waste of a '76,' he mutters, as he goes down the steps.

I look in the mirror in a reflex gesture – Oh God! is he going to tell me I look a mess again? was always my first thought when I heard his key in the front door – and am shocked to see how haggard I look. He returns.

'Don't worry, love, you look fine. Lost a bit of weight, haven't you? It's good. Suits you. Now listen: Kate's been going on about this new bloke of yours. She's very loyal – don't think she criticizes you – but I get the impression she doesn't care for him a lot. Who is he?'

'Polish. I've known him for getting on for two months now. He's about ten years older than us. Quite unlike any of our friends. . . sort of *mittel*-European intelligentsia type. Very serious; a bit humourless I suppose, rather laconic. Not your type, but mine.'

'What's he doing here?'

And so I tell Paul everything, wallowing in our former intimacy, which means that I don't have to make it funny; need not conceal my own disasters, yet can rely on the old shorthand of marriage and know that he will understand. Even as I tell him how much I love Iwo I find myself looking at Paul with nostalgia for the simple, undemanding cosiness of marriage. What's all this nonsense about sexy underwear and candlelight and having to double-check everything I say and analyse everything Iwo says? It's all so exhausting.

'Conce, do you honestly think he's right for you? Because

it doesn't sound like it, the way you tell it. You make it sound hell.'

'Look, right from the beginning I was certain that he was – well, saving your presence, Paul – the one man I'd been waiting for. I stumbled on him like a well in the desert and could hardly believe my luck. He was clever and attractive and he needed me.'

'So? What's gone wrong?'

'I don't know . . . in fact I never know whether I'm imagining it all. One time we'll meet and it's just fantastic and I'm up and flying . . . the next time it'll be awkward and stiff with long silences and it all seems like my fault and I come away feeling a complete fool.'

'He sounds like a sadist to me. One of those types who gets a kick out of proving his power over women because he can't actually make a go of a relationship.'

'Darling, don't, *don't* say that! You put my nightmares into words and I can't bear it!'

'Has he said he's in love with you? Can you talk about your feelings?'

'Never. I don't know why but that's taboo. I've never said I love him and he of course hasn't either, and doesn't, I think, love me.'

'But he fucks you?'

'Yes.'

'Earth-moving stuff?'

'Paul that's an odd sort of question to ask!'

'Think of us as just good friends. Is he a good fuck, or are you a *real* masochist?'

'He's a good fuck.'

'Now listen my dear ex-wife . . . no, don't look like that. I'm not being patronizing. I'm extremely fond of you and I flatter myself I still know you pretty well. Here, might as well finish the bottle. You are, if I may say so, a sexual innocent. Apart from me, and not counting the gropers in the back row who preceded me, you haven't been to bed with a great many men, I would think?'

'Depends what you . . .'

'Don't muck about, love. Have you?'

'No.'

'And especially not lately?'

'Some. Well, I suppose not that many.'

'Which makes you a pushover for any bloke with a hard-on and a passable line in intellectual chat. But apart from bed – yeah, I take your word on that – what do you have in common? Hobbies? Friends? Bird-watching? Does he like the kids? Make you laugh? Constance . . . whatever . . . sweetheart for God's sake don't *cry*.'

He gets up and beckons me over to the lumpy old sofa that has always sat in a corner of the breakfast room, where the children did their homework and cuddled cats and quarrelled with each other; and I get up too and fold myself into his familiar lap, and there I lay my head against his shoulder and cry and cry. I cry for us, so fond and close and irretrievably apart; I cry for me and Iwo, so much hope and love going to waste; and finally I cry for me, for the black pit of fear and loneliness and humiliation that yawns in my unwanted unmarried state. I cry for a friend, a lover, a husband.

When at last I have finished crying, Paul kisses my hot, swollen eyes and says, 'Every instinct tells me to make it better by taking you upstairs to our room and our bed; but it isn't *our* bed any longer, and I would make that lady waiting for me back home very unhappy if I did. But Constance, listen to me. If something's right, you *know* it's right . . . because it's easy, not difficult; relaxed, not tense; funny, not miserable. Because you're not in awe of the guy, like some kind of superhero, you know his faults and his weaknesses and you love him for them. When something's wrong it's no good torturing yourself. And you do know, really, that this one is wrong.'

'Paul, you don't understand. I know all that . . . and I love him. I just totally, helplessly, beyond my control, even against my will, love him.'

'Now you sound like a Barbara Cartland heroine. "But sire – or papa, or my Lord, or whatever – I love this man." "Why

100

then, Mistress Constance, he shall be thine!" Snap out of it, silly cow, and come back to real life; since apart from making yourself a misery, you're not doing my children a lot of good. Stop languishing in some romantic novel and start being a real, funny, liberated human being again. Next time Lulu and I have people round for dinner do you want to come along?'

'God forbid! One advertising man is more than enough for a lifetime!'

'Thank God for that . . . you sound like yourself again! Don't be rude and I'll see if lurking anywhere in my limited circle of acquaintances there might be someone quite uncontaminated by the advertising world.'

And so we kiss and part; and for a few days my sense of perspective is restored and I feel better, even quite indignant with Iwo. I hold brisk imaginary conversations with him in which I say, Stop mucking me about, Iwo and tell me what's going on! What do you actually feel for me, if anything? or, even more bravely, Who *are* all these Polish women who make such a fuss whenever you put in an appearance – Joanna and Marina and God knows who else?

Until he rings; and on the phone he is nice to me, his voice is tender and he says he's been thinking about me and needs to see me. Immediately the old addiction floods through my veins again, and my mind is clouded with the heady knowledge that I shall see him within less than forty-eight hours. Paul's sensible advice seems utterly misguided and irrelevant.

Iwo is uncanny. He knows the precise moment when he has pushed me to the edge; when I could almost bring myself to say that our relationship is making me unhappy and we had better stop . . . and at that moment, he will become gentle and attentive, full of little hints about what we can do together in the spring. These moments expunge all my past doubts. I reproach myself for having been foolish, self-indulgent, introspective; for failing to make allowances, expecting too much, too soon. After such a meeting my mind races away to the opposite extreme. I am buoyant, confident, positively audacious. I may even over-reach myself to the point of telephoning him. If I do, I am punished. He's out, and some strong, casual Australian voice doesn't know where he is; sometimes, not even *who* he is.

'Iwo? Who's he? Monty? Hey you guys, anyone know a fellow called Monty? Sheila here says he's Polish . . . What do you want with a Pole, lady? No, don't answer that! You want to leave a message?'

But that is the lesser of the two evils. It's worse when I ring and he does come to the phone.

'Yes, hello?'

'Iwo, hello, yes, are you there? It's me, Constance . . .'

'Yes, hello Constance.'

'I, well, just wanted to say hello, you know, and . . .'

'Yes?'

'Oh Iwo you are hopeless on the telephone! I just wanted to chat. What've you been doing this week? Shall I see you at the weekend?'

'This week has been much the same as all the others and yes, if you like we can meet at the weekend.'

From this cheerless conversation I retire humiliated, angry with myself and him. If I am interrupting something, why doesn't he say so? Maybe he can't. Maybe Joanna is at his elbow, blowing on his ear and smiling, centimetres away from my little pleading voice. If I'm not interrupting any-thing, why can't he make amiable conversation for five minutes? This man has now made love to me a dozen times, yet he still can't be civil on the telephone.

On the spur of the moment I decide to go and talk to Marina. She has known him for years and, despite having been his pupil, she manages to treat him as an equal. She's the obvious person to turn to for advice. She's practically a stranger to *me* but the important thing is that she knows *him*. If anyone can provide clues to the riddle of Iwo, she can. I grab a book, my purse, coat – so different from the preparation for meeting him – and I'm off.

I don't know the club's address, and wouldn't normally be

able to find my way there after just one visit. But I only have to recall that evening when Iwo brought me there, what I wore, where we met, and the rest follows naturally. I remember everything. I am a little abashed at entering this Polish haven without him, but this is submerged in the much greater fear that I may find him there. He is not.

As I reach the foot of the stairs Marina sees me, and a wonderful curving smile lights up her face.

'Oh, it's Monty's friend!' she says. 'I did so *hope* you would come back. I want to talk with you.'

'Me too: are you busy? Can we sit and talk now? Look, you must call me Constance . . . and please, can we call him Iwo? Monty sounds strange.'

'Constance: yes, of course. If more customers come I may have to leave you, but sit here and I'll get some coffee and pastries.'

Marina takes charge of the conversation, and doesn't allow me to feel embarrassed or intrusive.

'I was so glad when I met you that Monty — sorry, I *will* remember! — *Iwo* had found a good woman to love him. It is so necessary for a man. They are bad alone. For him, he makes this big step, he leaves Poland, and for what? He is poor and bored with a stupid job and . . .'

'It's not such a stupid job. You know he mends violins and things?'

'Is that what he tells you? Well, probably I should not say different: but the truth is, he packs for a musical instrument shop. Guitars and pop music things, they sell. He packs them in paper and cardboard for being sent away. How should he mend them? He knows nothing about instruments!'

I am dumb with the poignancy of Iwo's deception. To have gone from being an economics professor to a violin mender would have been bad enough; now I find he has actually had to go lower still. No wonder he can't make small talk about his working life. How crass I've been! Clumsy, tactless — oh, *fool*.

'It is not important. Look: I am a waitress. There is a

103

famous Polish writer who is often in here. He works as a postman. We all have to start right down. But Iwo: his mental state is bad, do you think?'

'Marina, I don't know. He isn't an easy man to get to know. Is he usually more cheerful?'

'No, not that. Professor Zaluski was never cheerful. But he used to be full of fire and beliefs, always talking about his work, having great big arguments with his students. He was very outspoken against the authorities . . . ever since I can remember, not just when everyone suddenly got brave. And now . . . he is very bitter, don't you find?'

'I thought it was *me*.'

'You? No, Constance, I think he is better since you. I tried to help him, to make him look forward instead of back, always, always back, to Poland.'

'Ah. Yes. I wondered about that. So you did . . . well, I mean, did you . . . sorry. I'm being rude.'

'No. I will tell you, because if I tell you the truth then you may believe there was no more. Yes, when we first found each other here, soon after he had arrived, yes, I went back to his room with him. It was strange for me. He was my professor once, and he is the age of my father. But he had known my fiancé – I had been a class-mate with his daughter: Henryka, the older one – and it was as though all the people we had left behind in Lodz were suddenly concentrated into just the two of us. So: yes, I made love with him. But it was only comfort we wanted, not sex. After that we could be just friends.'

'How can you be sure he felt the same?'

'I think so. Anyway, I have my boyfriend now, an *English* boyfriend, so it is no longer possible. And now he has you.'

'But does he want me?'

'Why not? Do you want him?'

'Oh Marina . . . you've no idea how much!'

'Well, all you must do is give him the things he needs. Comfort. Warmth. Love. Do you have children? It is nice if he is in a home sometimes. And let him have a nice time

'. . . you know, let him enjoy. He is too serious.'

'But does he want all that? He's so remote and . . . He frightens me.'

'Yes, he frightens me too. I think he frightens himself. Iwo I think is in love with our country, only he didn't know this until he had gone. He is like many Poles: I see it here, all the time. They become such patriots when they are away from Poland! But he can't go back, he must accept that his life is here. I have a nice English boyfriend who will marry me if I want to, and that makes me feel that I can belong here. Perhaps you do the same for Iwo?'

I am intrigued, though not surprised, to learn that she has a boyfriend. He must be unusual to attract her. She has already experienced so much: no ordinary, conventional Englishman would appeal to her. I'd like to ask more about him, but my immediate curiosity is focused on Iwo. I long to know more about his earlier life – what was his wife like? Did he sleep with his students? But just then a group of people comes in wanting to have a meal, and Marina has to look after them. I smile gratefully at her, and leave my phone number on a piece of paper.

As I prepare to go she seizes my hand and says, 'You will come back and see me again, won't you Constance?'

'I will, I will . . . thank you so much!'

Outside on the cold street I realize I am only a few hundred yards away from his house. Dare I go and visit him? I walk towards his street and stand a few doors down from the house, looking at it. I walk round to the back of the square, trying to make out which is his window and whether a light burns in his room. My heart thuds with nervous anticipation. This is ridiculous, I think, either stay and offer the comfort Marina says he needs, or go back home to Kate, but don't stand gazing up at what is probably the wrong window. I walk purposefully back to the house and ring the doorbell. A blast of light and raucous laughter. The Australians are there in force. Their noisy gusto pauses as they look at me expectantly.

'We do anything for you, lady?'

'Is . . . have you seen? . . . well, I wondered if Iwo, or Monty, is in?'

'I know you! The lady who's always on the telephone! Why don't you go up and take a look? Know which is his room? Yes, of course you do! Go on: give him a nice surprise!'

They mean to be kind, but they are overwhelming. Surely, if Iwo were there he would have heard my voice and put his head out? If not, perhaps he doesn't want to see me? Perhaps he has company already – Joanna? Anyway, I didn't have the usual bath and ritual dressing-up before I left. My lipstick has come off.

'No, no, thank you very much but it's all right. I was just passing and I wondered . . .'

'Come in and have a Foster's with us, why don't you?'

'No, honestly, thanks awfully, no I must go home.'

I escape. It is not the sort of ordeal I will risk repeating.

Perhaps they told Iwo that I had been looking for him: Hey Monty, you're a sly bastard. Nice little Sheila came round for you last night, where were you? No sign. Missed your chance there, didn'ya? Or perhaps he realized he had been short on the telephone; at any rate, a couple of days later he rings me, and it is time for the good policeman to take his turn. He enquires solicitously after my week: how are the children, how is the library, how am I and do I still want to meet this weekend? Shall we see a film? Shall we both consult *Time Out* and then compare notes this time tomorrow? If I had a shred of self-respect I would berate him for having been so abrupt. If we had a normal sort of relationship, relaxed and easy as Paul described, I would tell him that I had talked to Marina. But I don't do either: instead, I agree rapturously to look in *Time Out* and phone him back later.

With winged fingers I scan the film columns. I know his preferences and it is not hard to convince myself that I, too, want to see these films of intergalactic slaughter; these worlds, pre-historic or post-nuclear, peopled with blonde teenagers in well-rounded breastplates and designer lingerie. The film is unimportant: a pretext for meeting. I have other plans. Marina is right when she says I must make Iwo enjoy himself. I have thought of a way. It's a risk, though, he may scoff, as he did at the candles.

He meets me in central London in the early evening and together we hurry through the rain, through the cheerful weekend crowds, through the technicoloured neon reflections bouncing in and out of puddles, and into the plush passivity of the cinema. This time I let him buy the tickets, not least because he has chosen the film, which could have been computer-assembled from the ten commonest elements in American college-kid movies. He watches it with the fascination of an anthropologist observing the fertility rites of a new tribe and I, glancing sideways through my fingers, watch his attentive profile outlined by the bluish light from the screen. We leave the cinema in high spirits.

'Excellent film!' says Iwo, with real satisfaction. 'Now what?'

'Now I have plans for us. Let's go back to your room. You'll see . . .'

It is early December. The streets are cold and wet, the shop windows glittering. The tube is full of shoppers laden, even at this hour, with bulky plastic bags. I too am weighed down with a supermarket carrier. I have planned a picnic: a luxury picnic which we shall eat on the floor of his room. He will either shrug eloquently and make some dismissive comment or he will like the eccentricity of the idea, and join in. Luckily for me his good humour, prompted by the absurd film, inclines him to the latter. Midnight feasts in the dormitory used to be like this, tinged with the same edge of hysteria, but in those days it was the fear of matron's sudden entry that made us stifle our giggles as we gorged ourselves to nausea on tinned peaches and artificial cream, Mars bars, sweet sherry or cider and bags of crisps. But tonight Iwo is not going to be matron. He looks on with astonishment as I produce the delicacies I bought this morning: two bottles of wine, and a corkscrew; plastic cups and plates; smoked meat and sausages and fish; four kinds of cheese, with celery already washed and stripped of its fibres; apples and parsley and even salt and pepper . . . I have thought of everything. I sit on the floor surrounded by the food, and open the first bottle of wine. A grin spreads over his face — oh, it is so lovely to see him smile!

'Wonderful! What an idea!' he says. 'Pity we have no music. Well, you must imagine, at the far end of the room behind that curtain, four musicians in dinner jackets: a string quartet. They are going to play Mozart, don't you think? Yes. My dear, have you been carrying all this food all evening? I wondered what was in your bag.'

'It's much cheaper than eating out, and it's fun. If you didn't hate candles so much . . .'

'Who says I hate candles? Look, here, you want candles? I have some.'

He fixes three candles firmly in saucers, and they surround us flickering softly, making small points of orange in the gleaming glass of the wine bottles. Outwardly I am vivacious and talkative. I laugh as I tell him the story of my week — told to make him laugh about the people who have been in the library, Linda's problems with the exasperating Stavros, Kate's mulishness.

I can't bear silence, which has always seemed synonymous with disapproval, ever since my childhood. My father used to come upstairs after my mother had kissed me good night and switched the light out. He would sit mutely on the end of my bed in the dark heavy with disappointment at my behaviour. He might begin a sentence, 'Your mother tells me, Constance, that you've been rude again . . .' but his voice would trail away as though in despair, his lack of words a more eloquent reproach than anything he could have said. At other times I didn't get any clues at all; he would merely sit, and sigh. Eventually he'd get up, saying something like, 'I hope tomorrow I shall be able to feel more like kissing you good night . . .' and he would walk slowly out of the room, closing the door very gently behind him. He had no idea how much harm he was doing, after all, he hadn't hit me, hadn't even raised his voice. I am sure he thought of himself

108

as the kindest of fathers. I would be left lying in bed, clenched with remorse for the unknown sins I had committed, probably the same ones as usual: rudeness, showing off, ingratitude. But because my father had said nothing, the sins never felt forgiven or forgotten. My deep-seated anger and guilt remained. Iwo never accuses me of anything – how could he? I have done nothing wrong – but his failure to praise is far more damning. It means that everything I *am* is inadequate.

In the attempt to amuse Iwo I work out in advance what I am going to say. Nothing is spontaneous. On bad evenings my foolish remarks fall into leaden silence and leaden looks. Tonight, thank God, is one of the good evenings. Iwo, eating Polish *krakowska* sausages and smoked pork fillet on black bread and rye bread, sipping a glass of good white wine from Paul's – no, dammit, *my*! – cellar, cocks his head towards me and contrives to make me feel as though he is indulging me, when surely it is the other way round.

Because our relationship is discontinuous, each meeting becomes a separate event. It's hard to imagine us reaching that relaxed and happy state of people who telephone every day or two and chat about what's been happening, just to say that all's well. For every hour spent in Iwo's company there have been five of thought and planning. Tonight the stage is softly lit and the props are food and drink, but the dialogue is false. It looks like a scene from one of the films I love so much, *Pandora's Box* maybe, and if only I looked like Louise Brooks! Here we are in Jack the Ripper's attic room, black and white, a slanting beam of light from the window emphasizing his sharp cheekbones and the cut of her hair and chin. Amid this surreal menace my one-woman performance is all wrong. This cold picnic in a cold room with a cold man is a farce. Let's get drunk and replace the artificiality that I have orchestrated with one that's alcohol-induced. No: I can *pretend* to be drunk and ask him questions I couldn't risk when sober.

'This wine is good.'

'Mmm, isn't it? Pour me out another glass . . . Iwo: tell me about your wife.'

'We mustn't drink too much. It's late already.'

'Tell me *all* about her. What was she like? Do you think about her *all* the time?'

'What time is it? Do you want to sleep here tonight?'

'Yes. Go on Iwo, *answer.*'

'What about Kate? Are you happy to leave her alone?'

'She's not alone. Cordy's there. Can I have another glass of wine? You have one as well. What about *your* daughters?'

'If I drink any more I'm afraid I shall disappoint you.'

'You couldn't. Iwo, tell me . . .'

'Constance, what do you want me to say? That I think about my wife? Yes, I do. Not all the time. And my daughters? Yes. Now will you come to bed?'

It's no good. Even drunk – he must be a bit drunk – he's had the best part of the two bottles – his self-control never falters. In his orderly fashion he tidies away the remains of our meal, putting the plastic bag full of debris behind the curtain so that the gleaming floorboards are bare again. I sit on the edge of his bed and watch. He undresses, folding up his clothes. It's like a striptease, his slow, absorbed movements heightening my desire. When he is quite naked, shivering in the blue air of the room, he puts his arms around me.

'Now I am going to do the most erotic things to you . . .' he says.

Why do I invent a monster and torment myself, when the real Iwo makes love to me with skill and generosity? He leaves no part of me untouched. What does it matter if he doesn't speak? Why do I need words, when here, coiling around me, over and under, warm body and entwined limbs, is the proof that he wants me? And yet, I wish he would speak. I know that the words, 'I love you', uttered by either of us, would bring me to instant orgasm. But he doesn't say them, and I can't.

Sleep on, my love, in thy cold bed, never to be disquieted.

8

The good alternates with the bad. The ordinary is followed by new horrors that I hadn't thought of; and I thought I'd thought of them all. But to start with the ordinary, the comfortingly normal, the safe bits of my life: all of which I would overturn for him.

The library on Monday morning has more than its usual quota of pensioners escaping from their cheerless rooms. They come here because it's warm, and full of company. From the speed with which they get through their library books, I reckon some of these pensioners don't speak to anyone all weekend.

Not that they're all to be pitied. Take the huge and formidable Mrs Rowe, doing her usual trick of commandeering all the serious Sundays and monopolizing them by simply sitting down and spreading her skirts across the ones she isn't reading. She's so myopic she has to hold the relevant section right up to her eyes and peer at it from a couple of inches away. Perhaps that's why she likes to get them first, so that they don't smell of other people's dirty or nicotine-stained hands.

Some are in a desperate plight, yet manage to confront it without a trace of self-pity. Like my old favourite, Mr Southgate: he's in again this morning, looking for the reference books on law.

'Thinking of embarking on a life of crime?' I ask.

'Never left it!' he says.

He has recurring problems with his tenant. He's far too delicate to sully my feminine ears with the precise misdemeanours, but I'm given to understand, by those meaningful looks and pauses that indicate the physical functions, that nowadays the man not only . . . when he's been drinking, he's even taken to . . . as well.

'It's shocking. It's not right, and I won't have it in my house!'

Mr Southgate wants to find out his legal rights as regards evicting the man. I direct him to the reference section of the library, knowing that he won't in fact take action – the same tenant has been there for years – but understanding too that the mere act of doing something will make him feel better. I've suggested in the past that he should go and talk to the Law Centre or the Citizen's Advice Bureau, but his fierce independence, combined with his fear of authority in any form no matter how benign, precludes this.

One or two housewives want to look up Christmas recipes in cookery books or magazines. I recommend *Good Housekeeping*, and tell them it costs ten pence to use the photocopier. Linda wants to know if I've made my Christmas pudding yet. The morning passes sluggishly. The light beyond the windows is dark grey, and the rain is thickening into sleet. In spite of this I decide, on the spur of the moment, to go home for lunch.

I am in the middle of loading the washing machine when the phone rings. Iwo? Max? My mother? Three possible phone conversations have already flashed through my mind by the time I pick it up.

'Constance? I hoped you might be at home. This is Iwo.'

'Iwo! Already! Where are you?'

'In the workshop.' You mean postroom. 'Eating a sandwich. Tadeusz rang to ask if we – he invites you, too – can come to see a Polish play at the Centre. I said I'd check with you. He needs to book.'

'Iwo, how wonderful! In *Polish*. When?'

'It is a play about an informer, in Warsaw, in the early fifties. A time I remember. There'll be headphones to translate for you. He suggested Thursday.'

'Will Joanna be there too?' Damn. 'Yes, I'm free. Thursday will be fine. How kind. Isn't this weather foul?'

112

'I am in the basement: I can't see it from here. I don't know about Joanna. Does it make a difference?'

'No, no, of course not . . . I just wondered. Yes, please say yes for me.'

'Good. I will meet you at Ravenscourt Park, the tube station, at about seven thirty.'

'Fine, lovely, what fun, yes, see you then.'

'Your sandwiches are very good.'

'*My* sandwiches?'

'From last night.'

'Oh I see: yes, of course. I'm so glad. Iwo, you know there's this old man who comes into the library a lot? He was in there this morning, and . . .'

He interrupts. 'I have to go, Constance. You may tell me on Thursday.'

'Of course, sorry, it's not important. Thanks for ringing . . .'

'Goodbye.'

Well, maybe everything *will* be all right, after all. We're going out together publicly, as a couple, that's a first.

The sky outside my window casts an almost black light and heavy rain flattens the leaves into a slimy mass. I go upstairs to surprise Kate by making her bed for her, and leave a cheerful note welcoming her back from school before returning to the library. It's cold. I need my woollen gloves.

My ritual for getting ready before meeting him takes longer and longer. It didn't take me nearly as long to prepare for my wedding – but I was young and I thought Paul loved me. On Wednesday evening I go through Cordy's wardrobe as well as my own, trying on and discarding several possibilities, and finally decide on simplicity: high-necked black sweater, narrow black skirt and boots. This unrelieved black is relieved with some of Cordy's unconventional jewellery. On Thursday I come back from work to an empty house – Kate is spending the night at a girlfriend's house again – and the stillness and solitude calm me down. The rites of preparation are enjoyable. I lie in a scented bath, breathing

113

scented steam and trying out Cordy's henna rinse. Best if I assume Joanna will be there, and make a point of talking to Tadeusz. Then Iwo can do what he likes.

The Polish Centre could be in the middle of Warsaw for all the English I can hear around me. I watch the audience, trying to see whether they have anything in common with each other, or with Iwo. There is perhaps a kind of intensity in the way they talk and gesture and listen. Their smiles and arguments are passionate: or do I romanticize them because they are all Polish? The truth is probably that they could be any cross-section of people, some well dressed, some drab. Iwo looks shabbier than most.

He leans forward and watches the play with fierce concentration, nodding occasionally. I wear headphones, through which I can hear the interpreter's voice speaking in time with the actors. When he – that is, the hero – says, 'I can't live in another country, under another sky. . .' the words make me glance at Iwo, to see if he reacts to their relevance to his own situation, but he listens apparently unmoved. 'There isn't a man in Poland who isn't scared' – he and Tadeusz nod at one another. And, at the end, 'My country! Why did it always have to be so sad, so desperately, hopelessly sad!' My lover! Exile has made you joyless, and I do so long for joy.

I reflect, during the applause, that if I am fathoms deep in love, Iwo must be fathoms deep in grief. The sad country he has left is unknown to me, and the chance of reconciling our two obsessions is slim. But it does help me to put Joanna into perspective. It is Poland he loves and wants, not some other woman. My jealousy of her misses the point. Marina was right: what he needs above all is comfort, warmth, a reason to live in the present and stop yearning for the past. Oh, I know I can do that for him – and I take his arm with the confidence of our earlier meetings as we walk through to the restaurant.

As we sit down, Iwo and Tadeusz start talking Polish, so I turn to Joanna and ask her to help me with the menu. She recommends a dish called *bigos,* a thick, filling, smoky stew, and as Tadeusz turns his attention to ordering I look past the waitress and see . . .

'Iwo! Look there! Surely that's Marina!'

'You're right.'

He smiles brilliantly and goes across to where she is sitting with a young man. He comes back with them and we all rearrange ourselves to share the same, now cramped, table.

'This is my friend Peter,' says Marina. 'Peter Matthews.' He shakes hands all round and even sketches a small, un-English inclination of the head.

'Could you understand the play?' Iwo asks him.

'Those headphones were excellent, didn't you think? And Marina had explained the plot beforehand – it's very well-known, right? So I could follow it. As to whether I *understood* . . . I don't know whether any English person can understand.'

At once I grasp that he loves Marina, for he has interpreted the play through her experiences exactly as I had applied it to Iwo's.

'Peter,' says Marina, 'you realize this is *the* Professor Zaluski, who taught me at university; at Lodz?'

'Was she a *model* student?' Peter asks him, mock-sarcastic to conceal his pride.

Iwo sees it too, and answers. 'Oh, she was. That is to say: difficult, talkative, made every class into a battlefield . . . cost me very much trouble!'

'Hasn't changed, then,' says Peter.

Marina was not boasting when she said her English boyfriend would marry her. The problem is more likely to be whether she wants him. He isn't at all as I had imagined. In his early thirties, he's rather thin, his face angular and severe, and he wears a blazer and knife-edged trousers. Her dead fiancé would have been very different – but then, we marry who we can, and for a variety of reasons. She offers beauty and intelligence; he offers security. It's much the same exchange as between Iwo and me. So does that mean he, like Marina, is wondering whether he could settle for someone so much less good than he had before? But he

115

keeps insisting his marriage went cold years ago.

Marina is conferring with Iwo about his visa, and as she pauses to explain the situation to me I learn for the first time that it will probably not be renewed. Even though he has a job and somewhere to live, the extension could be refused. In the first wave of sympathy that the British felt for Solidarity, it wasn't hard for Poles to get entry visas. Even Home Office officials and immigration officers were touched by the courage of brave Polish workers raising their banner to confront the Soviets in the name of freedom. But three or four years later, that struggle is out of the headlines and those who were originally welcome now find their position insecure. Thus Iwo and Marina need to seek permission all over again, every year, and dare not leave the country for even the shortest holiday in case they are refused re-entry. The authorities have no reason to deny Iwo an extension to his visa, but . . . he knows others, equally blameless, who have been given notice to leave. What have they done wrong? They're not told. Perhaps a landlord complained anonymously, or a colleague. Perhaps they fell foul of some petty official in the DHSS. It may be anything, or nothing at all. I hadn't realized quite how urgently Iwo needs a wife, an *English* wife, who can give him permanent status here. If he doesn't marry me, or somebody, soon, he might be gone within weeks! Joanna swims back into focus as a very real threat: for she, as the daughter of a naturalized Briton, born and brought up in England herself, she would also guarantee him residence. His situation, mine, is more desperate than I knew.

'We are lucky that the British like us,' Joanna is saying. 'You'll be all right, don't worry. It's not as if you were black.'

'Quite right too,' says Peter, and his face turns spiteful. 'Far too many of *them* here. Thinking a British passport is a meal-ticket for life. Lazy buggers. Double the birth-rate of whites.'

Dear God! I think, the man's a racist. No wonder Marina's shining corn-goddess looks appeal to him. Can I challenge him, or would that offend her? But he is offending me.

'In the company of so many foreigners who are the grateful guests of your country,' Iwo is saying in a dangerous monotone, 'that is perhaps not a wise thing to say.'

Rather than watch them square up to each other, both needing to impress Marina, I interrupt and change the subject.

'Peter, how did you and Marina meet?'

'I picked her up!'

'He picked me up practically *inside* a *church!*' she says, 'nearly six months ago.'

'It was *out*side the Brompton Oratory,' says Peter, and as the two of them laugh and correct each other and tell the story of their first meeting I see that they *are* happy together – they're far more relaxed as a couple than Iwo and I – and it will probably work out for them. Lucky them. I glance across the table at Joanna, trying to gauge her reaction, and wonder how she feels about marriage and if she has a lover. She's surely in her mid-thirties, yet there's been no mention of a man. Could she – it seems unlikely, but she could I suppose be lesbian. Just then Marina gets up and heads towards the Ladies, so I follow.

I love the way women relax the moment they're alone together, even in a ladies' loo. I already *like* Marina far more than I like Iwo. She's a friend and an ally and he's certainly neither of those things.

'Peter obviously adores you,' I tell her.

'I must show you a photograph of Jerzy next time. My Polish fiancé.'

'Is Peter like him at all?'

'He lives at home, with his mother, works in an insurance company . . . no, he is not at all like Jerzy. He has had a simple life, he is a good Catholic, and he loves me. Which is surprising because he's very patriotic, very proud to be English. Falling in love with a foreigner is the most dangerous thing he's ever done in his life. I think he's still surprised at himself.'

'And you . . . ?'

'Constance, we must go back, or Joanna will think we're talking about her.'

'I'd actually meant to ask you about her . . . but some other time. You found my phone number?'

'Yes. Don't worry.'

'Marina, if you know about him and Joanna you've got to tell me.'

'*Yes*, once or twice, but don't let it worry you. I know him, and I promise you it isn't important! Come on. We must go back.'

Why did I insist? Now I have to emerge and look at Joanna – and they are, of course, talking together in our absence, heads close, while Tadeusz struggles to make conversation with that frightful little Fascist. Joanna's wonderful auburn hair swings over her face concealing her expression, making her words confiding, for his ears only. And to think I walked in here proudly holding his arm – look, everybody, this is my man!

Tadeusz grins at us.

'When two women go off to the Ladies together they always take three times as long! Well, have you decided about us? Do we get gold stars?'

'*Two* gold stars!' I tell him. 'One for the play and one for the dinner.'

'Well, if you are going to be one of us' – oh, leaping heart! – 'you will have to learn about us. We are sentimental, we are Polish, we live with our past.'

But Joanna interrupts, before he can give me more precious clues.

'Papa stop it, you will depress us all! Constance, take no notice. He's a tragic actor who is still waiting for his destiny. The theatre always makes him like this. Now he's going to go home and brood on the great soul of his country. Am I right, Iwo?'

'He will, and so will I,' says Iwo. 'Shall we go?'

We part in a flurry of smiles, handshakes, hand-kissing, cheek-kissing: several social conventions all going on at once, like a comic sketch. Iwo refuses both offers of a lift and, taking my arm, heads resolutely towards the tube station.

Half an hour later, less, we are together in his bed. He makes love to me in silence, as usual: but tonight it seems as though he is suppressing speech. Words burst like fireworks in my mind, beautiful explosive showers that I long to release and dare not. He embraces me, takes hold of me, turns me this way and that, rolls me to and fro, with a ferocity that is close to violence. The tightrope between pleasure and pain is taut and narrow, and we sway along it together, leaning one way and then the other. I have a strong urge to bite and scratch, to mark that smooth pale skin and startle him into making a noise. I bare my teeth against his shoulder, taste his sweat, part my lips against his flesh, graze it with my teeth.

'Yes!' he murmurs, 'Oh yes. . .'

That night he talks in his sleep: in Polish of course, and repeats the name 'Kika'.

I lie awake for hours under the pale night sky, my mind brimming with questions. But few nights are entirely sleepless, for in the morning he wakes me.

9

The following evening, walking back from the library, I
notice that already Christmas trees are beginning to appear,
leaning in resinous clumps outside the greengrocer's. Paper
cut-outs with red or green lettering saying 'Merry Xmas' and
'Season's Greetings' are pasted inside shop windows,
and woolly gloves, slippers, and knitted hat and scarf sets
now have the words 'Gift for Dad' pinned beside the price.
'Order Your Christmas Turkey Now!' says a notice in the
butcher's window; so I go in and order a goose. For how
many? Until now, Paul has always made a point of spending
Christmas Day with us, leaving his current girlfriend to visit
her parents or stay with friends or go skiing or do whatever
they did. Now I wonder whether I can invite Iwo to join us
this year. Will he want to share our English Christmas? What
will the children say? I order a large goose, big enough for
six, eight at a pinch. That should cover all possible permu-
tations. The Indian newsagent has paper streamers
festooned garishly across the shop and extra racks of
Christmas wrapping paper with Father Christmas and his
reindeer sledging downhill. I buy an Advent calendar for
Kate. In the end I'll probably be the one to prise open the
daily doors and peer at the tiny drawings on transparent
paper, as the dates progress steadily towards 24th December.

Kate is home already, and shrugs eloquently when she
sees the calendar. At least she doesn't reject it.

'I had a brilliant time at Amanda's, Mother. We sent off
this whole load of really weird Christmas cards to the boys
at her brother's school. They were like way-out cartoons saying, "It's a girl!" and "Peace on earth and goodwill to all
women!" and stuff like that. The boys are such sexist pigs.

And then me and Amanda sat up for hours talking. We want to give this really great New Year's Eve party . . .'

'Where?'

'Not here, don't worry, at Amanda's house. Her mum's already said we can. We were making out a guest list. We'll do the food and get everyone to bring a bottle . . .'

'A *bottle?* Darling, you're a bit young for a bottle party: are you sure Amanda's mother doesn't mind? I'd better give her a ring . . .'

'It's all *right* Mother. Oh Christ, you'll only go and spoil it and make her think it's going to be really wild and it *won't* be . . .'

'Will they be there? Her parents?'

'Course they will. I mean, we'll organize everything, we've got it all planned. Her brother'll do the disco and . . .'

'What time did you get to bed?'

'It wasn't late, Mother, honestly.'

'To sleep then?'

'Well, round about midnight, something like that.'

That means small hours. She'll get crotchety with tiredness soon. 'Darling, I must sit down and think about my Christmas present list. Why don't you start on your homework while I'm doing that? Then we'll have supper. Call me if you need help.'

Kate goes off to spread her school books in a messy semicircle over the dining room table. I make myself coffee and sit down to think about Iwo, and my Christmas list.

The phone rings and I leap to answer it.

'Hello? . . . Paul! How're things? Listen, you were really nice the other evening. I'm sorry I . . .'

'No problem. You OK? Seen him lately? Any better?'

'Yes, last night. I'm getting to understand him a bit, I think. It's all this business of being Polish that screws things up. Anyway, some other time . . . What about you? Are you seeing the children this weekend?'

'Not this one. Lulu and I thought we'd take off for a quiet weekend in the country before the countdown to Christmas starts. Soon everyone'll be getting drunk at agency parties.

There's a great place in the Cotswolds I know . . .'

'Yeah, I remember . . .'

'Not that one. Another one. Don't be so spiky. I'm ringing to ask you to dinner, but I could always change my mind.'

Dinner. He hasn't asked me for dinner before. I've been to his flat for Sunday lunch sometimes with the children or drinks on my ex-father-in-law's birthday: awkward, dutiful occasions when we all tried to make believe that in spite of the divorce we were still a close and caring family. It never worked. But I'd had the impression up till now that Paul's social life was more a matter of cocktails at the media clubs than dinner parties at his place. I hadn't realized Lulu was so entrenched. It's nice of him to ask me. I must have worried him.

'What dinner? When?'

'Saturday week. Be about eight of us, some you know, some you don't. Remember Andrew Lloyd-Simpson, from Oxford? Christ Church man?'

'Andrew? Good heavens . . . yes, I do remember him. What's he been up to all these years? Gosh, he was nice. He used to have poems in *Isis*, do you remember?'

'He still writes poetry. Published a slim volume last year. Faber and Faber.'

Good old Paul, never forgets a brand name. 'What's he doing nowadays?'

'Advertising.'

'Well, I'll manage to forgive him. Can I bring Iwo? Actually I'm curious for you to meet him. See what you think of him . . .'

'Certainly *not*. Whole point of this is to get you away from him, at least for one evening.'

'Oh Paul, I don't see him often.'

'Listen, are you coming? Saturday week? About eightish?'

'Christ, what'll I wear? Your friends are bound to be deadly chic.'

'Something red or black. Anything.'

'OK. Thank Lulu. I look forward to it.'

'Good. Seeya kiddo.'

Do I look forward to it? Lulu will probably be intimidatingly efficient, cook some wonderful nouvelle cuisine dinner, and I shall have very mixed feelings about seeing her act as my husband's partner and hostess. I go into the kitchen and prepare onion, bacon and potato hotpot for me and Katie, with plenty left over to warm up at the weekend if Cordy or Max drop in.

I spend the next few days in high spirits. I still love Christmas: not just for the children's sake, not just for the feasting and presents. I love the carols, the secrecy and planning, the lift that it gives to the mid-winter doldrums. Katie's school has a carol service and, although she pretends to find it all a great bore, I hear the high, clear notes of 'Oh Little Town of Bethlehem' or the lower register of 'Good King Wenceslas' drifting down from her room. I think about this year's decorations. We have always prided ourselves on not having to resort to twisted Woolworth's streamers or paper chains. Last year we decorated the house using a dozen rolls of silver paper, twisting it round the backs of chairs, smoothed glitteringly across the table and mantelpiece, adorned with ice-white satin ribbon and candles everywhere. This year I shall have to try to improve on that. Red and green would be nice, but how? Apples and holly and ivy and branches of fir? With green and red candles this time? Yards and yards of satin ribbon twining round the banisters, green and red again, and Christmas tree candles stuck into cored apples . . . yes. It takes days to decorate the whole house, but we never have a single fairy light anywhere, everything is lit by candles, with their mysterious old-fashioned smell and soft circles of guttering light. Lovely, oh it'll be *lovely!*

Then there's the children's presents to think about. Cordy will know what Kate wants; Kate will know what Cordy wants. Max will tell me himself. I scribble lists in the back of my diary. And Iwo? The excitement stops abruptly. I long to buy him special things: a warm, soft, expensive sweater; a thick duvet for his cold bed; a book about Vermeer, my favourite artist. I want to be extravagant: I want to be intimate. The problem is, how not to embarrass him? He has so little money; if he buys me anything at all it can only be a token.

As happens when I have recently seen him, I can think of Iwo quite sanely, even optimistically. He is like a drug to me. Only *he* is really in focus; the rest of the world grows hazy at his edges. This state of intensity lasts for a day or two after we have parted, but as time goes by, if he doesn't phone, I begin to be gripped by anxiety. My perception of him becomes distorted. After several days of silence, my craving has become so urgent that I can think of nothing else. I am tormented by brief flashes of memory which present him to my mind's eye: his walk; the angle of his head as he turns sideways to listen to me; the curious way he bares his teeth in a smile while he is talking, giving an air of humour or deprecating irony to his words. People in the library say constantly, 'Cheer up!' 'Don't look so worried!' or, kindly, 'Anything the matter, love?' The moment he telephones, I am better – and he does, and asks me if I am free on Sunday.

On Tuesday evening, as I'm about to leave for my regular twice a month visit to my mother, Cordy rings, sounding unusually agitated.

'Mother? Can you meet me this evening? It's urgent.'

'Darling, what's the matter? I can't really: I'm just on my way out to see Granny.'

'You can be late, for once. Ring her and say you're going to be an hour late. I have to talk to you. Not me – it's Max.'

'Is he all right? Has anything happened?'

'He and Judy have broken up . . . she walked out this afternoon. He called me just now. He sounds desperately upset.'

We arrange to meet in a wine bar and by the time I arrive she's there already, sitting hunched over a table with her hands curled round a glass of red wine. She tells me that things have been bad between Max and his girlfriend for several weeks now.

'I ought to have told you sooner, but you were so involved with your new bloke, I sort of never got a chance. He came over a couple of times last week and slept on my floor

124

because they'd been rowing so much. Then this evening he rang up – thank God I was *in* for a change! – and said he'd got back from work to find she'd moved all her stuff out and just gone. He cried on the phone, poor old Max.'

'Where is he now?'

'The other two in the house were going to take him out and get him pissed. I said I'd go round later.'

'Oh Cordy, *poor* Max. God I feel awful. Do you think he'd come home for a few days?'

'I doubt it Mother, quite honestly. You can try.'

And where was I when he needed me? Engrossed in my own obsession, to the exclusion of everything else: even the needs of my children.

As we share a bottle of red wine, Cordy fills in the details. Judy, a drama student, had dazzled Max by her flamboyance and intensity. He, slower and steadier, provided the anchor she needed. As time went on, be began to learn that her intensity could be deeply neurotic, and she started to blame him for anything that failed to go right in her life. Where once she had welcomed his imperturbability, recently she had begun to ridicule it. Max has never been good at losing his temper, and she mistook his calm for indifference. Cordy's eyes are bright with indignation on behalf of her brother.

'Jude's been a real *cow* to him lately. She's just left all the cooking and shopping and stuff to him – and Max is busy too, it's not just her – and used him as a tame skivvy.'

'Probably just as well she took herself off in that case,' I say. 'Will she be back, do you think?'

'Max didn't seem to think so. It sounds pretty final.'

'He cried? Oh Cordy, did he really cry on the phone?'

'I know, rotten, isn't it? At least he's got the other two. They'll look after him.'

'But what about me?'

'Not a lot you can do at the moment. I just had to tell you.'

'Will it ruin his Christmas?'

'Doubt it!' she says, and grins suddenly. 'It's his first big heartbreak, but he'll get over it.'

125

'Are you and Ben OK?'

'We're *fine*. Great. Don't worry about us.'

'No point in phoning Max tonight, if he's going out to get drunk. I'll talk to him in the morning and see if I can persuade him to come home for the weekend.'

'You do that.'

Outside on the pavement she gives me a great generous hug as we go our separate ways.

I arrive at my mother's for a belated supper, and have to try to conceal my anxiety from her, for she couldn't begin to understand Max's situation. The last thing I need is a lecture on the virtues of the old-fashioned ways. I watch her as she fusses about, blaming me for our spoilt meal, and wonder whether she finds old age any easier to cope with than I do middle age, or Max youth, or Kate adolescence. Her life has followed the pattern that could have been predicted almost when she was born: she must feel a certain satisfaction in having conformed to all those expectations. Whereas here am I, her daughter: a middle-aged woman with deepening lines and greying hair, yet ludicrously in love. How can a man love a woman unless he knew her when she was young? Women in their twenties have clear, confident faces nowadays, without the diffidence of earlier generations. In their late thirties they wonder how the years will reward them, but we in our forties begin to panic. Iwo has made me aware of my own mortality. Never, before I met him, had I examined my physical deterioration so ruthlessly, and seen that it was all I had feared. Yet his elegant skull is like a death's head, death itself.

'How's that new gentleman friend of yours?' enquires my mother brightly.

Cordy had guessed rightly that Max wouldn't want to come home, but he has agreed to drop in one evening: more, I suspect, for my sake than because he needs to see me. Meanwhile, there is Paul's dinner. Preparing to dress for that, I look through my wardrobe and am surprised to see how many clothes that he would recognize are still hanging there. For a moment I am tempted to wear the red dress which had inflamed the passions of Ron Rendle, Paul's former boss; but the memory of that fat, predatory hand along my thigh so put me off the dress that I have hardly worn it since. Might as well give it to the Oxfam shop. There is a floaty, crinkly black cotton number that Linda passed on to me, because it was too short for her. I still have nice legs; if I dress it up with shiny black tights and Cordy's jewellery I can probably get away with it. In half the time it takes me to get ready for Iwo, I set out for Paul's Hampstead flat. Silvery cones of snowflakes are eddying under the street lamps as I walk towards the bus stop, their weightlessness making a mockery of the squat blobs of cotton wool glued to shop windows. For once I don't spend the bus journey engrossed in my book, but gaze out of the window at the black outlines of trees receding through flurries of snow. By the time I ring Paul's doorbell my cheeks are icy and my best black shoes are wet, but my mood is ebullient.

'Constance!' Ah: no 'Conce' then, this evening. 'You made it! Terrific! Meet Lulu. Lu: Constance. Now don't you two spend the evening talking to each other or you'll make me nervous.'

Lulu looks apprehensive, but she smiles at me and her face mirrors the curiosity on mine. It's the first time we've met; and the children had not prepared me for her youth. She can't be out of her twenties. She's dressed like a sharp and chic little punk, her hair dyed black and cut short and angular around her pale, smooth face. She has large dark eyes and wears no make-up except bright red lipstick. In her sleeveless top and narrow black trousers, she is touchingly young. Together they shepherd me through to the drawing room — I am the first guest — where Paul hands me a stiff whisky. This is no moment to remind him that, as he perfectly well knows, I never drink anything other than red wine.

'Lulu, do you work with Paul?'

She does.

'Have you known each other long?'

Just over a year.

'Do you like the agency?'

Oh yes, she does.

Dear heavens, I think, give me a *bit* of help.

'I love your haircut! Where do you have it done?'

We are in the middle of a discussion about London's hair-dressers when the doorbell rings again and it's Andrew.

It is a shock seeing him after more than twenty years. His thick hair, which I remember smoothing across his forehead one evening when we sat in his rooms confiding in one another, now starts from the top of his head, above a high expanse of shining, domed skull. Yet he still looks like a poet: the problem is to discern the advertising man.

Whatever his thoughts on seeing me, his reaction is warm and generous. He puts his arms round me and gives me a real, enveloping hug, far removed from the usual chill social pecks on adjacent cheeks. He always was a dear man, even if, then as now, his clothes smelt faintly acrid with perspiration.

The dinner is well cooked and, like good guests, we eat it and praise it, conversing together first this side, then that. I play my part conscientiously because I know Paul is anxious for Lulu's sake that the evening should be a success. So I make social small talk . . . plans for Christmas? Going away? Miles and I decided we'd go skiing this year. Well of course it's different when you have children to think about. You *did* keep the children, didn't you? Yes, Miles's ex-wife got his. He misses them terribly of course but it does mean we're much freer. We have them for the odd weekend. I adore them. You work? In a library, really? What, something like the British Library or the London Library or something? Oh, oh I see . . . well it's a marvellous thing, isn't it, that anyone can read all those books absolutely free. *Do* they much, nowadays? From this I turn gratefully to Andrew, but even while I talk to him I am preoccupied with Iwo. Iwo's laconic manner, the austerity of his room, seem like cold water in contrast to the cloying liqueur we are now being offered.

I thought I was nodding and becking and smiling in a

convincing way, so I'm startled to hear Andrew say in an undertone that no one else can hear, 'What is it? What are you thinking?'

'Me? Nothing. Don't be silly. Go on.'

'You're miles away. Tell me.'

'When we were at Oxford, Andrew, and I used to come round to your rooms and pour out my heart about *him* there, what were you thinking?'

'I used to wish it was me.'

'Dear Andrew . . . how kind you are. No, seriously.'

'I am serious. I envied him.'

'No but did you think I loved him?'

'You said you did. It wasn't like my sort of love.'

'Wait . . . yes, it's coming back to me. Ann, wasn't she called?'

'That's right. Good memory. That nurse I'd met while I was doing my National Service.'

'What did it feel like?'

He pauses, and says slowly, 'As though I were Saint Sebastian, bleeding from a hundred arrow wounds. I felt like a laboratory monkey or the screaming Pope. I felt pain.'

'Why didn't she love you?'

'I never knew. Sometimes she'd be flirtatious and cuddle up to me and we'd talk about the future, and other times she'd be cold, but in a pert, flippant way, high-stepping and mane flowing, so that I was driven mad with longing.'

'Did she mean to torment you, do you think?'

'I didn't know at the time and I still don't. To think, I never went to bed with her!'

'It wasn't nearly so automatic, then, was it? Lots of people didn't. Paul and I took quite a while to get round to it.'

'I wrote a lot of poetry about her, of course. That helped.'

'I wish I could.'

'Could what?'

'Write poetry. Now.'

'Oh Constance . . . Still? Is it Paul?'

'Will you drive me home? Have you got a car here?'

'Yes.'

129

'Good. OK. Now we'd better be sociable.'

Time to change partners again.

The evening has relaxed. People are sprawled like dragonflies. Miles's second wife, fun-loving Meredith, is confiding her secret longing for a baby. Covertly, I observe Lulu, now that her dinner and the worst are over. What must she think of Paul's collection of sixties records: The Stones and King Crimson and other psychedelic musicmongers from our early married life? Johnny Rotten and Sid Vicious must be more her style.

Noticing me watching her, Lulu comes across to Meredith and me and says, 'You know it's Paul's birthday soon? I thought of taking him to Covent Garden . . .'

'I'm sure he'd love it, but would *you*?'

'That is a problem, right. He likes good solid stuff, doesn't he? – Wagner and the Russians, *Khovanschina*, that sort of thing – and I'm far more into the nineteenth-century Italians, Bellini.'

'Do you sing or anything?'

'Soprano.'

'What, professionally?'

'Well, I once thought I might, but it's terribly competitive. Nowadays I just sing for fun, and for the discipline of it. The exercises.'

She has put me down so subtly that Meredith hasn't noticed.

'Well as it's Paul's birthday treat you ought to book something he'll like. But since you obviously know more about music, I'd suggest something *you* like!'

'Would Cordelia and Max like to come too, do you think?'

'You'd better ask them.'

'Yes, I think I will, if that's OK by you.'

Paul comes and joins us, taking Lulu's hand, and says, 'What did I tell you two? No plotting!'

'You and Andrew were plotting too, looked like,' says Lulu.

I ask Paul if Andrew has changed since our Oxford years, since he struck me as being exactly the same.

'He's a bloody good advertising man nowadays. Creative director of Plumtree Roland Mathieson is worth a few K.'

Andrew drives me home. He's never been to this house before, the setting for my life. He sits in one corner of my sofa, his face like an over-restored portrait: time and texture obscuring the original. Behind it I see the smooth face of a fresher Andrew. Hearing him talk, watching his hands curved around a mug of coffee, is so powerfully evocative that I feel surrounded by his room in college where we used to sit. I would perch on the wooden window seat from which I could look down into the quad, and back into the darkening room at his pained face. I conjure up his table, piled with books and file paper; his shelves, books spilling out of them over the floor in untidy columns. Why were we in love with other people, and yet so close to each other? Ours was an entirely platonic relationship. I never touched him, except to comfort him, nor felt any nudgings of desire from him. Now, though in all common sense he would be a better man for me than my sad knight, Iwo, I feel only nostalgia.

'And what happened with Ann finally? Did it fizzle out?'

'It went on for years, even though we always seemed to be in different places. She in London, me in Oxford; and then when I came down to London to start work, she moved to a hospital in Birmingham. It was never simple. And then after a while it got really extraordinary.'

'Mmm?'

'Well, it's still not easy to talk about. I wrote some poems at the time, and later published one or two, and luckily everyone assumed they were allegorical.'

'Mmmm.'

'Constance, this will shock you. It ought to. It was shocking. It was very destructive. I think it did me a great deal of harm.'

'Mmmm? Don't talk about it, if it makes things worse.'

'How come I can talk to you like this when we haven't met for over twenty years, about the most painful episode in my life?'

131

'Because we're back in Peck, on a warm summer's evening, with people calling to each other across the quad. That's how *I* feel.'

'Ann's mother seduced me. To make up for Ann or something. One weekend when I was staying with them she came to my room and got into my bed. It was the middle of the night, and Ann was asleep just a couple of doors down. She might easily have woken up and heard us.'

'Do you think that was the whole point?'

'I think Pammy, her mother, was a bit baffled by me, probably wondered if I were gay. She herself had been widowed in the war, never remarried, she was still only in her mid-forties when I came along, didn't have a man in her life, fancied me . . . took me to bed.'

'How did you feel?'

'Guilty. Flattered. Shocked. We slept together regularly after that first weekend and it went on for ages, alongside my relationship with Ann. I was in love with the daughter and fucking the mother. Sounds like a young man's wet dream, but it was a nightmare. Damaged me a lot. Look at me, still not married . . .'

'But not because of that: those two?'

'Don't know why. Fact is, I still haven't married.'

He looks ungainly and neglected. Throughout the evening I've been intermittently aware of his sour smell: the smell of a man whose clothes aren't clean, rather than his body, in defiance of all the deodorized canons of advertising.

'Why did you feel so damaged? Is it necessarily wrong for women to sleep with men half their age?'

He laughs.

'Constance . . . ?'

'No, not me. I just don't happen to care for younger men all that much. Anyhow, today's young men aren't guileless and innocent: which I presume was the main attraction.'

'Yes, it is wrong for women to sleep with young men in love with their daughters. And Pammy knew how I felt about Ann. She put me into a double bind, so that I had not one but two of them to deal with, which meant, to get away

132

from. So there I was, starting out in advertising, chatting up the secretaries in the pub at lunchtime, sharing a flat in South Ken with three others, outwardly the swinging sixties man, making trends like follow-my-leader; and what no-one else knew was that I was utterly hooked on these two Medusas. Ann soon knew I was sleeping with her mother, I'm sure of that. It was like incest: we never discussed it. The whole relationship was about evading the truth, but I bet she knew.'

'Would she have cared?'

'To care she would have had to love me, or her mother. I don't think she loved either of us. I think they both enjoyed watching me twisting like a fish on a hook, wrenching my guts out in the effort to escape.'

'Poor Andrew.'

'Yes. Poor me. I say that not out of self-pity but quite objectively. I do think I was unlucky to get into the clutches of those two.'

'Perhaps you wanted it?'

'Constance, I don't believe in all that psychological crap. No, I didn't want it. But they were two powerfully manipulative women, and there's no doubt their relationship with each other was sharpened by what they were doing to me. They weren't going to let me get away.'

'If it doesn't sound too cold-blooded, I want to know how you did get away?'

'Some other time. Tell me about yours.'

'I am desperately in love with a man who doesn't love me. That's all.'

It is the first time I have stated it as a fact, even to myself. Iwo doesn't love me. Everything is not going to be all right, not all right at all. Andrew pats the sofa beside him, but he is not Paul, and I feel no impulse to snuggle into his comforting circle. I shake my head and, hands clasped around my folded knees, I tell him as briefly as I can the story of me and Iwo. When I have finished he sits silent.

Eventually he says, 'It's very late. I'm very tired. I don't think I can talk any more. I certainly can't say anything

133

helpful. But I would like to see you again. Now that we've started. Will you have dinner with me?'

'Give me a ring. Yes, I'd like dinner, but I have to get Christmas out of the way.'

'Ah, family Christmas?'

After he has gone, hugging me less spontaneously than at the beginning of the evening, I get undressed and think about him. Am I enmeshed in another version of the emotional coils that bind Andrew? But Pammy was wicked – or was she? Maybe she was just lonely and frustrated. Maybe the same is true of Iwo. He didn't ask for love; why can't I go to bed with him and shrug off the emotions? Could Andrew and I discover one another now, in the aftermath of what we have both learned? He, after all, is a man who knew me when I was young. He could love me. Never mind the speculation: look at the facts. I, now, here, thinking of these two men, am in bed alone. The sheets are cold. The clocks chime three.

10

Next morning Fred phones. I have been dreading this conversation, not least because I know I am too cowardly to meet him and tell him to his face that I shan't come to his room again.

'So when are you coming to collect your Christmas present?' he starts.

'Oh Fred . . . you haven't? Christ, you haven't got any money.'

'I didn't buy it. I wrote it.'

'Look Fred, I can't. You must have realized. We haven't seen each other for months . . .'

'Five, not counting the library . . .'

'Fred, look I've fallen in love with someone.'

'Oh.'

'I couldn't help it.'

'No.'

'Please don't sound so hurt.'

'Sorry.'

There is a long silence, down which his spoken and my unspoken 'sorry' reverberates. Then the pips go.

'Do you want to ring me back? You can reverse the charges.' I gabble in the ten seconds we have left.

'No point. It wouldn't have made any difference if I'd said I loved you.'

'Did you?'

'Yes.'

'Sorry Fred.'

We are cut off.

Once or twice during the day I wonder if Fred's 'love' can have resembled what I feel for Iwo; but Christmas is almost upon us, and cards and lists and arrangements soon push Fred out of my mind.

It is late on Sunday afternoon, and I am about to start on the long ritual of anointing myself for Iwo. My Christmas cards, which I have written and signed, 'much love from Constance, Cordy, Max and', have received their final flourish from Kate, and the envelopes are stacked in a pile on the hall table, to be posted when I set out. The Sunday papers are scattered over the carpet. In the grate, the first coal fire of the winter glows soporifically. The room is full of calm and contentment, and I go upstairs in a state of well-being.

The phone rings beside my bed, and Andrew's voice says, 'Constance? Paul gave me your number. I drove away with no idea of your address and not much memory of how I got you there last night.'

'I directed you. I don't know how you got home.'

'I can't believe we just shrugged off twenty-five years like that. It was extraordinary, wasn't it?'

No. Extraordinary is *our* word.

'Pretty incredible. I'm really sorry we lost touch for so many years.'

'I was away.'

'I've just been writing Christmas cards all over the world. That's no excuse.'

'Constance, *will* you have dinner with me? It's not going to screw things up with this Polish fellow of yours?'

'Why should it? I'd like dinner, though it'll have to be after Christmas.'

'I hate New Year's Eve parties: if you're not going to one, how about on New Year's Eve? I could pick you up and cook you a meal here at my flat.'

'That's a thought. Yes. Let me scribble down your phone number in case . . .'

I mean, in case Iwo should invite me to something. 'But yes, I think that's a lovely idea. Are you going away for Christmas?'

'Only to my sister's in the country. It'll be all right. Just a couple of days.'

'Right. Well, have a happy time, and I'll see you after that. Oh Andrew . . . it really *was* nice, last night!'

'Me too. 'Bye, Constance.'

I lie outstretched in my bath thinking, what a *nice* man he is, what a gentle, soft-voiced, dear man. So why has nobody ever married him? I must buy a book of his poems tomorrow: perhaps I'll find the answer there. I can tell Iwo I met a poet at dinner. Get him to tell me about Polish poetry . . .

The phone rings again. I shout, 'Katie! Telephone! Can you take it? If it's for me, say I'm in the bath!'

I rest my foot on the tap and am soaping my leg when Kate looks round the door and says, 'It's *him*. Do you want to talk to him or what?'

'Who: Iwo? Honestly? I'll talk to him.'

Wet footmarks follow me to the bedside phone, and I pick up the receiver with beating heart.

His cool voice, brief and low as ever, says, 'Constance? How are you? . . . Yes, yes, fine. I am sorry my dear but I have to ask you to postpone our meeting this evening. Do you mind? I am sorry to ring at such short notice, but one day later this week, perhaps . . .'

I cannot expostulate, or ask why, or sound even mildly annoyed. Laconic as he, I say, 'No, that's fine. Do you want to fix a day now or . . . ?'

'I'll call you in a day or two, shall I? And again, my apologies.'

I put the receiver down and stand naked, wet, and rigid with shock beside the telephone. My fragile equilibrium has been rocked by an earthquake. My self-esteem is falling like debris all around me. Did I think I was stable; content; secure; normal? My heart is thudding nightmarishly fast; the rest of me is motionless. As the water dries on my body I start to feel cold. I walk to the bathroom, let the bathwater out, wrap myself in a towel, and lie down on my bed. I changed the sheets this morning, in case. On the other side of the bed my clean clothes are spread out ready, the under-wear faintly scented from having been rinsed in perfumed water, my shoes side by side on the floor beneath. I pick up a book, put it down. Look at my watch, six o'clock. If I shut my eyes, will I sleep? Into my mind comes the recollection that Paul said Andrew's first book of poems was called *Journey to an Icy Land*. Where is Iwo going? Who with? And why did I think, for two or three days anyway, that I was normal? Like a diver, I swim in a different element, down, down, down. The water is heavy and sluggish around my limbs, gloomy before my eyes. This exertion is not natural. It makes my heart burst. The thought wriggles through my mind again: Does Fred feel like this? He can't.

During the week, my joy in Christmas has gone, but routine carries me through. Cordy's term ends, and she comes home: a marker buoy towards safe waters and firm realities. She spends hours talking to Ben on the phone beside the breakfast room, while I sit at the table wrapping presents or making decorations with Kate. Their conversations are funny, flirtatious, secure. I envy her that relaxation: not only because even at her age I could never have talked to Paul like that – being straightforward and open about love, work and sex. The only men with whom I could ever be really myself were those I didn't love or feel desire for: men like Andrew; or, in the last weeks, Paul himself. The men who are my friends get the best of me: those whom I love, especially if they don't love me, receive a distorted, unnatural version.

Paul and I talk on the phone about how best to combine our obligations to family and friends. In the end we make a deal. Paul will spend Christmas Eve at my house without Lulu but with Iwo. I will spend Christmas Day at his flat, with Lulu but without Iwo; and also with his father and my mother, who have nothing in common beyond the fact that they are widowed. This means that both Paul and I are with the children for both days of Christmas, and everyone sees everyone at least once. It seems the most satisfactory compromise: not least because Paul and Lulu will have responsibility for the most elaborate meal, Christmas lunch, when in the past both culinary and emotional crises have come to a head. It also means that I shall have the unsettling

– no, intriguing – experience of seeing Paul and Iwo together at my dinner table. Now all I have to do is ring Iwo.

Christmas makes me understand my parents better. When I was a child, our Christmas rituals were rooted in their rituals, when they were children. They handed down the family words for things, the special family ways of doing things, often with an anecdote that was retold every year. They hated the way that, as my sister and I grew older, these observances became an obligation and a source of embarrassment to us, which we performed grudgingly and self-consciously, if at all. Only now can I see that re-enacting the same ceremonies in exactly the same way recreates the magic feelings of one's own childhood, as well as affirming continuity with those generations of children past.

When I was five or six years old I saw Father Christmas and his reindeer sweep across the sky – saw them, really and truly saw them. I felt a sense of wonder and rightness – so, everything is all right and just as it ought to be. I used to feel the same when my children were small, watching their eyes and faces reflecting the bright candles on the Christmas tree. But nowadays, when the rituals are played out and the hallowed responses called for, it is their turn to make resigned faces and join in awkwardly. Yet none of us would want to dispense altogether with the ritual, and simply eat, drink, and be generous. Nevertheless, each year the trappings become more lavish. Gifts are more gorgeously wrapped, more numerous, and more expensive. Food and drink are plentiful, rich, stultifying. I spend hours adorning the house with evergreen and ribbons and candles and bright groups of fruit and berries, till it looks like the frame for a Victorian Christmas card. Yet it *is* beautiful, and the care with which I have created the illusion does succeed in conjuring some of the Christmas spirit. The children ask when we're going to decorate the tree, 'Christmas Eve, like we always do', and try to guess what presents they're getting. Slowly I crank up the magic, slowly the calliope

139

starts to turn. One evening, just before Christmas, uncertain flurries of snow swivel through the darkness, and Kate decides on the spur of the moment to go carol singing around the neighbouring streets. A few phone calls, a few friends turn up, and, self-deprecating and pessimistic, they set off to sing for charity. Well over an hour later, when the snow has thickened and the house is filled with the spicy smell of hot mince pies, they are back, shaking coins on to the table from a rackety Ovaltine tin, crowding round to count them, marvelling at the unexpected generosity of some, the parsimony of others.

'Was Fred in?' I ask apprehensively, dreading the answer.

'Don't know . . . Who is he?'

'That very tall thin man who I occasionally point out. The one who's often in the library.'

'Don't know him,' says Kate flatly, and I sigh with relief.

Cordy was right when she predicted that Max would get over Judy fairly quickly. I was prepared to find him pale and subdued, but the round of pre-Christmas parties has picked him up and whirled him along through late nights and dazzling young women, and he shows no sign of bitterness or depression. The young have an infinite choice of new partners. I don't think he's putting on a brave face, though I'm touched to hear that he plans to give Judy her Christmas present all the same. He chose it back in the autumn and has been paying a jeweller weekly for a slender brooch of Victorian jet which he knew would suit her dark, intense face. How generous he is! Most young men would have kept it and simply given it to the next girlfriend. I'm quite relieved that he's unattached once more. The four of them in their squat had moved so rapidly into domesticity that I had wondered how easy Max would find it to disengage himself.

'When I decide to get married it'll be quite different,' he says, 'but I don't suppose that'll happen for years.'

'What makes you say that?'

'Partly you and Dad . . . getting married so young . . . Partly me. I just know I don't want to settle down for a while. But that doesn't mean I can't take relationships

140

seriously. It was good living with Jude till it went wrong. Much better than just meeting a couple of evenings a week. We had a great time. Only in the end she felt hemmed in and I didn't.'

'Are you going to see her again?'

'Once at least. We're having a drink before she goes down to spend Christmas with her parents.'

'And that's when you plan to give her the brooch?'

'Yeah. It's nice, isn't it?'

'Anyone else looming?'

'*Mother!* Give me a chance! No, not really.'

'You could always come and live here for a bit . . .'

'I'm all *right.*'

I can't forget that he cried on the phone – my stolid Max. Meanwhile I only have a few days left in which to find a present for Iwo. On the telephone he had tried to decline my invitation for Christmas Eve, but for once I was bold, swept aside his objections, insisted that he should come. In the end it was probably his curiosity about Paul that made him acquiesce. Paul was equally curious about Iwo. Each knew a good deal about the other, but only from my perspective. The impression they created in the flesh would contradict much of what I had said. I want to give Iwo everything: but his present must be small and look inexpensive. At the last minute I decide on the classic dark green French café set: octagonal cup and saucer with gold rim; matching coffee pot and milk jug. He won't even know their origin; but to me they promise a holiday abroad together, and that means future happiness. I am giving him my dream.

On Christmas Eve I drink too many glasses of wine in the first hour, and after that the evening flashes past like a series of images in a ViewMaster . . . Paul arriving with a cardboard box brimming with packages; the girls greeting him with huge happy smiles, Iwo and Paul shaking hands, eyeing each other, drinking together, relaxing, animated. The evening is lit by the small flames of dozens of candles which give a swaying glow to the room, shadowy in the corners, golden around the focal points where candles are grouped

. . . and Iwo, as I have never seen him, laughing and happy, talkative, approachable, ordinary. Once the meal is over I sit dazed with relief and tiredness, watching as the people I love most enjoy the celebration. Firelight and candlelight, silver strands shimmering on the tree, music, everyone dancing and in my memory – which is blurring past and present – the image of a grave little girl reading from the Bible. Is it my daughter, myself, or my mother? The child stumbles over the archaic rhythm and I catch my breath and glance across the room at Iwo who, in a moment of stillness, looking at me, smiles. Really it's all so simple: I shall, at last, sit down by thee.

After this, Christmas Day at Paul's was bound to be an anti-climax: but the anti-climax is a relief after the high-pitched emotions of the last few weeks. I surrender myself completely to their hospitality and the children's love. Paul's father and my mother are touching in their anxious dignity; anxious to be important, to do the right thing; anxious to be reassured that they are loved; anxious not to seem old. What must they make of Lulu? Does Paul's father envy him the sexual freedom to renew his potency with a younger woman and still keep the affection and respect of his children? My mother cannot understand that Paul and I can be divorced yet apparently friendly and relaxed. Does she share Katie's dream, that we will somehow get together again and remarry? Do I, in all honesty: do I?

From Buck's Fizz we move on to pheasant consommé; then to smoked salmon. Lulu is like a young acrobat on the high wire, performing miracles, winning applause for her skill and vulnerability. She is performing only for Paul, but to win him she needs us on her side, too. So, I think: she wants marriage. Behind that white-faced, black-haired mask is a woman who wants a husband and babies. It is the un-doing of us all.

After lunch the older generation disappear for what Paul's father calls 'a little zizz', and my mother 'putting a new face on'. I too am dopey with wine and port. I loll back in the sofa and watch my husband with his young mistress. Why doesn't he marry her tomorrow? The answer must be that he still thinks he may do better, find someone richer, perhaps, from a better family? How choosy men in their mid-forties can be! But for now the two of them are happy. Paul has given her a gold chain whose links are made up of the letters L and U endlessly repeated: a charming, intimate present. He has given me a set of beautiful bookplates, mock eighteenth century, with urns and flourishes.

It is pointless brooding about Paul; I will brood about Iwo instead. He is at the Polish Centre, with Tadeusz and Joanna and Marina and dozens of other Poles whom he knows and I don't; and by now they are probably all awash with nostalgia, maudlin and maundering, singing hoarse patriotic songs and clapping one another on the shoulder or brushing away elderly tears with the edge of a cuff. Iwo will have gone to mass this morning, since he missed it last night – surely even lapsed Catholics go to mass at Christmas? – and will be feeling sentimental and guilty about his family. Does he have a grandchild yet? I must ask him. Perhaps he is gazing wistfully at a photograph of some tiny black-haired infant, trying to discern in its features some trace of his own. Has the Zaluski line come to this?

I hear Kate from next door. She's been sent to wake my mother.

'Granny? Wake up! Christ, the oldies are a dozy lot! Lu says, do you want a cup of tea and some Christmas cake? Go on: she made it herself.'

'I couldn't eat a thing. Well, a sliver: literally.'

'I'll tell her. Anyhow Ben's coming over in a second, and he'll eat masses.'

'Ben? Who's Ben?'

'Oh Granny.' A weary, patient drone, appropriate to dealing with the forgetful elderly. 'I told you this morning. Ben and another girl are coming here for tea then they're all going off for the evening. Ben is Cordy's fella. Boyfriend. You know.'

'Oh, Cordelia's . . . yes dear . . . Max too?'

'Yes Granny, Max too. I did *tell* you.'

'Yes, I believe you. What about you Katie?'

'I'm staying here with Daddy and Grandpa, for the night. He'll drive me home tomorrow. Told you that too.'

She is merciless. I must tell her not to be so hard on the old.

'Actually I do remember, only I'd forgotten.'

'How efficient Paul has been,' I say to Cordy. 'He's fixed everything.'

'You don't even have to worry about Granny. Dad's running her over to Kensington Gore', pronounced with mock upper-class languor, 'to visit Mrs Watkinson. The two old dears can witter on together about how frightful their grand-children are.'

'Darling! Don't be silly. You weren't frightful a bit. I love my wine glasses.'

'Good. *And* we washed up while you were asleep. Me and Max and Katie. The kitchen's pristine.'

I am mortified to learn that I too had slept. I thought I had only day-dreamed. Am I so middle-aged already, despite being fierce with love and desire? Here comes Max.

'Put some lipstick on, Mother, and look normal. My new girlfriend will be here any minute.'

'What? Ben's sister?'

'No, not Ben's sister. Nothing to do with Ben. Nobody's met her yet. Dad wanted to, so I thought she might as well get you all over in one fell swoop.'

'What's her name?'

'*I've* only just met her, just a couple of weeks ago. I sort of meant to tell you only . . . anyway. She's called Danuta.'

'What?'

'Danuta. Yeah, what a laugh: she's Polish.'

At this I really do laugh. I laugh and laugh, and so does Max, and we're still laughing when she arrives, which makes for a warm welcome. For ten minutes the little flat is crammed with people. For ten minutes the Christmas spirit overcomes everyone's unfamiliarity and shyness, as the gen-erations toast one another in sherry and Christmas cake; presents are admired; Ben finds himself talking to Paul's father – they are both First World War buffs, though in rather different ways; soft, pliant-looking Danuta is pleasing my mother with her gentle manners; I am congratulating Lulu on the brilliant success of the day; and Paul and Katie are quietly sharing one armchair, their arms around each other. But ten minutes is all that can be managed. The young refuse a second glass of sherry, become stiff as they render the obligatory thank-yous, and relax visibly as they go out through Paul's front door.

'What time . . . ?' I shout at their retreating backs.

'Late . . .' says Max.

'. . . if at all!' says Cordy.

I insist on going home by myself and walk most of the way, to look into people's lighted windows, and to sober up. Most people are watching television. The snow hasn't come back, but the air is damp and fresh.

At first when I enter the quiet, dark house I feel an impulse of self-pity, and have to resist the temptation to ring someone. Instead I make coffee and talk to the complaining cats as I wait for the dark pungent liquid to filter through. I carry the tray to the living room, light the candles on the tree and some of those around the room, and look at the presents still piled up on a side table. Iwo gave me a Polish dictionary. The message inside is written in Polish. It is the first time I have seen his handwriting. It is small, cursive, continental. He has written: *Jest to podróż według przewodnika poprzez trudnośći językowe jednak uwieńczone sukcesem, i przez dziedzictwo Polski jednego z Jej synów – Twój przyjaciel – Iwo Zaluski.* With the help of the dictionary I translate only two words: 'difficult' and 'friend'. I shall have to ask Marina for the rest. He is indeed my difficult friend . . . yet how happy he was yesterday, how unlike his usual self. If only I could suffer less and enjoy myself more, if only I could have fun with him. Maybe then he would drop his guard and let himself love me. What I told Andrew is true: Iwo doesn't love me. He nearly did; he wanted to; hoped to; tried to. Now, three months or so after our meeting, I have to face the fact that he doesn't love me, and the harder I try, the more unnatural and unlovable I become. One by one the little candles begin to flicker, and gutter, and fade. The dim room is aromatic with the scent of Christmas tree and evergreen, and the exotic smell of snuffed candles as I pinch my wetted fingers around the final two or three and leave it to darkness.

11

During the Christmas holidays Cordelia and Ben spend the night more or less alternately at one another's houses. When they're staying with me, they come down, yawning, to a late breakfast, stretching and glowing and healthy. That much I have managed for my children, I think, whatever my own emotional and sexual complications. They are not riddled with sexual guilt; nor are they mindlessly promiscuous. Neither Cordelia nor Max has ever pretended that they don't sleep with the people they love . . . and a few others as well: yet they both appear fresher and more innocent than I suspect I did at their age, when my preoccupation with the forbidden (and unperformed) act led me to scandalize my parents by dressing in stark Bohemian black from head to foot, the whole silhouette crowned by my teenage face looking bizarre with white lipstick and black-bordered eyes. I tottered on heels so high and fragile that they constantly snapped off in gratings and escalators. At any other time but the end of the fifties I would have been unmistakably a tart. As it was, half Oxford's virgins dressed in exactly the same way.

This is the Constance that Andrew knew; and indeed, he too was a virgin at the time. The changes of the past twenty-five years have benefited my children, but not me. I remain hidebound by the pre-pill morality and my parents' fossilized attitudes. My father saw me as his to guard and protect and deliver unsullied to my bridegroom. He did his best. He couldn't know that the man who demanded an unsullied bride was not the kind of man I would ever want to marry. The damage was done anyway; since whatever my progressive mind may have believed, my stubbornly unliberated body conveyed with every gesture that 'nice girls don't'. Paul tried to undermine my father's conditioning – hence the beautiful underwear, treasured but unworn. His, and my, failure to overcome those inhibitions was perhaps the main reason for the failure of our marriage. Paul was a sensual, stylish hedonist who believed pleasure was no sin. I remained a timorous, furious puritan. If Iwo and Paul ever discuss my performance in bed, which, thank God, is unlikely, they would be incredulous at how different are their two Constances.

Paul is dismissive about Iwo when I ring to thank him for our Christmas Day.

'Can't imagine what you're making so much fuss about,' he says briskly. 'Nice chap, quite intelligent, lousy dresser, perfectly easy to talk to . . . Nothing to torture yourself over. Feed him and fuck him and he's yours, I should have thought. And lucky him,' he remembers to add, kindly. 'What about my Lu? The kids seem to like her.'

'Oh they do: a lot. She's amazingly pretty . . . hey, is she in earshot?'

'Relax. She's out.'

'. . . *vachement chic*, seems bright, and nuts about you. My dear Paul: what more can you want?'

'It's a question of what I don't want. Babies. Lu wants babies, or at the very least *a* baby, and the thought of going back to sleepless nights and potty-training is more than my aged frame could bear. I've done all that, and the kids are wonderful, but I don't want to start again.'

'You've told her this?'

'Of course. And either she pretends she can manage without babies and all she really wants is me; or she says I'll change my mind.'

'Paul, how old is she?'

'She's twenty-nine, worrying desperately about becoming thirty.'

'I see. Hence the panic. So it'll all depend on whether you can live without each other.'

'Tried that. We separated for six weeks earlier this year,

148

and it was hell. Kept seeing her in the agency, and I don't know which was worse: her with red eyes or her with some other bloke going off for a drink. So we got back together again. But nothing's settled.'

'Can't help you, darling.'

'Now, what about you? You're having dinner with Andrew? Why don't you take the poor man off the shelf and marry him and live happily ever after?'

'For that matter, why doesn't Lulu?'

But this remark is not thought to be in good taste, and the conversation ends there.

Iwo is less forthcoming on the subject of Paul, but it is clear that he liked him, and was puzzled as to why we should have divorced. On the subject of New Year's Eve he is non-committal; so I phone Andrew and confirm that our dinner is on.

I am intrigued to hear what other revelations he may have for me: after all, there are still two decades of his life to catch up on. At the same time I mustn't seem so sympathetic that he misreads the situation. He didn't attract me then, and he doesn't now. The answer, I hope, is to affect the same outlandish make-up as was fashionable when we were at Oxford together, and thus emphasize the nostalgic friendly basis on which we meet. With luck he'll be perspicacious enough to interpret these complex signals. So I blank my mouth out with chalky pink lipstick, enlarge my eyes with black lines flicked up at the corners, and emerge feeling foolish when he rings the doorbell. The children find this teenage apparition hilarious; and its effect is indeed quite startling – from a distance. In close-up, my face has become tense and lined, with a deep frown between the eyes from constant reading. Andrew takes it all as a successful joke, and in high good humour we set off in the car for his smart bachelor address.

It is early still on New Year's Eve, but already the streets of London are thick with people, dressed up and in party mood. At zebra crossings and the lights they peer into the car and wave, and I laugh and wave back through the windscreen, happily. Suddenly all motion slows to a halt, the smile dropping slowly, my hand falling slowly down into my lap. Crossing the road in front of us are Iwo and Joanna, her arm locked through his, her face turned up towards him. She is talking. They are quite absorbed. They move in unison. They have not seen me.

Andrew is in mid-flow. He turns, laughing, for my answering smile, sees my expression, and the light falls from his face.

'Constance! what on earth . . .'

'Iwo. Doesn't matter. I've just seen Iwo.'

'Where? Which one?'

'He's gone now. Doesn't matter. Sorry.'

'But why . . .?'

'Look Andrew, I'm sorry and it's absurd, but he's with a woman. Now for God's sake go on with what you were saying.'

'Who?'

'Oh, a Polish girl. I've met her.'

'So she's a friend. Don't jump to conclusions. It's probably just a friendly evening out, like you and me.'

'No, Andrew, it wasn't.'

'Look Constance, I don't want to hassle you, but either you tell me about this now, or it's going to ruin our evening.'

So I tell him, in a tight clipped exposition of pain, about my fears, now all realized. About Joanna's youth and beauty and Polishness. About my jealousy: now all justified. I wish I could cry, but my father put a stop to crying for sympathy years ago. We reach the flat and park outside and sit in the car till I have finished.

'Right,' says Andrew, 'now for a drink.'

His flat is expensive, untidy, comfortable; a mish-mash of good family furniture and trendy adman's stuff . . . Italian light fixtures and lots of black and white and grey, with wire basket accessories. He hangs up my jacket, sits me firmly down on a huge puffy sofa and gives me a straight whisky.

'Now I'm serious, Constance: I won't have you ruin this evening. Drink that and shut your mind to Iwo and concentrate on seeing the New Year in with me. Music? What do you like?'

'Anything.'

'No, not anything. You can have jazz, opera, Haydn or Bach; Beethoven, Sibelius, or sixties rock. You can have Edith Piaf . . .'

'Mozart. Not opera: something religious.'

'Requiem, Coronation Mass?'

'Oh the *Coronation Mass* . . . yes . . . that!'

'In the Colin Davis version or . . . ah! Garbo laughs, but Constance smiles. Right?'

'Andrew, you're lovely. I have stopped thinking about Iwo.' For the moment. 'Now, dinner. Do you need help?'

'Watch!'

At the far end of the room is a long white roller blind. He pulls it up, and there is a miniaturized kitchen with a microwave oven. From the fridge he takes out a salad whose shades of green owe more to avocados and kiwi fruit than lettuce; and a bottle of champagne which he places on the dining table. I begin to feel apprehensive. What does he expect of me?

'Constance, do you realize I have become a fairly rich and rather lonely middle-aged bachelor? I have laid on this performance for quite a number of women whom afterwards I hoped never to see again. Give me the pleasure of doing it for you, and just enjoy, will you?'

Over dinner we plumb layers of news, gossip, and recollection. Andrew summons up images of us at Oxford, punting, jiving, arguing, celebrating in subfusc after Schools were over. Everything can be told, no questions barred. We quarry through folded seams of memory. He remembers me and Paul as happy young lovers more vividly than I do, since in my case those images are overlaid with our subsequent disillusion and parting.

'Why did you two break up?' he asks. 'I was in New York when it happened.'

I can be flippant, after all these years. 'Andrew, we were babies, Paul and I, when we got married. And then, right

151

away, we *had* babies. Max and Cordy were born before we were twenty-five. So there I was, smelling of milk and baby-shit; and there was he, all pert in his sharp little sixties suits with striped shirts and floral ties, and the next thing he noticed was that he had this secretary. Well, more of a typist. And she smelt a lot more enticing than me. Wasn't difficult. After that he was away. As the French say, it's the first one that counts. When you've been unfaithful once, there seems no real reason to stop. I never had a first one. Not till quite a long time after he left me.'

'Poor young Constance.'

'Not so young by then. I was, hang on, thirty-seven when he finally went.'

I stand beside Andrew as he makes coffee in his galley of a kitchen. It looks complete; yet it's not. There are no stores, no ordinary supplies like flour and jam and tins. No half-used jars of anything. The fridge is full of bottles – white wine and champagne and Perrier water – not leftovers like mine, or ingredients for the rest of the week. It is bleak in a different way from Iwo's disciplined bleakness, and it moves me more. We sit down, on the same sofa now, and I ask, 'What about you? What was Pammy's secret?'

'Very simple. She taught me about sex and *guilt.* Plus: do you remember me telling you about my mother? Probably not: long time ago now. She was widowed in the war, too, and brought up me and Rosemary by herself. We were genteelly poor: the worst kind of poverty, because it usually means that those around you are rich. So my grandparents sent me to public school, but in the holidays I never went abroad or skiing like everyone else: just home to Berkshire and the bridge parties and the Young Conservatives. No, wait, it's relevant. You know what's lethal about all that? Those women get status by manipulating men, though they actually despise them. My mother's friends used to sidle up to me and pretend to believe that I must have dozens of girl-friends. We were the most sexless household I ever knew. My mother, I'm willing to bet, never slept with a man from the day my father went off to get killed, when she must have been, what, twenty-six? My sister was a tennis club virgin. And me. I finally lost my virginity to Pammy.'

'Andrew! What a killer! How did you survive?'

'Well have I? Look at me. I can only relate to women in two ways. Either I love them and suffer – that's thanks to my mother and Pammy. Or I distrust and exploit them – my revenge on the bridge club harpies. The only women I have ever felt comfortable with are the very, very few who are my friends. That's why I'm so glad to have met you again.'

He tops up our glasses in silence: wine for me, another large brandy for him. The atmosphere grows tense with his pain and need.

'Tell me how you got away from Pammy.'

'I went on an expedition to Antarctica.'

'You *what?*'

'I know: bit extreme. I had been swinging from Ann to Pammy and back for years . . . until I was nearly thirty. And then my mother died, quite young: thank God. It meant Rosemary could get away from home and marry, and now she at least is normal. Our house was sold and we took half each and I put my half into an expedition to the South Pole.'

'Was it wonderful?'

'In many ways, yes. We were there for seven months.'

'Wait, I've got it now! "Great stone boulders are not here/ Clear blue mountains shape this land, steer my ship . . ." I thought all that was metaphorical. I didn't realize you'd actually been.'

'Constance! You don't know what a compliment that is!'

'I could quote you more: "Beloved Gorgon, kindest of torturers . . ." Paul said you had published some poetry, so I went out and found *Journey to an Icy Land.*'

'Lots of people buy my poems . . . well, lots: a few hundred, but I often wonder how many people actually read them. You did.'

'Did the Antarctic cure you of Pammy?'

'It certainly got me away from her. Icebergs really are blue, you know, it wasn't just a figure of speech. And penguins have a great sense of humour. Dead pan. No. Yes, it did cure

153

me of Pammy, of the relationship, if not its after-effects. From there I hitched a lift to America, and stayed on and worked in New York for more than ten years. Came back to London the complete media clone.'

'You're not.'

'No, I'm not.'

The conversation has become like Paracetamol for a headache. It takes away the pain, yet I know that somehow the pain is still there. When we have stopped talking, the image of Iwo with Joanna which waits, crystal-sharp, at the back of my mind, will scythe through these reminiscences and cut me down. So Andrew and I talk through and past midnight, pausing to open another bottle of champagne and wish one another better luck in the New Year, and I never feel awkward or reticent.

Finally, I have to say, 'Andrew, darling Andrew, you've got to let me go home. I'm dead. And pissed. Can you call a cab for me?'

'Wouldn't dream of it. I'll drive you home.'

And so he does; and outside my door he folds me very gently in his arms and with great tenderness he kisses me. He takes my hands, and kisses them, and then lays his own hand against my lips. Then he drives away.

I wrench my front door open and totter into the hall. I have had a good deal to drink. Iwo and Joanna. Shall I ring him and wish him a happy New Year? Then perhaps he'll tell me about his friendly evening with Joanna and then everything will be all right and I shall be able to sleep. He might suggest that as it's a Bank Holiday tomorrow we could meet. Even as I think the conversation I know it will never take place. He and Joanna are lovers. I have been a fool to kid myself. I once saw a motor cyclist die. It was in the days before crash-helmets were compulsory. The crash happened in less than five seconds, and the image was photographed with shocking clarity, to flash before my eyes for weeks afterwards. In the same way, the picture of Iwo with Joanna is by far the clearest I have of him. I recall to the fraction of an inch the precise angle of his body as he bent solicitously towards her to catch what she was saying, undoubtedly in their precious Polish. I recall his warm, tight grip on her arm – such a Continental gesture! – and the ease and confidence with which she smiled up into his face. Was there ever a time when I felt as sure of him as that?

I have been made a fool of. I am angry. I will be indignant. The young motor cyclist jack-knifed off his bike into the air and his last living expression was one of utter surprise, before he hit the road and his head rolled under the wheels of the lorry.

II

The Polish Obsession

12

All happy Christmases resemble one another, each unhappy
Christmas is unhappy in its own way, as Tolstoy might have
said. Last year I had an unhappy Christmas, alone among
courteous acquaintances to whom I was a duty. This year I
spent Christmas with a family, and shared in feelings of sentimentality and old customs and ceremonies fitting for this
occasion. I ate and drank well; had one woman and could
have had two, but I chose not to. I was not rejected.

It has been a good, cold winter, and I miss my fur hat with
the ear-muffs. The snow began to fall early in December, and
my room was very cold. I spent many evenings alone in it,
with a bottle of vodka for company. Vodka makes a better
hot-water bottle than the beer which the youngsters downstairs are always drinking. I sometimes accept a can, to show
friendliness, but vodka is too expensive to share. The three
of them – or is it four? – would empty my bottle in ten
minutes. But they bear me no grudge. Constance brings her
own wine, and would not, I think, want vodka. When she is
here I don't need vodka to warm me. She always wants to be
fucked.

I have been trying to decide what to write to Katarzyna,
who hinted in her last letter that if we are to get a divorce
after all this time, she would like to get it over and done
with. The vodka and I together have started many letters:
'My dear wife, I have met a woman here in London who
wants to marry me, and if I am to do this and thereby acquire
permanent status as a citizen of this country, I shall need
official divorce papers.' Sometimes I write, 'You will be
relieved to know that I plan to marry a Polish girl, so that if
one day you or the girls visit me, there will be no language

problems in my home.' But none of these letters is ever sent, because I have not made up my mind what I shall do. The third possibility, to go back home, looms larger all the time. I try not to think about it, because I know that the consequences would be unthinkable.

I miss the family preparations for Christmas. I seem to remember my childhood Christmases better than more recent ones. Perhaps everybody does this. Here in England they don't celebrate Saint Nicholas's Day, but as it approaches I remembered the terror and excitement that I used to feel as a little boy. Mama said he only visited good children, and I knew I hadn't been good all through the year. The question was, did Saint Nicholas know? Sometimes I would decide to confess all my sins in the hope that, being a saint, he would be merciful and forgive me, and give me presents just the same. In the end I always thought it best to keep quiet and hope he would be deceived, and it always worked. I learned very early on that, if you keep quiet, good people will think the best of you. In the years when we spent Christmas with my grandparents, Saint Nicholas would ride through the village in his red coat and hat on a sleigh, stopping at every house to distribute presents to us children and take a glass of vodka with our parents. In the magic of that arrival I would become a good little boy, and send up prayers promising to be good next year too. His bells could be heard ringing all down the street, and I would stand in the porch under the light dry-mouthed with anticipation as his sleigh rattled up the long drive lined with spruces. He would climb down out of the sleigh with a heavy sack slung over his shoulder, and swing it to the ground, and dig around in it, and pretend at first that there was nothing for me. Then he would say, 'Has Iwo been a good, loving child all through the year? Does he say his prayers every night? Perhaps he has forgotten something he ought to tell me?' And I would be dumbstruck with fear and doubt, and just as I was about to blurt out the sins I had committed, Mama would put her hands on my shoulders and say, 'Dear Saint Nicholas, our Iwo is a good boy. Have another look in the sack . . . surely you have something for him there?' And then when he had gone there was still Christmas to come.

There have not been many events in my life as a man that brought the same shivering of excitement as that sound of sleigh bells down the road. It must have had something to do with the uncertainty of never being sure I would get a present. Uncertainty still makes me tremble with fear and pleasure today. I am a natural risk-taker. Many of the things which others called brave were done to recapture that suspense. At one level, they were just childish games. The women who have excited me most were always those who might refuse me. Katarzyna I never completely learnt to predict. After weeks of silence, she could walk into my room one night in her slip. I never felt jealous about any woman, except her.

In the snow my feet are cold and wet. I cannot afford good boots and nobody in London wears galoshes. My shoes are thin, and they make my feet damp, which is bad for them. When I was a child I once had boots made of leather embroidered with flowers in many differently coloured wools. I was ashamed of them, because the town boys called me a sissy, but in the country all the peasant children wore them with their best suits and jackets, on feast days. These are the things I remember. I am not homesick. I don't want to go back to the Poland I left, but to the Poland before that.

The work I do here punishes my mind and my spirit. If I were doing it in Poland, well-wishers in the West would make me a *cause-célèbre,* write letters to the Ministry of Justice complaining that a distinguished economist should not have to work as a common packer in a postroom. But here in the West, it is freedom. I am a free man in a capitalist country. I work for my food and drink and self-respect. That basement is killing my self-respect. The men with their talk of football or racing, television or women, the crude women spread over newspaper pictures, the noise from their radio that never stops. They mean to be kind.

'Here, Monty, what you doing for Christmas? Going home for a little holiday, are you? See the family?'

When I say no, I cannot do that, I shall be in London for Christmas, they are concerned.

'Won't be on your own, will you? Shocking thing, on your own at Christmas. Here, Monty, want me to have a word with my Missus? Can't have you on your own, like.'

No, I have told them, I shall be among friends from the Polish community. We will celebrate in our traditional way. They are relieved. One of them squats down and kicks his legs clumsily forward, roaring and toppling over, and the others laugh.

'Be a drop of the old vodka going round, will there? What do you lot eat at Christmas? Turkey?'

The carp . . . the roast carp of my childhood!

'No, he eats fish don't you Monty? Yeah, I knew a Swedish girl once . . . gawh! . . . She said they ate fish at Christmas. Some funny fish.'

'Yes, mostly we had fish. When times were not too bad.'

They drink their tea and stub out their fags and turn their attention away from me to a young woman dispatch rider who has come down to pick up a Red Star parcel. They will spend two minutes talking to her and ten minutes after she has gone speculating about her. The general view is that women who take jobs like dispatch rider or bus driver are lesbians. This belief doesn't stop them propositioning her.

I make the hours pass by burrowing deep into my memory and recreating days in great detail. I may decide to recall a December day of ten years ago. I start by remembering my morning routine: what time exactly I needed to get up; how long it took to shave; what clothes I could select; what we would all have for breakfast; and then the walk to the bus stop. I remember the news-stand where I bought a paper; the shops I passed, the names above the shops, the faces of the shopkeepers. Sometimes I manage to recall the faces of regulars in the bus queue. I retrace the route to Narntowicza Street and the university; then walk in, past the porter's cubby hole, past the message board, past the crowd of students. I pause to remember some of them, and on a clear day I can wipe out Marina's London face and replace it with her rounder, softer face of ten years ago. If I am left alone to concentrate, I can follow my own path through the day till I am almost hallucinating. Once I even answered in Polish when one of the men spoke to me. This skill is the same that prisoners use, and it may be invaluable to me one day, even more so than now.

The streets of Lodz are dingy compared to those of London, the shop windows drab, with old-fashioned lettering, often painted with gold outlines on glass and unchanged for fifty years or more. I miss my fur hat, the one with the earmuffs. I had not realized how much colder the wind blows on a head of thinning hair.

These fantasies have the drawback of all fantasy. They give me the power to edit my past. I have tried to imagine a day when I argued with Alina or, more likely, Henryka, but I find I can't do it. The thought, I wish I had been less hard, keeps breaking in and will not allow me to play out the argument accurately. Because of these hours in which I control events I find the present less satisfactory. I can't make a real effort with Constance after a day filled with thoughts of Katarzyna. My Katarzyna. My wife. I miss you more than my hat!

They look at me, so probably I have a face. Of all the faces known I remember least my own. Here I live in a world of strangers. I have no family friends, no neighbours. The shop-keepers and newspaper sellers do not know me. But then, I no longer buy a daily paper. I am invisible, a citizen of nowhere except Poland: and not the real Poland, but the Poland inside my head. It is growing like a tumour. It fills my head and swells my brain cells. Perhaps it is a malignant growth? It may be. I will live inside my head. My food is bought in the shops at Lodz, even if it means queuing for an hour or more. It is cooked by my wife, so that I can eat stuffed cabbage with beetroot pickle, or apple and cinnamon cake. Being invisible and anonymous makes me wicked. If nobody notices me or talks about me, if I have no face to maintain among my colleagues and neighbourhood, there is nothing to stop me from doing as I please: in real life, just as

163

in my fantasies. Here in London I have no conscience. My only constraints are those of energy and money. I walk the streets like an invisible man in an American movie, passing spectrally through the crowds. No head turns to recognize me, nobody smiles. I am powerless and lonely. In Lodz, a network of gossip surrounded me. People I didn't even know noticed me: comrades of Katarzyna; schoolfriends of the girls; students from my classes. A thousand, maybe five thousand, sets of eyes monitored my progress. Necessity kept me faithful, on the whole, to my wife. The risks, when I dared them, were all the sweeter. One late afternoon in the classroom, the sun slanting across the wall and over the wooden battens pinned on to the wall, and on the floor between the desks, the labouring young body of Anna, or Kika, who frowned in just the same way whether it was over her work or my orgasm. In Lodz I paid for my pleasures with danger, itself a pleasure. Here, who cares? I squander half my wages in Soho and who gives a damn? I take Constance to bed one night, and Joanna the next, and no-one is any the wiser. Exile makes me wicked, but wrong-doing without risk or guilt loses its sting. My clothes don't matter any more, as long as they're clean and comfortable. In Poland, where what most people wear – of necessity – is shabbily uniform, I took pride in being smart, but here where everyone except the tramps is smart, I am shabby. Why waste money on clothes for strangers? Where is my self-respect, my grandmother would ask; and the cheeky boy who still lurks inside this grown man would reply, not in the cut of my shirt and trousers! Would that make her laugh, or would she clip me round the ear for it?

Grand'mère was kinder to her little dog than she was to me. The dog would sit on her lap, and her pearls would fall and mingle with his smelly fur, as his curly tongue stretched up to lick her face. But if ever I tried to give her a hug, apart from the formal salute at morning and bedtime, she would push me off sternly. 'Iwo! Be a little gentleman!' she would say, and then perhaps extend one small grey hand at arm's length for me to kiss. That fragile tyrant. She would die of mortification to see me packing in this basement dis-guised as Monty.

Mortification will not kill me, but it gnaws all the same. Another Ewa wrote:

Be careful of your thoughts
Which will leave you suddenly
Catapulting from the burning surface of your brain.

My brain burns, my thoughts leapfrog. Am I still normal? What would Alina say? Father, you have changed. You seem more savage and more inward than before. That would be astute. The animal in me hunts alone. The human mind in me thinks in silence more often than it speaks. I summon up pictures of myself as the focal point of a white lecture hall, rows of students before me taking notes, rapt with admir-ation at my audacity. How nimbly I leapt from theory to demonstrative fact! Did I? Were they?

Christmas is coming, and the fellows at work say, 'Coming for a booze-up down the pub tonight, Monty? Celebrate the festive season?' The management, our benevolent em-ployers, put an extra ten pounds into this week's wage packet, with a note saying, 'The management of Fordyce Music wishes all its staff the compliments of the season. December 23rd–26th inclusive may be taken as public hol-idays. Please report for work punctually on all other days.' I spend my Christmas bonus at the pub with the other post-room workers, and a couple of trim typists from upstairs. They giggle and flirt, and tease young Kevin, the postroom junior, who does weight-lifting at the gym in his lunch hours. I could tell them that they are wasting their time. We stay until the pub closes. Two of the lads have spent the last half hour with their arms round the waists of the typists, hands brushing their breasts as they leaned across the bar towards the next drink, and these four leave together, triumphant. Tomorrow the whole day will be spent exaggerating, or denigrating, the outcome. I walk more rigidly than usual to the tube station. In the morning my head aches. An ordinary hangover is almost a relief.

Katarzyna writes to say that my Christmas parcel has arrived safely. Three years and 900 miles apart, my wife and I are thinking along the same lines, for she writes:

Iwo, my dear husband,
You would smile wryly to yourself if you knew how I miss you. This will be a surprise to you, as indeed it is to me. Even an old enemy can be preferable to a new friend! Well, this is a harsh way to begin a letter of thanks for your generosity. The woollen things which you sent are very welcome, and their Western elegance is much admired! The food also arrived intact, I think. Good that you put an itemized list with your letter: I am sure it stops the customs officials from stealing. The girls are both well. I see them nearly every week. Alina's pregnancy is well advanced and I still can't get used to the sight of her, swollen with motherhood. She still seems like our teenage daughter to me, and I wish you were here to tell me this is nonsense. She must take care not to over-exert herself, so we shall have Christmas with Henryka and Stanislaw. We will toast you and hope you are celebrating among friends. If you have time, I wish you would consider the future. This letter is in no way meant to dissuade you from your desire to formalize the end of our marriage. Yet I would not want you to believe that I think of you coldly. I often think back over the years and wish I had been warmer to you. Well, the past is the past. May the Infant Jesus and His Holy Mother bless you at this time.
From your Kasia.

I have brooded over this letter. Kasia, a proud woman, is telling me that she still loves me and would like me to return. This after two years with almost no letters, and years before that when we were unwilling prisoners in the same cell. Is it because she is older and needs company? But if she were lonely she could go and live with one of the girls. Does she want a man to warm her bed, and will settle for me if I'm all she can get? I wish I could know. If it is truly *me* she wants I will return. What will they do to me, if I go back? I am not afraid of risk, but of boredom. Are Katarzyna and I now both so old that we will settle for grumbling at one another until we die?

Why should I stay here? If ever I believed the West would make me rich, famous, contented, or bring recognition for my work, opportunities to meet other economists and travel the world attending academic conferences — ye gods, how wrong I was! The West has given me a new understanding of myself, true. It is a self pared to the bone for survival, not fattened on luxury. And women. Can I build over the rubble of my past and make a start again with — whom? Constance would have me and so would Joanna; but do I want to be a husband again? Marina is too young, or I would set up home with her, and not leave her to that rat-faced young bigot. Her youth would warm my old age, and we share many memories. But my wife would laugh and my daughters would be ashamed. Nor am I sure she would have me. I am tempted to try. It is the thought of the ridicule of my former colleagues and her former class-mates in Lodz which stops me. An old man with a young wife is always a fool, and usually cheated.

Well, how about Constance? One, she wouldn't cheat me. Two, she is not stupid. Three, she has a comfortable home. Four, she or her friends would find me a better job. Five, the Home Office would get off my back. Now I am an outsider, and Constance would enable me to be an insider. Six, she loves me. Too much. I would be gobbled up by that hungry heart.

My life is a chess-board and I plot several moves ahead without seeing the clear strategy for a win. Both the queens are after me. I shall temporize and castle. From the safety of my room I will wait and see what move the others make. I still haven't written to my wife, and the empty bed is colder than ever. It snows outside my window. I am freezing, catatonic. Only my tumour throbs. I am a man in a block of ice, visible to the outside world, perfectly preserved, a lifelike specimen, but cold.

Constance rings, her voice tense with excitement. I am to join her family Christmas, no, she insists, I must. Very well then, I say passively, so be it. I will. She is happy and full of plans.

Joanna rings, her voice relaxed with false indifference. I love artifice in women. Joanna believes she must stalk me subtly, so that I do not notice. I am supposed to think I am pursuing her. My dear and desperate Joanna, your stratagems, and those of Tadeusz, were obvious the first time we met. A good Polish Catholic – oh yes you are! – does not sleep with a man unless she has plans for him. I am content to embrace all those who offer themselves to my surprised arms. I am grateful to them and to all the women who have let me enter their lives and their bodies. Does any man ever feel he has slept with *enough* women? The man who married his first love and has never been unfaithful to her, perhaps? Even he must be curious. I have not slept with enough women yet, and life wouldn't be worth living if I thought there were no more to come. Would I renounce all other women for my wife? Kasia, at this moment I would say yes: but I know that if we were together again I should do just what I did before! The interplay of glance with glance, the brushing of hand on thigh, the moment when I allow my erection to nudge, as if unconsciously, a woman's body, and feel by centimetres whether she moves towards me or away – Iwo don't kid yourself: you can't live without this!

I am to join Joanna's Christmas as well. Why not? I can eat two Christmas lunches; only I wish that *la veille de Noël* were with Joanna in the Polish way and Christmas Day with Constance, rather than the other way round. I can't have everything. I can't see the shape of my pregnant daughter, swollen with my first grandchild, my posterity, the child who will make me immortal. The blood of the Zaluskis in the veins of a Party worker's son! What difference does it make? So long as they give the boy a happy childhood – let him be loving and confident and feel himself cherished. Not like me. *I will not think of Grand'mère,* nor of *le grand seigneur,* proud and pitiless. I will think back instead to the little boy they broke, myself, when he was trying to be happy.

Christmas at my grandparents' house in Warsaw. A house large enough to feel grand, with a salon in which twenty people could sit without it being crowded, but small and intimate enough to remain a family house. It was only our home for three generations. No, let me do this, it's not the tumour, just memories. I came into the entrance hall, a very little boy, holding Mama's hand. Was there a butler? Did he bow? Or was it to Mama, when she was a child, walking ahead of the poor French governess, that he bowed? It doesn't matter. I am in the hall. The floor is tiled in black and white marble. To my right the staircase curls upwards and away, with wrought-iron banisters and a handrail that I had to stretch high to reach: but I liked the way the wood flowed like silk under my palm. Straight ahead I walked, from the hall, through double doors, into the drawing room, with its chandeliers and mirrors and the tall tiled stove. Left was the dining room, another chandelier, more mirrors; and right, the salon, panelled in wood, with the portrait of Grand'mère painted just after her marriage, a fireplace burning huge logs, and the high Christmas tree – higher than Papa – that scented everything with the smell of Christmas. Is that right? Yes, wait: the Christmas tree used to stand in front of the french windows so that when the curtains were drawn back, people could see our candles flickering and the fire dancing in the darkened room. No-one decorates their trees with real candles today: it's always those electric lights that smell of nothing but dusty flex. Real candles smelt of danger, as I secretly waited for them to set the branch above alight, or even the Christ-child on the very top. The tree's shadowy bulk seemed to fill one side of the room. I would gaze into the sky, waiting for the Christmas Star to appear. Grand'mère would sit in her winged chair and watch me open my presents, and then put them away for me to give to the poorer children after Christmas. *Then* I was allowed to kiss her. I was a privileged little boy and didn't need toys, did I? Those were for children less lucky than me. I shall never sleep with all the women I want.

And then, in the evening, we processed in to dinner. First my grandparents, and then my parents, and then me and my sister, the last year before she died, and then the governess and the nursemaid, to make sure that little Urszula ate. Not that she did, not even at Christmas. Was there family silver and fine linen and gold-edged Korzec plates, or do I imagine them? Do I imagine it all? It can't be the tumour, it's Christmas, my candlelit Christmas!

What a surprise it was, to find that Constance and her family had real candles too. Not just on the tree, which she had spoiled by draping it with silver strands and glass balls, instead of leaving it green like a wild tree in the forest that just happened to have flowered with candles, like a chestnut tree. Her whole house was full of candles, and their smell brought my childhood back, almost more vividly than I could bear. I sat in a corner of the sofa and talked to Kate, melting her sullenness by praising their decorations.

The other surprise was Constance's husband. I had imagined a fussy, bossy little man, whose self-importance would explain her anxious humility. Instead, he was a good chap; distant to me at first while he watched how I spoke to his children and treated his wife – his, of course, ex-wife – and then once he'd checked me out, friendly and complicit. What could Constance have told him that made him say to me while she was in the kitchen, 'She's a good girl you know, Constance. I'm more aware of it after eight years apart than I was when we lived together. When we were married, I mean. Just try not to let her become too complicated. She thinks too much. Have you noticed?'

'She is an intelligent woman . . .' I said guardedly.

'Of course. But she over-analyses. Her main fault is thinking too precisely on the event.'

'She has been very generous to me. So have your children.'

'Kate's the tricky one.'

'Ah,' I said, not knowing how Kate had described me to

her father, but remembering my covert jealousy of any man or boy who seemed to approach too close to Alina or Henryka.

'Try and make her relax . . . Constance, that is. She's best value when least complicated.'

Did he think me a simpleton?

'And your . . . friend?' I asked.

'It gets awkward, all this business, when your kids are grown up and at it themselves,' he says, man to man: we understand the problems.

'I suppose so.'

He beckoned Cordelia over, and she poured both of us another drink. He was more relaxed with his daughters than I ever could be with mine. He could hug them unself-consciously, as though they were still just little girls rather than young women. I was always uneasy about my daughters' sexuality. Their little breasts alarmed me. I seldom hugged them once they'd changed from girls into women. I was afraid of being aroused by those forbidden breasts.

Constance sat at the head of the table, with Paul and me on either side of her. She was high-coloured and flirtatious, showing us off to one another, basking in our attention. The food she had cooked was delicious – goose and red cabbage – and since Paul had brought champagne and I vodka soon we were all a little drunk. By the time the meal ended, Constance was leaning towards me in open invitation, but I felt inhibited by the presence of her husband – ex-husband, as if the man whose children she had borne could ever really be 'ex' – and couldn't respond to her advances. Paul left the table and danced with his daughters, first the little one and then the older, and finally with both of them together. Max stood before his mother saying, 'OK then Mother, might as well show them!'

When they danced together I was surprised how good they were. The boy moved well and Constance became almost abandoned. She laughed and swung her head and body, fast or slow, whatever the rhythm, until you would not have thought she was a mother dancing with her son. She would have ended the evening equally happily in bed with either of us: Paul or me. I knew it would not be me. Even with his implied permission, I could not have made love to another man's wife after spending the evening at his table, eating his food and drinking with him. Perhaps I was just making excuses, or perhaps it was the soft body of Cordelia – whom I held in my arms when, later, we all danced together – that I secretly coveted. I have taught too many young girls.

Finally Kate made them all calm down while she lit new candles on the tree and gave out presents. The resinous smell and the packages tied with bows and the church bells ringing outside made me nostalgic again, though I had been avoiding sentimentality. What good are the carols, the sweetmeats, the samovar, the midnight mass? Then I was a child, and not a happy child, not at the time, and now I am a middle-aged, almost an old man. We think we are free to celebrate, copulate, deceive, forget. We are trapped. I am trapped. The tumour grows. A thick yellow poison as sweet as honey fills my senses with the past. How can I sleep with this woman who only wants to give me a future? Because I am afraid of becoming old and lonely and sexless. I don't want to turn into one of those men with twisted faces, who mutter to themselves as they carry out obsessive errands that nobody needs. I don't want to be a man whom nobody touches except by accident. Will Constance save me from being old, unfucked, and mad? Will Joanna?

Tadeusz, next day, is more direct than Paul. After we have eaten Christmas lunch with their friends, and the women are in the kitchen, he puts his hands on the table, palms upwards, and says, 'You know it would make me happy to see my daughter married.'

'Yes.'

'She is nearly thirty-five. I don't know why she hasn't married yet. She is a good-looking woman, and not just in her father's eyes?'

'No, more than that. Joanna is a beauty.'

'She's not one of these strange, modern women, who

172

reject motherhood, and say they don't want a husband and would think it demeaning to run his home.'

'No, she will make someone a good wife.'

'Have you thought about it, my friend?'

'Tadeusz, you flatter me. I am an old man.'

His right hand clenches into a gesture of virility. 'Not too old.'

'Not too old to make love to women, thank God. But too old to start again, with a young wife and family. Children. Babies. Anyway, I have no money.'

'Rely on me.'

'What makes you think Joanna wants me? Maybe she wants to get away from Poland, from this Polish heritage that drags . . . ? Maybe she wants to be *English?*'

I understand what he is saying. But if I were so certain that I wanted to stay here, I could marry Constance, without the problem of children.

'Tadeusz, all men worry about their daughters. Mine are married, and I worry about whether their husbands beat them. You know Alina expects a child in the spring?'

'Congratulations, my friend! You will be a grandfather!'

'It is too late to start all over again. I would look a fool, becoming a grandfather and then a father myself.'

'I have watched Joanna. I won't say she loves you, I don't know if she does, but . . . think about it, Iwo. Here she is! Tell her your good news!'

Joanna's eyes light up, and she swings eagerly towards me, smiling.

'What good news? What is it, Iwo?'

'My daughter is with child. It will be born in the spring.'

'Congratulations!'

Gravely she kisses me on both cheeks, and her hair sways towards me, scratchy and fragrant. In a flash of lechery I long to see her head bent over me, her face hidden behind that curtain of hair. I will have her tonight, grandfather or no grandfather. I rise in expectation. They are toasting me. With upraised glasses we salute new life.

In the evening we all go – Joanna, Tadeusz, her aunts – to

the Polish Centre, to join the other wistful expatriates who together will create a travesty of our vanished Christmases. Schoolchildren in national dress sing Polish carols; the restaurant has made a special effort; the women have baked; there are fir twigs on the tables in front of each place, and candles again, more candles, and the Polish eagle clenches its beak and claws and bends its fierce eyes on all of us. The old people reminisce, their crinkled eyes fill with rheumy tears, the women smile and sway. The young are patient and impatient. I close my mind to all thoughts and plan to detach Joanna from her relatives. She toasts me in vodka, brandy, and wine, her eyes sparkling. She is at her best when she feels desired. She wants me too, as husband and home-giver. Why not? I don't want to be old and lonely and unfucked, and Joanna can save me from all that and let me be Polish as well. I want you naked in a dark landscape, dense with bronze chandeliers, vases . . .

I fuck Joanna as if I were raping Poland, purging my furious homesickness on her barren white body, and she cries out in Polish and loves it.

13

The end of the year is cold. My room is cold. The postroom is glum with anti-climax and boredom. I spend my time composing letters to Katarzyna, not yet knowing what I want to say or how I want her to respond. I will write two letters and send whichever seems the more convincing.

Constance rings, still full of Christmas, and asks me what the inscription in front of her book means and whether I have plans for New Year's Eve. I have forgotten what I wrote, but I invent something. If I start the New Year with her, will that tip the balance towards her and away from Joanna? Perhaps I should spend New Year's night alone, waiting for the mirror to show me the face of my future at midnight's stroke? I say nothing, and Constance is too sensitive to press me. She senses the increasing distance between us. And yet I have tried to love her, to squash myself into the shabby, comfortable role of a second husband, to please her friends and appease her children. I am cold and stiff and tired of pretending. I want to be mad. Then I could shed responsibility for my old age, my feet wandering feebly forward, my mind travelling confidently back.

What was it like being the economics professor that I was, the figure in the vanguard of Communism, glibly re-interpreting the world according to the new orthodoxy? What was it like, to have seen through God and dispensed with superstition, what was the rational Iwo like? I would get up after a night spent in my bed, the bed I chose when I married my wife, between sheets darned and turned but made of good rough linen. I would wash and shave in a bathroom that had not been used by strangers. I would dress in clothes I selected from a wardrobe in which every garment reminded me of past events. They were not expensive but they were my own: dark jackets, duffel coat, a warm muffler, my fur hat. I would breakfast on bread and sausage and hot, bitter coffee while my daughters or the radio spoke to me of the day's events in Polish. When I left my home, my departure was noticed. Someone called after me: 'Iwo, don't forget to ask at lunchtime about getting the telephone mended!'; 'Daddy, will you bring me some drawing pencils?'; 'Papa, tonight you have to hear my music for the examination, don't forget!' I was a person, don't forget.

It is not security I need, but continuity. Any woman would make me secure, but only my wife is continuous. Can I, more than half-way through my life, forget thirty years or more as an adult and start again?

My dear wife,
It is four years, almost, since I left, and to my dismay I find I am less and less able to accommodate this new life I chose. I have read your letter many times, and I am filled with visions of Alina as a mother, you as a grandmother. I wish I could share this new family with all of you. Is Janek taking care of her? Has she enough of the right things to eat – whatever they are – you craved coal, unless that is another fantasy of mine. I am often bewildered nowadays, and I have difficulty untangling real memories from those I have invented. It seems to me that you and I were happier together than I knew at the time, and it is hard to think of myself as some other woman's husband, though, believe me, there are those who would willingly marry me. And what about you? Have you another man in your bed? Not men – those, dear Kasia, were always there, and I knew and didn't know, but now I know – but a *man*? Or are you perhaps . . . I cannot put it into words. Write to me, tell me your thoughts, embrace my daughters since I cannot, and ask for everything you need. I earn good money here and shall soon be promoted and earn more,

176

so don't be afraid to ask for everything you need. Real coffee? Warm clothes? What do babies wear?

My blessings to you all as the New Year begins. I am, your loving husband,
Iwo.

In the end I have written, not about Constance or Joanna, but about Katarzyna and myself. Have I ever pleaded with her so nakedly before? Is it enough? I don't care if she has grown older and uglier – I want the warm, familiar smell and breathing of my wife in my bed.

Joanna rings and, by pretending to be melancholy at the end of the year, forces me to cheer her up. We agree to meet and celebrate with strangers. At any rate it must be better than hearing the Australians getting drunk, shouting and vomiting and jamming the pay phone in their efforts to make it provide them with free calls home.

Symbolically, I scrub and sweep my room clear of the old year before setting out to meet Joanna. She is in a new coat, red, and full of good humour. My spirits lift as I see her, and we link arms like an old married couple and stroll cheerfully through the cheerful streets. I had a glass or two of vodka before setting out, and Joanna's breath smells tart yet sweet, as though she had already hailed the New Year, but in spite of this we sit among the English in a pub and take it in turns to buy drinks for each other. Her fluent English always surprises me. I forget that she is not a stranger here, like me.

'Are you ever curious about Poland? Do you ever feel you don't quite belong here?'

'Yes . . . no. Of course I'm curious, about my family, my parents' home town, about the whole Polish side of me. I feel very Polish: do I look Polish?' And she strikes a pose, showing her fine profile to its best advantage, tipping her head back just enough to expose her throat and remind me how she looks *in extremis.*

'What does Polish look like? In Lodz no-one would take you for a foreigner, but then, here they don't either.'

'No. I have an English voice and I went to an English

school and have English friends: only my culture is Polish. It's odd, isn't it, that I have stayed so close to my father? Do you think it's wrong?'

'For him it must be good; for you . . .?'

'Well?'

'In Poland of course it would be normal, for all sorts of reasons. You wouldn't get a single flat, if you were in Poland. Not unless you were a *nomenklatura:* a high-up Party member. And your aunts would never let you go!'

'They won't let me go here, either. They are a problem, Iwo. I feel trapped, the only young one in a household of elderly people. They still see me as a child.'

'So leave . . .'

'I'll come and live with you!'

'You wouldn't like that much either.'

'I don't know . . . whenever you were in a bad mood I could go and talk to all those young men downstairs . . .'

'I'm sure one of them would take you in now: you don't need me!'

'Ah, but you need *me.*'

'I am quite clean and tidy, aren't I . . . and hardly ever lonely.'

'No, Iwo, I don't mean to domesticate you. But you are . . . not lonely . . . but alone. You are becoming obviously a man who lives alone.'

This idea frightens me. Is it so obvious?

'You are teasing me, Joanna. You are unkind, making fun of an old man`. . .'

'Did you know that when you aren't paying attention you talk to yourself?'

'Is that bad?'

'Does my father do it?'

'I expect so.'

'No, he doesn't.'

'So: I need you to stop me talking to myself. What about you Joanna? Do you need me?'

She has been waiting for this question, or something like it, and I have fallen into her trap. She commands my attention by remaining quiet for a long while before answering. The noisy pub rackets around us, but Joanna creates our own silence.

'It's my turn to buy the drinks . . .' I say; but she stops me.

'Yes. I do need you. You know I do. Not just because I should get away from my father and stop being the baby of the household. Nor do I necessarily want children. I . . . I very nearly love you, Iwo.'

'My dear Joanna. You do me too much honour.'

'Does Constance love you?'

'She has never said so.'

'But she does?'

'She may do, yes. She has never said so.'

'She looks as though she does. She watches you all the time. She is very jealous of me.'

'She knows nothing about you.'

'Maybe not: but she is perceptive.'

'What can she suspect?'

'That I am your mistress, Iwo. And that I almost love you.'

It is a generous declaration. I know I am being churlish in not offering her some warmth, some implied promise of hope.

'Joanna. You do not know how difficult I am.'

'I can see that you are difficult. I don't like easy men.'

'I am so much older than you.'

'I am used to older people. Don't think that I have not had young men after me.'

'I am sure you have . . .'

'I have . . . and I have still. I'm not a simple woman, either. Do you know that I have loved women, too?'

This I had not guessed, but, as always, am immediately excited by the image of two smooth women's bodies embracing one another, with myself invisibly watching.

'Do you prefer women?' I ask her.

'No: in the end I prefer men.'

'Good.'

We smile at each other, and she leans forward and kisses me in the corner of my neck and says, 'Let's go? Come on!'

and we go out again into the late night London streets. We decide to go and look at the Thames, somewhere near Big Ben, so that we can hear midnight strike and feel the New Year flooding in. It is a fine, dry night, and the noise of people spilling out of the pub recedes behind us as we walk into Embankment Gardens and up the steps to Hungerford Bridge. Side by side we lean on the railings and look down into the water. Joanna has said all that she planned to say for the evening, so we stand in silence, looking across the river. It eddies beneath us, full of patterns and sounds. I gaze in a fixed focus of concentration. My thoughts and senses hang motionless, until behind me I hear the great bell strike, twelve times, and as the last reverberating chime throbs away into silence Joanna turns towards me. Her mouth parts and her eyes close.

I can't respond. I can kiss her, I will fuck her, but I am engaged only in actions, not with my head or my heart. I am amazed that I, a catatonic man, am apparently loved by these two women. I would, if I were normal, feel flattered, even conceited; or perhaps guilty that, having solicited the love of Constance, I am unable to respond to it. I feel nothing, except lust. What has crippled me? Was it my grandmother, frowning on my childish affection and turning it to formality and cold courtesy; or my timid, fearful mother, in awe of everyone including, finally, me; or was it my wife's infidelities, or my own? I get only sexual relief from pleasure and feel no enthusiasm for anything. My joys are all retrospective and my appetites are momentary and impersonal. I don't care whether it's Joanna or Constance in my bed, and would be satisfied most of all by the spectacle of them making love to each other. I feel like a zombie in the country of the living. I am getting to fear myself – like now: I have walked with Joanna for nearly an hour, guided by her through unfamiliar streets, till we are almost back at the house where I have a room; yet I don't remember hearing what she said, or whether I answered.

'Have I been talking to myself again?'

'Not a word. Nor to me.'

'I'm sorry. Do you mind?'

'No: I was thinking about my New Year resolutions.'

'Have you made any?'

'Yes. I shall decide my life this year, one way or another. I shall steer it forward, and not just drift any more.'

'Good for you! Anything else?'

'Yes. I shall have fun.'

'Very good. Now I must think up some resolutions.'

'Have mine.'

'All right. Why not? The second one is more difficult.'

'Oh yes, Iwo, yes: fun. Let's have fun together. What a funny word for fucking. Fun. Is fucking fun? Not really. Not often. Shall we fuck for fun?'

I can't bear myself. I can bear the separate parts of me: Iwo the cock; Iwo the husband; Iwo the Pole; Iwo the economist, though I don't care for Iwo the postroom worker. But I can't bear the composite man all those parts together make. I don't think I ever could. How did Katarzyna endure me, or the girls? How can Constance think she wants me, and why does Joanna expose her nakedness so boldly to my cruelly distant eyes? I watch her and listen. I wonder how she feels, or what it must be like if the turmoil of her body is matched by some activity of her mind or emotions. I myself am quite silent, quite in control, and apparently quite good at what I'm doing, for she cries in crescendo, 'Fuck me, Iwo, oh Christ fuck me, come on, fuck me . . .' – easily loud enough to wake all the Australians, if they were around, which, perhaps fortunately, doesn't seem to be the case.

'Happy New Year, Joanna. Sleep well.'

In June 1944 they finally liquidated Lodz ghetto. I remember it perfectly clearly. The streets were filled first with noises and cries and then with bodies in attitudes of abandonment and then with a great silence and a guilty atmosphere that wafted all through the city, like smoke. This tumour is bursting my brain, making fissures across the surface of my skull like those cracks that craze my ceiling. I must paint over them again. Well, sleep . . .

There was a simplicity in people, when I was young.

Today, everyone is as American kids say 'full of shit'. These thoughts are prompted by a film I see a few days later, with Constance. It is an old film, black and white and stilted, but it preserved that directness and innocence I remember from my childhood. They are prompted also by a fall of snow which has covered the garden and the roofs outside my window with whiteness, and muffled all noise. That, too, is a brief return to simplicity. Lodz was such a dirty city that snow only stayed white for a couple of hours, and then gradually became speckled with black grains of dirt from the mills. This snow is whiter for longer, but its fall means that during the next few weeks my room becomes even colder. I haven't been warm since the night of the film, when Constance stayed here. Her warmth in my bed was welcome. It comforted me. I wondered for a little while whether I couldn't just surrender to the intensity of her need and drift, letting her draw me into her life. But by morning it was already obvious again that it isn't possible. She left me sadly and unwillingly, saying she would be late for work. I telephoned my boss and said I was ill and would need to take a few days off work. 'Just be sure you bring a doctor's certificate with you once you decide to come back,' he said peevishly. He was only guessing. Lots of people get flu and are off sick in January; and I need time to think.

Joanna said that this year she'll change the direction of her life, and I told her I would, too. A different kind of work would do it, and in a better job I might start to earn more money, and then I would have more choices. I have stopped believing that I will ever be an economist again. When I first arrived here I used to go to the reference section of the local library, and read the financial pages of the newspapers and *The Economist* every week, to try to keep up with events and become properly Western in my analysis. It was harder for me then than it would be now, since my English has got much better in the last four years. But I have become intellectually lazy. I no longer make the effort. I have stopped writing notes towards . . . a lecture, a symposium, an article or economic model. By working in a postroom I have become a postroom worker. Torpor makes me leaden. My brain is dull and my limbs are sluggish. I must find some way of becoming more energetic. Since I gave up swimming I take no exercise.

The Pakistani who owns the late-opening grocery tells me he has made a resolution to keep fit. He is pot-bellied, with sunken eyes, exhausted by the long hours he keeps. He has to greet everyone pleasantly in the hope of making his customers loyal and preventing them from shopping at the big supermarkets.

'What will you do?' I ask him.

'Only sport I can play is cricket!' he says. 'I have too big belly for young men's games. My son's school has squash courts, very energetic, but for me it will have to be something slower I think! My son says to me, why not try weightlifting?'

It is a comical picture, this small, pear-shaped man like some cross-legged contemplative Buddha, heaving iron bars with weights. But I say, 'Good idea. Where will you go? Perhaps I need something like that.'

And so I found out from him the name of a sports centre, near here and very cheap. Perhaps I can keep my mind under control if I discipline my body, exhaust it with sweat and effort. And anyway, I might need to be in top physical condition if . . . Enough of that.

I sit on my bed facing out of the window, and discover how quiet the house is during the day. They must all go somewhere. I am quite alone, and nobody on earth knows that I sit here, looking out of the window on to bare trees and ragged bushes, while snow drifts and melts on the slush and birds sit in the branches as motionless as I am. Now that I have found somewhere to exercise I ought to plan when to go. First I shall think about my life when I was a man and a husband and a teacher.

What time did I get up in those days? Well, it was at seven if I was in a good mood and looking forward to the day. How did I get up? The trams would disturb me in my sleep, from

183

the time they started to rattle through the streets just before six. Sometimes Katarzyna would need to start early, and I would hear her clattering in the kitchen as she slammed the kettle on to the stove and ground beans and chicory together in the coffee mill. Or it might be the sound of the lavatory cistern from the flat above, making the pipes thrum and shudder. In the summer it would be sunshine and birdsong. If I hadn't got out of bed by half past seven, the alarm clock on the other side of my room would finally compel me on to my feet. So: it's sometime after seven and I'm up. Out of the door and into the bathroom for a piss. I peer at myself in the mirror, inspect my hair and teeth, and wonder whether today is one of the days when I can call out to my wife about breakfast. Sometimes she will simply answer, 'Make your own! I'm not your servant, thank God!' but on good days she will answer, 'All right then, what's your fancy this morning? I bought some jam from a peasant woman, plum jam, do you want that with your bread?' I wash and shave and go into the bedroom to dress. What shall I wear? Who am I seeing today? My underwear is shabby, but who cares, while my shirts are still good? Thank God I have never become fat. I could still wear the clothes I had thirty years ago, if I wanted to. I weigh the same now as I did then; only some-how my flesh makes fine dry folds around my body when I move or turn, and it seems paler and greyer than when I was young. I decide to wear my dark brown trousers with the tan leather jacket, and my good brown shoes. As I walk into the kitchen my wife looks up, takes in my appearance, draws her own conclusions, shifts an eyebrow up and down, and turns away. I help myself to bread and white butter and coffee, but she goes out of the room before I can make up my mind what to say to her. She cannot help leaving a warm, friendly smell behind her. She was always a clean woman, who only smelt of sweat after making love. She was both uninhibited and fastidious: an unusual combination. I loved to roll her to and fro, and watch the sweat begin to glisten between her breasts and on her upper lip, till finally we were both coated with sweat, her face and throat

184

reddened, and her black hair lay in sticky tendrils across her forehead and between her thighs. I preferred it when we used to make love in the mornings, before the children woke. I never have the energy nowadays to make love in the mornings. But I used to, all the time.

Did I think, then – ever – that I *loved* my wife? The question seldom occurred to me. I desired her, married her, lived with her, fucked her, fathered children. What had love to do with that? Now, when I look back, I see that I did what I could instead, I *lived* her. It came to the same thing in the end. Now I don't even have the inclination to live Joanna, or Constance. I can't be bothered to share their experiences with that absorption that women require. Except, perhaps, for Marina . . . I might be able to live Marina; but she is too young.

In the evenings the telephone rings downstairs, and sometimes one of the Australians comes and thumps on my door shouting, 'It's some girl asking for you, Monty! You want to talk to her?' but I always reply, 'No, say I'm out.' Not ill: that would bring them hurrying round full of concern and remedies. Why was I afraid of being alone? It suits me. Joanna gave me a diary and I am starting to write in it. It is so long since I wrote anything more than a short letter that my handwriting and my style are awkward, like someone for whom Polish is a foreign language.

My room is very cold. I have no coins to put in the meter so the fire stays unlit. Today I stayed in bed mostly, just as though I were really ill. I am not ill at all. When I was a child and told lies they would often come true; so perhaps I will get ill now. I am waiting for Kasia's letter. If she will take me back, will I go? I am afraid. It is easier to think about Poland than to go back to it. My fingers are stiff. That's why my writing is so clumsy. Nor have I spoken to anyone yesterday or today, though now when I buy the milk and some bread, I will speak. I shall remark on the cold.

185

The days are long and dark, and after a while I stop bothering to put the lights on. Into this mid-winter rigidity the arrival of Marina is shockingly violent. She comes running up the stairs and knocks on my door, and I'm quite unprepared. I don't even know what day of the week it is.

'Monty! Are you mad! Why haven't you ever come to the phone! I've had to take time off to come and see you! What's the matter? Are you ill? Oh, Iwo . . .'

She comes to the bed and puts her arms round my shoulders. I would embrace her, but I am ashamed of my threadbare vest.

'Not ill at all. I have been taking some time off. What day is it?'

'Sunday. Have you eaten?'

'Of course. Not today: but yesterday. Nothing is wrong with me.'

'Everything looks wrong with you! I've been worried about you! At first I thought you might be staying with . . . your English friend . . .'

'Constance? No.'

'No: so then I rang Tadeusz, but he said they hadn't seen you since Christmas. Oh Monty . . . Iwo, what's the matter?'

How beautiful she is! She has the colour and warmth of a brown egg, smooth and rounded. Her eyes are grey and anxious. The room is so cold that her breath lingers in the air after she has spoken. She lays her cheek against mine, and although she has come in from outdoors, it feels warmer than my face. I haven't shaved.

'Marina, you shame me! Hand me my shirt so that I can get up.'

'Let's go out and have lunch! Shall we go to the Ognisko? Or to the Polish Centre? I can't take you to my place. But you must eat a proper meal: hot food. And while you do I can ask you about Peter.'

'Why? Has anything happened?'

'He is talking about marriage. Oh Iwo, it makes me miss Jerzy so!'

'Yes, I know. I'm the same.'

'Get up! I'll go out, shall I? Can I get you some shopping? You ought to eat fruit in the winter. I'll buy you some oranges. They'll cheer the room up, too. You can put them on the windowsill.'

Together we walk to the Ognisko. The day is white and blue. It is invigorating to walk briskly beside Marina. For a while the outside world becomes real to me again. In Marina's healthy, normal company I realize how mad I have been for the last few days, and it frightens me. I didn't know one could slip away so fast.

'. . . February already, and Peter wants us to get married in the summer, June or July and. . .'

'*What* month did you say it was?'

'February. What did you think?'

'January.'

'Monty!'

'Marina, my dear, can the old joke lie down and die now? Will you call me Iwo all the time?'

'Sorry – yes, if you want – but February! It's bad enough not knowing the exact day of the week, but the *month* . . .'

'I must have taken more time off work than I realized. I'll go in tomorrow.'

'What have you been doing for money?'

'I don't spend much. Bread, butter, sausage, coffee. Occasionally plum jam. Razors. Stamps.'

'I'll pay for this lunch.'

'I am glad you came and rescued me.' I couldn't have faced anyone else.

'People have been worried about you.'

'How do you know?'

'They asked about you in the club, my one, I mean; I haven't been to King Street. And Constance rang me. She said she hadn't seen or heard of you for weeks.'

'I took her to the cinema just the other day.'

'She said it was January the 5th.'

'Perhaps. What did you tell her?'

'That I'd come and see you and ring her back.'

'But she didn't come and see me herself.'

187

'She said she was . . . afraid to come. She was nervous of what you might say.'

'Why should she be nervous? I'm not frightening.'

'Well, you can be, sometimes. You're important to her, and that makes people nervous.'

'Are you nervous of me, Marina?'

'Not any longer. But I've known you for years.'

'Yes.'

It is good to walk in the fresh air, Marina's head bobbing along at my shoulder level, her hair sparkling in the sunshine. Her company fills me with well-being.

'Here we are. Have you been here before?'

'No.'

The Ognisko turns out to be a substantial house – very English, with panelling and plasterwork ceilings, an elaborate fireplace in each room, and an imposing stairway leading up from the hall – filled with Poles all speaking Polish. Beautiful, formal, courteous Polish . . . No! Obsolete, irrelevant Polish, a language made pedantic by distance. It's obvious from their intonation that some of them haven't spoken it in their homeland for half a century. Their accents are stilted, almost foreign. Marina's freshness makes them look as though they might crumble into dust at any moment, alone with their exquisite memories.

'Well, my dear, this place brings out the old Marxist in me!'

'How funny, me too! That's why I don't come here a lot. They're charming and lovely but they're like puppets aren't they? Look at their painted wooden faces and jointed arms! But never mind: you'll get an excellent lunch here. Better than my place. Real *barszcz!*'

'For that I can put up with a few pretensions. Do they have *zywiec* too?'

'They do!'

'Marina, you are wonderful. Now, why are you thinking about marriage?'

The waitress, also Polish, brings me the beer, and then our soup and a hot, nourishing stew. I eat ravenously, looking at my food so as to concentrate on Marina's words without being distracted by her face.

'I want to stay here in England. I like it here. I feel free. But you know the constant feeling we have to live with. Will the Home Office renew my visa? If I want to go on holiday, will immigration let me back in? I've had enough of all that. I'm sick of drama and adventure and uncertainty and living on the edge – *sick* of it!'

'It's easier to lead a dangerous life against a familiar background. An ordinary life that might end next week, that's got no glamour, but it's harder. Sorry . . . Why – what's it got to do with your marriage?'

'I want a home. You've never seen my room, have you?'

'No . . .'

'Well, it's a bit better than yours: at least I have somewhere to cook, and a carpet on the floor. Look, I'm almost thirty. First I lived in my parents' home. Then, briefly, with Jerzy . . .'

Marina and Jerzy. Gilded youth. He was dark and angular as a stork, either shouting at her or kissing her. He was never one of my students: he was studying film, but he would come to parties with her, or pick her up after class. Reckless with brilliance, he behaved as though he would live for ever. But not even a crazily idealistic youth of twenty can get away with open defiance; not even if he has Marina drumming up support for him. In the end they were the most prominent pair of students at Lodz. He hanged himself on his tenth night in prison. After that they let her cross the border. They probably thought she was broken. Perhaps they were right.

'Iwo, I never thought I'd hear myself say it: but I want to be *ordinary.* I want to live somewhere comfortable, somewhere I can invite my friends to, give parties.'

'Do you take it for granted yet, living without fear? I don't. I am still compelled to orderliness. I am terrified at the thought of what the boss may say tomorrow. I'm the one that's broken. Marina – tell me about Peter.'

'Professor Zaluski, you know about Peter. Yes, he is what

he seems. Don't you hear what I'm saying? I want to be married. *Married.*'

'To Peter.'

'Why do you force me to say it? All right: I know he's not brilliant. He's not a romantic figure. But he'll never die in a prison cell!'

'My dear . . . I am sorry. I understand. You are braver than me.'

'I know I don't love him like I loved . . . Jerzy. But I'm a homeless person in his country, and that makes us equals. I need him. And he really loves me. Where's your well-known cynicism, Professor? You should be telling me we make a perfect match!'

'I mean it. I admire your courage. But it also makes me sad.'

'You get nostalgic about your past; now you're getting nostalgic about mine! Iwo, look, you're the only person in London who knew me in my other life . . .'

'You don't need my permission to marry.'

'No. But I should like your blessing.'

'You will miss Poland.'

'*No!* That's where you're quite wrong! In fact if I can help it, I won't ever speak Polish again once I'm married, let alone teach it to my children. What's the point of all this . . . ' She waves a hand at the *ancien régime* eating cheese pancakes all round us. '. . . neither English nor Polish, one thing nor the other? What do they want, why are they wasting their lives? It won't bring back their youth, and that's what they're nostalgic for: for being *young* again. I've been young, and it was terrible. I want to be middle-aged, ordinary and busy. I don't want to be a desiccated spinster sitting here in fifty years' time, remembering the glorious 1970s.'

'You're very hard on us.'

'Not us: them! You don't have to get like that either. Get married, make a new home, enter a family, get a job – oh of course you could! Teach mathematics or economics or languages; write articles, do a book – *anything.*'

'Such energy!'

'Don't smile at me like that. Do it! We have to live, Iwo, as best we can: that's the one essential thing. You're not living. Oh Christ. Sorry. Only I do mean it.'

I smile again and take her hand, which tenses and then relaxes under mine.

'Marina, I have to let you pay because I have only a few coins left. Then let's go and look round the museum here. There are some embroideries you would like, and a tiger. You are right. Get married. If you do it in church, I will be there.'

'We will invite you.'

We leave the Victoria and Albert Museum at closing time. The streets are quite dark, and I dread going back to my room and diary. Although I'm almost sure she will refuse, I can't help asking Marina if she will come back with me. Whatever excuse I give, the reason is that I long to hold her in my arms. I remember hair, remember the shadow of a cheek, fragile fingers and the weight of a sleeping hand.

'No,' she says, 'I'm going over to Peter's for supper.'

She leaves me at the front door of the house where I live, and I watch her back as she walks down the street towards the tube station, under the street lamps. I was mad when she came this morning, and in spite of everything she has left me sane: at least temporarily.

People nourish themselves in order to live, I was repeating to myself; human life has great importance. The value of life surpasses the value of all the objects which man has made. Man is a great treasure, I was repeating stubbornly. This is water, I was saying. I was stroking the waves with my hand and conversing with the river. Water – I said – good water: this is I.

I experienced ecstasy once in my life. It was one summer when I was a boy of about nine and we were spending a month with my grandparents in the country. One hot day we all picnicked in the shade beside a stream. I had just learned to swim. After lunch the grown-ups wandered off or fell

191

asleep, and I took my clothes off and slipped into the water, which was quite shallow and very cold. Trees hung low over the stream and the sun flickered through their leaves and shimmered on the surface of the water. I swam with a slow, strong breast-stroke, rhythmical as a rower, cleaving the water with my hands, shrugging it aside and pulling my body forward with the outward curve of my arms. Cleave, pull, glide . . . point the fingers; cleave, pull, glide. The afternoon was coiled and still, the only movement that of the water parting around me as the warm sun on my shoulders alternated with cool gloom beneath the overhanging trees.

The stream turned a corner and when it became too shallow I stood up and looked at the quiet fields on either side of me. Then I turned round and swam back. Nobody noticed I'd been away. That was my ecstasy – the only ecstasy in my life.

Next day I go back to work, and have a hard time convincing the fellow in charge of the postroom that I have been ill for over three weeks. In the end I have to talk him into ringing Marina, and she pretends to be my landlady and talks convincingly of how worried she's been about her poor Monty. Old Tom scowls and curses but can't quite bring himself to sack me. He threatens to do so if I don't bring a sick note next day; but the local doctor is an easy-going fellow and that can be arranged.

That evening I get back feeling better for having returned to normality. On the hall table, cluttered with unwanted mailings and printed cards from window-cleaners and mini-cab firms, is a thin envelope in Katarzyna's handwriting. I take it up to my room. I put it on the bed and go for a piss and wash my hands. I take a glass from underneath the napkin on my chest of drawers and pour myself a vodka and look at the envelope. It was posted ten days ago. It is dark outside, and raining. I fetch a knife and slit open the letter.

Dear Iwo,
Thank you for your letter and your New Year wishes. It

sounded as though you had celebrated the New Year a little too well! You are not usually so sentimental. Perhaps one of these other women has softened you up! It's more than I could ever do: have you forgotten that? Must I remind you that for the last five years that you lived here, we hardly spoke? By all means use your memories to keep you warm, but don't confuse them with the truth! I bear you no ill-will, but you must make up your own mind what to do. I shall go my own way, with or without legal permission, much as I always did! It won't hurt me, or the girls.

It is good of you to offer to send us more things, but you were very generous at Christmas. Some warm stockings, fine wool are best, would be welcome, and good baby clothes are hard to find. We are all knitting coats of many colours! Any shop will tell you what babies need. Don't be embarrassed to ask. But none of these things is essential.

I am glad to hear of your promotion. From violins to cellos? Perhaps one day they'll let you repair a double bass! Smile, Iwo, smile! You were always melancholy after Christmas.

The food situation is getting a bit better here. Things are still very expensive, and the queues are as long as ever, but we have supplies back in the shops. Whenever there's any fresh fruit to be had we all get it for Alina. She is blooming and we all need vitamin C!

Look after yourself, and tell me your final decision soon.

Your affectionate
Katarzyna

She is as capricious as ever, hot and cold by turns. Should I believe the cold tone of this letter, or the warmth of the last one? Although I have a non-existent marriage with an absent wife, she still torments me. Is she just playing games with me? What am I to believe? I am filled with lustful thoughts as if it were thirty years ago and we had only just met.

14

I have hired a television. It costs me nearly ten pounds a month, but it saves money on everything else. Now, if I feel like laughing I can watch the comedy shows; or music if I feel like music. There are nightly programmes about politics. In the postroom they talk about what's been on television the night before, and now that I have a set I can join in their conversations, which are mostly about snooker, or the plots and characters in soap operas. Their wives watch the soap operas and they watch sport. Sometimes they also talk about the news, criticizing the Prime Minister as though she, too, were a character in a soap opera. It never seems to occur to them that politics might be a struggle that involves them, nor even that the struggle has any importance. It's not – as I used to think – because they are wary of expressing political views in front of the foreman. They have no dialectical vocabulary.

The basement is airless and even when it rains I prefer to get out in the lunch hour. The flicker of the neon lights and the throbbing of the central heating pipes set up electrical currents in my head like the thickness in the air before a dry storm. I often go to Soho Square and sit on one of the benches there, or on a seat in the lee of the gardener's hut if it's very wet. The other day it was raining so hard scarcely anyone was about except a few people under umbrellas hurrying to lunch or the book shops. Yet a girl of about seventeen, dressed all in black, was walking slowly round and round the square, taking no notice of the rain and apparently weeping. Sometimes she stumbled with her head down, looking at her shoes, and then she would tip her head back, up into the rain, so that I could see her face distorted by emotion, her eyes screwed up hard against the rain and her tears. After watching her for several minutes I became so distressed by her pain that I walked towards her and took her arm and led her firmly towards the shelter. She shook her head and moaned 'Oh Christ!' but I ignored this and she did not resist. She seemed very young, with angular hair dyed crudely black and a black leather jacket that stank of cigarettes, even in the rain.

'It's all right,' I said. 'I'm not a strange person and I won't hurt you. It's all right. You are so wet.'

She sat with drooping head watching the rain roll down from her hair and drip on to her knees. After a while she took out some cigarette papers and tobacco from her jacket pocket and with red, trembling hands rolled herself a cigarette.

'Your hands are very cold,' I said, and although she didn't answer, she jerked the skimpy little cigarette towards me.

'No thank you, I don't smoke. Would you like a cup of hot coffee to go with that? Shall I buy you a coffee?'

She shook her head again and said indistinctly, 'Never take sweeties from strangers,' and lit the cigarette. She inhaled deeply, occasionally giving a hiccuping shudder like a child who has been crying for hours.

'I'm Polish,' I told her. 'In my country I was an economics lecturer. Are you at school still? Or have you a job?'

'Sixth form college,' she said, and stopped again.

'I have a wife and two daughters at home,' I said to her bent head. Her hair made starry spikes where she had run her fingers through it, and her scalp showed whitely through.

'My daughters are grown up and married. Have you got a family? Brothers and sisters?'

'Sods,' said the girl, and started to cry again.

'My name is Monty. Really my name is Iwo but English people call me Monty. Do you want to tell me what you're crying about? My lunch hour is over soon and I must go back in ten minutes so you could talk to me for that little time. I am sad too. Perhaps we will both feel better. I am sad because I don't know whether I want to go back to Poland or stay here and I can't decide. It depends if I love my wife and I don't know. I have perhaps never loved anyone . . .'

'I love someone, he's called Martyn, he's very handsome, his face is all bony and he's got this really thick hair . . .' the girl started and a shudder ran through her again.

'I've never been in love before, but with him I fell in love the moment I saw him. I only met him a few weeks ago. He started at the college this term. He'd been thrown out of public school, he said, and he's come to the college to do his A Levels like me. He's really, you know, laid back, he doesn't fool about like most boys and he really knows about things like jazz and French films and stuff like that. All the girls were after him as soon as he arrived and he's got this really posh accent. I'm not a snob. He's tall and he wears ever such nice clothes and his parents have got a lot of money only he doesn't get on with them so he's got his own place. He has this flat, right? And after we'd been going out a few times he asked me to move in with him, that was two weeks ago.'

She stopped and seemed about to cry again, so I asked, 'And did you? And what did your parents say?'

'Not my parents, my dad, I live with him. He was mad. He was fucking mad and he said if I went I needn't ever bother to come back so I went. That was two weeks ago.'

There was another silence while she relit her cigarette.

'My wife didn't throw me out, I left of my own wish, I fled from Poland, after December the thirteenth. But we had been living like strangers under the same roof for years. We shared the same flat but we slept in separate rooms. The girls had left home by then.'

'So anyway I moved in with Martyn and it was lovely. He has this really nice flat because like his parents have got pots of money. Course I've been with lots of blokes before, I started when I was thirteen, but never like this. I really love him. I got frightened of him because I loved him so much, and so I couldn't be a laugh or anything like I usually am,

196

and I got dead jealous if he didn't come back with me after college. Three times last week he didn't and once he came in after midnight and I gave him real hell, and then on Monday he did it again and I'd spent the whole evening on my own in his place crying, and I didn't even know who to ring and ask, and I couldn't do my work either. Then when he did get back he didn't want to like, go with me, you know? I mean he slept with me, he had to there's only this one bed, but he wouldn't . . .' She started to cry again.

'I have to go in a minute,' I said. 'My lunch hour is supposed to end at half past one.'

'Yeah. I don't care. What the fuck anyway?'

'So you had a row . . . ?'

'Row? All night long. We made it up in the morning, I thought, but since then he hasn't you know, and this morning when I was doing his coffee he said perhaps I ought to go. And I can't. My dad'll never have me back and I love Martyn just so much, and I've got tickets for this jazz concert next week because it's his birthday and I love him, I really really do, I really do.' She got up and lurched away from me into the rain and walked out of the square on to the street. I didn't run after her. I let her walk away. After a minute or two I also got up and walked back to Fordyce Music and that basement.

In the evenings I watch more and more television. It has become a sort of hibernation, and means that I go out even less than I did. News pictures of the miners' wives shouting furiously in support of their husbands remind me of Katarzyna, my wife. How splendidly she spoke at rallies, reckless and single-minded, without a fragment of doubt. She always remained convinced that the doctrines of Communism were inviolable; it was the leaders who were flawed. A government of Katarzynas, a party of Katarzynas, would indeed have produced a Utopia! She is incapable of hypocrisy or self-interest. Belatedly I recognize her nobility. The miners' wives shout or shake their fists into the camera, spit their defiance at the police, and all those wives are one wife: my own. How is it possible that I never recognized her qualities while I lived beside her? As though her lovers reduced the largeness of her spirit! Besides, did I really care? I was jealous – but did I care? My pride was clipped but I never asked myself why she needed to take other men to her bed. Now at last I want her in her entirety: but even if I can convince her of that, will it make any difference? There are television programmes about Poland; re-creations of the events at the Gdansk shipyard, interviews with Walesa, and during all of them my eyes dart like frantic little fish across the screen, searching the crowd for the face of my wife. Often I think I see her, and then I pay attention to the commentary and find the film was shot in some place where she couldn't possibly have been. I fear the return of the tumour. Thoughts of Poland are insidious, and draw me into daydreams that overwhelm my waking hours.

Constance telephones, and I agree to meet her. It is a long time since I saw her, and I have almost forgotten her existence. I tell her blatantly that I have no money; that I have just sent a parcel of food and clothes to my family, which is true, but she assures me that this is unimportant; she will pay.

Down in the underground there are more miners than ever, shaking their plastic buckets covered with stickers that say 'Coal Not Dole'. They respond cheerfully to those who throw coins in with a word of encouragement, and equally cheerfully to those who spit, sometimes in tones of extraordinary malevolence, 'Fucking Scargill! Ought to be bloody locked up!' But few people challenge them directly. In the rhythm of my head I sense a slow crescendo. I feel it in the miners, too: they are accelerating towards what will be an astounding victory or a crushing defeat. The strike has lost its timeless feeling; events are moving towards a conclusion. I have the same sense about my own affairs; I have resolved my dilemma without consciously knowing how I have resolved it or what I am going to do. Now I must wait and let the decision rise to the surface of my mind, and then wait again to see how it translates itself into action. I move passively with the momentum of events, not really thinking, waiting for them to engulf me.

Constance is vibrant with energy. She looks bright-eyed and vivid, but her voice is nervous.

'Iwo! Don't you look *well*? Marina thought you'd lost weight but you haven't! Isn't this weather foul? How are you? Gosh, it's ages since we saw each other . . . must be, what, over a month?'

'Perhaps it is. You too look very well, Constance: the winter suits you.' She glows with pleasure and I am touched to see her made happy so easily, and draw her arm into the crook of mine and let her guide me to the cinema where she has booked tickets.

'I would have come over to see you when you were ill, Iwo, but Marina said you'd specially asked not to be visited, so I didn't. But I would have done otherwise. Did you have plenty to read? I actually enquired at our library about some Polish books for you but then of course I had no idea what you'd have read or which authors were any good so I . . .'

She tails off anxiously, so eager to please, so ineffectual.

'My dear, I have been a recluse, but now I have emerged, all the better for my retreat. Tell me something about this film, before we get there.'

She knows everything about it: the career of the director; the private lives of the stars; she will tell me the plot if I want her to. She has chosen an American film for us, which is a pleasant surprise, and I prepare to surrender to some other man's patriotic fantasies.

In the restaurant afterwards, a stone's throw from my position in Soho Square, she softens with the warmth of the food and thick red wine.

'Have you ever been hungry, Constance?'

'Only when I've been trying to diet. I've never *had* to miss a meal because I couldn't buy the food. Oh Iwo, have you been eating properly? You must eat properly, it's terribly important, especially in the cold.'

'I was thinking how different your life has been from mine. It's like the men where I work. They have no concept of struggle, it seems to me.'

'I don't know: look at the miners. Some of them were probably quite complacent until a year ago. Now look at them.'

'In Poland we have seen the earth shake. For the last twenty years, thirty, more, for as long as I can remember, the struggle has been constant. Ordinary things are hard all the time. Buying things is hard. Teaching is hard. Talking with friends is hard. A knock on your door is hard. I think I have come to need that, that tribulation.'

'Your life doesn't seem exactly easy now. Not even mine is entirely without its problems . . .'

'My dear: look at us. You have arranged the evening and taken care of me: and I don't have to wonder why; if you can be trusted; if I should guard my tongue, or whether you will start to question me about one of my students or friends. Here, on this menu, we can have whatever we choose. There are no shortages. The other people eating here . . . they're nothing to be afraid of. They can overhear us and it doesn't matter. No-one wonders why we are speaking in French . . .'

'Iwo! I meant to tell you: I've been learning Polish! With your dictionary; and with an old lady who sometimes comes into the library.'

She makes me feel guilty: she must be doing this for me.

'Good day my name is Constance and I lives in England,' she says painstakingly in my mother tongue. 'I have three children, two is girls and one is boy. What is your name?'

Suddenly I am tired and bored and I feel a great longing to catch the tube from my usual stop and let it carry me home to bed. The film and the food have relaxed me and I know I could sleep now, without thoughts or dreams. But the wine has made Constance skittish.

'Shall we go? Shall I get the bill? It's nearly midnight. Are we going to my house or what?'

You go to your house and I'll go to mine, I want to say; but the most I can manage is, 'I'd rather go to my room.'

'All right then. I warned Katie I might not be back. She's got a friend staying the night. Iwo, how was my accent?'

Appalling. 'Not bad at all.'

'Really? It's a terribly difficult language.'

'I hope you aren't learning it on my account.'

'No, I'm enjoying it. And the old lady – her name's Magda, she's wonderful – she really enjoys teaching me.'

'I may not be here all that much longer. Don't learn for me.'

In the silence she signs for the bill and smiles glassily at the waiter, who fetches our coats. We leave the deep plush warmth of the restaurant and swing open the doors into a cold night.

'Where are you going? Is it for long?'

'I don't know. I might not. I'm still thinking about it.'

'I see. Well. What does Joanna think?'

'I've no idea. I haven't discussed it with her. I told you, haven't decided anything yet. I shouldn't have mentioned it.'

She is silent at that, and silent on the tube, and silent as far as the front door of the house. Then she says, 'I can always catch a taxi home . . . I don't have to . . .'

'What nonsense! You will stay, I hope,' I have to say, and of course she does.

But as I sit on my bed and watch her undress, a longing for human contact takes me by surprise. It is weeks since I held a woman's body in my arms, in my bed, and Constance smells sweet and her flesh is warm.

'I'll warm your side . . .' she whispers, as she slides between the cold sheets and shivers. As I undress, the prospect of being welcomed into bed makes me glad of her presence. I kiss her to stop her talking; her breath tastes of wine. Her body arches towards me, and I find that the old mechanisms work, they still work, the flag is hoisted up the flagpole to the sound of a solitary trumpet.

Towards the end of February snow falls hard for several days, making the streets first clean and then mucky. Waking up one morning to find a snowstorm whirling down from a high white sky, I lie in bed watching the crystallized trees and black, huddled birds, and sink deeply back into childhood. Each morning they would begin with the announcement of the temperature. 'Minus fifteen Celsius' the grown-ups would say, and sometimes, with bated breath, 'Minus twenty degrees Celsius' and, very rarely, 'Minus *twenty-five* degrees Celsius! Iwo, mind your nose doesn't drop off!' 'It can't, it's impossible,' I would insist, but they'd wag their heads and with long faces tell stories of children whose noses had got frostbitten without their even realizing it, and dropped off, leaving them for the rest of their lives with faces like lepers. Fingers and thumbs and even toes were liable to the same disfigurement if I didn't wear my warm scarf, my warm gloves, my galoshes, drink my warm milk and come in when I was called. With threats and blackmail they controlled my days, cutting short my play and using my ignorance to fill me with fears. Why do people tell lies and talk nonsense to children? What they didn't know was that I disobeyed most of their commands – took off the gloves and scarf and defiantly exposed myself to Jack Frost. My fingers turned first blue and then yellowish-white with cold and stung with pain, but I didn't become a leper, so their bluff was called.

After that I skated and sledged for as long as I wanted, especially during that magical time towards sunset when the blue winter dusk wiped out all shadows and made the snow-covered ground look perfectly smooth. My sledge would skim this glittering surface and for those fifteen or twenty minutes – the brief time between whiteness and darkness – each bump that went shuddering up through my backside along my spine came as a shock, because my eyes hadn't anticipated it. Tense with bravado, I went faster and more recklessly than usual, dashing into danger, *wanting* to fall off and break a limb. I never got more than bruises. My mother used to bathe them with witch-hazel, and its pure, healing smell is the perfume I associate with her. She wore scent in the evenings, but I preferred her in witch-hazel. She had to anoint me secretly, because my father and grandmother accused her of coddling me and making a fuss. The secrecy made the smell enticing. Grand'mère I associate with bitter aloes, which she painted on my fingertips to make me stop biting my nails, and eau-de-Cologne, with which she washed her ears. Her house smelt of beeswax and the lemon water which the servants used for whitening marble, and logs for the fire. Smell is the most primitive of the senses and snow one of my earliest memories. It wafts me backwards in time. A little boy lies here in bed, cosseted in plump starched sheets and feather pillows, a night-light beside him, watching the snow.

Jack Frost gets me in the end: thanks to the London winter. Being without a warm scarf and gloves, I develop a genuine bout of flu and am forced to stay in my room. I lie in bed for days, sick and self-pitying, haunted by unresolved events from my all-too-present past. How can I help being in thrall to my childhood? Raw perceptions were branded on my senses, while my emotions were exposed to a complicated rhythm of pleasure alternating with pain. The love of the grown-ups around me was pleasure; their disapproval was pain. Love and disapproval seemed meted out at random. Had those years been all misery they might at least have given me the tough hide of a realist, which is to say, a cynic. As it was, my heart was cramped by the timidity or harshness of the people who ruled my boyhood.

I began by fearing and obeying my father. Next I hated him, because he tyrannized us all in the sacred names of discipline and duty. Finally, I despised him, realizing that he was a bully, a cowardly man behind the erect façade. He was contemptuous of tenderness, which he called sloppiness, and love, which he called sentimentality. Today at last I understand why: the tiny, tyrannical figure of his mother, my exquisite Grand'mère, was reason enough. I wish I could forgive him for the harm he did me . . . especially now, when I am becoming like him in so many ways.

As for the settings against which these dramas took place: far from being timeless drawing rooms they turned out to be as flimsy as plywood. In one decade the family house and hierarchy collapsed. By the end of the war my grandparents were dead – luckily for them – my ineffectual mother was frail in health, and my father reduced to being a worker among fellow-workers in the publishing house he had once headed, which now became a conveyor belt for shoddy propaganda.

The lesson I learned in these crucial years was: do what you want and confide in nobody. Yet in spite of myself the search for harmony and kindness still goes on, and still occasionally seems to have found its happy ending. A complete cynic doesn't believe in happiness, and therefore doesn't bother to pursue it. I am still capable of yearning for Marina, or detecting in Constance, for a while at least, that same intelligent heart which as a small boy I treasured in my mother. I am half a lifetime away from closing my eyes and calling out for my mother. I am an ageing man in a strange house and this flu is making me ache. To hell with self-pity! To hell with the past, and with all phantoms and shadows and silhouettes and ghosts!

I'm sick of being sick. Flu is at its worst, not in the days when one is most ill – those pass in a haze of sweat and boredom, and are hardly different from standing in a queue for hours on a hot summer's day – no, the worst of flu comes afterwards, with the depression and weakness. In this state I have no resistance to nightmares. Those maudlin daydreams about my childhood were infinitely preferable to these images from my adolescence. In old churches in the country, frescoes with black visions of hell-fire and purgatory have sometimes survived for centuries: maleficent demons grimacing at their victims, who are twisted into caricatures of pain. These images, I learned, are exact, not melodramatic. We have no need of hell when this world does its job quite satisfactorily. The hurts inflicted by my family, which distorted me for life, were good training: they helped me to survive what I witnessed later. I did not believe I could become a man, after what I had seen as an adolescent, and yet I did. One does, unless one happened to be Jewish.

That's as much as I can manage now. I'll have to talk about something banal. But I'll come back to the nightmares – I have no choice, since they always come back to me.

It's only my thoughts that burn. Outwardly I am not warm. People have sometimes called me enigmatic or inscrutable, which fills me with a mixture of incredulity (me? Iwo, the small boy who craves approval, enigmatic?) and satisfaction, since I know that inscrutability is a baffling and attractive quality. Women like a man to seem unfathomable.

Marina phoned me yesterday and asked me to stop by the club, as she had something to tell me. I knew what it would be, and of course I was right: she has definitely decided to marry that oaf, Peter. She even has a flashy engagement ring, which she shows me with bravado.

'My dear, it is a beautiful ring,' I say. 'Now everyone who sees you will know that you belong to some generous man.' I know that will gall her.

'It's not new,' she says, 'it belonged to his mother. She gave it to him for me. It's her way of saying that she approves of me, I suppose: though after having had him to herself for so long she must dread him going. So it was generous of them both.'

She is clever, and I smile at her in recognition of the fact.

'Will your fiancé allow me a congratulatory kiss?'

'He's allowed all the others . . . one more can't make any difference.'

My lovely and defiant little Pole, you're going to be wasted, I think, as I kiss her smooth brown cheek.

'Has Constance spoken to you?' she asks.

'Not for a week or two . . . whenever I saw her last.'

'She's giving a small party for us, to celebrate our engagement. I know she's going to invite you. Iwo, you will come, won't you?'

Constance is giving a party for Marina? I'm astonished. But then, who else is there? Me, I suppose: and she knows I couldn't do it. The club might have organized a party for her: but then it would be impossible to keep all the elderly Polish airmen away, and an engagement party of veterans would be depressing. So . . . yes, Constance. She is kind – and she must be closer to Marina than I had realized.

The party is on a Saturday evening. It is strange to arrive

at Constance's cosy English house and find it full of the intense babble of Polish voices.

Constance herself greets me in Polish, with a sentence that has been carefully rehearsed: 'Welcome to our celebration of the betrothal of our dear friend Marina.' Its archaism must be due to the age of her teacher, but I manage to bite back a smile.

I take her hand and kiss it, saying very slowly, 'Thank you. It is an honour to be here.'

She smiles vaguely. I presume she understands.

At the same moment her forbidding younger daughter comes and pushes a glass of wine into my hand saying, 'Well? Aren't you even going to come and say hello to them?'

Marina looks like a young Polish peasant woman, ruddy from fresh air and farm food, her eyes sparkling and her movements full of vigour and candour. I can hardly bear to turn from her to the pinched face of the fellow who stands beside her, complacently accepting the congratulations of her friends.

'My dear Peter, you are a very lucky chap indeed,' I tell him.

'I know that. I hope Marina is considered lucky as well?'

Ignoring this arrogant remark, to which the only honest reply would be, Certainly not! I ask instead if he plans to learn some Polish.

'Like Constance, you mean? No, we've decided that our household will be a proper English one. Marina's English is pretty good already, you wouldn't know, probably, but it is, and it will get better the more she has to speak it. For the time being I plan to have her go on working, but as soon as we start a family she can give up waitressing and devote herself full-time to me and our children.'

The little man is intolerable. I find myself almost wishing he were doing it to provoke me, but I fear he's always like this. In Lodz he wouldn't have got within a hundred metres of her.

I see Marina moving towards a group of young English people – presumably Peter's friends – but I wander off before she can try to introduce them to me. Tadeusz is surrounded by a group of elderly Poles, Jewish mostly, who have glasses of vodka in one hand and are gesticulating vehemently with the other. They are arguing – it's hardly possible, but they are – about the validity of the Polish Government in exile here. Standing in pearl-grey double-breasted suits, they are so unaware of their absurdity that for an instant I sympathize with Marina in her desire to put all this futile nostalgia behind her. Then I remember what caused them to leave Poland. I remember the mad parties during the war. Whatever else was happening, we were young. We packed our youth into a single room, round a single candle, and while a girl's voice sang, unaccompanied, or to scratchy music from a wind-up gramophone, we would couple: all of us together, in that one room, bodies grappling on the floor with no possibility of privacy. Why pretend, when everyone was doing the same thing? Do it now, in case tomorrow you're dead. Besides, the rooms were so cold that most people were fully dressed, including overcoats. These old men were those young men once, or their parents. The more layers of fantasy they can interpose between themselves and that reality, the easier it is for them to forget: and if those layers mean a shabby-imposing building, which they call 'the Castle'; and a group of self-deluding old men, whom they call 'the government in exile', grouped around a nonagenarian, whom they call 'the President' – well, so Kafka lives!

Constance is beside me, her hand clinging to my arm, her voice cheerful and vivacious. 'Iwo! Don't look so melancholy! Don't you like parties? What you need is another drink. Hang on, where's Katie? . . . Katie, darling! . . . Now Iwo, has anyone talked to you about making a speech? Because it seems to me it would be nice if . . .'

'Do you really think Marina and Peter want speeches? Can't they just enjoy a pleasant evening with their friends? I will make a speech if you really think it's necessary, but . . .'

'Would her father? If Marina were back in Lodz now, would he want to say something?'

'I'm not her father. Have you asked Marina what she thinks?'

'Peter was the one who suggested it. Don't worry. I'll go and ask Tadeusz. Look, Joanna's all on her own. Why don't you . . .?'

'I told you. If you think it necessary I will make a speech.'

'Right. Good. Excellent. Give me a few minutes to get the champagne out. Kate! . . . Look! . . . Iwo's glass is empty.'

She goes off unhappily. She doesn't know what she's asking. How can I simulate pleasure in this preposterous engagement?

'Kate? Can you keep a secret? Then listen: just keep filling up my glass. That's right. And again. Good girl. Thanks.'

Later that evening, well into the small hours, I lie in my bed alone and angry. Marina I can't ever have again. But tonight, either Constance or Joanna would have been welcome. Constance was dancing with some young man half her age and although she embraced me all too publicly and urged me to dance too, I could see that it would be hours before she was ready for bed. I left before midnight. As I stood at the open front door, I caught sight of Kate, circulating among the guests, and beckoned to her.

'I owe you a secret, don't I?' she said as she arrived, a half-full wine bottle in each hand.

I bent towards her, to humour her maudlin adolescent confidences. Her eyes glittered.

'Shall I tell you?' she said flirtatiously. 'Shall I, really?'

'Just as you like,' I said, so she beckoned me closer, and fastened her hot mouth to my ear.

'I hate you,' she said softly. 'We all call you the Undead. But I hate you.'

I straightened up and smiled at her conspiratorially.

'Don't worry,' I said, 'I won't tell anyone.'

'I knew you wouldn't,' she said, and swirled on her heel, back into the thick of the party.

Joanna and her father gave me a lift home, she sitting primly upright in the front seat, gazing straight ahead, and although I stroked the back of her neck invisibly under the

208

warm sweep of her hair, she didn't respond. So here I am, horny and alone. I shift position and reach beneath the sheets; but not even a furiously effective hand-job sends me to sleep. Finally I get up and compose a letter to my wife:

My dear Kasia,
Do you I wonder remember a young student of mine, about eight years ago, called Marina Dubinski? If you don't, ask Henryka. They were class-mates at school. I have just attended a party given to mark her engagement to an Englishman. Marina sends you and the girls her kind regards.

In your last letter you urged me to make up my mind, and gave me no clues as to which way you hoped I would jump. Well, I'm coming home. Not just home to Poland. Home to you. You are my wife, and that means for life. I finally understand that. I finally mean my marriage vows.

I know it's a risk, but I have always loved risks. The girls' husbands will take care of things for me. The girls will be glad that we are together again. And I want to see my grandchild, and hold him in my arms. It must be very soon now. It is good that Alina has plenty of vitamin C. I will make a little package of pills and send you some more, so you can all benefit from them.

Other than Marina's engagement I have no news. My visa expires in three months' time, in June. That should be long enough for us both to prepare for the idea of being together again. Kasia: really together, man and wife.

Send my love to our daughters. Embrace them from me. Please write to me as often as possible. Tell me your thoughts. Are you afraid, too? Don't be.

We shall be all right.
Your loving husband,
Iwo.

*　　*　　*

I feel perfectly calm now, without regrets. So this is what it took, to show me that I loved my wife? How many complications I have had to unravel to reach this final simplicity. Now that I have put words to the force that has driven me all these months, I am not even impatient. Curious, yes. Will I get my job back? Or will I go to prison? Will I be arrested at the border, or betrayed by one of my former associates? But that's impossible. No-one knows.

I sleep like the dead.

15

The following day I telephone Constance and offer my formal thanks for the party.

'Wasn't it fun?' she bubbles. 'You should have stayed. We danced for hours. Didn't Marina look wonderful? I'm even getting to like Peter. The last person left after four or something. What are you doing today?'

It is a Sunday.

'Nothing much. I just wanted to say thank you.'

'By the time I'd finished clearing up – Marina and Peter stayed on and helped, in fact they're still here – it was practically breakfast time. Do you have any plans for Easter?'

'Easter? When is it?'

'Oh Iwo . . . next weekend!'

'I hadn't realized.'

'On Easter Monday they always have a fair on Hampstead Heath. For years we used to take the children. It's quite fun really. Merry-go-rounds and stalls where you can win goldfish and that sort of thing . . .'

'Let's see what the weather's like.'

'Yes, great, it's a deal. If it's sunny, we'll go to the fair.'

Why not? Time drags on a long weekend.

During the week I go to the sports centre the Indian guy told me about. I remember the school gymnasium when I was a youth: a big, old-fashioned hall with a parquet floor and panelled walls, above which were ranged the parallel bars. There was a shabby leather horse with iron hoops that made your hands tingle. I used to strengthen my arm muscles by hanging suspended from the long ceiling ropes with padded rings on the end of them. I would grip these, bend my elbows, and gradually winch myself up until my

211

arms were rigid at my sides. Then I'd hold this position as long as I could, till my muscles shivered under the strain and the rings shook in mid-air.

I must be physically fit, to deal with whatever may happen. The place is cheap, and the changing rooms are rough, but the instructors are good and there is a range of modern equipment that I've never seen before. I am given a programme of exercises and weight-lifting, and take satisfaction from extending my body till my muscles ache, knowing that I will need these resources of stamina and strength. Many of the regulars at the gym are unemployed, and have become obsessional about perfecting their bodies – for what? They sweat and strain and crack their biceps as they shape themselves for work they are not offered. The gym is lined with mirrors. Each man is engrossed in his solitary narcissism, glancing sideways at himself and comparing his sleek triangular body with those around him. Afterwards, in the showers or changing rooms, they talk a jargon of incomprehensible figures.

'I got my 1600 under 7 today. I'm aiming for 6.30,' one will say; and another, 'I can't push the ab reflexor higher than 45. Mike says if I keep working at it, it'll come.'

None of them drinks or smokes. Their self-respect is linked to a physical efficiency which apparently needs no justification. For me it may be the difference between life and death. A sprint of one or two kilometres . . . a stretching routine that keeps me fit even in a cell . . . there will be buckets of water, or other things, that I can use as weights. If nothing else, I will achieve a muscularity that can still surprise Katarzyna. I have goals to aim for.

My optimism is ended by a letter from her, which must have crossed mine. I open it casually one evening when I get back from work, knowing she can't have had time to receive and answer the news of my homecoming.

Dear Iwo,
I am sorry to send you bad news, but you have to know. Alina's child was still-born yesterday. It was a boy. He

212

seemed normal, and the birth, though long, gave no hint of trouble until the end. Alina is still sedated, and hasn't really understood yet. Please don't think you must come home. There is nothing you could do. They are both young, and can have many more children. There is nothing more I can tell you, and to wish you a happy Easter would seem a bitter jest.
Katarzyna.

My heart contracts for my daughter. I sit hunched up, curled over on the edge of my bed, arms around my empty chest. Alina! Oh my distant flesh and blood. Later in the evening I walk to the late-night shop in the Earls Court Road, buy a bottle of vodka, and carry it back to my room. There I sit stonily drinking. It takes half an hour to finish, and another hour to work. I stretch out on my bed, fully dressed, eyes open, staring at the glaucous moon. My daughter is without child? I think: there was a child, a male, and now there is no child. At last I take my shoes off – bang! bang! – and lie stiff and straight and close my eyes. Deprived. And why shouldn't you be deprived? Those better than you were deprived.

In the next days I dull the pain by transporting myself back to the times, twenty years ago, when they were children. The mornings were Katarzyna's job, but I enjoyed the clatter and urgency of breakfast, as the little girls worried conscientiously about their overalls, their exercises, or the letter to teacher. With newly combed and plaited hair they would set off together, oblivious to me within a few steps of leaving, absorbed in the rivalries and gossip of their classmates. Sometimes I watched their backs from a window: Henryka upright and responsible, Alina hurrying along to keep pace with her. Then my own world would claim me. Was I happy then? Not that I knew. Yet the sounds and smells and the very air in the room from those mornings saturate my senses.

There is a man in the postroom, a few years older than me; a little, round, good-natured man whose face shines with sweaty goodwill, the butt of everyone else's jokes. He is uxorious, devoted to his daughters, coming in every Monday morning with proud accounts of his latest feats of DIY on the suburban house where he lives. He has discovered that I too have daughters, and he worries about me.

'You OK, mate?' he says one morning. 'Everything all right back home? How's the family?'

'I heard from my wife last week . . .' I begin, not knowing how to continue, but already he is beaming with approval.

'Writes regular, the Missus, does she? That's the spirit! Like me in the war. Regular as clockwork, me and the Missus wrote to each other. Every week. I'm not much of a one for letter-writing, not normally, but those letters . . .'

'She didn't say much. A short letter only.'

'Never mind, it's the thought that counts. Be going over there this summer I suppose? Gives you something to look forward to. Makes the time pass a bit quicker.'

If he had known that I was expecting to become a grandfather, perhaps I could have told him, but I've never mentioned it – not wanting the showing around of photographs and pronouncing of Polish names that would follow – and so I smile and let his kindly platitudes roll over me.

The week is a short one, since we don't work on Good Friday. I have rejected all attempts to involve me in plans for the Easter weekend. I have nothing to celebrate, and would be a kill-joy. For three days I sit in my room, brooding about my dead grandchild. I cannot grieve for a baby I never saw and cannot imagine – it's so long since I saw a new-born child – but a great line pointing into the future has been severed, and the darkness ahead has closed in again. I try to find words to tell Alina how much I care, but in the end write only a short, formal note that will seem callous to her. It is easier with Katarzyna, for she feels closer to me than she has done for years. In a long letter I repeat my intention to come home. It feels as though these intervening years have been a war that has kept us apart, and now I am returning like a soldier from a distant battlefront. I comfort her, tell her how eagerly I look forward to seeing her, ask her to cook my favourite dishes, promise to bring presents for everyone. I even smile to myself as I write the letter. Oh my dear wife.

I try to cancel the meeting with Constance, but she over-rules me. She is childlike with excitement, and after all it will only be for a few hours, and then I can leave, or stay and fuck her if I feel like it. Keyed up by work-outs at the gym, my body is filled with an energy of its own that seems detached from my state of mind.

Easter Monday is a dull day, with rain lurking behind low grey clouds, and I half expect Constance to ring and cancel our meeting. But she doesn't, and so I leave the house for the first time in three days to have lunch with her. Kate hides her enmity behind a civil greeting and immediately retires to her room with a group of schoolfriends.

'Oh Iwo, it's so good to see you!' exclaims Constance, as she draws me into the kitchen. 'Have you had a lovely Easter weekend? What have you been doing?'

'No,' I answer flatly. 'I have been in my room, writing letters.'

She stares at me, disconcerted, and in the pause I add, 'My wife wrote to tell me that our daughter's child is dead.'

'Oh Iwo! Not the baby? Oh God how terrible. I am . . . Why did it . . .?'

Her face shows real pain, and yet she knows she can't offer comfort.

'It is all right, my dear. Do not concern yourself. There will be more children. Shall I call Kate down?'

She moves stiffly back to the stove and without looking at me, says, 'Just shout up to Katie, five minutes, will you?'

On an impulse I climb the stairs to the top of the house where the girls' bedrooms are, and knock on Kate's door. The chatter from inside stops, and after several seconds her voice calls, 'Come in!' Four or five young girls are sitting on the floor or leaning against the bed. Pop music thumps from the gramophone, and from the smell in the air they have been smoking. Kate looks at me with hostility.

'What does Mum want?'

'She sent me to tell you that lunch will be ready in five minutes.'

'Have I got to help?'

'She didn't say so. May I be introduced to your friends?'

'Emma, Jo, Rachel, Suzie. OK? Tell her we'll be down.'

Why does she hate me so? I am not unkind to her mother. I have tried to be pleasant to her and the other two. I don't threaten the relationship with their father. Christmas seemed a happy time. What is there about me that she can hate so much? I am not usually unsympathetic to young girls.

The Heath that afternoon is a hubbub of noise and fairground music. Girls are screaming on the swings and dodgems, children shriek and cling to the roundabouts, mothers look anxious and fathers hand out coins and get irritable with everyone. Only the teenagers really enjoy themselves. Ostentatiously relaxed, they smoke and stroll through the crowd, their bright clothes dimmed beneath anoraks and leather jackets. Kate and her friends are on the look-out for boys, but offhand when they do catch their attention. I am astonished at their language. 'Fuck off, stupid cunt,' Kate will fling from the side of her mouth at some harmless youth whose looks or clothes displease her; and then all five giggle and look back at him contemptuously. Is this how the young flirt today?

Constance says, 'Katie, darling, I have asked you not to . . . I mean, it sounds so awful . . .'

And Kate says, 'Yeah, sorry Mum,' until the next time.

Yet Constance appears to be happy. She holds tightly to my arm – 'We mustn't lose each other in this crowd' – and wants me to shoot for goldfish at the rifle range, or lob rings on to pegs. She looks into the faces of everyone and is buoyed up with vitality.

'It's really just like a Renoir or something, isn't it?' she says. 'Or . . . no, I know! . . . it's like that marvellous ending to *Les Enfants du Paradis,* you know? When the crowd goes bobbing and dancing past regardless, with the balloons, and her in that carriage . . .'

'I suppose all fairs are much the same,' I reply; and cut her off before she can start on Brueghel. Her face becomes still for a moment.

'Iwo, you don't feel I'm being heartless, do you? I know you can't be enjoying anything much. And yet . . . all the same . . . you can't just stay in your room and brood, you know.'

'No. I was aware of that.'

'Shall we . . . leave the girls here at the fair and . . . walk across the Heath a bit? Perhaps to Kenwood? Would you prefer that?'

'What is Kenwood?'

'Oh darling, that *house* . . . you know . . . that house we . . .'

'Just as you wish.'

We leave the chaos and litter of the fair, the smoky hot dog smells and the dawdling families, and strike out across a rolling expanse of grass. Constance is quiet for a while, but not with an easy silence that allows each of us to pursue his own thoughts; rather a tense, frowning silence. It is a good ten minutes before she can bring out the question that has been preoccupying her.

'Your . . . I suppose, it must be soon . . . don't you have to renew your visa fairly soon now?'

'I am only here on sufferance. I've always known that. Why do you think Marina is marrying Peter?'

'Because he *adores* her, Iwo! And she, she says she's very fond of him.'

'But her original reason was to gain resident status.'

The branches of the trees are encrusted with buds. The clouds are low, slate-grey.

'If they . . . the Home Office . . . after all, *you* could always . . .'

'What?'

'Iwo. *Marry someone.*'

Now I am silenced. I owe her some explanation. I did — though it is some time since I remembered the source of our acquaintance — advertise for a wife; and Constance, in

217

replying, was acknowledging her desire to be married. We haven't alluded to it since. I have no intention of marrying her, surely she has realized that? Of course I am aware that she loves me. I can't make any definite statement of intent, and until I have received Katarzyna's letter, can't announce my firm decision to go home. I've told nobody that; nor would I choose to tell her first. We walk for several minutes while I turn over in my mind what to say, and just as I am about to begin, Well, my dear, I didn't think it needed putting into words but if it does, then . . . she herself breaks the silence.

Turning to me with a false burst of energy she smiles and says, 'I don't know whether you'd gathered that Katie and Co. are going back to Jo's house?'

'No. I hadn't.'

'Why don't we go home now and I could cook us supper and we can have a nice relaxed evening together? Or do you have . . .?'

I had not planned to stay with her, but she has made me feel mildly guilty and so, matching her unreal smile, I agree.

As it turns out, it isn't such a bad idea. She cooks a decent meal; we eat together in the breakfast room and she produces a bottle of solid red wine and offers me vodka afterwards. The drink relaxes me and makes Constance talkative, and I am reminded of her pleasing intelligence and occasional wit. But I don't want to spend the whole night at her house, in case there is a letter for me next morning; so when she bends down to pass me coffee I cradle her breast as her shirt swings forward.

'Why don't we leave all this and take our drinks upstairs?' I murmur against her throat, and at once she picks up her glass and mine and leads the way. I watch her firm arse seesawing ahead of me as she climbs the steps, and rise in anticipation. In the bedroom she turns to face me, and I unbutton the top of her shirt and slip my hand inside. Empty mind, rigid cock, moaning woman, creaking bed, short sleep. Then I just make it to the tube station in time to catch the last train. Not, in the end, an unsuccessful day.

218

The following morning there is still no letter. It is too soon, of course. Five days for my letter to reach Poland; a day or two for Kasia to reply; five days back . . . it won't be till the end of this week, at the earliest. My own impetus is now so powerful that it's hard for me to realize that practical matters like the post move at their usual pace. I can begin to make plans. Regardless of what the Home Office says, I shall go anyway; best to say that I am simply taking a holiday – relatives in East Germany, perhaps? – and then cross the border and, what? I can think about that later.

Meanwhile my grandson is still dead.

When I was a child and some bad thing happened – I was due to go to the dentist, or had to fight a boy at school that day – I used to wake up to a few seconds' peace of mind; and then I would remember that some cloud hung over me. It's the same now. I wake up clear-headed, and then like a shadow the memory blackens my consciousness: the boy is dead. There is no baby. As the days go by its death oppresses me more, not less, and the pain lies more heavily. It is an increasing struggle to be normal, get to work, exchange a few words with the others. I take to going to the gym every day, working myself so hard that I come off the floor after an hour red-faced, my singlet soaked in sweat. I run for longer and longer on the relentless treadmill, five minutes become ten, and the speed increases too. One day a young man comes up to me as I stand gasping for breath.

'You don't want to overdo it old son,' he says. 'No good pushing yourself too hard. You can get a fucking injury that way.' I tell him I'm training for the London marathon, and he claps me on the shoulder. 'Good for you! Bloody marvellous! Take it easy.' Do I look so old? I sluice myself afterwards under a cold shower, gasping, punishing, numbing the mind and shocking the body.

There is still no letter on Friday, and none on Saturday either. Somehow I have to get through a long empty Sunday. Why don't I just go now, in a week or two? Why wait for a letter? There are two reasons: one, I have to save up for another few weeks before I have enough for the train fare;

and two, I cannot leave before Marina's wedding. On Monday there is no letter, and I stay at home to wait for the second post. None comes. After lunch, not that I eat lunch, the phone rings in the hall, so insistently that in the end I go downstairs to answer it. It is the fat, friendly guy from work.

'God! Bloody good thing you're there!' he says. 'Listen Monty me old mate, you're in a spot of fucking trouble. Tom's hopping mad. Says if you don't come in tomorrow you're for the chop. Shouldn't push your luck, if I was you. Anything up? You poorly or what?'

'No,' I tell him, and thank him for warning me. I'll be in next day. I'll make an excuse about the Home Office.

Next morning, before I leave, the letter comes. I tear open the envelope. There is one sheet of paper inside. Katarzyna's bold writing covers barely half a page: its message could be contained in a sentence. She does not want me back. I have been imagining things. All she ever said was that she missed me, and I have built castles of fantasy on this polite banality. The girls have their own lives now; my return would only complicate matters for all of them. She does not want me back. 'I have set in motion the formalities for a divorce. Marry one of those women there in England who want you.' To ram the point home she signs her maiden name: Katarzyna Slowik.

The letter needs no reply and I do not send one. But as the days pass I realize, almost joyfully, that it makes no difference. My intention is set. How could I expect her to understand from my stilted letters that everything between us is just as it was thirty years ago? I shall never pin her down and so will never get bored with her; none of this has changed. I keep referring to the Christmas photograph taken six years ago, but it is not the stout, middle-aged woman who reminds me most of my wife, but Alina. My daughter was twenty when that picture was taken; Kasia when I first met her was twenty-three; but young women looked younger in those days. They were girls then until at least eighteen, clumsy and boisterous, with bouncing plaits. I was her first man. She had kissed other men, but I was the first to make love to her. Make love . . . we made love like carpenters make furniture! We created love with our hands. When we began she was just another conquest to me. But her sexual surrender was the least of our achievements. Making love together was the literal building of love. We put it together, laboriously at first, improved it, constructed it, and finally accomplished it. Love was there; we had made it. Through fucking her I knew her and, by knowing, came to love her. I never understood this before. How simple and accurate language is. How obvious: we *made* love. I've fucked plenty of women, but my wife is the only woman with whom I have ever *made love*.

I will remind her, when I'm back, of our days in the countryside that first summer. We used to meet early on Sunday mornings and bicycle away from the rubble of the town, the boarded up and bombed out houses. We might be stopped and asked to show our identity cards to the military police, and then I'd wink and make a conspiratorial gesture, and they'd let us go. We'd pedal along the pot-holed roads until they became country lanes and finally grassy paths. Dropping our bicycles at the edge of some deep meadow, we would fall into the long grass. We made love in the open air, sometimes in the rain, and in the late dusk we cycled home with our hair full of grass seeds and our clothes stuck with burrs, and spent the rest of the week scratching mosquito bites. Kasia, her plump body flattening the stalks, would complain that it wasn't fair, the woman had to put up with roughness against her skin while the man was cushioned by her body and didn't suffer. In time I taught her that there are other positions, and most of them are hard on a man's knees.

After Kasia's letter very little changes, except that I no longer want to fuck. This gets me into trouble with Joanna who voices her resentment, and with Constance, who expresses careful, elliptical concern. I'm not worried. The gym burns up a lot of physical energy; I sleep better at night and without the need for vodka, which saves me money; and I am leaner and harder than I have been for years. I start to make detailed plans for my return home. I write to both the girls, but not my wife, telling them when I am coming, and that I shall take the train. In my letter to Henryka I confess, 'so that there will be no lies between us when I see you again', my part in the deaths of Kika and Jerzy. I tell her that I gave Kika the list of addresses for dissidents in Russia, and did nothing to try to save her when she was arrested. Also – this one is more difficult, since it is just possible that she might send news of it back to Marina – I admit that I was indirectly responsible for Jerzy's suicide. She must make what she will of that.

When my daughters were little girls at school, who was there who could tell them the truth about their country and its past? Even the teachers didn't know the truth; it wasn't their fault. So children grew up under the great lie. I shall change that, and they will at least have the choice: take it or leave it. Believe me, or the powers that be. If I begin with this truth about myself, they may believe that all the other things I tell them are also true. What more can I do for them?

I have no idea how Henryka and Stanislaw will respond to this, but one thing is certain: it will alert the authorities, who do of course read my letters, and they can work out for themselves at which point I shall cross the border. From East Berlin there's only one place: Frankfurt an der Oder . . . unless I go south, to Dresden, and from there to Wroclaw . . . I pore over a map, murmuring the Polish names. I shall have hardly any luggage. Most of what I need is waiting for me at home. It will be good to wear my old clothes again.

Back here in England I wake up happy one morning and realize that it is the first of May. I am happy because of a dream I had last night. I was in the garden of a house that my parents had lived in long ago, before the war, so I must have been a very small boy. In my dream it is recognizably the same garden, but filled with flowers of such brilliant colours that they shimmer in the air. There are several animals as well, an oddly assorted bunch – a hippo, and a couple of ordinary farmyard pigs, and lots of chickens, and a fox – but they are all serene and harmonious. The garden is filled with a celestial humming sound, rhythmical and pulsating, which flows from the mouth of a nun. She is at the top of the garden swaying and smiling in her black and white habit. Above her head a goldfish is flickering through the air, more like a humming-bird than a fish, making figures of eight in time to the music. Its scales gleam as they catch the light. This gentle scene throbs with sweetness. It fills me with such contentment that I wake up and find myself smiling. I used to have dreams like that in my childhood. I take this dream to be a good omen.

Tadeusz invites me for an evening at the Polish Centre, and I listen while everyone talks of fresh arrests and imprisonments. The authorities are playing cat and mouse with the supporters of *Solidarność*, academics and dissident writers. They put them in prison and then, apparently at random, let them out again, using some phoney amnesty as a pretext. It's the usual tactic – good policeman, bad policeman – keep them guessing and you produce such insecurity that even good actions make the victim suffer. So, for the benefit of the West, some people are arbitrarily released while days later others, just as arbitrarily, are arrested.

Tadeusz and his cronies are greatly exercised about this, and my indifference seems callous. But I can hardly tell them about my dream, let alone that I am about to return to Poland. Tadeusz still has hopes of me for Joanna. To please him, I agree to partner her at Marina's wedding. It will give us the appearance of a couple, but she needs that status and it doesn't make any difference to me. A few days after that I shall be on my way back to my wife.

I haven't told anyone at the postroom that I am leaving, either, in case the foreman uses it as an excuse to dismiss me, but I no longer bother to make myself pleasant to them. Only the fat fellow still tries to talk to me. He says I should look after myself better, or go and see a doctor, or, best of all, find a woman to take care of me, but anyway I should stop counting under my breath as it's driving the others mad. I ignore his platitudes and in due course he too gives up and leaves me in peace. Sometimes in my lunch hour I walk up to the square and look for the black-haired girl who cried once, in the rain, but I never see her. She'll be back with either her father or her boyfriend. I'd like to satisfy my curiosity and know which.

I prefer to write in my diary rather than talk to people. I shall take it home with me, to show Kasia she had no reason to be jealous. It has become, recently, an extended love-letter to her, and a recollection of our love. Much of it is erotic. The thought of her waiting excites me very much.

> You have black curly hair on your head and under your arms and around your nipples, and it makes a line down your belly and flowers between your legs, and I will kiss all of it and watch it darken and become damp with sweat as we make love. You give off a strong, feral smell when you lose control and become female under my hands. I shall lick you into shape. I shall be starved for sex, like a man who has been in prison for four years. We will shut ourselves up inside our flat and fuck until we are too sore to fuck any more.

What could the authorities charge me with? Conspiring to overthrow the state by force? That would be a joke. I haven't even been to look at the Castle – though I shall go before I leave, so that I can tell my compatriots how our esteemed government in exile is housed. They can't think those dreamy old men have anything to do with modern Poland? Most of them probably, in their hearts, dislike *Solidarność* as much as Moscow itself! Maybe the authorities will decide I have been in England to raise funds for the workers' struggle? That's a laugh too. What do the English know about Poland's struggle? The liberal sympathies of the West have turned out to be a sour joke that has curdled in my mind. They'll have difficulty claiming that I must have been in touch with the Underground. After those two deaths in prison – both suicides, both students close to me – the Underground has little love for me. They mistrust coincidences. So what can the authorities get me for? Ah, how ironic! I see that four years in England have left their mark.

I am beginning to think like an Englishman. They don't need facts. They will invent, search my flat, plant papers, question my wife, my daughters, my former colleagues . . . and, of course, me.

In the war, when I was a youth, I saw people being killed, or being taken away to their deaths. I saw many corpses – habitually – they became ordinary to me. What must that do to a learning mind, such casual familiarity with death? It can make you into a necrophiliac. The only difference between me and most people is that I admit it. Death is not a taboo. It becomes a need. You miss it, and need to re-create it – if necessary, in yourself.

My diary again:

I have doubled the amount of time I spend at the gym. I now go there early in the mornings before work as well as in the evenings after work. My heart and lungs pound to bursting with the workload I impose on them. I can now run 1,500 metres in just under six minutes, and 5,000 metres in less than half an hour. I can do two sets of twenty press-ups and twenty chin-ups. This physical fitness makes me mentally calm and perfectly in control. I sleep better than ever. I have memorized my exercise routine, and could improvise much of it without equipment, if necessary, in a bare cell. It is concentration, counting, and repetition which matter. I now count my steps to the tube station from the gym, and at the other end, from the tube to work, and count stairs as I run, not walk, up and down them. The repetition of numbers is comforting and imposes a discipline. It also helps me to detach myself from what is going on around me. Kasia, you are all I have left now (one). My daughters are married and lost to me (two). My grandson, my posterity, is dead (zero). England has failed me; other women have failed me (three). But I still have my numbers and my wife. My wife, the one love in the world. Wife is life, life is love, love is lust, lust is lost, so – I must, I must come full circle.

I shall sit
immobile
my eyes fixed
upon the heart of things

Not me, Kasia: that's Zbigniew Herbert. He couldn't stay in the West, either.

III

Dissolution

16

I am becoming addicted to humiliation. I can no longer persuade myself, even on good days, that Iwo will ever love me, let alone marry me. I don't know by what definition I love him. We are more like strangers now than the first weekend we met. Since Christmas I have seen him precisely five times, and two of those times he didn't even want to make love to me. *And yet* . . . I think about him more than ever and compulsively invent conversations with him in my head – they never take place, of course.

One day, instead of going to the library, I take a very early tube – leaving Kate to see herself off to school – and wait outside his house to check if he still goes in to work. I hang around in the road, walk up and down, and eventually buttonhole the postman. 'If there are any letters for Mr Zaluski,' I say, 'I'm just on my way to see him . . . I could take them!'

The postman looks at me as though I were dotty and says, 'That's all right, Missis, I'll just put them through the letter-box, if it's all the same to you.'

In fact there is no letter for Iwo. By ten o'clock when he still hasn't appeared, I bang on the front door, which is opened by a tousled young Australian. Iwo's room is immaculate and empty.

I shut the door firmly behind me, lock it, and stand in the middle of the floor with pounding heart. Now what do I do? For all I know, he's just down the corridor in the bathroom. I have no desire to look through his private things, but I want to feel like him. I want to do what he does. I take my shoes off and stretch out on his taut white bed. Here his body rests at night. His head dents this pillow. His eyes see those trees. I am terrified that he will return, but I can't hurry away. I turn my head and look across the room. At the far end, the white gauzy curtain is drawn across the cupboard where he keeps his things, and the chest of drawers in which he found the photographs of his family that he showed me the first time I came here. How confiding he was then, quick to explain, to draw me into his past and tell me its names. The curtain shimmers slightly, then flutters in a draught, and at the same time I hear steps on the stairs. I can feel myself going white. After the footsteps have passed I stand up, straighten the bed to its former perfection and leave the house.

This episode gives me a new fantasy to work upon. I've always been better at expressing myself on paper than in speech, so I draft wonderful letters which I might have left behind for him. Sometimes they are flamboyant and metaphorical: why does this room look like midwinter when outside it's warm and bursting with spring?; while other versions are confident and decisive: Iwo, your bedsitter days are over! I have decided to buy a new house, smaller but more central, and I want you to help me choose it and then 'Come live with me, and be my love' (English quotation!). I polish a number of variations on this letter to such a fine, artless elegance that it's all I can do not to send one; but of course I don't, and I always knew I wouldn't. Yet the illusion of action gives me temporary relief from the pressure of frustrated energy stored and growing within me.

My obsession with Iwo moves like a cloud across everyday life, blotting out more and more of it. In the library I have ceased to look interested and available for conversation or enquiries. I spend as much time as possible either doing my Polish exercises for Magda, and trying to memorize long columns of Polish words; or else reading Polish history, poetry, trade union affairs and the political broadsheets which I order from libraries all over London.

'You doing an Open University course on Poland or what?' asks Steve one morning during our coffee break.

'Yeah,' puts in Linda, yawning; 'thought I might try one,

too. Maybe something on the ancient Greeks? Stav bangs on about them all the time.'

'Constance?' repeats Steve.

'No. Not exactly.'

'That's *right,* course you have, I'd forgotten . . . you've got this Polish fella, haven't you?' says Linda, perking up at the sniff of gossip. 'How's it going?'

'Not very far, at a guess . . .' I say, trying to look wry and offhand.

'Bloody foreigners! Don't know why we bother with them! Yes I do.' She turns to Steve, who is wearing his concerned male feminist expression indicating discreet but non-aggressive sympathy.

'. . . It's because you lot are such wallies nowadays! You "my-turn-to-do-the-nappies" brigade: you're hopeless! A right turn-off!'

'Linda, it's not fair to drag Steve into it. Just because you think men with big muscles and tiny minds are macho . . .'

The conversation is steered safely away from Iwo. Linda and Steve will argue the merits of old sexism versus new, improved equality, till the cows come home.

One great consolation is that nowadays Cordy is around more often than usual. She's cramming for her finals and it's easier for her to work from the comparative peace and quiet of her bedroom here than in the communal chaos of the house near college that she shares with four or five other students. Sometimes she'll walk through the breakfast room to put the kettle on for yet another cup of sweet Nescafé and find me hunched up on the sofa.

'How's it going? On schedule?' I say.

'Yeah, doing OK. Coffee? *You're* not, by the look of you. Not bloody *Iwo* again . . .?'

All three of them are now openly splenetic about Iwo: heaven knows what they must say among themselves.

'Cordy, a, it's no business of yours; b, I'm sorry but I love him; and c, I can't help it. Don't call him that . . .'

'Sometimes I think *I'm* forty-four and you're the one that's twenty-one,' she says.

231

While we wait for the kettle to boil she tells me about her Ben. She sounds secure, happy in their mutual, uncomplicated love. They meet mostly at weekends, 'take in' a film or two, perhaps a party, spend a couple of nights together and go their separate ways on Monday to work during the week for their coming examinations. I look at her as she stands looking at me, her face reflecting concern for her suddenly mad mother, though her mind is still on her revision notes. She is barefoot; her strong, slightly grubby feet planted firmly on the black and white floor. She always loved going barefoot and, as a child, the first thing she did on coming home from school was to tear off her shoes and socks and leave them in a wrinkled heap by the doormat. In consequence her feet are wide and her toes splayed, but they are good, healthy feet. She is a good, healthy young woman, more sane and balanced than I have ever been, except briefly, during the child-bearing years of my marriage, when I thought I was doing what women are meant to do.

Oh my lovely, four-square, casual daughter: have I managed to spare you that emotional and sexual baggage that has lumbered me and led me to this state of ludicrous anguish; those outdated, irrelevant trappings of sexual puritanism, social class and female marriageability that I have lugged about all my life, outwardly denying they matter, inwardly strait-jacketed? Do you make love without guilt, claiming your due of pleasure and giving it in turn without modesty or shame? Can you meet a man without covertly checking up on his marital status, and becoming arch if he's 'free'? The long shadow of my parents looms over me still. 'Is he a nice boy darling? What does his father do? Well, if you don't know you must *find out.*' They couldn't quite bring themselves to ask whether the hapless youth 'respected' me, but I knew the question was always there. When my father learned that I had lost my virginity a few months before I married Paul, but with Paul, of course, he erupted with indignation. 'I would rather have heard that you'd committed *murder!*' he said; and I knew that he meant it. Had I been a murderess they would have stood by me, loyally

232

convinced of my innocence; sat white-faced and brave throughout my trial, and confronted the cameramen outside the court tight-lipped, wan, no comment. But the loss of my chief female asset was a far greater disaster, and my father felt as though *he'd* been robbed.

I have tried not to burden Cordy with any of this, and looking at her now it seems possible that I have succeeded. Beside her stands the spectral figure of myself at the same age: rigid, self-conscious, signalling correctly with Braemar twinset and real pearls, meticulous accent and deferential manner. Cordy, by comparison, is relaxed, her clothes falling shapelessly around her soft, uncorseted body, all her limbs at ease. Her face, though, is bright, alert, individual – in vivid contrast to my useless, middle-class, all-purpose smile.

And now here I am half a lifetime later, still playing a part: this time that of the operatic heroine overcome with grief and unrequited love. Yet however unreal it may look, and worse than unreal, absurd, the pain is as acute as though I were suffering from a perforated ulcer. At best I am gnawed by a soft, searching ache; at worst, great flashes of lightning stab me with new humiliations.

One of these occurs when Marina phones me to talk about her wedding and reveals – deliberately, but with great tact – that Iwo will be partnering Joanna.

My first instinct is to say petulantly, Well it's clearly going to be a very Polish event, you won't want me intruding, but I manage to suppress this childish reaction. 'Why her?' I ask.

'Constance, you mustn't take it to heart. He's just saving Tadeusz's face, hers too, of course, by not letting their Polish friends see that she hasn't got a man to escort her. Whereas you . . . everyone knows you've been married and got children and so on.'

'I daresay he's been seeing her a lot lately. He certainly hasn't been seeing me,' I complain.

'He comes alone to the club about once a week. I haven't seen them together since Christmas. I get the impression he's become very solitary. He looks very fit, but his mind is somewhere else. Not on Joanna.'

233

There is a pause, during which I wait for her to supply more details but she says nothing, so I gather up the shabby cloak of my good manners and say, 'But how are *you*, Marina? Looking forward to the wedding, being married, all that?'

Another pause, longer this time. Then she begins to speak, in slow, disjointed sentences.

'Oh Constance. I don't know if I want to marry Peter. It will mean that I have given up hope. Solidarity, you know, offered us hope for a new, free Poland. Those were very important, very beautiful feelings. Life in Poland was harsh, we spent many hours queuing, and what we could buy was poor. We didn't have your choices, but Polish women, especially the young women, were becoming equal. Whoever got home first did what needed doing. Sometimes I cooked or washed for Jerzy, sometimes he did it for me. There was an excitement, a newness in life that made up for the harshness. And we had our writers. Polish litera-ture has always stood guard over human rights and our national pride. Now . . . I wrote to my mother, you know, and told her I was marrying an Englishman. It was hard to describe Peter in words that would convince her I loved him. Then, when I sent her a letter with the date of our wedding, she wrote back and said, "I shall think of it as your marriage to Jerzy". Oh Constance . . . I am losing so much!'

'Is your mother coming over?'

'No. I can't afford to pay her fare – even if she could get a visa – and Peter hasn't offered.'

'*Ask* him.'

'I can't. He is spending all his savings on furniture for our flat, on equipping a wonderful kitchen for me, on our honey-moon – he won't tell me where we're going, says it's a secret – I can't ask him for yet more money. He wouldn't even be able to talk to her. She doesn't speak more than a few words of English, and he can't speak any other language.'

'I'll pay her fare, Marina, if you like.'

'Dear Constance. You are very generous, but no. Iwo will

234

represent my past and that's all I want. Is it a bad sign, do you think?'

'You've never been as proud of Peter as he is of you. It was always him pushing for the marriage.'

'I have tried . . .'

'We ought to meet, Marina. Do you have a free evening soon?'

'This week I'm off on Thursday.'

We meet at a place she suggests: a Polish club in Kensington called the Ognisko. It has not been easy for her to see me alone. Peter is accustomed to sharing her evenings off, and Marina has to promise that he can join us for coffee at half past nine, so we hurry through our meal and our conversation. Concentrating on her, I hardly take in the people around me, who are mainly Polish, with the fine, elegant bones I have come to love. Their voices are sibilant with emotion, in contrast to their faces, which tend to be dignified and static. Poles do not smile easily.

I sense that the trap has closed around Marina since I last saw her. Peter is asserting ownership as though fearful that she might elude him, even now, a month before their wedding. He must be regretting that it was booked so far in advance; but they are marrying at the Church of Our Lady of the Dolours in the Fulham Road, and summer weekend dates are not easy to secure. She has lost weight since the evening of our party and the soft curves of her cheeks and chin have become more angular. She looks as beautiful as ever, but older.

'I keep asking myself why I was so keen to marry him. Suddenly I can think of far more reasons why I should not.'

'Well, let me give you some reasons why you might want to, and then you can tell me why you don't. He is a good, honourable, decent man. He will not hurt you, abandon you, cheat you, or let you down. He will give you a home: a house, with rooms, with objects that will make your life more comfortable and spacious. Above all, he will give you children.'

'I can't have children.'

'What?'

'I had an abortion, in Poland, when I was seventeen, and then after Jerzy died, another. I saw a gynaecologist the other day, and she told me she had her doubts. I had a test. It's most unlikely I shall ever have children.'

'Have you told Peter?'

'Yes. I don't think he was all that sorry. He is very possessive. I think he would rather have me all to himself.'

'Do you mind very much?'

'Yes. Very much. Very much.'

She begins to cry, tactfully, with restraint, so as not to embarrass anyone in this crowded, ornate dining room. Her eyes glisten and sparkle with tears, which she wipes away.

'Never mind, Constance. Let's talk about you. You don't look happy, I have to tell you.'

'I never see Iwo. That's why. And when I do, he's so changed, he's quite different from when we first met.'

'Yes, I find him changed, too. He's very abstracted. His mind doesn't seem to be in the same place as his feet.'

'It isn't just me, then?'

'Oh Constance . . . of course it isn't *you!* I suspect he's ill with homesickness. A lot of us go through it. He'll get over it. Be patient with him. When I'm married I'll ask you both to dinner. Often.'

'So you think you will marry Peter?'

'I have to, don't I? I know that really. I am just playing with the idea that I could get out of it. He is everything you say, and I ought to have realized that perfect happiness with the perfect man is a fairy tale. And even if it weren't, what would my perfect man be doing chatting up a waitress in the basement of the Polish Airmen's Club, huh?'

'You met Peter at church.'

'You don't think I'm allowed to go to church by myself nowadays? No, it's all right Constance, I've come to my senses. You've even cheered me up. I'll be OK. I'll marry him. I don't want to turn into a Joanna.'

'Oh Marina, meeow!'

'She is going to be a cross middle-aged spinster in a few years' time.'

'Is that why she's so set on Iwo?'

'I suppose so. He thinks so. Don't worry, he won't marry her. Look, here's Peter. Darling? Here we are!'

Behind him stands Iwo.

I gaze at him. Time pauses, like my heart, and moves on. It is five weeks since I saw him. Over and over again during those weeks my mind has tried to assemble his features or conjure up his stance. Iwo in the flesh is overwhelming, and I feel myself colour as though my own physical reality were coming to life. Blushing, tongue-tied, dry-mouthed, trembling, I am aware of Peter bending to kiss Marina on the forehead, of Iwo lifting her hand to his lips, then nodding to me, while Peter's clipped, nasal voice is saying, 'Hello my dear . . . Mrs Liddell . . . am I late? I bumped into your friend Monty in Exhibition Road and assumed he was on his way to meet you both. He said he wasn't: but here he is anyway!'

Peter looks none too pleased at his intruder, but must hope that he can palm us off with each other.

As the four of us sit uneasily around the table over coffee – uneasily because Peter would rather be alone with Marina; who might want to finish her conversation with me; while I certainly want to be alone with Iwo, though he looks as though he would be happiest by himself. I think, she's right: he does look fit. But he looks different. He is more inaccessible than ever. How wonderfully his face is moulded on to his skull! How self-contained he is: not fidgeting with his hands, as Peter is: nervously tangling and untangling his fingers as though itching to get at Marina; nor staring around him at the other diners, as I had been doing; nor feeling obliged to join in the little froth of social pleasantries that Marina is trying to whip up. He just *is:* and in being, is perfect.

A waitress comes over with the bill, hoping to move us to the bar so that she can clear the table. Marina and I engage in an argument over who is to pay, which I win, and then – trying to prevent Iwo from leaving us – I suggest a drink.

Everyone declines, but Iwo says, 'Come Constance, the happy couple must want to be left alone. I will take you to the tube station.'

We walk briskly side by side through the late-darkening streets, flanked by grand, stuccoed buildings. I stare miserably at my feet. Where are those fantasy conversations, now that I need them? Where is the cheerful bravado of '. . . and then come live with me, and be my love'? I watch the little shiny bows on the toes of my shoes twinkle incongruously to and fro. Iwo doesn't offer his arm, as one happy afternoon on Hampstead Heath he did, and Boadicea wouldn't have had the courage to reach out and take his hand. We walk in silence towards Earls Court underground.

I remember an evening like this nearly thirty years ago. I was seventeen and he was my first love: a handsome boy with a craggy face and a heavy lock of Teddy boy hair curling over his forehead. He was tall and he liked jazz and jive and my parents would have disapproved of everything about him. He wasn't really interested in me, but I had found some pretext for offering him a 'spare' ticket to see a modern dance company and he had agreed to come with me. The performance was a disaster – he hated it, and I could find no words to justify having liked it – but as we came out of the theatre he said, grudgingly, 'I'll walk you to your station.'

Then, as now, my head buzzed with conversational openings, all of them unspoken. Then, I had been wearing a brand-new pair of shiny black Italian shoes with uncomfortably high stiletto heels and elongated toes. I had watched these toes preceding my feet like medieval jesters' shoes and in silence we had walked along the Embankment from the theatre to Waterloo station, suburban entrance. It was almost precisely the same distance, too: perhaps half a mile. For half a mile I looked at my feet and played a searchlight into the corners of my mind in case some brilliantly witty remark might lurk there to break the tension and make him laugh and spark off an interested response. None did, and after a while he said, 'You're very serious, aren't you? I wish you'd stop looking at your feet . . .' Just as now, Iwo says, 'Relax, Constance. They'll be all right.' Both times, I expect, I half laughed and said, 'Gosh . . . sorry . . . I mean . . . yes, I know . . .' Only then, I was seventeen and it was forgivable. Now that I'm forty-four it's absurd.

It is hard to convince myself that this secret Constance isn't blatantly obvious to outsiders. Yet Iwo's remark shows that he simply assumed I was silent because I was worrying about Marina's future. He can't see the inner panic that has never subsided. The plain little girl in her flesh-pink National Health glasses who knew she came a long way behind her vivacious younger sister in everyone's affections – *that* self-conscious, awkwardly clever child is the ugly duckling still waddling along with me. In due course I was surprised to find that lots of people thought me funny, affectionate, generous and good company; but the people whose opinion mattered – my father, my husband, my lovers – weren't fooled. Their power over me was rooted in my sexual insecurity. I never had much trouble with the male world of authority, which was easily outfaced and outwitted. I acquired the skills of competence: a fairly simple matter of advance planning, lists, and debt-balancing. I wrote long letters to bank managers accompanied by pitifully small cheques and promises of greater to come. I could deal with teachers and doctors and, eventually, solicitors and accountants, and, last of all, an employer and colleagues. My children took it for granted that I was adult – I was their mother, I must be – and thus forced me to grow up. Yet, as she pointed out the other day, sometimes my daughter Cordelia feels, quite rightly, older than me. Is it all a matter of confidence, instilled by love? Guided by the failure of my own childhood, I decided when I became a parent to do the opposite of everything my parents had done. Not criticism: praise. Not frugality: lavishness. Not rules: trust. It was risky and occasionally disastrous. But by and large I loved them, complimented them, encouraged them, defended them and hoped that everything else would fall into place.

When I get home I find a scribbled note beside the telephone: 'Andrew Lloyd-something, not Webber unfortunately, says ring him any time up until midnight.' It's only just after eleven, not too late to talk to him.

I dial his number which is on the same exchange as Iwo's, sinking down into the sofa with the telephone and a cat on my lap, settling in for a long session. It's weeks since we spoke.

'Constance,' he says, 'thank you for ringing. How are you?'

'The same . . . No: a bit worse.'

'Poor lass. Want to talk about it?'

'Well, yes, sometime . . . but tell me first why you rang.'

'A pretext, and then a confession. The pretext is to ask you to this play at the Mermaid . . .'

'Rave reviews . . .'

'Yes, I managed to get tickets for Saturday. Like to come?'

'Love to. Providing the children haven't committed me to anything.'

'Don't give me that crap. You mean, provided the magnetic Pole doesn't ask you out that evening.'

'All right. Yes. I'll definitely come. You are funny. Now what do you want to confess?'

'It's difficult on the phone. I . . . Last night I had this dream. It was about you.'

'Dreams sometimes . . .'

'Yes. This was one of those.'

'Andrew, don't rush to . . . I didn't dream about you. Didn't dream about anybody.'

'Are you about to go to bed? Can I come and see you?'

'*Now?*'

'Any reason why not?'

'It'll be midnight by the time you're here.'

I acquiesce, flattered, curious, and in need of someone to sympathize, someone I can tell about Iwo.

Half an hour later he arrives, bringing his own whisky and Perrier. I welcome him at the door with a deliberate 'old friends' embrace: big smile and a chaste kiss on each cheek.

We exchange the usual formalities: 'How's work?' 'Oh, same as ever, you know . . . going away soon?' 'Yes, France, end of July.' We are English, we know the conventions. 'How's your mother?' 'Well, I suppose . . . that reminds me, I must give her a ring.' Until Andrew sits and bends his grave, domed gaze upon me.

'I'm sorry to come so late.'

'It's all right. I'm wide awake. I spent the evening with Iwo.'

Be warned.

'Constance, there is no way to say this except straight. I had this dream about you, about us: a very erotic dream . . .'

'What happened?'

'I said erotic.'

'Now, or in the past?'

'Not at Oxford. *Now.*'

'Poor Andrew!'

'Constance, don't insult me by joking. It was extra-ordinarily vivid and at the same time terribly obvious, *sensible,* almost.'

'Sensible *and* erotic?'

I am being defensively light-hearted because I dread what he is going to say next: I love you, I have always loved you, ever since I met you again at Paul's place . . . how can I tell him that, to me, he has always been completely sexless?

'Andrew, can I have a glass of your whisky?'

He goes to the sideboard, fetches a tumbler, pours me a whisky, tops it up with Perrier, sits down again, beside me this time, and says, 'Constance, you have *got* to come to bed with me.'

'*Got* to?'

But even as I sit there thinking, this is embarrassing, this is hopeless, how am I going to extricate myself? I feel the first uncurling of a tendril of desire.

'I told you, I've just spent the evening with Iwo. You know, because you kindly lend me a shoulder once a month or so, that I am besotted with him.'

'I am besotted with you.'

The tendril sends out a shoot.

'You make it very difficult for me. I don't want to . . . Oh, Andrew, you're such a good friend and now I shall lose you!'

'No. You will gain me.'

He takes my hand. The shoot produces buds, the prickling of lust. The conditioning of twenty years is being undone by simple frustration, as my body responds to the whisky, the late hour, and the presence of a man. He puts his hand firmly, not flirtatiously, on my breast.

'Constance. Come to bed with me.'

Quite suddenly I decide to surrender. I can't see how he is going to get out of this situation, and the truth is, I do want to be made love to. I get up from the sofa, and for a moment he looks at me, wary and puzzled – am I going to throw him out? – and then as the silence deepens he stands up and puts his arms around me, enfolds me, and for the first time in our lives we kiss.

Reader, I go to bed with him. Why? Because being wanted is an irresistible force after weeks and months of being ignored. Because I am living on a high-wire of emotional tension in which *nothing happens.* The hope for a release of the physical tautness which Iwo induces, the relaxation of my face from lines of strain into the softness of gratified desire is why I go to bed with him. I need to be stroked, held, murmured to, loved: but although Andrew does all that, and more, it doesn't work. How could it, when drumming through my mind like rain on a roof are the words, 'Iwo, oh Iwo, my Iwo, please Iwo . . .'

Andrew doesn't spend the night in my bed. He comes, sleeps a little, and goes, after leaning over the bed with great tenderness and whispering, in case I am asleep, 'I'll give you a ring tomorrow. Darling . . .'

As soon as I have heard the front door slam behind him, and the engine of his car rev up and roar away, I switch on the bedside light and get up. Filled with still undischarged energy, I wash, clean my teeth, pick up my clothes from the floor, fold them, and finally go down to the kitchen and make myself tea. What am I to say to Andrew tomorrow? He must surely know that our attempt at sex was a failure. I didn't even try to pretend, to gratify his masculine pride or ease his embarrassment or simply bring the whole process to a climax. I *wanted* to be moved. It would have been a wonderfully simple solution if Andrew and I could have fallen suddenly, happily, into bed and into love. But the rain drummed in my head and left me quite detached from his gentle, grateful love-making.

Next day the phone rings immediately after breakfast, and I nearly leave Cordy to answer it, for I haven't yet decided what to say to Andrew. But in the end I pick it up, thinking, tell him the truth; you'll just have to tell him the truth. It is Iwo's voice.

'Constance, ah, I have caught you before you go to work . . .'

'*Iwo!*'

'My dear, I am sorry about last night. That young man encountered me by chance and would not be refused. I had no wish to interrupt your evening. But then you looked so anxious and strained, I didn't want to leave you.'

Kindness! Dear God, I had anticipated anything but kindness!

'Iwo . . . how nice of you to have noticed. You're right.'

'Marina is an intelligent woman and she has made up her mind. *She* knows she doesn't love him, but need is a better basis for a marriage than love, don't you think? It's something we should discuss, to set your mind at rest.'

'Iwo, where are you? This is an extraordinary conversation to be having at twenty to nine in the morning, when' – oh, I am daring! – 'you haven't spoken to me properly for weeks.'

'No, I have been very preoccupied. This weekend? Do you want to meet?'

'Of course.'

'Saturday?'

'Fine. Ring me.'

'I will. Goodbye.'

243

Light-footed as Mercury I speed around the house and trip off to the library. I smile at all the shopkeepers along the way, as they sweep the pavement or arrange displays outside their shops.

'Morning, my dear!' they call out to me. 'Lovely morning isn't it?'

'*Heavenly!*' I reply.

My way is clear for action, after weeks of inertia. All through the spring I have been sluggish, heavy-footed, pulled down by my doleful thoughts. And now Iwo wants to talk to me about marriage! I don't care if he marries me for need, if the Home Office is being difficult over renewing his visa, I love him. I decide to spring-clean this weekend. Perhaps I should put the house on the market and start to contact estate agents for details? Plenty of time for that after I've discussed it with Iwo.

Meanwhile, I ring my mother, and confirm our regular meeting. For years, we have met every second and fourth Tuesday in the month. When my marriage was breaking up, Paul told me that he had always known those nights would be clear for his adventures. 'Second and fourth Tuesdays will always have a *frisson* for me!' he said. The old pang shoots through me still. I am to go round to her flat, and she will make me a 'proper tea', making it sound as though it would be my only square meal this month. Well, I can tell her some good news about Iwo at last. I haven't told her much, but she has read between the lines and been con-cerned for me, and for her grandchildren. My father died too late in life for her to have any experience of other men; her life is a peaceful round of bridge at the club and trips to Harrods or the Royal Academy. Is it possible to leave behind all desire for love and sex, to look at men dispassionately, as though they were of the same gender as oneself?

Kate is spending the weekend with my sister whom she loves, and her cousins. They are younger than she is, so she can patronize and bully them – a rare treat for a youngest child. On Saturday morning I start spring-cleaning at eight, a whirlwind of virtuous and purposeful activity. As always, there is the unexpected bonus of becoming involved in the work, so that it ceases to be a chore and becomes a source of pride and pleasure. After three hours I am hot and bothered, pushing back the hair from my forehead with a yellow rubber-gloved hand, but the kitchen and breakfast room are spotless and orderly. Just as I think about putting on the kettle for a coffee, the phone rings – great: that'll be Iwo! But the voice on the other end of the phone is Andrew's.

'Constance! How are you?' Tenderly. 'I know I promised to ring you yesterday, but I was in such a whirl I . . . anyhow, about tonight . . .'

Oh God. I had absolutely and completely forgotten. My mind thinks faster than the speed of light. Elaborate lies are invented and rejected in the seconds after his pause. Mother ill? Child hurt? Neighbour in suicide bid? It will have to be the truth.

'Dear Andrew . . . Christ I hate doing this . . . Andrew I can't manage this evening after all.'

Heavily, he asks, as he is entitled to, 'What has happened? It must be Iwo?'

'Yes.'

'He wants to see you tonight?'

'Yes.'

No point in hurting him more by telling him that I had clean forgotten about our theatre.

'You know I'm obsessed. That means I behave quite unscrupulously.'

'So it seems.'

'Oh Andrew . . . will I see you again?'

'Why?'

Mind races off again. Need to discuss things. No. Want to say sorry? No. 'A friend of mine, a Polish girl, is getting married in a couple of weeks' time. At the Catholic church in Fulham Road. All very formal, with a reception afterwards. Could you possibly come with me to that?'

'I should have thought Iwo was your obvious escort.'

'He's going to be in a group with another Polish family. Andrew: will you? Please.'

'Yes. Talk to you some other time. Pity about tonight.'

'Yes . . .'

'Goodbye Constance.'

Iwo loves – who knows? I love Iwo. Andrew says he loves me. Who loves Andrew? Probably somewhere there is, even now, a woman hearing her phone ring and wondering if it might be Andrew. I hope she has a good evening at the theatre.

I spring-clean all day, scrubbing my guilt into floors and polishing it off windowpanes until they're so clean that the whole room looks lighter. Iwo telephones and we arrange as always to meet outside the tube station. Lovingly I wash my favourite objects in hot soapy water – the yellow crystal bon-bonnière, the cerulean blue vase, the three dancing children – and arrange them, sparkling, in new places. I also make fresh arrangements of flowers and fruit on the side tables and shelves in the drawing room, and gaze around the sweet-smelling rooms with satisfaction before going upstairs to lavish the same attention upon myself. When Iwo comes back tonight both the house and I will be as immaculate as is possible for a Victorian semi and a middle-aged woman. The clocks have been wound, corrected and synchronized and are all chiming seven as I leave, shouting over my shoulder into the empty hallway, 'Bye-bye all of you!' for the benefit of passing burglars. My knees ache from kneeling and my hands still smell faintly of bleach as I head into the May dusk. It is my favourite time of day: the light concentrated low down in the sky, sharpening details of the young leaves and old brickwork with its slanting gold.

Iwo is waiting for me even though I'm five minutes early. He takes my arm and guides me down the Earls Court Road, through jostling groups of young, mainly foreign young, for Earls Court, not Soho, is London's bazaar. We skirt Iranians urgently pleading their political cause to anyone who'll break step to listen; Australians, tall and gregarious, arguing about where to get the best exchange rates; and passing decorously through this minefield of male glances, the black-eyed women – inscrutable behind beaks and veils – whom Allah will protect from defilement. The only English people seem to be sullenly handsome young gays displaying their wares in studded black leather, registering every bleep of warning or interest emitted by other passing males.

Iwo says, 'This evening we have to talk, don't you think? So shall we find somewhere to eat?'

'Fine,' I say breathlessly. 'Great. Yes. Anywhere.'

'There's a new Italian place just down the road from here, round the corner. It's said to be good. Shall we try there?'

As he pushes open the glass door the noise hits me like a wall of Babel. Some interior designer with an eye on Milan has devised the restaurant as though deliberately to hinder the activities of everyone using it. The white tiled floor is easy to slip on and difficult to clean, and does nothing to blanket the sound of fifty or more people talking in a confined space. The walls are roughly plastered and scrape like a grater. The tables are glass, with multi-coloured tubular legs, matched by the tubular arms and perforated seats of the chairs. It would have been hard to think up more ways to frustrate and inconvenience both waiters and diners. In spite of this there is a queue of people just inside the door, which we join. To communicate with Iwo I have to lean towards him and practically shout.

'Looks promising! Always go to busy restaurant says old tourist proverb!'

He smiles and nods. What a crass remark, I think. What an awful place. Why don't I simply suggest we try somewhere else? Impossible. He chose it.

Eventually we follow a waiter who pilots us narrowly between tables to share with another couple. It is a further ten minutes before the menu, our order, and the wine arrive. We can only hear each other by leaning right forward. It's privacy of a sort. In any case, the couple next to us is American and when they hear Iwo ordering in his foreign

247

accent, and then the two of us speaking French – *'Alors, écoute, c'est difficile mais . . .'* Iwo begins – they evidently assume that we can't understand English.

'Will ya take a look at that guy?' says the man *sotto voce*, that is, in a modified shout, as he slides his eyes across Iwo's shabbiness, and I frown at him angrily, in Iwo's defence.

'Honey, I said, d'you like my *hair?*' says his wife. 'These British hairdressers . . .'

Hear me, feel me, my mind sings to itself, *touch me, heal me . . .*

Iwo leans closer. I wish I hadn't chosen spaghetti *alla vongole.* The banality of life's crucial moments.

'When we met we were both very honest,' he says. 'We met because we both wanted to be married. I hope I was quite straightforward with you about my reason?'

'Your visa.'

'Yes. Also I told you that I was still technically married.'

'But that it was unimportant. I remember you saying that your marriage had been dead for many years. You and your wife lived side by side like strangers.'

'Is that how I put it?'

'That's what you said, yes. That you stayed together because in Lodz it was difficult to find a flat. You told me that sometimes all she said in a week would be, "Have you used my milk?"'

'Did I?'

'*Yes,* Iwo, you did. Why? Isn't it true?'

'You seem to remember word for word, so I suppose I must have said it.'

The American next to us is stentorian and confident, master of the world. Have they ever felt uncertain? A graduation ring, a credit card, and that'll do nicely? Iwo eats in silence. I jab my fork into a can of worms.

'Why're we eating Italian in Britain when we'll be in Florence tomorrow?' says the woman with the youthful hairstyle.

'Venice, honey. That's what our schedule says. Venice, Italy.'

'So long as it's got the Michelangelo. The David and Goliath.'

'Sure, sure.'

So sure about everything, and I'm so unsure. *I wanna be loved by you, just you and you alone . . .* Someone once told me that the songs we hum or hear in our heads unconsciously reflect our inner fears. Could it be true, or is it just psycho-babble?

Iwo says, 'What I told you was true, as I then believed it. But I have learned that the truth can be hidden very deep. We often get it wrong.'

What is he going to say? I was happier cleaning my house. To travel hopefully is better than to arrive.

'It didn't seem like that at the time. I remember thinking how honest we could be with each other. About our child-hood and feelings and. . .' Oh Iwo, remember that moment when you first stretched out and took my hand? My voice trails away. Already I know I have lost. *A fine romance,* sings my mind, *with no kisses . . .*

'It is true that I hoped to be able to love you, Constance, or at least marry you. I needed to, and you offered, most generously, to let me enter your life . . .'

Is there sauce round my mouth or parsley between my teeth? I look directly at him, desperate for the suspense to end.

'Iwo, for God's sake come to the point.'

'I cannot love you, I cannot even marry you, because I have realized how much I love my wife.'

'So? She's in Poland. Or are you going to try to get her out?'

'I am going back to Poland.'

Thud. Like an express train crashing, there is a ghastly clatter and scrunch as one impossible oncoming event col-lides with another. Crash, shudder, whirr, silence.

'I didn't mean to hurt you, Constance. You never told me what you felt.'

From sprawling disorder a cry of pain emerges.

'And what did *you* feel? What in the name of blazes did *you* ever feel, Iwo? Tell me!'

'Hope. Gratitude. Perhaps affection.'

'Affection? Gratitude? Jesus Christ, I've been insanely in love with you since the day we met.'

'Yes. If I'm honest I suppose I have to admit that I knew that. You didn't hide it. I tried to pretend I didn't know because I didn't want it to be true.'

My love, then, was always absurd and unwanted. And, if *I'm* honest, I always knew that.

We look at each other bleakly, in silence – or as near to silence as this hell-hole allows.

'Coffee?' he says. 'Or shall I get the bill?'

'The bill.'

'There is coffee at my place.'

Hope flares, and is immediately quenched.

'I think probably I'd rather just go home.'

He pays the bill, for once I let him, in pound coins and lots of small change. As we get up to leave a new crowd of chattering young immediately takes our place.

Outside in the street I gulp down the fresh air. I am shaking. My legs are trembling. He takes my arm. Just like the first time we met. It is less than ten minutes' walk to the tube station, and yet I can hardly bring myself to speak. Finally I ask, 'When are you planning to go back to Poland?'

'I thought, immediately after Marina's wedding.'

'So *soon?*'

'In about three weeks' time, yes.'

We shall never make love again. Nor in bed fright thy nurse with midnight startings, crying out, Oh! oh, Nurse, oh my love is slain . . .

'Constance, will you believe me, I am truly sorry I have made you unhappy.'

'Of course I believe you. It's my fault, too. I should have told you long ago, I suppose.'

'No. I always knew. I would have liked to be able to love you.'

250

'Then why didn't you?'

We stop outside the tube station, still thronged with people.

'It has been a curse over my life. I have never made any woman happy.'

Dance, dance, dance, little lady, dance, dance, dance, little lady . . .

'What will happen to you in Poland?'

'I don't know.'

I saw him, I, assailed, fight, taken, stabbed, bleed, fall and die.

'Will your wife take you back?'

'I don't know. But I hope so.'

'Will I see you again?'

'Of course. At Marina's wedding.'

'I mean, apart from that?'

'I don't know.'

'I must go. Ring me.'

In the tube there is a drunk, or perhaps he's just mad, released from a mental home under Mrs Thatcher's policy to live in the caring community. He comes and straphangs above me, looking, grinning, peering, roaring, performing, hiccuping. I sit locked up tight and nothing he does startles me into action or forces me to change my seat. In the end he shambles off to loom over someone else and I just sit. Were it a month, a year, or ten, I would thy exile live till then; and all that space my mirth adjourn, so thou wouldst promise to return.

On Tuesday I go to visit my mother. She lives in one of those scruffy squares on the fringes of South Kensington where everyone is either going down or coming up, and the former derive comfort from despising the latter. Mother lives in a basement flat, forever quoting the words of the estate agent who called it 'light and airy', as though that were nearer the truth than her own daily experience of it as cramped and sunless. Even so, she lives better than some of her friends, ex-pats with leathery faces now sitting in one room hemmed in by brass and cane and memories. My father's modest legacy, the fruit of a lifetime of prudence, has at least saved her from *that.* Empty McDonald's boxes bowl along the gutters and into the area steps, but nothing more threatening happens than the attempted rape of one Pekinese by another. Anyway, Mother doesn't keep Pekes. She has cats. And it *is* SW7.

'When Daddy died, tell me, how did you get over it?'

She is startled. The question seems almost indecent.

'Well, darling, we'd known it was coming for a long time. We were . . . *prepared.*'

'I don't mean before, when you were together, I mean *afterwards,* when you were alone.'

But woe is me! The longest date too narrow is to calculate these empty hopes.

'One . . . mourns . . . naturally . . .'

She pronounces it 'moorns'; oh, the dreadful gentility of grief!

'I know that, but how did you *go on?*'

'Darling, whatever is the matter?'

To her astonishment and mine I burst into tears, gasping and retching, trying to turn my face away and mutter, 'Sorry' and 'Don't know', and eventually she comes across to the armchair where I am sitting and kneels beside me and puts her arms awkwardly round my knees, waist, anything she can reach, murmuring, 'There, there' and 'Never mind', till I judder to a halt. She goes and gets me a clean handkerchief and when we have both settled back into our separate armchairs I say, 'I'm sorry. I had no idea that was going to happen. I never cry. Daddy stopped me, years ago.'

'*Daddy* did?'

'Yes. It was the only way I could get the better of him. He was so strong. The one thing I could do was refuse to let him see me cry.'

'Your father, *strong?*'

'Of course. Terrifyingly so.'

'Your *father?*'

252

'Oh Mummy, do stop repeating yourself!'

'You amaze me, Constance. Your father, God bless him, was the weakest man I ever knew. He couldn't say boo to a goose!'

'Well then why was he forever saying it to me?'

'*I* used to tell him what he had to say to you when you'd been . . . *rude* and naughty . . .'

'Why didn't you say it yourself?'

'That was *his* job. After all, I did everything else. Cooked for you, looked after you, made sure your clothes were clean and ironed – this was well before the days of your "Women's Lib", you know – I did everything for you and Stella. *His* job was to punish you. Tell you off. *Discipline* you.'

'Come to think of it, he wasn't much good at it. He usually sat on the end of my bed and said nothing. But it made me feel so guilty, imagining he knew all the things I'd done wrong . . .'

'Typical! That's just like Daddy. I used to tell him exactly what he must say and now you tell me he just used to sit there in silence! That's absolutely typical.'

My poor father, not an ogre at all, but nearly as fearful as I had been myself.

'Well, what about his views on sex then? He was appallingly strict with us both. All that stuff about going virgin to the altar, making boys respect you . . . Why did he dish out all that rubbish?'

'Constance, dear, it *isn't rubbish*. It's quite right and very important. It never did you any harm.'

I sigh. How can I begin to explain to her now, after all these years, the unspeakable harm it did?

'Oh yes, Mother, I think it did quite a lot of damage. But don't let's talk about all that now. It's far too late.'

'It's only just five. You're being absurd to get so upset. Is it your new friend, that Polish gentleman or whatever he is? You haven't talked much about him lately: how is he? How's it . . . going?'

'Look: I brought some *petits fours* as a treat. Shall we sit down and have tea?'

'*What* a good idea! You know, Cordelia rang me the other day . . .'

She is on safe ground, as she chatters away proudly about her grandchildren, enabling me to observe how skilfully they edit their lives so as to present her with a version that she will find acceptable. *She* has edited my life. The Authorized Constance. But unfortunately for her, more unfortunately for me, I became a woman in the decade of the Revised Version; woman according to Germaine Greer and Gloria Steinem, Kate Millett and Betty Friedan and Jane Fonda. To me they were names to conjure with, but my mother hadn't even come to grips with Doctors Freud and Spock. I was reared according to the strict principles of Doctor Truby King: meaning that, from babyhood onwards, being 'good' was equated with punctuality – regular meals, bowel movements, and bedtime. There was only one flaw in this tidy routine, summed up in the lines girls used to write in autograph books when I was at school: 'Be good, sweet maid, and let who will be clever.' For I was clever, there was no denying it, and however hard I tried to be good the cleverness would out. Instead of playing with dolls and helping Mummy in the kitchen and keeping my room and my clothes and face and hands nice and clean, I would be crunched in a corner absorbed in a book. My mother tried her best. She urged me to go *out,* go for a walk, join the pony club, the tennis club, the Young Conservatives; she tried to teach me the proper way to make pastry and gravy and my bed; she bought me pastel twinsets and tweed skirts; she made me wear gloves and an elasticated corset called a roll-on; she instructed me never to buy cheap shoes or handbags because 'you can always tell a lady by her shoes'. But in spite of her best efforts I remained more interested in Jane Eyre or Becky Sharp or Héloïse and Abélard.

All these precepts I threw over when it came to bringing up my own daughters, but not all the cleverness in the world could save me from my early conditioning and so I grew up into a conventional rebel. The guiding emotion of my first twenty years was guilt, and its counterpart, secrecy. I rebelled by sleeping with my boyfriend and conformed by marrying him. I rebelled by marrying a man who was lower-class, by my parents' lights, and conformed by staying at home to look after him. And then, just as I was turning into a good wife and mother, *he* rebelled by leaving me and asking for a divorce. After that, feminism got the upper hand – it had to; I had to earn a living. Paying bills is very liberating. Even then I became a 'good' feminist, wearing boilersuits and Oxfam clothes and rejecting make-up for a year or two until my outrageously, gloriously punk teenagers taught me that you could be brash and glittery with fake everything without compromising on liberation.

That's why the gulf between me and my mother now yawns so wide that as we sit facing each other across the damask-covered tea table with its Spode tea service and real silver, our only safe topic of conversation is cats. We compare notes on flea-collars and tinned cat food and my turbulent burst of crying is not referred to. Yet she needs to be needed. She worries about me. She must also, surely, be curious about Iwo: for I had hinted, early on in the relationship, that I had met a man whom I might marry. This would be a great relief to her. She has never come to terms with my divorced state and longs to be able to tell her Kensington friends that 'Constance is getting married again . . . yes, *such* a nice man . . .' Instead, we talk about the cats. But as I stand outside her front door and just as I am about to climb the stone steps to pavement level, she says, 'I *do* miss him, you know, Daddy. I often talk to him.'

'Do you, Mother?' I say, astonished, for they never talked much while he was alive.

'Yes. When I have my little drink at six, I tell him what I've been doing during the day. Silly, isn't it? Well darling, off you go, or you'll be late with the children's supper.'

Off I go. She is growing old and she is alone and nobody touches her except by accident. It will happen to me as well.

17

Marina's wedding is less than two weeks away. I have
offered my house for their wedding reception, but I live too
far from Fulham for this to be practicable and, in any case,
the members of the Polish Airforce Club where she works
have insisted that she should hold it there. Peter has
accepted this – after all, it's the last time she will appear in
a Polish setting – and has also agreed that Iwo and I should
be *in loco parentis* for the day. In preparation for this I now
spend an hour five times a week taking Polish lessons with
Magda.

The room she lives in – just one furnished room – lurks
on the top floor, and there is no lift. Curtains, once purple,
are so shabby that the light shines through them. Her
spoons are silver, which she must polish twice a week, and
make the coffee that they stir taste better, lending it their
quality. As for herself, Magda's hard to describe. She sits
here in this room of faded, pock-marked velvet, rising above
its meanness and giving it dignity by her own splendour. On
either side of her hang pictures of her boy, smiling and
stupid with embarrassment. His cheeks have been coloured
pink by the photographer, so that he seems to blush.

Magda is one of those women who are uniquely
mittel-European. They have no English equivalent. She must
be in her late seventies, but although she has lived through
some of the grimmest events of the century they have not
dulled her optimism or soured her view of human nature.
She is Jewish, and her strong features and piercing gaze
make her stand out in any English bus queue. Her table is
covered with the latest novels and biographies which she
orders from the library – that's how I met her. She also

256

borrows classical records and a changing selection of paintings to brighten up her walls. She is all alone, the last of her family. Her husband disappeared one day in 1942 with their son – 'they were picked up in the street where they'd gone to try and scavenge some food' – and she never heard of either of them again. She spent the rest of the war in hiding: moving from one precarious refuge to another, relying on the frail goodwill of neighbours, buying silence with the last of her jewellery. But she survived, managed to make her way to England, and found a job as a sales assistant in the hosiery department of a big store. She worked there for nearly twenty-five years. It must have been as demeaning for her as Iwo's job in the post room; yet she is totally without self-pity: on the contrary, she is grateful to England. Now she lives on a tiny pension, supplemented by occasional pupils like myself. Although she doesn't smile easily she brims with warmth. Her voice is resonant and her concerns never trivial. She is Mother Courage, and I learn much more from her than just her difficult language. Our lessons, now that I have an elementary vocabulary, take the form of laborious but impassioned discussions about the miners' strike, Greenham Common, and the behaviour of the people she observes around her. She cannot understand the apparent indifference of the English towards their children: not that she condemns them; she literally cannot understand them.

'You are a good woman, a good mother,' she says, carefully choosing simple words and construction. 'Can your daughters go out alone at night? Can they drink alcohol or smoke cigarettes? Are they rude to their grandparents? How is it possible to allow such things?'

Haltingly, I try to explain. Times have changed. My daughters at thirteen and twenty-one are more mature – mature? oh, right – than I was at twenty, even twenty-five.

'That cannot be,' she answers fiercely. 'Maturity only comes with experience and responsibility. While they live with you and take your money they are children, and must show respect and be obedient.' She studies their photographs and smiles.

'They are lovely girls. I am sure they will make you proud. They will find good husbands, lead fine lives . . .'

Her only son is dead.

She is curious about Iwo – her son would be about his age – whom she has never met. I try to describe him, becoming so tongue-tied that I have to lapse into English, and she says, 'I know his type. He is proud, so proud that real life can't touch him. He has created a Poland that never was, nostalgic for the "good old days" of Hapsburg rule. They were *bad* days. Don't break your heart over him, my dear: he is a relic of a way of life that he has only imagined.'

I try to protest, but she stops me.

'I know those old Polish aristocrats. Ruthless, pleasure-loving egoists. Believe me, they didn't live beautiful lives. They exploited everyone to gratify ever more meaningless whims. They were cold, stone cold. Yes, their façade was perfect, but behind that formality they were brutal. To everyone except their own kind. Tell him that, my child: make him answer that. He cannot.'

In pleading Polish I say, as I have said to many people these past weeks:

'What can I do? I love him.'

'Love him? No you don't! You are seduced by his dream-world. He treats you with the same superiority and contempt that his ancestors treated their servant-girls. No, Constance, he is not real, and you are lucky that he doesn't want to marry you. Go to this wedding – Marina sounds a lovely girl – but smile and dance with all the *other* men.'

The lesson is over. She puts a record of Bach's piano concertos on her elderly gramophone – 'Listen: his music is truly celestial. It was composed for God to hear.' – and brews us each a tiny cup of thick, sweet black coffee. Magda personifies self-respect and joy. Having had to discard everything irrelevant she has pared her life down to the simplest and best human qualities: energy, imagination, tolerance. And paradoxically, I think she is happy.

* * *

Marina has given her landlord a month's notice and, not wishing to be married from the room which she has occupied for the last three years, and which was one of the main factors impelling her into wifehood, she packs her stuff for Peter to take to their new flat, and moves out. She is to spend the last night before the wedding under my roof. He drives her over and drops her off at my house before going on to his stag party.

'Don't worry darling,' he tells her, 'I won't drink too much. I'm looking forward to an early night.' He smiles at her tenderly, and I retreat into the drawing room as they embrace for the last time as single people.

'Let's get pissed!' Marina says to me, the moment my front door has closed behind him. 'Let's drink too much and talk too much and celebrate my last night as a single woman!'

Together we totter down the cellar steps and grope around among Paul's carefully stacked bottles of wine. The maturing clarets are hidden away at the back, and by the dim light of one bulb we peer at their labels.

'How about a '75?' I say. 'Look . . . this should be good: a Pomerol. Château de Bel-Air. Or . . . hey! Look at *this*, Marina! A '70 St Emilion! I bet Paul didn't realize there were any of these left!'

'Will he be angry when he finds out it's gone?' she says.

'Oh what the hell! Why should the best wine always be reserved for the men? We'll drink it!'

She carries the wine upstairs and opens the bottle, and it and she wait and breathe and unfold while I sit at the breakfast room table preparing the meal. For her last supper I have chosen rich but finicky dishes: a cold Roquefort quiche to start with, then loin of pork with a prune sauce, a pale green salad, and finally strawberries that have been absorbing vanilla sugar and a glass of Tokay since this morning.

'Here, give me that knife,' I say bossily. 'You don't want your fingers smelling of garlic for the next forty-eight hours do you?'

Instead, she peels the courgettes lengthwise for me until

their shiny skins are variegated dark green with lime-green stripes, and chops parsley and mixes vinaigrette.

It is almost the longest day of the year, and the garden beyond the back door is still suffused with warmth, even at half past eight. The cats crouch in the grass, their ears semaphoring to catch every promising rustle. The sky is that unnaturally deep blue that comes when dusk changes from early into late.

'Let's eat outside?' I suggest. I unfold the spindly garden furniture and cover the table with a starched white cloth. It gleams, turning pale blue as the light falls.

From the surrounding gardens we hear fragments of other people's conversations. The teenager next door says, '. . . I hate being a girl. I've always hated being one. I always — wanted to be a man – well, a boy when I was at school – I'd much rather be a man . . .'

The voice of her friend drifts across: 'Oh I shouldn't bother, in ten years' time all the blokes will be wearing make-up anyway . . .'

'Here, Jools, d'you think I ought to do my toenails, now everyone's barefoot and sandals and stuff?'

From the other side, Mrs Williams, known as 'Mrs Jubilee' because she organized the street party in Jubilee year, shouts out of the back door to her children. 'What you lot doing out there? Come on in now. It's long past bedtime. You come in now and I'll give you a nice Crunchy bar to eat in bed. Harreee! Nicky! Hurry up or I'll tell your dad.'

The children amble up the garden.

'Look Mum, we found a butterfly.'

'What've you done with it?'

'Killed it. We can take it to Miss for the nature table.'

Screened by the high wall which surrounds the terrace outside my kitchen window, Marina and I idle over our meal in the cooling evening.

'What sort of cooking will you do for Peter?'

'English. I want to learn to cook English food. I don't want to run a Polish household. Nor does he.'

'But won't you always feel Polish?'

260

'I don't know. I hope not. Of course, I can never forget my language, but . . .'

'Is this Peter's influence?'

'*No,* Constance, you're too hard on him. He's a sweet man you know, really, underneath . . . all that.'

'What do you mean "all that"?'

'You mustn't forget, he's lived all his life with his mother in Ealing. His father died when he was a little boy. Just the two of them, in half a house, poor, decent, good Catholics. He was terrified his mother would marry again. And she, I suppose, has dreaded him getting married. But he's never suggested she should come and live with us. We shall be quite near, of course – lunch every Sunday . . .'

'Does she know about . . . you?'

'You mean, no children?'

'Yes.'

'Peter said he'd leave it a year or so after we were married, and then tell her. In case of a miracle, he said.'

'Does he believe in miracles?'

'Constance – you mustn't think I am conceited, but – he thinks *I'm* a miracle. He says.'

I bet he does, I think. Can't believe his bloody luck.

'It is not bad to have a man who loves me like that.'

Shall I risk it? Yes: 'Marina, can I tell you what perhaps your mother would be telling you? You *still* don't have to marry him. Because I sense . . . you don't honestly love him, do you?'

I make a business of lighting candles and fitting the round glass chimney over the candlestick to stop the flames blowing out, so that Marina can decide how to answer.

'I don't love him. No. Not nearly the way I loved . . . you know . . . but then, I didn't expect that, ever again. But I will. I shall change him, you'll see. He thinks he's going to change me; but I shall change him more.'

'How?'

'Little by little. When he's not living with his mother, he won't have to listen to her narrow ideas every day. That's a start! First I shall try and get him to show his feelings more.

261

Then, I shall ask him questions, get him to discuss things with me. You wait. Little by little I shall make him softer and more relaxed. He will learn not to be afraid of everybody who isn't like him. I will teach him, I hope, how to *enjoy*. Now, he just wants to be invisible. What matters to him most is not to stand out, never to offend. I think he can be happy, I think he has that possibility.'

Lucky old Peter! I think. She's taking him on as her family, her country, her pupil, her life's work. She has a generous spirit.

'Coffee?'

We carry the plates indoors while the kettle boils and, when the coffee is made, we settle in the breakfast room, Marina curled in the lap of the ancient sofa, me sitting at the table.

'Don't let's have the light on,' I say. 'Nicer to watch the candles burn down. Anyhow, you must get to bed fairly soon.'

She looks at me in the flickering stillness.

'What about you, Constance? I've never really understood why you love Iwo so much.'

'Mainly, I suppose, because I thought he might marry me, because I thought he needed to.'

'But why do you need to? You've got this house, your children, a job. . .'

Why indeed? Because a man is safe-conduct through this man's world. A lone woman is open to exploitation, ridicule, and attack. She has to be forever on her guard, conciliating, avoiding, anticipating trouble, because being alone means being exposed. Women are biologically designed to be vulnerable: soft-fleshed, soft-breasted and bellied, they need a man to protect them from predators. You can learn kung fu and judo and anti-rape tactics; you can wear shapeless, colourless clothes to disguise your pliable body; but still you must be wary — and not just of rapists: the everyday threat is more banal than that. Builders, doing a job for a woman on her own, will 'fix' the leak in the roof with a few licks of cement, and then overcharge, and then when the drips continue to stain the ceiling will say, 'Well, lady, what do you expect? What you really need is a whole new tiling job. Cost you, of course . . .' Late-night taxi drivers — if you can get one to stop for you — will take it for granted that a woman who has to go home by herself will be grateful for their leering compliments; in fact, you sit on the edge of the seat, waiting for the journey to end, nervous in case it ends badly. What about all those correct, safe couples at parents' meetings, who glance covertly at you and avoid your solitary figure, the wife whispering in explanation, 'You remember, I did tell you, she had that rather attractive husband . . .' shwush, shwush, as your private catastrophe is reduced to a public cliché. It gets worse. You're awkward to accommodate at dinner parties — they've got to find a spare man and so few of them are around — though you probably still qualify for an invitation to their parties: a wedding anniversary perhaps, or somebody's fortieth birthday. But you accept, trying not to think stupidly optimistic thoughts. You face the ordeal of entering a roomful of people on your own; attach yourself — smiling at everybody and nobody — to a group, and work out who belongs to whom. An unclaimed attractive man is always a rarity, and if you find one you try too hard to be funny and intriguing and he senses this, and becomes evasive, and starts looking over your shoulder. Your smile slides away and so does your lipstick and you end up with some maudlin type who's drunk too much and transfixes you with his wandering story. So you thank your host radiantly for a lovely party and wait for your mini-cab. More tales from no-man's-land? What about the nutters on the tube, lurching into you with fumbling hands and incoherent oaths? The lone man in the cinema who edges towards you . . . is he sliding his hand under your thigh or do you just imagine it? The pervert who rings in the small hours, waking you from sleep, to whisper obscenities. Even if a woman manages to cope with all this, she finds herself called a 'hard bitch' because she lacks the one essential female attribute: vulnerability. A woman has no right to be strong. Be weak, dear lady, and let the men be strong. A woman alone must be a victim, for how else can you describe someone who only wins approval by being passive, weak, and acquiescent? If she becomes strong then she is too like a man, and men don't want her. She is a victim on a sliding scale from neglect and pity down through contempt to violation. There are exceptions. Magda is one. But I'm not as brave as Magda.

And those are only the public reasons. The private ones? I want a man in the mornings and the evenings. I want him in my bed at night: yes, of course, to make love, but also to hold and to have sleeping beside me. I want a man for tenderness. I want a man to whom I can unfold the daily journal of my life, telling it to make him laugh, sympathize, or understand. Paul, in leaving, took away from me the cast of characters from his working life, and left all their stories unfinished. I liked that soap opera of office intrigues and romances, seen through his eyes. I liked to watch him embroidering the story as he told it for me, much as I had earlier told bedtime stories to the children. I liked tucking up into him at night, even when we made love less and less: I liked the secrets of his physical presence, his smell, his habits, his illnesses and imperfections. For me, since I want to be part of a couple, the choice is to become a lesbian or a wife. I couldn't be a lesbian. I like women, love my women friends a lot, but I don't want to fuck them. That's why I need to marry.

Marina is still looking at me expectantly, as though I had only paused.

'I've been on my own for, what, seven or eight years now. I'd like to be a couple again. Life is easier with a man.'

'Yes . . .'

Yes, she knows that, too.

'Oh Marina – we must be mad! We were going to get drunk and be daft and irresponsible. And I was going to tell you very solemnly all about your duties as a wife, and warn you that there are certain services every husband expects . . . And here we are, grave as widows! Perhaps it's just as well. Marriage is a serious matter. But let's have one last drink. Brandy? There's even some vodka left over from the last time Iwo was here – God knows how long *that* was.'

I am lying. I know exactly. It was Easter Monday, over two months ago. Two months since I made love to him.

'Vodka please.'

I take our glasses across to the sofa and sit down beside her, stretching my arm along its bumpy back, picking at the stray threads torn by cats and children.

'What do you want to know?'

'Everything, Constance. Tell me my future. Can I change him? Have I the patience to last for a lifetime? *Will* I learn to love him? What if I'm unfaithful? Does it matter? If it happens, do I tell him? What must I do to make it work? Everything, I want to know everything . . .'

As darkness encloses the guttering candles on the table, the sky outside seems to get lighter, with the long midsummer radiance of June. It's the time of the corn goddess, but this ripe young peasant is a long way from the pagan rituals of her ancestors. Exiled, barren, she is deprived of her roots and her tongue by accident of the place and date of her birth.

'Marina, tomorrow morning, early, you should telephone your mother. Let me pay for the call. But book it now.'

She leans across and puts her arms round me. How sweet she smells.

'That would be *wonderful.*'

'You're in Max's bedroom. There's a telephone up on the top landing.' I have prepared the room for her as though it were for her wedding night, rather than the last time she will sleep alone. There are flowers and candles beside her bed, a snowy white duvet and pillows plump and soft as ducks, and laid across the bed my present to her: a nightdress of intricately pleated white cotton, as elaborate and virginal as anything a village maiden would have stitched for her bottom drawer.

'Go to bed Marina. Everything will be all right.'

*   *   *

Next morning we hardly have time for a calm breakfast together before the chaos begins. It is almost entirely a telephonic chaos, most of it incomprehensible as well, being in Polish. Every five minutes the infernal instrument rings and my simple Polish is stretched to breaking point. Everyone wants to wish her luck and check the morning's arrangements: how to get to the church; what time the service begins; they are right, aren't they, the reception is at the club afterwards and should they bring anything? Marina darts between bathroom and telephone in her underwear, wrapped in a towel, with wet hair, hair-dryer, but won't let me leave the phone off the hook so that she can get dressed in peace.

Suddenly it's half past ten. Andrew has offered to pick us up at eleven-fifteen and drive Marina to Iwo's, who will take her up the aisle, and then come with me to the church in Fulham Road. Marina is ready, wearing an apricot-coloured linen suit, and I have to rush to catch up. From downstairs I can hear her voice on the phone bubbling away. It seems that the only person who hasn't rung is Peter. As Andrew arrives she pulls one last, marvellous surprise. She must have got up early to pick fresh flowers from the garden, and these are woven into a little chaplet which she wears perched on top of her upswept hair. Very few young women could carry off such ingenuous simplicity. We both gaze at her as she descends the stairs, and Andrew says, 'You look very beautiful.'

In the car after we have dropped off Marina, I say to Andrew, 'I am . . . sorry . . . about the other night. The theatre. It was dreadful of me.'

His gaze fixed on the road, he replies, 'Yes. I'm sorry too. But I daresay a quick death is better than a slow one.'

'Does that mean . . . not that I'd blame you . . . have I wrecked our friendship? Does it mean we can't be friends?'

'I hope not. But it means we can't be lovers. Not that we ever could. My fault, probably. How could a dream compete with an obsession?'

'You are good to take me to this wedding.'

'I'm lethal at my job, you know. Real New York stuff: no holds barred. A killer in creative think tanks. I just can't be tough with women. I don't suppose it could have worked anyway. Us as lovers.'

'No . . .'

'I'll drop you here and find somewhere to park. You go in. I'll join you.'

The organ is already rumbling like distant, melodious thunder as I seat myself and wait for Marina to arrive on the arm of Iwo.

The unfamiliar Catholic ceremony forces me to concentrate, and as I sit and stand and kneel and watch her back view I find myself praying for her. I lost the habit of praying in childhood, and now I find myself using the same childish, almost pidgin language. Please God, make Marina happy, no, make them both happy, but specially her. Please God, let it all work. Iwo stands stiffly next to Joanna in the pew in front of me, and I add my uncertain prayers for him. Please God, make Iwo find what he's looking for, preferably with me, but if not then with his wife, and please let her welcome him and make them be happy too. And, since no-one listens to a marriage service without recalling or imagining their own, I think about Paul and me, and my young hopes, so desperately innocent, curdled by reality. It is odd to think that Andrew was present on that occasion, too. I remember walking up the aisle towards the rigid back of the man I was about to marry and thinking trustfully, How extraordinary: now I shall never kiss any man but Paul again.

What is Marina thinking? What, I really want to know, is Iwo thinking? Around me the deep Polish voices rise and fall, mostly male, for the club members have turned out to a man, it seems. Everyone's here except young Lochinvar. The frail voices of elderly Polish women tremble on a register above the men's as they cross themselves, and genuflect, murmur and move in unison like solemn grey and black birds swept up and down by unseen winds. Marina's voice is steady; it is Peter who scarcely speaks above a whisper.

The priest, in his stiff white brocade vestments, seems to be the centre of the ritual, the rest of us mere onlookers, deferring to his superior knowledge. His sonorous voice and unsmiling expression are more appropriate to a funeral than a wedding – which intensifies my feeling that Marina is being sacrificed to the young man awkwardly pushing a ring on to her finger. Oh God, forgive me these grudging thoughts! I do want them to be happy really . . .

My attention wanders back to Iwo and Joanna, standing far enough apart not to touch even at the elbow. She is wearing an expensive coat and a small, shiny hat: no doubt she hopes the wedding may weaken his resolve. Does she know he's going back to Poland? Does she know how soon? She could not possibly care as much as I do! Oh *God,* let me get *married* again! Not for the procreation of children but for the – what does the Book of Common Prayer say? – something about mutual comfort and society one to the other.

The service proceeds to the long nuptial mass, which I don't understand and can't share. People smelling musty and moth-balled in their best clothes brush past on their way to the altar, and again on their way back, and I smile and try to look holy, as they do. All these decorous, shuffling footsteps and downcast eyes: what are they thinking? Iwo doesn't take Communion either.

At last it ends. Marina walks shiningly down through us all, and Peter relaxes and smiles. Before leaving the church I make a little bob, in deference to all those genuflections, like a republican who can't help acknowledging the passing of royalty, and we find ourselves milling about in the street with passers-by skirting us irritably just as though nothing particular had happened: as though two entirely different and separate people had not just vowed to stay together and look after each other every day for the rest of their lives.

They leave in Peter's car after a few hasty photographs have been taken outside the church. A wide white nylon ribbon makes a fluttering V for victory along the bonnet. A few people attempt to throw confetti; a few curious onlookers stare into Marina's face as she sits smiling beside her husband, remembering to give a special wave to his mother. 'See you in a minute!' Peter calls out, and then the car disappears into a mêlée of lunchtime traffic.

Ten minutes later we're at the club where, although it soon fills up, the Polish contingent and the English guests stand at opposite ends of the room, eyeing one another. Peter introduces me to his mother, a stout lady with a strained expression that might be due as much to her corset as to the emotion of seeing her only son bind himself to another woman.

'Peter says you've been ever so kind to Marina,' she says.

'I haven't been kind – it's been a joy getting to know her. I do think she's a wonderful woman. She'll make him very happy.'

'She's certainly a very nice-looking girl. As for the rest, we'll just have to wait and see, won't we? See how it turns out, whether she can learn to do things the way he likes them. I've always done my best for him, that I know.'

'It can't have been easy. But then, Marina hasn't had an easy life, either.'

'No, well, she's a long way from home, isn't she? Can't expect to be just accepted straight away. These things take time.'

'Marina understands that. And I know you'll help her.'

'I'm sure I'll try. Can't do more than that.'

A tray is offered, with thin slices of smoked Polish sausage wrapped round pickled gherkins, and rye bread cut into small squares on which morsels of cheese and black olives are impaled with toothpicks.

Peter's mother looks at them and says, 'No, thank you very much all the same.'

She's afraid they'll dislodge her false teeth, I think viciously. Or stain her new turquoise gloves.

'Will you excuse me?' I say to her. 'I must go and talk to Marina's economics professor . . .'

'Oh well, I'm not clever enough to talk to *him*,' she says.

And I think, too right you're not, lady; and immediately afterwards, but then, nor am I.

Iwo and Joanna are standing in a small group of Poles, including her father. Tadeusz raises my hand to his lips.

'How splendid you look for the occasion, my dear! You do Marina credit!'

'You are most elegant,' says Iwo.

I introduce Andrew to everyone I know, and have my hand kissed by a number of courtly Polish gentlemen. One or two thank me gravely for my kindness to Marina. The noise rises to a hubbub as trays bearing glasses of champagne are circulated with which to toast the newly married couple. Iwo makes his way to the far end of the room, beside Peter and Marina; and holds up his hand for silence.

'Ladies and gentlemen!' he begins, in the heavily accented English that I had almost forgotten. 'You will forgive me that my English is not so good, that I will first speak in Polish and then my good friend Tadeusz will translate for our English friends and Marina's new family.' He waits for the cries of 'Shame!' and 'It's fine!' to die down, before commencing in his own language.

I have never seen him speak in public before. His voice carries strongly around the room, and the rolling phrases, whose meaning I can follow though not word for word, bring smiles and nods of agreement from the assembled Poles. Marina stands with downcast eyes, holding Peter's hand. Iwo praises the bride and groom, refers gravely to the mother country that they – and so many of those present – have been compelled to leave, then lightens the atmosphere again with a joke I half catch, about how Peter will have to be a better and sterner teacher than he, for Marina was never a docile student; and finally, his voice raised almost to a shout, he holds high his glass and proclaims, 'Peter! Marina! Happiness!'

He is echoed by a deep harsh roar from all the Poles in the room: 'Peter! Marina! Happiness!' as heads tilt back to drink the toast in one full-throated swallow.

After this speech has been translated into English, and those guests from the groom's side of the aisle have responded with a rather more muted echo, first Peter makes

270

a short reply, and then, to everyone's surprise, Marina turns to him and says, 'May I speak?'

'It's not usual,' he tells her; 'you don't have to.'

'I only want to say a few things,' she says. 'And in English, for I have become an Englishwoman today. This is the last Polish occasion in my life, and perhaps the last time I shall be in a room with so many Polish people. I would like to say that I am grateful to this country, this free country, for having taken me, and all of us, under its wing. In Poland, where we were forced to live a lie, we dreamed of coming to the West, and being able to live in truth. For me that dream is doubly fulfilled today: thanks to my husband. To him, I pledge my love and duty as his English wife. And to all of you, my gratitude in sharing this day with us. And so, for the last time, I say: God bless Poland!'

This time the echo is more of a murmur. 'God bless Poland!' say the old men and women. In front of them all, Marina reaches up to kiss her new husband.

No half measures, I think. She has cast the die indeed, in front of them all. She is brave and beautiful and humble. I cannot meet her eyes or I shall cry.

The champagne, or perhaps the emotion of nostalgia, has loosened everyone's inhibitions, and tentatively the two sides begin to mix. Marina introduces some of Peter's friends to the elderly gentlemen from the club, and both groups bend their heads towards each other in puzzled goodwill. Taking my cue from her, I walk over to Iwo's corner and introduce Andrew first to him and then to Joanna. She by now is bright-eyed and dishevelled; she has taken off her stiff little hat and is laughing with the abandon of slight drunkenness, tossing her glossy hair across her sidelong face and then back, with a flash of her taut throat. Iwo seems to be unaware of this flirtatiousness. It soon becomes clear that Andrew is not. He stands fractionally closer than necessary, and his voice lowers so that only she can hear clearly. At first Joanna's animation includes them both – 'Iwo, tell this ignorant Englishman that in Poland, women are different!' But when she sees that Iwo will not pander to her wish to

271

play them off one against the other – 'I am sure, my dear Joanna, that you can tell him much better than I' – she bends all her attention towards Andrew. Iwo places his hand almost imperceptibly in the small of my back and steers me away. He begins to talk Polish to some old ladies dressed in black, with black headscarves folded triangularly around their pale, seamed faces; and soon I smile vaguely at them and drift away. The champagne is insulating me from my own reactions. I am content to stand alone in a corner of the room, watching as an anthropologist might watch a strange tribe. I observe that the Poles touch each other a good deal, but smile more rarely; while the English shun all contact, but smile all the time. The Poles interrupt shamelessly, two or three often talking at once and no-one is offended, while the English nod and wait to be quite sure the speaker has finished. For once I find myself looking *into* people's faces, not merely at them; and I seem to see in the Polish faces a combination of self-confidence and candour which the English lack. The guests from Peter's side are defensive, correct, missing nothing. They will have a fine tale to tell their mates at the pub, their hairdressers, the girls in the keep-fit classes, or whoever makes up their safe circle.

Meanwhile one of the wedding guests has produced an accordion, and starts to play: softly at first; soon with increasing speed and emphasis. The Poles murmur the tune, the murmuring swells with clapping, and finally the clapping is matched by insistent stamping feet. Marina glances anxiously at Peter, for she can see that his friends are looking ill at ease. At that moment an old man approaches her, bows with great dignity, and evidently asks her to dance. Peter nods and smiles his permission and Marina, flushed and excited, moves into the centre of the room, where the guests are backing against each other towards the wall to clear a space. Her partner bows, stamps his feet, and then slowly raises her hand to his and together the two perform a dance like a couple in a dream. Their faces are serious, the old one so deeply lined, the young bride so smooth and firm, both with pursed lips and eyes on each other. He could be

272

her father, her grandfather even; and in this solemn dance he seems to be giving her in marriage far more than Iwo did when he escorted her stiffly up the aisle. Is it a dance they both know, or are they improvising as they dip and spin, loose hands, clap, and join again? The accordionist ends on a bravura crescendo that stops abruptly on a thrumming chord, and the two dancers salute each other, catch their breath, and break into laughter, happy at their combined skill, as the guests applaud. Even Peter's mother is smiling, archly indulgent – and then my gaze shifts to Andrew and Joanna. They are looking at one another, intense, secret, rapt. A cocoon of mutual anticipation shimmers around them.

'Iwo,' I say, 'when Marina and Peter have left, can I go with you?'

He looks across at Joanna, sees what I have seen, and nods. 'Yes,' he says.

Soon after this we are on the street together, waving the newly-married pair towards their unknown destination. Peter's mother is sniffing tremulously, but she has plenty of concerned supporters: she doesn't need me. Andrew and Joanna make their excuses and drive off together – impossible to be discreet on such an occasion and, in any case, why bother? – and Iwo takes my elbow in the familiar manner as we walk away from the club.

'Well, that went off all right, didn't it?' I say tentatively.

He hardly bothers to acknowledge my remark, but asks, 'Your friend . . . is he a good man? Tell me about him.'

In a rush of protective warmth I recount the story of my friendship with Andrew; his long bachelorhood – 'Why? Does he prefer to go with men . . . or boys?' – his current loneliness in the tidy, empty flat. I tell Iwo that he is a poet, which is approved, and an advertising man, less acceptable. I say nothing about our recent encounter.

'Good. Perhaps something may come of it for them both. Joanna needs a good man. She is also sometimes lonely. Like us.'

Surprised and made brazen by this rare admission, I say, 'Can we go to your room, Iwo? It isn't far.'

'We could sit in the park, in the sun . . .'

'We could, yes.'

'All right. If you wish.'

We head towards the house where he lives.

His room is, as always, austere as a bleached bone. The bed has the tidy, anonymous look of a hospital bed; the floor is swept; the curtain drawn across the end of the room ripples in the light like sun on water. Soon he will be gone, and its emptiness will be complete. This may be the last time I am ever here with him.

'Iwo, please, do me a favour? Can I spend your last evening here with you? Before you go? Sorry to ask. Would you like it?'

'I know I have made you unhappy, Constance. Believe me, I never wished to be unkind.'

'Of course you didn't. Don't worry. But please let me.'

'It is a very generous offer. I leave next Thursday.'

'So *soon*? Oh God . . . I hadn't quite realized it was *that* soon.'

'Now that Marina is married, there seemed nothing . . . there was little reason to stay. I bought my train ticket yesterday, at lunchtime, and told my employer I wouldn't be coming back.'

My face, my body, are as though turned to stone. I can only look at him, no longer able to hide my feelings. For that matter, could I ever?

'I am sorry, my dear. I don't think you understand.'

Understand? I have never understood. To understand means, literally, to feel supported from below; to bestride certainties; to be buttressed by knowledge. My love for Iwo tried to take root in imagination, guesswork, and fantasy: all of it probably wrong. I have been standing on air. This time my thoughts are slow, and in the silence we stare at one another. Then he takes a step towards me, two, three, and puts his arms around me, without speaking.

I stand rigid, held in a gesture, not an embrace, until all my control sags and I say, 'Iwo, shall we go to bed?'

An image flashes into my mind – Joanna and Andrew

coupling rapturously – and as I dismiss it guiltily I hear Iwo murmur into my hair, 'I think it would be better not. I am bound to disappoint you.'

But thou wilt never more appear folded within my hemisphere, since both thy light and motion like a fled star is fallen, and gone.

Walking like an automaton through the sunshine towards the tube in my best clothes, my mind knotted and my emotions brimming, I realize that I am not far away from my mother's flat. On an impulse, for the first time in years, I decide to visit her unannounced, and, now that I have a source of comfort, I almost run through the streets towards her. I stumble clumsily down the steps and press hard on the doorbell, breathing heavily, knowing that the moment I see her I shall cry: Oh Mummy, oh Mummy it hurts, please make it better! Where does it hurt, darling? Here, here, it hurts *all over*. Now Constance, pull yourself together and don't be a silly girl. Tell Mummy clearly where it hurts most and then we'll put some TCP on it . . .

She stands in the doorway, incongruously smart. Her eyebrows shoot up at the sight of me, but she recovers instantly – as, indeed, do I. Ah, the English self-control!

'Darling! What a lovely surprise! I think there's some tea left. Come in . . .'

Leading the way, she walks through to her small drawing room where, amid her best teacups and slivers of lemon and thinly-sliced cucumber sandwiches, an elderly man is rising to his feet.

'Constance darling, you remember Uncle Leonard, don't you? Leonard Elphinstone?'

'She won't remember me, goodness no! But I remember you, *very* well.'

He is wrong. I do remember him. Uncle Leonard and Auntie Janet. They used to play bridge and tennis with my parents when we were all young: when, come to think of it, my mother must have been younger than I am now.

'I do remember you, though. And Auntie Janet.'

An expression of conventional grief comes over his face,

and my mother says hurriedly, 'Auntie Janet died a couple of years ago, Constance. *So* brave. It's been a very difficult time. But Leonard's been wonderful. Oh yes you *have,* Leonard!'

Deference has been observed towards the dead.

'Well my dear, *you* look very smart. Been lunching with an admirer, hm?'

'Not exactly, Mr Elphinstone.' I will *not* call him Uncle Leonard, yet I can't bring myself to utter his naked Christian name. 'I've just come from a wedding.'

'A wedding!' bubbles my mother. 'Darling, how lovely! Whose? Do I know them?'

'No: some Polish friends of mine.'

'Splendid chaps, the Poles. Lot of them fought in our Air Force in the last war . . . Did you know that, Constance?'

'Really?' I say, and drink my tepid tea quickly, thwarted in my search for consolation, wanting now just to be left alone.

My mother is talking about the grandchildren and he winks at me. 'Very much the proud grandmother, eh? And quite right too, from all I hear. My young feller-me-lad emigrated to Canada, so all I see of *my* grandchildren is a lot of shiny photographs.'

Poor old thing: so he's lonely, too. Well, isn't everyone?

The human condition. Old age, decrepitude, resentment, memories.

As I leave I notice in the hall a carrier bag full of freshly ironed shirts. 'Goodbye Mother,' I say, kissing her formally on both cheeks. 'Thanks for the lovely cup of tea.'

She looks anxious. 'You're *sure* you're all right, darling?'

'Fine,' I say, flashing a big bright smile. 'Just a bit pissed, I expect. See you on Tuesday . . . 'Bye!'

But woe is me! The longest date too narrow is to calculate these empty hopes.

18

The aftermath of a death must feel like this. The loss has changed your life irrevocably, yet the rest of the world goes about its business impervious. Iwo leaves me for ever on Thursday, Thursday of *this week*. Wednesday evening will be the last time I see him. I have failed. All he wanted was a wife, any wife, and still I wasn't good enough. What help is poetry to me now; what use my books, my library, my stalwart friends? In a way it would be easier if he *were* dead. That would also put an end to everything, but I wouldn't be to blame. This way, I shall have to live with the thought of him in Poland, with his wife. Well then, Katarzyna, I give you what I could not keep. Be kind to him.

I wish I could have believed Paul when he said that what was wrong was not what I offered, but Iwo's ability to take it. But I remember how we met: that first afternoon on the Heath when the trees burned. He reached out to me then, eager to share his sense of self and learn about me and mine, and I thought I had found my soul's dear wish . . . It hasn't worked, and I am numb with loss.

Sunday is interminable. Katie's with Paul. Cordy's bent over her books, inaccessible. I try to read the Sunday papers, usually such a treat, but after a sentence or two my concentration falters and I stare blankly into the ominous brightness of the summer day, its heat too heavy to last. I wander through the house and garden, barefoot, unkempt, sticky in a faded T-shirt and loose cotton trousers. I finger my address book, wondering whom I could ring. Nobody. I languish out, not live the day. I take salad and a glass of iced lemonade upstairs to Cordy, who barely looks up.

'Great. Thanks. Later. *Hot . . .*' she says.

I go down again and lie in the garden, but the sun gives me a headache and the grass itches against my bare skin. With the coming of evening the house cools but the pressure is still there inside my head. The telephone rings, so loudly that I jump, and I rush to pick it up.

It is Max, his voice strong and happy. 'Hi Mother, how're you?'

'Fine darling. You?'

'Yeah, great. Smashing day, wasn't it? Danny and I went to Richmond Park. Took a picnic. Got pissed and lay in the sun. My arms are all burnt.'

'A picnic. How lovely. How is she?'

'Look: it's a bit short notice but we thought we might come over and have supper in the garden with you some-time this week. Wednesday would be best, or Tuesday?'

'Wednesday I can't. Tuesday.'

'OK then. Want us to bring anything? Bottle of wine?'

'Don't bother. There's still a surprising amount in Daddy's cellar.'

'Right then. Sevenish? Eightish? You say.'

'Any time. Be lovely to see you both again.'

Their visit will be a godsend, taking my mind off my farewell to Iwo, if only for a few hours. Max and Danuta have been together for six months now, and despite her parents' objections she has moved in with him. How ironic, if after all this I were to acquire a Polish daughter-in-law! But the young are in no rush to marry and I don't suppose those two have even discussed it. In their twenties they still have so much time and so many choices . . .

On Monday morning I wake up to find the weather has broken. It's much cooler, and it is starting to rain. Rain patters on to the pale green lime shoots springing from their truncated boles. The peonies are at their height, fatly glori-ous, their texture magnified by raindrops. People come into the library with damp hair or shaking water from their umbrellas, and joke about the English summer.

'Just in time to ruin the last week of Wimbledon – typical,

isn't it? Never fails. Still, we got two weeks. All you can expect.'

'Winter begins officially next week,' I say, trying to match their cheerfulness. For me, it has begun already.

Katie's school sports day is a sodden disaster, the games-field streaked with muddy skidmarks. The parents have to make do with PE displays in the gym and indoor sand-wiches. Kate is furious. Running is one of the things she's really good at, and for all her adolescent precocity she's still enough of a child to care about winning races. Paul is annoyed too. Having arranged to take this Monday afternoon off so that he can be seen to do the decent, divorced father act and cheer Katie on, he now sits fuming as other people's children perform wobbly gymnastics.

He drives us home in his latest shiny car – 'Firm's car,' he explains – and goes upstairs to say hello to Cordy. She, her examinations already under way, is haggard with last-minute revision.

'She can't really have done as badly as she's predicting?' he asks, sitting spreadeagled in the old sofa with a glass of white wine in one hand and Katie curled into his shoulder.

'She's just trying to prepare us for the worst,' I tell him reassuringly, 'so that whatever her results, it'll come as a relief to us that she's got a degree at all.'

He nods. 'Can't be easy, us with Firsts and all that.'

'I don't think we've ever put any pressure on her, have we?' I ask.

'I don't know about you. *I've* made it bloody clear that it's a hard, cold world out there, and if they want jobs they'd better get a damn good degree. How're things with young Tim?'

'Ben.'

'Whoever. She serious about him?'

'They seem to get on very well, yes: but what's that got to do with her exam results?'

'If she's going to be a wife and mother of six it doesn't matter what she gets. If she wants to be a media whizz-kid it makes a hell of a difference. Competition's shit-hot nowadays. Even the secretaries have degrees.'

I am astonished how untouched Paul is by the changes in the lives of women of his own generation: the changes that our divorce made in my life. He seems to take for granted that I, once his mousey, stay-at-home wife, now earn my keep and that of our children, as well as running the household single-handed. Yet it doesn't occur to him that the same might happen to Cordelia. He pays lip-service to the language of feminism in his advertising campaigns because he must, but other than that he remains sturdily indifferent to the New Woman.

'You're Neanderthal, do you know that?' says Kate grumpily. 'Why should Cordy and Ben get married? They'll be like Max: live in a squat or buy a flat or something and just *stay* together.'

'Well, we'll see . . .' says Paul. He strokes her hair and she snuggles down again. 'So, young lady, now that you're out of training, where would you like to eat?'

We decide, as we always did in the past, to go to the small Italian restaurant down the road. The food isn't up to much, pretty awful in fact, but it holds memories of birthday celebrations for years back, and they always make us welcome. Kate goes upstairs to change out of her school shorts and Aertex shirt, and I'm just about to follow her when Paul stops me.

'Stay here. Have a glass of wine and talk for a minute. I've got news for you, and I want you to help me tell the girls.'

'Paul! What?'

'Sit down. Here. Want a fag?'

'You ought to know by now that I've given up smoking. It's been nearly eight years. What news?'

'Lulu's pregnant.'

'*Darling!* Er . . . congratulations?'

'I was pretty appalled at first. Can't honestly say I fancy going back to sleepless nights and nappies.'

'So? What are you going to do?'

'I tried for a while to talk her out of it. But she's determined to go ahead. She says she'll have the baby whether I get involved or not. Did *you* know she was that keen to have a child? I mean, she went off the Pill without telling me!'

'I only met her that couple of times over Christmas: how should I know? But didn't you?'

'I knew she was feeling broody. But I thought she'd wait until we'd sorted ourselves out.'

'And when was *that* going to be?'

He grins. 'I suppose you're right. No reason for me to change the status quo.'

'So she's forced your hand?'

'A bit. Not that I don't love her. I do. Well, I hope I do, because we're getting married.'

'So it *is* congratulations!'

He smirks, and I see that he is not unhappy at the prospect. The wedding is to be next month, and the holiday they had already planned for August will become their honeymoon. Lulu is nearly four months pregnant – with *my husband's* child. The thought of it makes me lonely. I had hoped to have a chance to talk to him about Iwo. Now I can't. Instead I have to smile, and kiss him, and tell him I'm sure our children will be thrilled – but will they? – and all the time I'm remembering the births of our babies. How young we were then – how unprepared for parenthood! This baby will be born into an affluent household, complete no doubt with nanny and daily cleaner; with half-brother and -sisters. It's being born so that Lulu can have what she wants: a husband, *my* husband. I am angry and jealous and envious and confused, but my smile stays fixed in place. This is it. He's really gone from me now. He belongs to another woman and another family. I am on my own, no Paul, no Iwo. My father died five years ago, and now there is no male in my life.

We hear Katie and Cordy coming down the stairs and I say quickly, 'Don't say anything to them just yet. I'll think about how you ought to break the news. It's bound to be a bit of a shock, but they'll be pleased in the end. Don't worry . . .'

He flashes a grateful nod as the two of them bounce in. My lover, my husband, my mother: one by one they step outside

281

the roles I have allotted, refusing to be what I need them to be and pursuing their own, so much more satisfactory, lives.

On Wednesday I'm tempted to take the day off, but realize that if I do it will only mean eight empty hours in which to brood about the coming evening. Better to spend the time in the library and hope to be distracted. In my lunch hour I hurry to the shops, buying the last presents I shall ever give Iwo, to accompany him on his train journey away from me. The rain sweeps warmly, softly down.

As I get ready to see him for the last time, bathing and washing my hair and putting on my scented underclothes, I know that for once I shall let him determine the conversation. I can't behave as though nothing were happening, or put a brave face on his going. All I know is that I won't embarrass him by 'making a scene', as my parents always described any show of emotion. I feel turgid, passive, fatalistic: a swimmer going under for the third time, already half-drowned. There is nothing to gain by struggling.

The journey to his house on foot, by bus, and by tube takes exactly as long as it always did, and I shall arrive exactly at eight, as arranged. Will we go out and eat a final meal together; or walk through the wet streets while dusk lasts, and then go to the Polish café, not Marina's, the other one, where we first met Joanna? Will we stay in, sit on the floor or the bed, and talk, able finally to be honest with one another? Will he try to explain why he could not, could not love me? Or will we go to bed together, and make love one last time? I only know that *he* must decide.

I try to dawdle the few hundred yards to his house, delaying the moment when our final time together will begin – and then realize I'm losing precious moments, and make up by hurrying. I stand outside the house. I press the doorbell. A rangy Australian girl opens it, tanned and loose-limbed. 'Oh . . . good evening . . . sorry: Iwo's expecting me. The man on the first floor.'

She turns and yells behind her towards the open door of the kitchen. 'Bobby! Who's Ian? Do we have an Ian?'

'Not Ian,' I say. 'Iwo. Don't worry. I'll find my own way.'

One of the Australians emerges, flushed and bright-eyed, shutting the door on the laughter behind him.

'Oh, hello lady! You're looking for the Polish fella, aren't you? He's gone.'

'No,' I explain. 'No, it's tomorrow he's going. I came to . . . well . . .' and I hold out my bag full of things I've bought for Iwo. 'I brought him stuff for the train.'

'No lady, he's left. Went this morning.'

'He can't have done. Look, don't worry. I'll just go up to his room. Sorry; didn't mean to bother you . . .'

'Please yourself,' he says, standing aside, and I climb the stairs.

I knock on the door of Iwo's room but there's no answer, so I push it open. The room is unrecognizable. A shabby carpet, still showing creases from having been unrolled, covers the floor. There are curtains at the window. The two ceiling tracks have gone, and the bed has been moved to the wall opposite me. In the centre of the room stands a battered table that I haven't seen before, flanked by a couple of wooden chairs. On the table is a dark green octagonal saucer brimming with cigarette stubs. There's a sleeping bag under the window, and a couple of half-unpacked suitcases have overflowed around it. Apart from its white walls, the room bears no trace of Iwo.

The Australian girl has followed me up the stairs and is standing behind me. 'Help yourself to a look,' she says. 'Nice isn't it? Me and Brend arrived today. You knew the last fella here or something?'

'Yes,' I answer. 'Yes, I did.'

'We're over for the summer. Boys fixed up for us to live here. We'll stay a few months, till it gets cold, then move on.'

'Yes,' I repeat. 'Cold. Wet now. Gone.'

I brush past her and walk stiff-legged down the stairs again.

The young Australian reappears, saying, 'See? Told you so. Went this morning . . .' And then, seeing my expression, his own changes and he asks, 'You all right, lady?

283

'Everything OK? Look, we're having a party. Welcome the girls. My name's Bobby. Come and join us. Cheer you up.'

'No. Thank you. Better go then.'

He glances down and catches sight of the bottles in my carrier bag.

'Come on now, lady . . . what's your name?'

'Constance Liddell.'

'Constance, come on, join in the fun! Have a little drink! Seen you around lots of times and never asked you for a . . .'

'No, I think I'll be off now, if you don't mind. Thank you.'

He stands aside, then leans forward and opens the front door. Dusk is beginning to fall, and the rain still patters gently on to the warm pavements. A cooling wind is blowing, rustling the leaves.

I walk away from the house and, after a hundred yards or so, stop. He has gone. He's already in the train. He didn't say goodbye. He knew I was coming, and didn't even ring to say goodbye. Perhaps he left a note? They would have told me. Perhaps not. I turn and run clumsily back to the house, ring the bell, bang on the door. The same tall girl opens it.

'You again!'

'Did he leave a note for me? Was there a note?'

'He left some money for the landlord in an envelope. Nothing else.'

'Are you absolutely sure there wasn't a note?'

'Look pet, the way that room was left, I'd have noticed a postage stamp!'

'So no envelope . . . nothing?'

'No. Sorry.'

I turn and walk away again, hearing the door close a few moments later. I head automatically towards the tube station. After a while I notice how heavy the bag is. I put it down, leaning it against a tree, and stop to think. Inside it I have packed a picnic for Iwo, to sustain him on his long train journey. A few last luxuries from the West. Brown bread with smoked salmon. A pound of sweet, dark red cherries. A packet of black bread, already buttered and wrapped in cellophane. A quarter of smoked sausage. I had debated whether to buy him a sharp knife, but decided there was bound to be someone on the train who would lend him a knife to slice it with. A bottle of red wine. Half a bottle of vodka. And my final presents to him. I had spent a long time thinking about those presents. In the end I bought him an anthology of English verse, and wrote inside, 'To Iwo — I have asterisked the ones that mean most to me — I hope you will like them too. Thank you for that first afternoon on Hampstead Heath. All love, Constance' and the date, written out in full just below the inscription. The other present was an odd one; I hadn't been sure that he would even understand it. I bought him a collection of Posy's cartoons from the *Guardian* and wrote inside, 'Dear Iwo — This is what you missed. I shall miss you. Constance' and the date again.

I stand for some time looking down at this bag. In the end I leave it where it is, leaning against the tree, and walk away, towards the lights and clamour of the Earls Court Road. I hope somebody finds it who needs — well, the food and drink at least. Not the books. I don't want the books back. What use are books?

In a little while it will be dark. The wind is blowing from the west, and the rain falls softly. Christ! That my love were in my arms, and I in my bed again!

THE END

KISS AND KIN

Angela Lambert

'A HIGHLY READABLE NOVEL ABOUT LOVE AND
LOSS'
Express on Sunday

Life for the newly widowed Harriet Capel is not
expected to hold any surprises. It will be spent watching
over the vicissitudes of her children's marriages and
relationships, and looking after the grandchildren. That
is, until she sees Oliver Gaunt again. He is her daughter-
in-law's father. The relationship between the parents-in-
law has always been difficult since their children's
wedding day and few words have been spoken. When
they meet, they do not at first recognize one another, but
the physical attraction between them is powerful and
instantaneous. As their love affair gathers intensity and
pace, so do its consequences for the family as a whole.

In *Kiss and Kin*, two generations walk a dangerous
tightrope between fidelity and parenthood, each
guarding past and present secrets, the revelation of
which, in the white heat of passion, may destroy the
carefully erected boundaries of tradition and propriety.

'A WRY LOOK AT LOVE AFTER THE MENOPAUSE . . .
CANDID AND ENTERTAINING'
Mail on Sunday

'SPIRITED, SHREWD AND STYLISH'
The Scotsman

0 552 99736 6

BLACK SWAN

A RATHER ENGLISH MARRIAGE

Angela Lambert

'A BRILLIANT TRAGI-COMEDY . . . A SHARP AND TRULY
SYMPATHETIC WRITER'
Penelope Fitzgerald, *Evening Standard*

Roy Southgate and Reginald Conynghame-Jervis have nothing in
common but their loneliness and their wartime memories.

Roy, a retired milkman and Reggie, a former RAF Squadron
Leader, are widowed on the same day. To assuage their grief, the
vicar arranges for Roy to move in with Reggie as his unpaid
manservant. To their surprise, they form a strange alliance,
based on obedience, need and the strangeness of single life.
Then Reggie meets Liz, a vibrant but near-bankrupt woman of
irresistible appeal, while Roy and his son's family grow
gradually closer. Marriage, it seems, however far from ideal, can
be a great protector against isolation.

'SWEEPS THE READER ALONG ON A TIDE OF GOOD
HUMOUR . . . THIS BOOK IS REMARKABLE FOR ITS
SHREWDNESS, PATHOS – AND ITS HIGH SPIRITS'
Observer

'A PORTRAITIST WHOSE VISUAL DESCRIPTIONS AND
OBSERVATIONS ARE EXACT AND OFTEN MOVING . . .
ALREADY A NOVELIST OF DISTINCTION, WITH THIS
NOVEL SHE PROVES THAT HER REACH IS UNIVERSAL'
Scotland on Sunday

'WARM, WELL-OBSERVED AND OFTEN VERY FUNNY'
Time Out

'ANGELA LAMBERT IS NOT AFRAID OF TELLING A
STRAIGHTFORWARD STORY AND IN GOING RIGHT TO THE
HEART OF HER CHARACTERS . . . *A RATHER ENGLISH
MARRIAGE* IS OBSERVANT, WRY AND ULTIMATELY
POIGNANT'
Financial Times

0 552 99741 2

BLACK SWAN

A SELECTED LIST OF FINE WRITING
AVAILABLE FROM BLACK SWAN

THE PRICES SHOWN BELOW WERE CORRECT AT THE TIME OF GOING TO PRESS. HOWEVER
TRANSWORLD PUBLISHERS RESERVE THE RIGHT TO SHOW NEW RETAIL PRICES ON
COVERS WHICH MAY DIFFER FROM THOSE PREVIOUSLY ADVERTISED IN THE TEXT OR
ELSEWHERE.

99630 0	MUDDY WATERS	Judy Astley	£6.99
99619 X	HUMAN CROQUET	Kate Atkinson	£6.99
99537 1	GUPPIES FOR TEA	Marika Cobbold	£6.99
99670 X	THE MISTRESS OF SPICES	Chitra Banerjee Divakaruni	£6.99
99587 8	LIKE WATER FOR CHOCOLATE	Laura Esquivel	£6.99
99624 6	THE COUNTER-TENOR'S DAUGHTER	Elizabeth Falconer	£6.99
99657 2	PERFECT MERINGUES	Laurie Graham	£5.99
99774 9	THE CUCKOO'S PARTING CRY	Anthea Halliwell	£5.99
99681 5	A MAP OF THE WORLD	Jane Hamilton	£6.99
99736 6	KISS AND KIN	Angela Lambert	£6.99
99741 2	A RATHER ENGLISH MARRIAGE	Angela Lambert	£6.99
99739 0	NO TALKING AFTER LIGHTS	Angela Lambert	£6.99
99742 0	THE CONSTANT MISTRESS	Angela Lambert	£6.99
99771 4	MALLINGFORD	Alison Love	£6.99
99392 1	THE GREAT DIVORCE	Valerie Martin	£6.99
99688 2	HOLY ASPIC	Joan Marysmith	£6.99
99709 0	THEORY OF MIND	Sanjida O'Connell	£6.99
99608 4	LAURIE AND CLAIRE	Kathleen Rowntree	£6.99
99763 6	GARGOYLES AND PORT	Mary Selby	£6.99
99753 6	AN ACCIDENTAL LIFE	Titia Sutherland	£6.99
99700 5	NEXT OF KIN	Joanna Trollope	£6.99
99780 3	KNOWLEDGE OF ANGELS	Jill Paton Walsh	£6.99
99673 4	DINA'S BOOK	Herbjørg Wassmo	£6.99
99723 4	PART OF THE FURNITURE	Mary Wesley	£6.99
99642 4	SWIMMING POOL SUNDAY	Madeleine Wickham	£6.99
99591 6	A MISLAID MAGIC	Joyce Windsor	£6.99

All Transworld titles are available by post from:

Book Services By Post, P.O. Box 29, Douglas, Isle of Man IM99 1BQ

Credit cards accepted. Please telephone 01624 675137,
fax 01624 670923 or Internet http://www.bookpost.co.uk.
or e-mail: bookshop@enterprise.net for details

Free postage and packing in the UK. Overseas customers: allow
£1 per book (paperbacks) and £3 per book (hardbacks).